hide me darling

Maree Rose

hide me darling

by Maree Rose

Apologies if I missed any, please reach out to me on social media if that is the case.

Playlist

I know how much you all love a
good playlist to set the mood...

For your listening pleasure:

https://tinyurl.com/hidemedarling

PLAYLIST

Almost Touch Me - Maisy Kay
Devil Inside - CRMNL
Love into a Weapon - Madalen Duke
Monsters - Tommee Profitt, XEAH
Whose Side Are You On - Tommee Profitt, Ruelle
Will I Make It Out Alive - Tommee Profitt, Jessie Early
MONSTER - Chandler Leighton
Be A Hero - Euphoria, Bolshiee
Welcome To My World - Tommee Profitt, LYRA
Be Careful - Tommee Profitt, Laney Jones
Don't Save Me - Chxrlotte
My Heart's Grave - Faouzia
Through the Dark - Kevin McAllister, IOLITE

Welcome To Your Nightmare - UNSECRET, MAYLYN
Here Come The Monsters - ADONA
Born To Die - Euphoria, Bolshiee
My Kingdom - Simon, IOLITE
Fortunately - Bellabeth
RAGE - Samantha Margret
Make Me Believe - The EverLove
Villain - ARCANA, Zack Merci
Hide and Seek - Klergy, Mindy Jones
Find You - Ruelle
Every Breath You Take - Chase Holfelder
Who Are You - SVRCINA
This Mountain - Faouzia

I know why you're here…
It's that fantasy of being fucked hard by
a couple of obsessed masked stalkers who will
kill for you but won't tell you their real name…
That's okay, I understand…
We all hide who we are in the darkness sometimes,
but be careful who might be hiding with you…

Prologue

S ometimes I wonder what it would be like to be normal. To have a life where everything is all sunshine and rainbows. Unfortunately, I know the truth about the world, and once you know, there is no turning a blind eye.

It's hard when you grow up and follow the same path as your mother. It feels like I'm in her shadow, even if I am my own person. Agent Alexandra Darling was amazing at her job... and I will prove that I'm amazing at mine.

I am Detective Hydessa Darling. Because of my mother, I know the evil that lurks in the shadows. I have grown up surrounded by the reminder that no one is truly who they say they are, not even the good guys.

My parents didn't believe in raising us with delusions of how the world truly is. They always said that the places we go are battlegrounds where light and dark are in constant conflict, and each of us has a bit of both inside us. They didn't shelter me or my sister from the harsh realities; instead, they prepared us to face them. While other kids were learning to ride bikes and play tag, we were learning survival skills, training in self-defense, and figuring out how to understand the complexities of human nature and just how easy it is to hide evil.

I know the darkness that calls from deep within the soul, because it calls from deep within mine. And though I don't consider myself evil, I don't consider myself good either. Not even the daughter of the great Agent Darling can outrun her demons, and I have a feeling mine are coming for me soon.

I remember the first time I realized I wasn't quite like other kids. It was in middle school, when I was around eleven. A group of students were picking on a boy smaller than them. Everyone else looked away, not wanting to get involved, but I couldn't stand it. As I sat there and watched others turn a blind eye, my anger grew until the shadows within me demanded I unleash my anger on those bullies.

They never touched that small boy again.

As I grew older, I became more aware of the storm that would command the fury within me. There were times when that darkness threatened to overwhelm the light. Times when anger, resentment, and despair felt like they would consume me and take everything good with it. But I learned to channel those feelings, to use them as fuel rather than letting them control me. It's a delicate balance, one that requires constant vigilance and refusal to give in.

I often wonder if there's a point to all this. Is there a purpose to the struggle? Or is it just the way things are, an endless cycle of light and dark, good and evil? My parents say that it's our choices that define us, not our circumstances. They believe that even in the darkest of times, there's always a choice that can bring out the light.

I don't know if I believe them.

While I know the darkness is a part of me just as much as the light is, I don't think I can always control which one presents itself. And perhaps that's the true challenge: not to banish the darkness, but to coexist with it, to find harmony between the two and know when to let the rage loose.

But who could love someone who embraces the darkness within themselves so readily? My dads adore my mom. They are still obsessed with her twenty-five years after having me and my sister. If love doesn't come with the same obsession that my dads have for my mom, then I don't want it.

Growing up, their love was like a beacon, a shining example of what true, utter devotion looks like. They never hide their feelings, their passion, or their commitment. It is intense and all-consuming, and I couldn't imagine settling for anything less.

They found a way not to fear their darkness, but to let it shield them. It's what makes my mother so good at her job and why so many people look to her for answers. Her sixth sense about others and their intentions is unparalleled in the world of crime solving.

My sister, Seanna, chooses not to think about it and embraces the darkness; she spends her time in the arms of strangers she meets while partying, living life to the fullest and taking on whatever jobs she can within the family business. She will cross whatever line she needs to in the name of justice. She believes that a love like what our parents share will be impossible to find, so she refuses to look for it.

She says she's just being realistic, that the world isn't made for fairy-tale romances and epic love stories. Seanna laughs off the idea of finding someone who would obsess over her the way our dads obsess over our mom. Instead, she throws herself into the moment and the fleeting connections that come and go with the night. It's her way of coping, of dealing with the darkness within her.

Sometimes, I envy her ability to live in the now and to embrace the shadows without fear or hesitation. She seems so free, so unburdened by the weight of expectations and the hopes for a love that might never come. Yet, I also see the emptiness in her eyes when she thinks no one's looking. The loneliness she hides behind her carefree facade.

I don't want to look like that.

I want the kind of love my parents have, the kind that endures through every storm, that sees the darkness and still chooses to stay. But the fear of never finding it gnaws at me. What if I'm destined to walk this path alone, forever battling the shadows without someone to share the journey with?

Still, a part of me hopes that somewhere out there is a person who can see both the darkness and the light within me, and love me not despite them, but because of them. Someone who understands that the darkness isn't something to be feared, but something to be embraced.

Maybe one day I will find a way to accept that part of me I try to keep buried deep, and it will bring me everything I hoped for. Maybe even more.

Chapter 1
Hydessa

I love a good mystery, and murder can be a beautiful mystery sometimes.

The blood arching in a way that tells a story, or the splatter that gives away the murder weapon. Tiny details that seem insignificant but paint a bigger picture.

I always thought that those were weird thoughts to have, but I still have them. We don't condone crime, but we do believe that it can tell us a story if we only look hard enough. I thought we were the only ones who looked at death and hoped it would tell us a story. We want to be captivated by every single piece of the puzzle, turning the pages until BAM. We solve it.

That is, until I stumbled across these blog posts. I don't know what it is about them that makes me want to drive out and see these crime scenes for myself, but they have me captivated. A mystery I want so desperately to solve simply from a few words on the screen of my tablet.

Dear Readers,

And another one bites the dust… I mean, I love a good Queen song. Doesn't everyone? But I love a good murder even more.

Another week, another victim… this one was even pretty, too. Blonde hair and sweet smile. Just enough loneliness in her eyes that you could see she had no one just by looking at her.

She rolled into town on the tourist bus just like all the others, with a bag big enough to see she wasn't completely homeless. But then, anyone who can get a ticket out here generally isn't at the time they board the one-way trip. I saw her looking for a job, but the help wanted signs are few and far between here.

The way her body lay out on the street, the blood glistening in the moonlight. It made it look like the stars in the sky were part of her and not light years away.

She was captivating, mesmerizing. The wounds she endured only added to her beauty, telling a story no one will ever know.

What do you think, readers? Do you think she cried? That she screamed and wished she had never come to this town as her blood spilled on its pretty streets? I'll keep those answers to myself for now until that special someone finds me.

And I know they will find me. I'm not really hiding. This town calls to the best of us. It's pretty on the outside, but it's rotten to the core. After all, some of the best villains wear a mask.

Until next time readers…

X X   X X

The screen of the tablet in my hands casts a bright light in the dim room. Narrowing my eyes, I read through the blog post again. Nothing in it gives away any details of who the writer could be or the town itself. All the little details that I need are missing. But what has me paying closer attention is the fact that this isn't the first death they have reported on and based on the timing between each, I don't think it will be the last.

Clicking through, I look at some of the other stories this same person has written. All very similar to one another with just enough detail to know exactly what was happening, but not enough detail to know who or where.

The weirdest part is, I can relate to each word they write, as if we were connected somehow. Which terrifies me, why would I feel connected to someone who from what I can tell takes innocent lives. Do I understand them because it's my job to hunt down these types of people, or is it something deeper? Something I don't want to discover about myself yet?

Sighing, I look up at the wall of my office. There are images of victims and criminals, crime reports and news articles, then all kinds of notes pinned to it, covering most available spaces.

Murders and murderers I investigated recently, my most recent case coming to an end only today. I have been on the city police force for years now; I worked my way to being a detective, and as much as I wanted to join the FBI like my mother before me, my parents felt it would be more beneficial for their organization if I stayed on the force instead. So, like the good daughter I am, I obeyed.

But it feels like a never ending cycle of death and disappointment. As much as I help the organization take care of the criminals and killers that slip through the system, I also see it when the system fails the innocent more visibly being on the force. I see the abused and the dead first hand. The fury at the perpetrators burns within me each and every day, only for me to be constrained by bureaucratic bullshit.

Justice isn't really justice, and I think that's what hurts the most. That is what has me wanting to break the chains I hold on my darkness and set it free. I want it to be real and I want to be the one to deliver it.

Most of the time though, I sit in the background while my mother and fathers take the lead. All too often I supply the information to them, and another team is sent in. I don't even get to see retribution served. But the families I talked to in order to find the truth, they never seem satisfied by the ending. The scales of justice inside me feel off balance. Lately, it's as if I'm going to break from all the death and darkness that outweighs everything else in my life.

If only I could live in the world my sister lives in, one where she ignores it all. I know she isn't happy like that, but even the ability to pretend might help the chaos in my mind not feel so overwhelming.

My sister and I have never been strangers to the evils of this world. Even when we were young we would see images of crime scenes pinned to walls. It was part of life. Initially, our parents had tried to shield us, but they then decided we needed to know the reality of the world.

I remember the first time I saw those images. The blood, the violence, the senselessness of it all. It shook me to my core. But instead of turning away, I found myself drawn to it. Not out of morbid curiosity, but out of a need to understand, to find a way to bring some semblance of justice to the chaos.

As I stare at the wall now, I can feel the weight of all those lives, all those stories. Each photo, each report, is a life touched by darkness. A life that, in some way, mirrors my own internal struggle. The thought is both sobering and motivating.

I look back at the tablet while trying to piece together this puzzle. I can tell their lack of details is a way to protect themselves, but it also means the mystery remains shrouded in shadows that urges me to shine a light on it.

Quickly, I realize I have two choices: I could ignore what I have found and pass it off as someone with an overactive imagination, concentrating instead on the immediate cases before me from my work as a detective. Or I can dive deeper into this mystery, hoping to uncover something that could prevent more tragedies and maybe help find that real sense of justice my mother always seems to find when she wraps up a case.

I could help these people. Really help them and maybe for once ensure real justice was given to these victims.

Choosing the latter feels right, despite the exhaustion that tugs at me.

So even when my eyes threaten to fall closed, I begin to compile the information from the blog. Everything I can find myself which, as it turns out, isn't much. It's tedious and meticulous work, but it's the kind of work that has always brought me a sense of purpose. Putting everything I have gathered into a secure email, I send it to my parents as well as my Uncle Max.

Since before I was born, my parents, along with their friends, have run an organization that targets corruption and those who take innocent lives. Uncle Max isn't actually our uncle, but another one of their friends, and an IT genius. If anyone can find details that I haven't been able to find, it will be him.

With not being able to tell where the blog is coming from, I can't even check to see if the local law enforcement are looking into this or just how large the case is. Are these all murders by the same person, a serial killer, or are they just different incidents in a corrupt town the blog writer mentions?

It could already be something on the radar of the local police, and if it is, that's great. They can solve the mystery. And if not, then my parents can send a team out there to deal with it.

Checking the time, I see that it's almost midnight. My limbs feel heavy from how hard the last few days have been. The case I just finished had me chasing down a sadistic asshole by the name of Eddie Sawyer. The case should have been simple, once we identified him as the lead suspect, it *should* have been cut and dry. But then he decided to try and run. It took us two days of twenty four hour work to track him down.

When I found him in an alley after a local butcher shop told us his whereabouts, I was *fuming*. A part of me was happy when he decided to try to attack me with a butcher knife. Shooting him probably shouldn't have given me the thrill that it did, but I haven't claimed to be normal for a long time. It was strange how the anger and frustrations that just seemed to build and build over the duration of the case began to bleed from me as efficiently as his chest wound bled for him.

The adrenaline rush from taking down Eddie, of seeing his blood spread across the ground beneath his dead body, has left me feeling both exhilarated and drained. In the quiet of my office, the reality of what I do and who I am settles over me like a heavy blanket. The shadows on the wall seem to whisper the same doubts that creep into my mind during these still moments. That the darkness is all I am, that they all deserve to die for what they have done and I am its instrument. I am the weapon that the darkness wields to avenge lost souls and no one could ever love me for that.

Leaning back in my chair, I let out a long breath and close my eyes for a moment, the weariness washing over me. The faces of victims and their families flash behind my eyelids, a stark reminder of why I do what I do. *No, that is not all I am. The darkness may be buried deep inside of me, but it's the light that guides my hand also. And it's that light that pushes me to keep going, to keep fighting, even when the odds seem insurmountable.*

A soft ping from my tablet breaks the silence. It's a response from Uncle Max, much faster than I expected. It's brief but reassuring.

UNCLE MAX

> Got it. I'll dig into this and get back to you soon. Stay safe.

I smile faintly at his words. *Stay safe.* It's something my family always says, knowing full well that safety is a luxury we can't always afford. But it's the thought that counts, the reminder that we're not alone in this fight.

I shut down the tablet and lean over to turn off the lamp on the desk. Movement outside the window makes me pause for a moment in the darkness, my body going still as I look intently at the surrounding property and forest that backs onto my parents' land. When my sister and I grew up, our parents built small cabins on the land for us so that we could have our own spaces to do whatever we wanted with. I loved that they built them close to the trees because it brought back so many good memories of Seanna and me. Plus, I can see her cabin from mine and that always brought me a sense of comfort.

Her cabin lights are off, so I can only assume she is already asleep or out at a nightclub living another carefree night. What I don't see is anything else out of the ordinary, no more movement. I take my time to look back and forth, searching in the shadows as the feeling that eyes are on me begins to make my heart race. But I don't see anything.

I frown to myself, because I could have sworn I saw something. Or maybe I'm just tired and overwhelmed. Stifling a yawn, I decide to dismiss it, but I check the locks as I close my office door and make my way to the other side of the cabin where my bedroom is.

It's small and cozy, a two-bedroom retreat with a simple but functional interior. It has all the amenities a young adult could need: a compact kitchen with modern appliances, a lounge area with a comfortable sofa and a modest entertainment setup, an office cluttered with case files and my personal tech, and a bedroom with a connected bathroom. Everything is done in neutral colors, giving the place a calming, understated feel.

I left the colors and walls as they were when our parents gave the cabin to me, appreciating the simplicity and tranquility of the design. In contrast, Seanna changed hers to dark grays and bold reds, making her space as intense as her personality. She once told me it felt fitting for her place to match her heart.

I enter my bedroom and immediately strip down before heading to the bathroom for a quick shower. The hot water does wonders to ease the tension in my muscles, the steam enveloping me like a comforting embrace. I stand there for a few moments longer than necessary, letting the water wash away the grime and the heaviness of the day.

Killing people can really take a toll on you. Plus I always feel like there is a layer of death on me that needs to be thoroughly washed down the drain after a job like this.

As the droplets hit my face I close my eyes, picturing what the blogger wrote about one of the women. Her clouded eyes, still wide open. The way her lips were parted, purple tinting the corners in a glow that almost made her appear otherworldly. Shivers dance along my spine as I shut off the water.

After drying off and pulling on my clean clothes, I feel slightly more human, but the exhaustion is still there, tugging at the edges of my consciousness. I crawl beneath the covers of my bed, the sheets cool and welcoming. Sleep and exhaustion bear down on me, and it isn't long until I give into it.

I have no idea who wrote those posts, but I can't deny that they intrigue me. It is almost as if someone recognizes the same beauty in death as I do. But there is one difference between us that has me questioning my involvement. I want to stop these killings and bring justice to the dead. What could this writer possibly want? Is it purely for attention or is there another purpose?

The quiet sounds of the forest outside is the last thing I hear before I drift off.

Chapter 2

Hydessa

DAD

Come up to the main house for breakfast.

MOM

Please... you forgot the please...

DAD

frowning emoji

PAPA

Ignore the grumpy one munchkin, come and have breakfast with me and your momma anyway *winking emoji*

I snort and drop the phone onto the covers beside me, scrubbing my hands down my face in an effort to wake up. With a tired groan, I swing my legs out of bed and stretch, feeling the stiffness from yesterday's exertion. The warmth of the covers tempts me to crawl back in, but the enticing invitation of a proper breakfast with real coffee spurs me into action.

As I shuffle towards the bathroom to freshen up, I can't help but smile and shake my head at the exchange between my parents. It isn't out of the ordinary for them to banter in our group chat.

Moments like these remind me of the warmth and love within my family, despite the darkness that often surrounds us.

I have the next couple of days off work after the way the last case ended, and I feel like my body needs it. One good thing to come from a shooting, I guess. It may have been a justified shooting, but the bureaucrats love their paperwork and red tape.

After washing my face and putting on some casual clothes, I lock up the cabin and make my way up the path to the main house. I can already see my mom through the large windows at the back of the house, sitting at the dining table and nursing a large mug of coffee as though it's her only salvation. I don't blame her; I inherited her love of the liquid gold and my dads know how to make it just the way I like.

As I open the glass doors leading into the dining area and kitchen, one of my dads steps up behind my mom and leans down to nuzzle her neck. "Hey, little darling," I hear him whisper to her.

I huff at them, but a smile still pulls at my lips. The love my parents have for each other has always been so full of devotion. Truth, Dare, and their little darling. My sister and I grew up hearing their nicknames for each other, and they ended up sticking with us.

I don't know their full story, and I cringe at the thought of knowing any details that might scar me for life. Bottom line is, they don't shy away from displaying their affection for one another. But I do know they went through a lot together and came out the other side of it inseparable, already pregnant with me and my sister.

My papa, Truth, straightens up as he notices me. "Good morning, sleepyhead," he teases, his eyes twinkling with amusement.

"Morning," I mumble, making my way to the coffee pot. They know better than to speak to me before the black drink has passed my lips.

I pour myself a mug and take a long, appreciative sip, feeling the warmth spread through me. "Thanks for the wake-up call."

My mom chuckles. "We thought you might need a little extra motivation this morning," she says, her eyes warm.

I take a seat at the table, and the smell of freshly cooked bacon and eggs fills the air. "You guys didn't have to go all out," I say, but the gratitude in my voice is unmistakable.

Dare, my dad, comes over with a plate of food and sets it down in front of me. "Nonsense. You need a good breakfast after the week you've had," he says, kissing the top of my head affectionately. "Besides, we wanted to talk about the information you sent over last night."

I raise my eyebrows in curiosity as Dad retrieves another two plates from the kitchen, placing one in front of Mom with a kiss to her cheek before sitting down. Papa huffs and rolls his eyes, moving to retrieve the last plate, the one for him, from the kitchen where Dad left it.

"Has Uncle Max found something?" I ask.

Dad points a fork at my plate, saying, "Start eating first, then we can discuss it." He has always been the overbearing one, but I know he does it out of love. I roll my eyes and start digging into the eggs and bacon on my plate.

"According to Max," he starts once I have eaten half of my food, "the person posting on that blog is bouncing their information all over the place. Not even he could pin it down, which says a lot in itself. I don't understand half of what he said, but he was able to find the general location of where the blog was posted from."

I smile at the news. "So, is someone going in to take the person responsible out or help assist law enforcement?"

Mom sighs and sets her knife and fork aside, only for Dad to growl at her. She gives him a look that he simply narrows his eyes at before she focuses on me again. "Max was able to find the general location, but not the specific person. No reports have been filed that we can find so we assume law enforcement isn't involved or doesn't know."

I nod, chewing my crispy bacon and savoring the taste. My mother exchanges a look with Papa before continuing. "Someone needs to go in to investigate discreetly and find the person responsible without raising a lot of alarm. It's a small island not too far from here, luckily, but it is very popular with tourists," she says.

Dad continues to stare her down until she growls back in frustration and picks up her fork again to return to eating. While they give each other challenging eyes, Papa looks at me with a grin, and I have to suppress my laughter.

"Who do you think would be good to send in?" Papa prompts.

I tilt my head and frown. "How come you're sending someone else instead of going in yourselves?" I ask. "This one feels important."

Mom grimaces, and I already know what she is about to say before she says it. I've seen that look enough growing up. "I have to head to Chicago. There's a serial killer up there that the local guys asked for help with," she responds.

"Well then," I say, leaning back in my chair. "You'll need to send someone who has proven themselves good enough. What about one of the new guys, Bodhi or Thorne?"

Dad exchanges a look with Mom again before turning back to me. "Well, given the delicate nature of this investigation, we need someone who can blend in with the tourists, but also someone who understands the kind of danger we're dealing with."

"And someone who can handle themselves if things get complicated," Papa chimes in.

I take another bite of my eggs, thinking it over. "It sounds like a job for someone with a mix of field experience and the ability to go undercover."

"Exactly," Dad says, his eyes fixed on me meaningfully.

I pause, fork halfway to my mouth, as the realization dawns on me. "You want me to go."

Mom reaches over and squeezes my hand. "We wouldn't ask if we didn't think you were the best person for the job."

I sigh, setting my fork down. "Why not Seanna? She has all the same skills as me."

Papa laughs, shaking his head. "Seanna has the subtlety of a sledgehammer sometimes. We need finesse for this one according to Max. This island is small, anyone new will draw attention naturally, especially if they aren't there for a vacation. And playing a tourist won't have them confiding in you."

"Plus," Mom adds, "she's currently tied up with another case. Something about a drug ring in the city."

Dad looks at me with a frown. "You brought this case to our attention, don't you want to see it through? It's not like you don't have the vacation time available. You barely ever take time off unless it's forced on you."

I sigh again, but this time with a sense of resignation. "Of course, you're right. I do want to see it through." I take another bite of my eggs, trying to mentally prepare myself for the task ahead.

Dad's expression softens slightly. "We know it's a lot to ask, but we have complete faith in you. You've proven yourself already."

Mom nods in agreement. "And remember, you're not alone in this. We are always only a call away."

Frowning, I realize I still don't even know where I'm going. Sure, I have wanted this opportunity to prove myself to them for a while now, I just wasn't prepared for it to be today. "What's the name of this place I'm going to anyway?"

"It's called Amity Island," Dad responds, his tone serious. I have to struggle for a moment not to laugh as I see Mom and Papa exchange an amused look.

I clear my throat to swallow my own laughter before asking, "Should I be wary of sharks?"

Papa snickers and says, "You should always be wary of sharks, both the animal and human variety, but this isn't *that* Amity Island."

Mom shakes her head at him before focusing on me again. "That one doesn't actually exist, but this one does benefit from the hype surrounding the name. There is a constant tourist presence there, so you need to be careful. Make sure to use your other identity and when you go out at night make sure to wear your mask."

My other identity. The fake name and identification that both Seanna and I use so we can swap out on jobs whenever we need to. So much for taking a few days off to rest.

I finish my breakfast in silence, letting their words sink in. This investigation is no different from any other, so I don't know why I feel nervous.

It's nothing new to hide behind a mask when I go out on jobs for my parents. Ever since I was little, I learned to love the anonymity it brought me. It's why I sometimes pretend to be my sister even now.

It comes in handy to have an identical twin sometimes.

After breakfast, I help clear the table, my mind already racing with plans and strategies. Mom and Dad both hug me goodbye and wish me luck, while Papa pulls me aside before I head back to my cabin to pack.

"Don't forget, you can always call Uncle Max if you need technical support," he says, his voice low and serious. "He's a wizard with computers and can help you track down almost anything."

I nod, appreciating the reminder even though that's why I sent the case to him in the first place. "Thanks, Papa. I'll keep that in mind."

He gives me a quick hug. "Stay safe out there, munchkin."

"I will," I promise, starting to feel the familiar blend of excitement and nerves that always accompanies the start of a new investigation.

As tired as I am, they're right; I do want to see this to the end. There is something about the blog that calls to me, and I need to solve this mystery myself. Not just the murders on the island, but the way I feel so connected to them.

Once I'm back in my cabin, I call into work to request the time off. I think my captain actually sighs in relief, thinking I'm taking some time to rest and recharge. Little does he know I have no rest or recharging on the horizon. I then spend the rest of the day looking into Amity Island.

It seems like a picturesque tourist town with a main strip of shops, a beach on one side, and a fishing port on the other. For an older established island, there is still a forested area in the center that hasn't been knocked down to make way for more vacation homes. It's almost like they wanted to preserve that piece of nature. But that doesn't mean there aren't plenty of short-term vacation homes and lots of resident houses. However, there are very few longer-term rental properties, and only one of those seems like it's available immediately.

I don't want to limit myself by staying in something short-term, and renting a long-term house will perhaps get me on the right foot from the start with the locals. Plus given I don't know how long it will take to get to the bottom of this mystery it seems the most logical direction, so I call the number on the property listing. It's a friendly female voice on the other end, she seems very nice when she informs me that yes, the house is available.

"It's lucky you called when you did! It just came back on the market," her bubbly voice comes through the phone.

"That's great to hear, I would love to take it before it's no longer available."

She emails me the paperwork, and I lock it in for a month with the ability to extend if I need to. With the accommodation sorted, I start packing, making sure I have everything I need.

When I take out my fake identity, I pause to look over the identification as I shift the cards around in my wallet. Taylor Delafield. The picture makes me look so innocent, so... not me.

It's moments like this when I wish I could just be the normal person who is on this card instead of hiding my identity behind a fake name. With a sigh, I shove the ID in its spot and check my tablet.

Uncle Max has sent me all the details he was able to find on the town and how far he had been able to get with identifying the blogger. It's one thing reading about the town on their own website, and another reading about its secrets he was able to uncover. I guess it would be bad for a tourist town to advertise its deep, dark secrets. But, I'll find them out all the same.

As night falls and my nerves build, I grow restless. My mind and body are filled with swirling chaos, and I need an outlet for my nervous energy before I have to focus on the investigation.

This is the only thing I love about the city. It may be full of darkness and people wearing masks, but that means there are some places where I can blend in and feel normal for a change.

Pulling out one of the dresses that I stole from Seanna, I put it on along with some makeup and then I head out. It's rare that I take a leaf out of Seanna's playbook, but tonight feels like the right time to let off some steam. For the next few hours, I will no longer be Hydessa or Taylor. For the next few hours, I will be Seanna Darling, party princess.

At least, until I get what I need.

Chapter 3

Hydessa

The club is already bustling when I arrive, music thumping and lights flashing in sync with the beats. I'm instantly let in, the bouncers only seeing my twin when they look at me. I chose this club because I know it's one she frequents.

Seanna is known as a party girl and she owns the attention she draws. It's nice to pretend to be her because only then do I feel like I can embrace my confidence.

Letting myself get lost in the crowd, I dance and move as though I don't have a care in the world. Just like her.

It's almost freeing to shed my usual demeanor and embrace this carefree persona that Seanna wears so easily, even if just for a little while. Once the thrum that was buzzing under my skin begins to dull, I head to the bar to grab some water. I'm not here to get drunk, just fucked.

I smile as I lean over the bar, making sure to show off my assets to the men near me. It's humorous to me how easy it is to draw a mans attention at a place like this. They are here for one reason, and tonight it just so happens that I am here for the same one. Well, that and dancing.

There is something about the way the music pounding through me almost helps regulate my heartbeat, slowing it down so the world feels easier to absorb. The flashing lights, the dark dance floor, and the way you are surrounded by people who are all moving to the same beat is freeing.

Making small talk with a few strangers, I enjoy the anonymity and the temporary escape from reality. I let some of their touches linger until I find the right vibe. I've found it's important to see how men will treat me before I take them somewhere. Are they quick to touch and pushy if I try to remove their hands from me? Do they pull me in and refuse to let go when I try to step back? Or do they look and don't touch until I lead them to?

It isn't long before I'm back on the darkened dance floor, letting my own identity get lost in the crowd.. I don't bother looking too closely at the nameless faces surrounding me—it's too dark anyway. Before the second song is over, there are hands gripping my hips from behind. He seems almost hesitant at first, not even pressing his body against mine, but I can feel him trying to match my movements.

Slowly, when I lean back into him, he pulls our bodies together, and I feel a hard chest against my back. Sweat prickles at my face and neck as the temperature rises. I can now feel every inch of the man holding me, his body much taller than mine by about a foot.

Reaching back, I wrap my hands around his neck as his hands slide further around the front of my body. One hand rests just under my breast while the other hovers dangerously close to my pussy, but I don't care—this is exactly what I want.

The movement of our bodies against one another has my whole body heating up and turned on. I needed this escape, and I'm finally about to get it. Grinding my ass back harder against his cock, I move to the music. He groans deep in my ear, bringing his hand up to twist my face around to meet his lips. It's not the best angle, and the kiss is harsh and messy, but I don't care. The urgency and intensity only adds to the thrill, making my heart race faster.

When I surrender to his lips, he tightens his grip, pulling me closer. Then his mouth is trailing down, his breath hot against my neck.

"You're incredible," he murmurs into my ear, his voice low and rough. I shiver at his words, feeling a thrill of excitement rush through me. Letting myself get lost in the moment, I forget all about the investigation, the island, and everything else. Right now, all that matters is the pulsating music, the heat of this strangers body against mine, and the intoxicating feeling of being desired.

His hands start to explore more boldly, one moving to cup my breast while the other slips under my dress, fingertips brushing against my thigh. I arch my back, pressing even harder against him, relishing the friction and the sensation of his growing hardness. He takes the hint, his hand slipping further up until he's teasing me through the fabric of my underwear.

I moan softly, the sound drowned out by the music, and turn my head to capture his lips in another fierce kiss. His hand finally pushes the fabric aside, fingers sliding against my wet heat. The sensation is electric, my pussy now throbbing to the beat of a different song. I grind against his hand, desperate for more.

Without breaking our rhythm, he maneuvers us off the dance floor and towards a dark hallway at the back of the club. He opens a door to what I can faintly see is a storage room. When he goes to turn on the light, I quickly say, "No lights."

He chuckles before pulling me back into him and whispering, "Will you at least tell me your name?"

"Seanna," I respond instantly, and he repeats it softly, but I don't really want soft. I don't bother asking his name; I don't want to know it.

The moment I manage to find the front of his pants in the dark, he grunts as I start working on opening them and freeing his hard cock. He swiftly takes back control the moment my hand wraps around his length and moves me so that my back is pressed to a free section of the wall.

I nearly let out a whimper when he tilts my face up to meet his lips. He kisses me quickly before I hear the sound of him opening a condom wrapper. Moments later, he's lifting me by the backs of my thighs while pulling up my dress. I move my panties to the side just in time for him to line his cock up to my pussy. My head falls back against the wall when he finally sinks inside of me.

The height advantage allows him to press deep, and I wrap my legs around his waist to lock my ankles and pull him closer. The music from the club outside is muffled here, but the bass still thrums through the walls, adding to the intense rhythm between us.

My hands clutch at his shoulders, nails digging in slightly as he begins to thrust. Every movement is driven by a mix of desire and urgency, each thrust pushing me toward the edge. He keeps one hand braced against the wall for support, the other gripping my thigh to keep me in place. His mouth finds mine again, and our kisses are a chaotic mix of teeth and tongues.

"God, Seanna," he mutters, his voice rough with need against my lips. "You feel so good."

The dark, confined space heightens every sensation. The concrete against my back suddenly jolts me into the past, right into the memory of holding my gun and aiming it at the murderer. The way the breeze blew against me, almost as if nature itself was encouraging me forward.

My hands ball into fists in the stranger's shirt as I forget all about him. All I can think of is how much I had wished I had a knife in my hand instead of that damn gun. How I yearned to stab him with it and watch as his eyes widened in horror, seeing the same darkness he used upon his victims reflected in my eyes as he took his final breaths.

His blood would splatter across the pavement as the beast within me took over, delivering the sweetest kind of justice there is. Death.

"Does that feel good?" The man's voice rips me from my daydream, ruining all of the momentum my body was beginning to build.

Was I about to come thinking of murder?

I clench my teeth as I try to push that thought away. Instead of responding to him with words, I tighten my legs around him, wanting him to go deeper, harder. I need the pain. I need to feel this deep within my dark soul. The rhythm of his thrusts becomes more insistent, more demanding.

Each movement pushes me closer and closer, but something isn't quite right. The friction, the heat, it's all there, but the final peak remains just out of reach. I can feel him getting closer, his breath coming in short, ragged gasps against my neck. My body responds to his intensity, but it's as if my release requires something more.

His pace quickens, and I can sense his climax approaching. With a final, deep thrust, he shudders against me, a low groan escaping his lips as he pulses inside me. His grip on my thighs tightens momentarily before he relaxes, breathless and spent.

I try to steady my breathing, frustration bubbling up from deep inside me because this is not what I needed. I did not come out here tonight to be teased and brought to the edge just so some stranger could get off instead.

He pulls back slightly, his lips brushing against my ear. "That was incredible," he whispers, his voice filled with satisfaction. "Did you come?"

Seriously, if you need to ask, then you already have your answer.

I force a smile that he can't really see, not wanting to ruin the moment for him because that's the kind of person I am. "Yeah," I reply, my voice a bit hollow. "It was great."

He lowers me gently to the ground, both of us adjusting our clothes in the darkness. The intimacy of the moment is already vanishing, my mind is already drifting back to reality, to the investigation, and to the nagging feeling of dissatisfaction that makes me want to scream.

He lingers for a moment, probably expecting more, maybe a conversation or a cuddle, but I can't stand to prolong this any further. I offer a polite nod and a faint smile before slipping out of the room. The thumping bass of the club instantly engulfs me, providing a much-needed distraction from the hollow ache inside.

As I make my way through the crowded club, I feel a surge of frustration. The whole point of coming out, of pretending, it was supposed to make me feel better. It was supposed to satisfy me and clear my mind for what is to come. I shove through the throng of bodies, ignoring the curious glances and the occasional touch from strangers. The pulsating lights and the pounding music blur into a cacophony of sensations, only heightening my agitation. Everything about the club suddenly feels suffocating. I need to get out, to breathe, to find clarity.

Finally, I burst through the exit and into the cool night air. The relative silence outside is a stark contrast to the chaos inside, and I take a deep breath, savoring the coolness as it fills my lungs. For a moment, I just stand there, letting the tension slowly seep out of my body.

But it doesn't last long. The annoyance of my failed mission still simmers beneath the surface, a constant reminder of the confusion I can't seem to escape. I have to grit my teeth and dig my nails into my palm just to make my feet carry me forward.

I start walking towards my car, each step heavy with the weight of my thoughts. The streets are relatively quiet, the distant hum of the city providing a stark contrast to the pulsating energy of the club.

When I reach my car, I pause for a moment, leaning against the door and letting out a deep, weary sigh. The cool metal under my fingertips feels grounding, a small anchor in the whirlwind of my mind. I unlock the car and slide into the driver's seat, the familiar scent and feel of the interior providing a small measure of comfort.

Sitting there for a moment, I let my hands rest on the steering wheel with my eyes closed. The night's events replay in my mind, the anger of the encounter in the storage room mingling with the weight of everything else in my life. I need to get home, to sleep, to clear my head and regroup.

This was supposed to make me feel better. All I had to do was pretend long enough for someone to make me come and then I could go to sleep peacefully without a thousand thoughts in my head.

Turning the key in the ignition, the engine roars to life, and I pull out onto the quiet street. The drive home is uneventful, the city lights blurring past as my mind drifts. I focus on the road, on the rhythmic hum of the tires against the asphalt, trying to push away the lingering dissatisfaction.

Finally, I arrive back at the cabin, the familiar sight of it offering a sense of relief. I park the car and step out into the crisp night air. The silence here is a welcome change from the sounds of the city. The door creaks softly as I push it open, making my way inside. I kick off my shoes and head straight for the bathroom, stripping along the way and throwing my panties in the trash, the lingering smell of the man from earlier already souring my stomach.

Turning on the shower, I let the water heat up before stepping in. Once the bathroom begins to steam up, I allow the hot spray to help soothe my tired muscles. Maybe this is what I need instead of running into the city for release. I'm not Senna and I think I need to stop pretending to be in order to get some relief. The encounter in the club now feels like a distant memory, replaced by a sense of emptiness and longing.

As I scrub my skin clean, I try to push away the nagging thoughts that threaten to consume me. But right now, all I can think about is the hollow ache inside, the emptiness that only seems to grow with each passing day.

Eventually, I step out of the shower and wrap myself in a towel, the steam from the bathroom swirling around me. I catch a glimpse of myself in the mirror, my black hair hanging limply down my back and my blue eyes looking overly large against my pale skin.

Shaking my head at myself, I quickly dry off and pull on a clean sleep shirt and underwear. Padding barefoot into the kitchen, I pour myself a half glass of wine, hoping that it will work to take the edge off instead. Carrying the glass and my phone to the couch, I curl up with my legs underneath me, gazing out through the large glass windows at Seanna's cabin.

A soft light shines in her living room. As I hit dial on my phone, I watch as her shadow approaches the window, looking back toward mine. The phone barely rings before it's picked up, but she doesn't speak first.

"If I hide..." I whisper into the phone.

"Then I'll seek..." comes her reply, her voice holding a mixture of concern and curiosity. "Are you okay?"

I take a deep breath and blow it out slowly. "No, I'm not," I admit quietly, my voice barely above a whisper. "I... I went to the club tonight."

There's a moment of silence on the other end of the line, and I can almost hear Seanna processing my words. "The club?" she repeats, her voice laced with surprise. "Why?"

"I'm leaving on an investigation tomorrow. It was a... distraction," I reply, the words feeling heavy on my tongue. "I needed to escape, even just for a moment."

Seanna's concern deepens, her voice softening. "And did it help, pretending to be someone else for a while?" she asks gently, knowing the answer before I even speak it. Seanna is aware of me using her name when I need to, but she also knows that it's my way of escaping myself sometimes.

"No," I admit, feeling a lump form in my throat. I recount the encounter I had with the man at the club as she listens patiently. "It just made everything... worse. I feel so... lost, Seanna."

There's a heavy sigh from the other end of the line, followed by a pause as Seanna gathers her thoughts. "I'm here for you, you know that, right?" she says finally. "Our parents already told me all about you heading out tomorrow, by the way. Maybe this investigation is what you need."

"What do you mean?" I ask, confusion lacing my voice as I try to make sense of her words.

Seanna lets out a soft chuckle, her tone gentle yet firm. "Think about it. It's a small island, and you need to be discreet. When in Rome, as they say... take the time to maybe live a normal life for a little while. You're on vacation, so have a vacation. I mean, obviously, you'll have to do your thing at night, but you know what I mean."

Her words sink in slowly, and I find myself nodding despite the lingering uncertainty. Maybe she's right. Maybe I do need a break from the constant chaos of my life, a chance to breathe and just... be. No back to back investigations that keep me up until the early hours of the morning only to arrest a murderer, only for it to take years for the case to go to trial before they're finally put away.

"Yeah," I reply softly, a small smile tugging at the corners of my lips when I realize I get to do everything on the island my way. "Maybe you're right. Thanks, Seanna."

"Anytime," she says warmly. "Now, get some rest. You've got a big day ahead of you tomorrow."

With Seanna's words echoing in my mind, I end the call and stand up, watching as she moves away from her window and further into her cabin. Finishing the last of my wine and turning back toward the kitchen, a strange shadow catches my attention just outside the window above my sink.

Frowning, I move closer, but there's no movement, just shadows and darkness. An eerie feeling settles over me as I continue to stare.

Come out, come out wherever you are. Seanna's voice echoes in my mind from when we used to play as kids. Hide and seek has always been our thing, but Seanna never liked to hide and I never liked to seek, so we kept our roles the same even when our parents tried to encourage us to take turns.

It would never work though. Seanna hates small spaces and putting her bright personality in a secret place never sat well with her. For me, being out in the open felt too vulnerable, like someone could jump out from behind a corner at any moment.

The shadows outside stay perfectly still and eventually I sigh, realizing my imagination is in overdrive. Moving to the kitchen, I rinse the empty glass before double checking all the locks and turning off the lights as I make my way to my bedroom.

Sliding between the cool sheets I contemplate taking my frustrations into my own hands, but quickly dismiss the idea for the night. I don't want to be even more frustrated if I couldn't even get myself there. So instead, I close my eyes and wish for sleep to help me hide for just a little while.

Chapter 4

Hydessa

The drive to the island feels long, with my nerves on edge the whole way. But the first glimpse of it as I cross the bridge takes my breath away. The picture I had found on the internet did not do it justice. The bridge is raised enough that the descent to the island side offers a spectacular view of the relatively small town.

I catch sight of a beach on one side and boats on the other. A pointed bluff with a raised lighthouse marks the ocean-side tip of the island, adding to its charm.

My first task is to find the strip of shops along the beachside where most of the tourists congregate. It will be a good introduction to the town, plus I need to get the keys to my new place.

After finding a parking spot, I make my way to the little real estate office. The jingle of a bell rings when I push through the door and a slim brunette with her hair in a bun greets me with a smile, her brown eyes shining from behind the wire frames.

"Hey there, how can I help you?" she asks.

"Hi, my name is Taylor. I think we spoke on the phone yesterday. I'm here to pick up keys to the house I'm renting," I say, holding my hand out to shake hers.

She has a strong grip, and her smile only gets brighter when she realizes I'm not another tourist. "Oh, Taylor! Yes, I remember. Welcome! Let me grab those keys for you."

As she moves behind the counter, I take in the small office space. It's cozy, with a few potted plants and photographs of various properties on the walls. The scent of fresh coffee lingers in the air.

"Here we go," she says, handing me a set of keys. "The house is lovely, right near the heart of the island and away from all these tourists and their parties. You'll love it."

"Thank you," I reply with a smile. "I'm looking forward to settling in."

She nods, her expression warm. Pulling out a map she marks where I need to go to get to the house and gives me a quick run down on the local businesses in the area.

"If you need anything or have any questions about the area, feel free to drop by. We're here to help."

"I appreciate that," I say. "I'm sure I'll be in touch."

With the keys in hand, I step back outside. The sun is climbing higher in the sky, casting a golden glow over the beach and the shops. This island, with its picturesque charm, is going to be my new home for the next few weeks. And with it, the hope of finding some answers.

Maybe even some peace.

From what I can tell, pretty much everything is walking distance, but the address of the house I'm renting is the furthest from the main part of town. I decide to take a stroll through the area first to get a lay of the land before heading up to the house. The air is filled with the salty tang of the ocean, and the sound of seagulls mingles with the chatter of tourists. The strip of shops is bustling, offering everything from souvenirs and beachwear to quaint cafés and seafood restaurants.

As I wander, I make mental notes of places that might be useful or interesting later on. There's a small grocery store, a bookstore that looks like it could hold some hidden gems, and a charming bakery with a tempting display of pastries on the further side.

The pastries and coffee smell too appealing to pass up, so I push through the door and into the warm space. The aroma is divine, and I immediately feel more at ease. The bakery is at the end of the shops, away from the hub of tourists, and I'm happy to see that it isn't as busy as some of the other cafés. The few patrons inside look more like locals, chatting quietly among themselves.

Behind the counter stands a beautiful blonde woman. She's wearing a pretty green wrap dress that accentuates her curves, drawing attention to her figure. I'm sure her looks work in her favor when she does get any tourists down this way. But it's her peculiar hazel eyes that truly catch my attention. The bold colors in them don't detract from the fact that underneath that pretty smile lurks something not quite so friendly.

Or maybe I'm seeing things because of the people I am used to in the city.

"Hey there, hun! What can I get for ya?" she asks, her voice warm and welcoming.

"Hi," I reply, trying to shake off my unease. It's hard to explain sometimes, but it's like the shadows that live under my skin know when they are in the presence of others. It's as if there is a tug in that direction, no matter how firmly I try to keep my feet planted. "I couldn't resist the smell. What do you recommend?"

She beams, a touch too eagerly. "Our croissants are a must-try. Fresh out of the oven. And the coffee is excellent, if I do say so myself."

"I'll take one of those croissants and a coffee, then," I say, smiling back.

As she moves to prepare my order, I glance around the small space. It's cozy, with wooden tables and chairs, and walls adorned with cheerful artwork and photographs. A small bulletin board near the entrance catches my eye, filled with local announcements and flyers. It might be worth checking out later for any useful information.

"Here ya go," she says, handing me a plate with a croissant and a steaming cup of coffee. "Enjoy!"

I thank her and find a seat by the window where I can watch the world go by as I eat. The croissant is indeed delicious, buttery and flaky, and the coffee is just what I needed.

As I savor the last bite of my croissant, the woman comes over, her smile warmer this time. "Need another coffee?" she asks, noticing my empty cup.

I glance down, realizing I finished the coffee without noticing, distracted by watching people outside. Grinning, I reply, "Yes, please. I think this is going to be my new favorite go-to every morning."

Her smile widens, becoming more genuine. "Are you visiting for long?"

I nod and glance back out at the passing people, concocting a story on the fly. "Yeah, I just rented one of the houses closer to the forest. Thought I would see if I liked it here before settling permanently."

Her face lights up with excitement. "You're renting the old Baker house? You should have said something and I wouldn't have charged you the tourist tax," she says with a laugh.

I glance at the couple of other people still at their tables, but she just laughs and waves a hand. "They're locals, hun, don't stress your pretty head. I'm Allegra, by the way. Welcome to Amity Island."

I smile back, feeling a little more at ease. "I'm Taylor."

"Nice to meet you, Taylor," she says, refilling my coffee cup. "If you need anything or have any questions, just let me know. I pride myself on knowing all the good gossip around town. Almost all the locals come here at some point during the day."

I raise an eyebrow, intrigued. "Oh really? So, you're the person to talk to if I want to know anything about anyone?"

Allegra chuckles, her hazel eyes glinting with amusement. "Absolutely. This island might seem quiet, but there's always something interesting going on. And I hear things." She taps her ear as if I didn't know that's where we processed sound. It makes me feel included in an odd way.

"Good to know," I say, taking a sip of my freshly poured coffee. "I might just take you up on that offer."

She leans against the table, her demeanor friendly but with a hint of something more as her voice lowers to a whisper. "You do that. People come to Amity Island for all sorts of reasons. Some are just passing through, but others are looking for something. It's the ones who are looking that usually have the best stories."

"I guess we'll see what kind of story I end up with," I reply, glancing out the window at the bustling street.

"Indeed," Allegra says, straightening up. "Enjoy your coffee, Taylor. And welcome again to Amity Island."

As I sip the fresh cup I can't help but appreciate how good it tastes. Once I've had enough of the people watching, I glance back around the room. A flyer on the bulletin board catches my attention.

There is going to be a carnival in town for an annual celebration along the waterfront in a week. I can't remember ever going to a carnival, but it seems like something someone living a normal life would do. Even if I solve this investigation quickly, maybe I could do what Seanna suggested and actually spend some time living a normal life here. Taking the time to escape the city might be good for me.

Besides, the locals are sure to be there and it would be an easy place to accidentally allow myself to bump into them and get to know them. I can start creating a list of suspects as soon as I know people's names.

It still baffles me that the local law enforcement has no idea about these murders, yet the blogger always makes it seem like the bodies are left in plain sight. Do they murder them just to write a post about them and then dump the bodies? Are they cleaning up for someone else? Or is the whole town hiding this secret in order to make sure tourists don't stop visiting?

My thoughts are interrupted by the sound of the door opening. Two men enter the bakery dressed casually, but the weapons and badges around their hips make it obvious who they are. For a moment, I think about my own badge and weapon hidden in my car.

"Mornin' Allegra," one of them says in greeting. I estimate him to be in his late thirties, maybe early forties, with sandy blond hair and laugh lines creasing the skin around his eyes. The second man is a bit taller, around my age, with black hair and a physique that suggests he spends too much time at the gym. His tattooed muscles are on display in a way that I'm sure is eye candy for most of the female tourists—if they aren't deterred by the perpetual frown that seems to be stuck on his face.

"Morning, Sheriff. Morning, Eli," Allegra responds with a grin.

Eli's frown deepens. "I've told you before, Ally. It's Deputy while I'm on duty."

She laughs, clearly unfazed. "Sure thing, Eli. How can I help you two this fine morning?"

I have to hold in a snort from the way Eli's face twists while Allegra pretends not to notice.

The sheriff, who seems more relaxed than his companion, gives Allegra a warm smile. "Just grabbing our usual and checking in. Anything interesting happening in town?"

"Same old, same old," Allegra says, but her eyes flicker towards me briefly. "Well, we do have a new resident," she adds, nodding in my direction.

That smirk I was wearing suddenly vanishes.

The sheriff glances over and gives me a friendly nod. "Welcome to Amity Island. I'm Sheriff Daniel Brooks, and this is Deputy Eli Carson. If you need anything, feel free to reach out."

"Thank you," I reply with a smile. "I'm Taylor. Just moved into what I've been told is the old Baker house."

"Ah, the Baker house," Sheriff Brooks says, a strange look entering his eyes as he watches me carefully. "That's a good spot. Quiet and close to the woods. You'll like it."

Deputy Carson gives me a curt nod, his expression still serious and his scowl deepening. "What made you come out this way?" His tone is as hard as his features, making me shake internally.

But I refuse to let that show. After all, I'm friendly Taylor who is looking for a fresh start, not Hydessa who is searching for a murderer or two.

"Needed a change in my life," I say with a shrug. "Besides, it's impossible to find a place that has a beach and trees within walking distance of each other without spending a fortune."

Eli eyes me for a moment but the sheriff seems convinced.

Allegra hands them their coffee and a couple of pastries. "Here you go, boys. Stay safe out there."

"Thanks, Allegra," Sheriff Brooks says, taking the bag. "See you around, Taylor."

With that, the two officers leave the bakery and Allegra turns back to me, her smile never faltering.

"Don't mind Eli," she says. "He's a bit intense, but he means well. It's why I tease him so much. Sheriff Brooks, on the other hand, is a sweetheart."

"I gathered that," I say, chuckling. "Thanks for the introduction."

"Anytime, hun. And remember, if you need to know anything, just ask. Enjoy your coffee."

As Allegra moves to help another customer, I take another sip of my warm drink.

I can already see that this little island is completely different from home. In the city, you are one among thousands of strangers who couldn't care less about you. But here, everyone seems to know everyone else, so surely someone knows something about who is murdering people on the streets of Amity Island and getting away with it.

As I leave the bakery, the morning sun is warm on my skin. The air smells of salt and coffee, mingling with the distant scent of the sea.

The interactions from the bakery play on repeat in my mind as I look around at the mix of tourists and locals on the island. This investigation isn't going to be simple. This town has its secrets, I can already tell, but how deep and dark are they buried? How long will it take before I uncover them all?

My main focus is on finding the blogger and stopping the murders, but I have a strong feeling there is so much more to uncover along the way.

Chapter 5

Hydessa

D eciding to settle into my rental home before I explore more, I return to my car and drive the short distance further into the heart of the island and away from the beach. Pulling up to the address, I stare in awe.

The information on the website didn't have any exterior images and only a few interior ones. It was enough to know that it would suit my purposes for however long I needed to stay here. But now, looking up at the large house, I'm wondering if I should have taken one of the short term rentals instead.

The place looms before me, its dark brick exterior giving it an imposing presence. The white trim offers a stark contrast, making the structure stand out even more against the backdrop of the dense forest behind it. The trees seem to crowd in on the house, their branches intertwining to create a thick canopy that blocks out much of the daylight. It's beautiful and eerie all at once.

For a moment, I wonder if it's the oldest or the first house that was ever on the island. It looks far bigger than all the others I have seen, and it is separated from its closest neighbors by a good distance.

I step out of the car, the crunch of gravel under my feet breaking the silence. The air is cooler here, the scent of pine mingling with the salty tang of the ocean. I take a deep breath, the smell is so different from what I'm used to at home, but somehow I like it even more.

Unlocking the front door, I push it open with a creak. The interior is just as impressive as the exterior, with high ceilings, hardwood floors, and large windows that let in plenty of natural light. The furnishings are tasteful and comfortable, a mix of modern and vintage pieces that give the house a welcoming yet sophisticated feel. I wander through the rooms, familiarizing myself with the layout. There's a spacious kitchen, a cozy living room with a fireplace, and several bedrooms, each with its own unique charm. It's large enough with enough hidden spots that I feel like I could get lost in it.

I set my bags down in the largest bedroom upstairs which offers a view of the forest. The bed is inviting, covered in a plush duvet and soft pillows. I can already imagine myself sinking into it after a long day. But for now, I have work to do.

First, I get to checking every square inch of the house for any surveillance. I have seen enough crimes in the city with hidden cameras and listening devices used in rentals that I have learned to be careful. You never know who is watching or who could be listening and it is up to me to ensure this case stays silent until I have found the murderer or murderers.

Maybe even then it can stay silent. I can take them out and dispose of them the same way they have with all their other victims. They can rest beside all of the bodies they already took from the world.

As fitting as that may seem, I don't know if my parents would approve of it. And at the end of the day, I am out doing this job for them.

Once I've cleared all of the rooms, I head back to the main bedroom to unpack a few essentials. Once it feels like I am a little more settled, I make my way back to the kitchen and brew a fresh pot of coffee, thanking whoever decided to leave a small supply of the liquid gold for me.

The aroma fills the house, adding a touch of warmth to the otherwise still atmosphere. I sip my drink as I stand by the window, looking out at the forest. There's something about this place that feels both peaceful and unsettling, a perfect reflection of my own inner turmoil.

Picking up my laptop bag and taking that along with my coffee to the small office setup, I feel a sense of purpose settling over me. There are far more rooms in the house than I will ever use, but at least they have an office set up in one of them with a large iron and glass desk. Placing my bag and coffee onto it, I look around the room for a moment. The walls are a medium gray but offset with the white trim and a large window that takes up most of one wall, looking out at the forest.

Frowning, I carefully move the desk further away from the wall it faces, allowing me more room to move in front of it. As I open my bag and take out the pile of papers I have inside it, I consider how best to organize the information I have. I don't have any photos yet to work with, but I do have some information already.

Looking at the first sheet of paper, the blog post I saw that started this obsession, I frown and glance back up at the blank wall. I can't use pins—I can only imagine how unhappy the real estate office would be with me if they came in to find the wall full of holes after I leave. Reaching into my bag again, I pull out a roll of tape and start taping the pieces of paper to the wall, being sure it doesn't pull at the paint.

I also take out a pad of post-it notes and start writing little notes to stick up on the wall as well.

Did no one hear the screams? Did the killer clean up the blood so no one saw it? Where are the bodies? Could someone be covering it up? I place a map of the island in the center, looking over areas that could be potential murder sights. When I finish my coffee and step back to survey the wall, it's like a makeshift investigation board. The questions and notes taped to the wall are starting points, breadcrumbs leading me deeper into the mystery of Amity Island.

My stomach growls, reminding me that I haven't eaten anything apart from the croissant earlier. It's already past lunchtime, so I grab my purse and the house keys, lock up and start to walk toward the beach again.

There isn't much noise this far away from the main tourist hub, and it's almost peaceful. It isn't long before I'm passing other houses and see the occasional person here or there who offers curious looks and waves in greeting. Everyone I have come across so far seems polite and friendly. If I didn't have the intuition towards evil that I do, I wouldn't be able to imagine that there is someone here killing people based on the front everyone puts on. It only takes twenty minutes at a leisurely pace to reach the beach, but there is still a decent walk along the beach to reach the strip of shops and the main tourist area.

Taking off my shoes, I bury my feet in the sand and breathe in the smell of the sea. Having lived close to the city for my entire life, I have barely spent any time at the beach. There is something about it that calms the soul.

Taking my time, I walk along the water's edge. There are a few people out this far, taking advantage of the quieter areas to swim and do some beach fishing. Like all the others I have come across, they smile and wave even though they don't know me. It feels strange but nice.

It feels *normal.*

Eventually, I reach the main town, taking in more detail than I did last time. There are other buildings surrounding the main tourist ones and cafes that I hadn't noticed.

Towards the outer edge near the bakery I visited this morning, there is an industrial looking gym that I make a mental note to check out soon. There are also a bunch of tourist shops with souvenirs along with the cafes and restaurants, and what looks like a little doctor's office toward the center next to the small police station.

Further along the street, a little tattoo parlor is tucked in between some boutiques. On the water side of the street there appears to be a lifeguard stand with a large balcony. I can see a couple of people keeping a watchful eye on those in the water which makes me feel like they are concerned about safety.

Next to that there are several custom surfboards on display along with some used boards in a stand. From my angle, I can just make out the front of the building that has art on display through the glass windows. I get the impression that the artist is the same one that created the beautiful surfboards.

Deciding to try a small seaside cafe that catches my eye, with tables set up outside under colorful umbrellas, I find a seat at one of the tables with a view of the ocean and order a seafood salad and a cold drink.

As I wait for my meal, I pull out my phone and review my notes, thinking about how to proceed with my investigation. The blog posts still nag at me, but they aren't going to provide me with any more detail than what I already have. I need to learn the ins and outs of everyone on the island and survey the area to see if any location could match up with the small hints from the posts.

Judging from how long they have been posting, it has to be a long term resident and not someone simply visiting on vacation. But there are still a lot of residents, a lot of personalities to learn about.

It could be any number of people, though; there is no detail on how the killer interacts with their victims. Do they actually get to know them or are they simply people who are in the wrong place at the wrong time?

The blog gave details that these victims are almost all homeless, the mention of having no one is a clear indication that they are targeting people who won't be missed.

Because it won't draw attention to them and the island? Because they think that they will get away with it the longer no one investigates? Are they relying on it not being investigated and if so, why post the blog?

My food arrives, and I dig in, savoring the fresh, tangy flavors. It's a nice change from the usual hurried meals back in the city. As I eat, I overhear snippets of conversation from the other diners—mostly small talk and vacation plans, but occasionally, something about the island's history or local legends.

Once I finish my meal, I go inside to pay at the little counter. There is an older woman there with her brown hair tied back behind her neck and kind brown eyes as she offers me a friendly smile, her badge says her name is 'Lily'. "How was it, dear?" she asks.

"Amazing, thank you. I can honestly say I've never had seafood that tastes so good before," I respond, and her smile widens.

"I'll have to let Jonah know you said that."

I tilt my head curiously, wondering if Jonah is the chef. Lily chuckles and clarifies, "Jonah is one of the local fishermen. We only source local seafood, and he supplies our little slice of heaven here almost every morning."

I smile as she hands me my change. "Please do. I'm sure I'll be back here again soon."

"See you then, dear." She nods as I turn away and leave the cafe.

I make my way to the little grocery store near the real estate office I spotted earlier. It's not overly busy inside, which I assume is because most tourists rely heavily on the cafes and restaurants.

An old lady with short salt and pepper hair behind the counter is serving a customer while a young boy helps bag up items. They all glance at me as I enter, but I just smile and take a basket before strolling down one of the few aisles. I can hear low voices talking amongst themselves as I pick up more coffee and basic essentials for sandwiches, along with some snacks. Lastly, I grab some wine before making my way back to the front.

"Well, if it isn't our newest resident," the old lady says with a smile, and I almost want to duck my head as the heads of the few other people in the store turn in my direction. "Don't be shy, I'm Gladys. You must be Taylor, aren't you a pretty thing," she says as I put my basket on the counter in front of her. I blush slightly.

"Nice to meet you, Gladys," I respond as she starts to scan the items in my basket. I feel someone step up behind me, almost overbearingly so, and I shift so I can look without being too obvious.

"I wouldn't get too attached, Miss Gladys. She looks like a city girl. You know they don't last long around here," comes a deep male voice.

I focus on him while still keeping an eye on the rest of the store. The man behind me is a little taller than me, his brown hair short and shaved close to his head on the sides. He's muscular with tattoos and wears a tight shirt with a construction company logo, jeans, and heavy-duty boots. Dirt and dust from an already busy workday covers him. His face isn't unfriendly but also not open and friendly either. He seems wary and jaded.

Just like me.

"Oh, hush, Rye. Nothing wrong with city girls. You forget I was one once upon a time," Gladys responds with a wave of her hand in his direction. A smile pulls at Rye's lips, probably thinking about how long ago that must have been, as he dips his head to her in response.

A couple of other people in the store have stopped to watch. One is an older gentleman with gray hair who seems to find humor in our conversation. The other is a man who looks to be in his early thirties, with messy sandy blond hair and a few days' worth of stubble.

He looks rugged with tan skin, like he spends too long in the sun, but it's the deep scowl on his face that catches my attention. His focus isn't on me but on the man behind me. When his green eyes meet mine, he simply turns and enters one of the aisles.

Should I take that as a sign I should be wary of Rye? There is obviously more to the look, but I doubt I'll find out what it is right now. I don't even know who that other man is.

Gladys finishes scanning my items while I am focused elsewhere and, with a smile, she says, "Ignore Rye. Don't let his hatred of city girls scare you off."

She shoots him a glare before taking my money and giving me my change. The young boy, who looks like he could be Gladys' grandson, hands me my groceries in a paper bag. I thank them both and make my way out of the store pleased that I am already getting to know people and clearly making an impression.

The more I can get these people to know me, trust me, the more likely it will be that I can get to the bottom of this town and complete my mission.

The sun is starting to lower across the sky, casting a deeper golden glow over the beach. I take my time walking back along the shore, enjoying the serene atmosphere and the calming sound of the waves. By the time I reach the house, the sky is a deep orange, and the forest behind the house is a silhouette against the fading light.

Unlocking the front door, I push it open and step inside. The house is quiet and still, a stark contrast to the bustling beach and the lively cafe. After putting the groceries away, I head straight to the office, where my makeshift investigation board awaits. The questions and notes taped to the wall seem to beckon me, and I need to add the information to it I learned today.

It would also help me pass the time until darkness fell across the island. Until I could go out again and see what was hiding in the shadows.

Chapter 6
Hydessa

I've been watching the sun set from one of the windows in a bedroom on the second story of the house. It's beautiful, such a stark contrast to the wall I created in my makeshift office. With bated breath, I watch as the lights on the waterfront start to shut down and the island turns from one of gleaming color to blackened shadows.

That's when I make my move.

Tying my hair back, I put on my black pants and black hoodie. My blue eyes get covered with black contact lenses, gloves and a skull mask finishes the look. With the hood up, you can't tell it's even me, which is exactly the point.

The mask is custom-made to fit my face and will disguise my voice if I ever speak to anyone with it on. Not that I do. I make a point of staying hidden in the shadows normally, as invisible as possible to prying eyes. My parents taught me to blend with the darkness, to hide in plain sight, and I'm good at it. I couldn't avoid drawing attention to myself during the day as someone new, but at night I will be one with the islands shadows.

This is how I am able to catch the bad guys. While most people are tied up in bureaucracy, I let a sliver of my inner monster loose at night. Just enough that it can peek through the cracks, but not enough to give it control. I gather evidence, then watch my prey, waiting for them to give me what I need to put them behind bars.

I think this is one of the few times I truly feel like myself, balancing the dark and light inside of me.

The day my dad, Dare, gave me the skull mask that everyone in the organization wears to protect their identity out on a job, I remember feeling like he could see inside of me. Like he knew what I was struggling with deep in my soul. It was one of the few moments that the blackness under my skin pushed towards him, as if it were seeking out an old friend.

It was a moment I will never forget because it was one of the few times in my life that I didn't feel alone in my fight to balance what was right with what was necessary to protect others.

Leaving quietly out the back door of the house, I use the forest for coverage to get as close as I can to the waterfront again. The forest sweeps in an arc, almost as though it is trying to touch the lighthouse and then cradling the beachfront area, stretching and curving around to the end of it. When the trees stop hiding me, I keep to the shadows, taking the path between buildings until I can see the once-busy stores and cafes. The streets are mostly empty now, with only a few people milling about, likely the late-night workers heading home or the occasional insomniac taking a stroll.

I keep my movements smooth and deliberate, every step planned to avoid detection. My parents always said that if you think like a predator, you'll become one, and I've taken that advice to heart. The skills they taught me, honed over years, are second nature now. I melt into the shadows on instinct, becoming one with the darkness.

The primary target tonight is the small police station. Not to break in—no, that would be too reckless—but to observe. To learn the rhythms and habits of the officers, see how they patrol and when they take breaks. If I'm going to uncover anything about this place and the supposed murders, I need to know what the local law enforcement knows, if anything.

It's clear they aren't investigating anything according to Uncle Max, but are they covering it up so that the towns name doesn't sour? Do they have a secret task force looking into it on the side while keeping no paper trail?

I find a spot behind a thick clump of bushes with a clear view of the station. The lights inside are on, but the front desk is empty. Scanning the area, I note the positions of the security cameras. They're minimal, probably relying more on the low crime rate than on actual surveillance.

After an hour of watching, I see the sheriff step outside, stretching and yawning before lighting a cigarette. He leans against the wall, looking out into the night but not really seeing anything. His routine seems casual, almost too relaxed for a place that's had multiple disappearances. He either has no idea, or he is very good at concealing his concern for the situation.

I wish I could simply have arrived as the detective I am and asked the sheriff upfront about what I know, but sadly, I also know that even law enforcement can't be trusted at times. The sheriff seemed like a friendly face and a nice man, but even the sweetest person could hide a heart of evil. After all, Dahmer was able to charm at least sixteen men long enough to kill them and snack on their corpses.

Never trust a charming face should really be my motto.

Movement out of the corner of my eye catches my attention, a soft light emanating from the building I saw earlier on the beach with the art and surfboards. It looks like all of the boards have been put away for the night, and the lights are out except for one room on the upper floor where there is a large window. I can just make out the side profile of a man sitting in front of a canvas painting.

Getting a little closer, I notice a little more of the details in the dim light. His dark hair is messy, as though he's run his fingers through it repeatedly, almost shaggy with a slight curl at the end. I can see the dusting of stubble along his jaw that seems clenched in concentration as he applies red paint to the piece he is working on.

I can't see the piece from where I am, but when he turns to dip his brush into the pain I can see the art across his bare back. There is a large tattoo that spans across his skin, a bird of prey of some kind, and the sight fascinates me.

I stay there for a moment, watching the artist work. The intensity of his focus is palpable even from this distance, and I wonder if he may have seen something from that window that could be useful. Artists often see the world differently, notice things that others might miss. I make a mental note to approach him later, perhaps under the guise of admiring his art if he has it on display.

Turning my attention back to the police station, I realize that the sheriff had disappeared while I was distracted. I curse silently under my breath, annoyed at myself for losing track of him and getting distracted.

Quickly refocusing, I scan the area around the building. It would be safe to assume he returned inside the station, but I don't like not knowing for sure.

I split my attention between the police station and the artist's studio for another hour. However, it becomes apparent that I won't gain any significant new insights from this vantage point tonight. With a sigh of resignation, I decide to move further along the street.

Most places have already closed, leaving only a few establishments with lights still on. The tattoo parlor catches my attention as I pass by. Through its windows, I glimpse someone inside, meticulously cleaning the space. The person appears heavily tattooed themselves, their movements precise and thorough, black hair pulled away from their face by a hair tie and showing off the shaved sides. I can't make out the details of his face from this distance, but I make a mental note to come back tomorrow.

Continuing down the street, I notice the gym next. Its windows are reflective, preventing me from seeing inside, but the glow from the glass entryway suggests activity within. The deserted streets amplify every sound, making each step feel louder than it should. I remind myself to keep to the shadows, avoiding unnecessary attention.

With nothing else catching my attention, I decide to return to the house to write down my observations for the night. Quietly, I make my way back, staying hidden until I am under the cover of the forest.

I'm almost at the back of the rental house when a shift in the forest shadows makes me pause. Instinctively, I narrow my eyes and scan the darkness surrounding me. The silence is eerie, not even the sounds of nocturnal creatures can be heard.

My mask suddenly feels stifling against my face, and a shiver runs down my spine. Someone is watching me—I can almost feel it, like a phantom touch—but the sensation passes fleetingly, leaving me uncertain if it was real or imagined. Almost like back at my cabin, but this was more intense.

Remaining perfectly still, I listen intently for any sign of movement in the forest. Seconds stretch into minutes, but there's nothing—no rustle of leaves, no snapping of twigs. With cautious steps, I continue towards the house, my senses heightened and on alert.

I almost slam the door behind me when I make it back inside the house. Instead of turning on the lights, I quickly discard my disguise under the cover of darkness, removing the hood, gloves, and skull mask.

I feel like I can finally take a breath when it's all off of me. The coolness of the room is a welcome relief after the tension of the night and the stifling feeling of being watched. Once I tuck the attire away, I flip on the light and make my way to the office, sitting down at the desk and taking out a notepad and pen to record my observations.

Taking careful notes, I am sure to go over in detail everything I know about the various businesses along the waterfront. Once the list is made, I flip to another page to make a note for each person I have come across so far and leave room to add more as I continue to watch them.

Some pages have more details than others, like Sheriff Brooks, Deputy Eli, and Allegra. But then others have minimal detail. The artist whose name I don't even know, the worker at the tattoo shop, and the others I have only seen just have their jobs listed with a brief description of their appearance.

You never know when you will need to recall someone's eye color or a certain tattoo. If I can catch even a glimpse of the murderer in action, maybe it will help me narrow it down. They probably wear a mask, but their build is important which is why I note that Allegra is curvy and that Eli is slightly taller than the sheriff who walks with a bit of a slouch.

Everything is important, even if it doesn't seem like it at the time. Which is why I make these lists, so I don't forget anything.

As I jot down the last details, I ponder my next steps. The eerie feeling of being watched in the forest lingers in my mind. Was it just my imagination, heightened by the adrenaline of the night's activities, or something more? I will have to be more vigilant in the future.

Reaching over to my tablet, I press the button to light the screen and check the time, noticing that there's a notification there. Thinking perhaps that Uncle Max may have found something, I pick up the device, bringing it in front of me and unlocking it.

Except, it's not Uncle Max. It's the alert I set up two nights ago.

Dear Readers,

It's amazing how some people can be so unobservant to what happens around them. They don't even see the life leaking out of someone oh so close by.

But then this one didn't make a sound, didn't scream or cry, all that could be heard was the soft gasping of breath until it rattled and stopped. It was like she had already given up before the knife cut through her pale skin.

She didn't even get a chance to live a proper life, barely an adult and already abandoned by everyone. This time, the sand absorbed her essence, the tiny grains stained red. Her dark blue eyes were a pretty reflection of the dark water, her brown hair like night and day to the sand.

Did you hear her gasps for breath? No, you didn't. You arrived too late. You just missed her when you appeared like a ghost, trying to become one with the shadows.

But we know you're here… creep around town all you like… you won't see us until we want you to. But don't worry, we see you.

Until next time…

<u>X X</u>   <u>X X</u>

My stomach drops. *What the fuck… Are they talking about me?*

Chapter 7

Hydessa

I struggled to fall asleep after the new blog post. Not only because I just missed resolving this investigation quickly, but because of the other details that the blog revealed.

There is more than one of them. Their use of the word *us* and *we* made that clear.

Why had I never once considered that there is more than one person behind all this?

After that revelation, I looked back over all of the historical blog posts, but I was right, there had been no clues previously. No little details at all, not like what they gave away last night.

If I hadn't already been here and knew where the blog was coming from, the details of the sand would have been another hint that I previously didn't know.

Are they actually going to feed me more information now that I'm closing in? But why? Do they think it's fun to make me chase them? Is it about the thrill for them? Do they think they will get away with this? How did they even know I was here?

The sun can only just be seen creeping into the sky when I tie up my running shoes. I am dressed in leggings and an exercise top, my black hair pulled into a hair tie and away from my face.

I normally run with music playing, but today I don't want any distractions. Especially not after the way I felt those eyes on me. Each time I scan the trees through the window, the feeling tries to return. It's making me paranoid.

The events of last night replay in my mind—how close I had come to finding the killer. *How late had I actually been? Hours? Minutes?* Shaking my head to clear the thoughts, I grab my keys and some money, step out the front door, and lock it behind me. I start to jog down the quiet street in the direction of the beach.

The rhythmic pounding of my feet on the pavement helps me focus. I need to think strategically, consider the dynamics of a group rather than a single individual. *How many are there? What roles might they play? Who is in charge? How do they communicate and plan their actions? Is it a collective decision to post the blog and leave bread-crumbs?*

As I make my way past the now partially familiar buildings, my mind races faster than I can keep up with. I need to adjust my approach. If there is a group, I can't just focus on one suspect at a time. I need to consider connections and patterns among multiple people.

One person on a small island getting away with murder is one thing, but how could multiple people hide their actions in such a small close knit town? Any one of the people I have met could be part of this, or none of them could be. I need to watch for inter-actions, subtle signals, and anything that might indicate a larger conspiracy.

Reaching the beach, I slow to a walk, letting the sound of the waves calm my thoughts. The early morning light casts long shadows on the sand, and the scene is almost serene. But somewhere out there, the killers are likely planning their next move.

Was it here on the beach last time? Is the same sand I'm walking over really just another crime scene?

Today, I decide to start by revisiting the places I observed last night. The artist's studio, the gym and the tattoo parlor are my first stops. I need to gather more information to put in the profiles I began building last night. Their routines, their behaviors, what hand they tend to write with—everything matters.

I also plan to keep my ears tuned in to everything around me. Surely someone knows this latest victim, maybe I could overhear a snippet of conversation with a clue to who she was. There is a decent number of tourists on the island, enough that one disappearing here and there isn't noticed. But the numbers are now adding up to double digits, surely someone has realized something by now.

I pick up my pace again and jog towards the bakery. The lights are shining brightly, and it looks like there are already a few of the locals inside with the same idea as me. The smell of freshly baked bread and brewing coffee reaches me even before I step inside, making me release a happy sigh.

When I push through the door, Allegra greets me with a grin. "Morning! If I knew you liked to run, I would have invited you to run with me in the mornings," she says, her voice much too cheerful for this early hour, especially when I haven't had any coffee yet.

I smile in response, glancing around at the few people already seated at tables with their coffee.

"Umm, at exactly what ungodly hour do you wake up to run and still get here to caffeinate people?" I ask. Her laughter draws the attention of everyone in the room.

"Don't tell me you're a night owl. There are far too many people around here that enjoy the darkness more than the beautiful sunshine," she responds, and for a moment, my heart races. I know she means it literally, but it still cuts a little too close to my own personality. She doesn't seem to notice the effect she's had on me as she continues, "Same as yesterday, hun?"

I look at the display case for a moment before responding. "How about a slice of that banana bread instead? It looks amazing."

She grins with pride as I hand her the money and turn to head toward one of the vacant tables by the window.

Suddenly, I'm forced to pull up short so I don't physically run into the man standing behind me. His deep green eyes are assessing, and it takes me a moment to place where I've seen him before. He was in the grocery store the day before, the one scowling at Rye.

Standing in front of me, he tilts his head as though to acknowledge me, but doesn't say anything as I step past him and make my way to the table.

"Morning, Jonah," Allegra says cheerfully. How can she be so cheerful all the time?

I pause when I realize I know that name. This must be the man who supplied the café I ate at with the amazing seafood.

My mouth waters just thinking about it as I settle into my seat, taking a moment to observe the room. Jonah moves to the counter, exchanging a few quiet words with Allegra. She turns to start preparing the coffee and Jonah walks over to stand near my table.

"It's Taylor, right?" he asks, his voice carrying a raspy undertone. He looks at me curiously.

I smile and nod. "Yes, that's right."

"How are you liking the island?" he inquires.

"It's... interesting," I respond, and I swear his lips twitch in amusement. It's kind of adorable.

Allegra comes over with my coffee and banana bread, placing them on the table, and handing Jonah a to-go cup.

"Anything else you need, hun?" She directs the question to me.

I shake my head. "No, this is perfect. Thank you."

When Allegra heads back to the counter, I take a sip of my coffee, savoring the warmth.

Jonah remains standing by my table, his curiosity apparent. "What brings you to the island?" he asks, taking a sip from his to-go cup.

I hesitate for a moment, debating how to respond, though I'm sure my pause is suspicious as fuck. "Needed a change of scenery." I say, keeping it vague.

Jonah's eyes narrow slightly, as if weighing my words. "Interesting choice. Not many people move here just for a change of scenery."

I smile and shrug, hoping to deflect his curiosity. "I guess I'm not like most people."

He nods slowly, still watching me closely. "So, what is it you do for a job then? Don't tell me you're one of those independently wealthy girls. You don't really strike me as the type."

Somehow, I don't think that 'I chase murderers and the scum of the earth' would be a good response, given my need to fly under the radar. Thankfully, Allegra interjects from the counter, her tone playful yet pointed.

"Don't go harassing the poor girl with twenty questions this time of the morning, Jonah. Especially when she hasn't even finished her first coffee."

Jonah's lips twitch again, and he nods in Allegra's direction with mock deference. "Yes, Ma'am," he says, his voice laced with amusement before looking back at me. "See you around, Taylor." As he turns to leave, I can't help but watch the way his strong body moves. It's as if he owns the presence of the gravity around him.

I let out a slow breath as my heart rate slows down again. As much as I tried not to show it, questions make me nervous. I know I typically ask questions for a living, and my goal here is to get to know these people and gain their trust. That does come with some give and take, which means I need to make sure my story is straight in my mind for when others ask the same things. I know I have a cover set up, but it's rare that I have to use it, so it doesn't come naturally just yet.

I finish my coffee and banana bread, quickly falling in love with this place. Allegra has the green thumb of baked goods, I might actually get addicted.

Looking around the room, my mind races with strategies for the day. I wanted to explore some more of the businesses that I had seen the previous night. Now that the blogger revealed someone was killed on the sandy beach, I feel like the closer places are a good place to start looking. It is still early in the day but this end of the strip of shops is where the gym is, so that will be my first stop.

Getting up from my seat, I wave goodbye to Allegra as I step out of the bakery, the fresh morning air greeting me once again. The gym is just a short distance away, and I make my way there with purposeful stride.

I replay my cover over in my mind as I walk, refamiliarizing myself with it in case I'm asked again. I'm a project manager from the city, I've had one too many big, tough projects recently and I just need a change in pace. The island is the fresh start I need to settle down now. *No need to tell anyone my projects are murderers and criminals.*

The gym is a modest building with a sign that simply reads "Island Fitness." As I push the door open, the familiar sounds of clanging weights and the rhythmic thumping of running shoes on treadmills fill the air. The smell of sweat and rubber mats hits me immediately, a stark contrast to the bakery's warm, inviting aromas.

No one is at the reception desk to greet anyone but everything is quite open. I can see a few people giving me curious looks, including one man who taps someone on the shoulder and points in my direction. When I get an eyeful of the man as he turns toward me, I can see why there are so many women here this early in the morning.

He is pushing two hundred pounds of pure muscle while tattoos decorate his pecs and down both arms. His bare abs emphasize the freaking eight pack he has. His black hair is cut close to the sides of his head, leaving the top longer.

I am forced to hold back a laugh when he runs his hand through his onyx locks and a woman on a treadmill almost falls over. He notices immediately and flashes a grin in my direction.

"Hey there, welcome to Island Fitness," he says as he walks toward me, his voice surprisingly warm and friendly. "I'm Makai. Are you looking for a day pass?"

"Actually, I'd like a week pass," I reply, motioning down to my running attire. "I've already had a run this morning."

Makai's eyes flick to my running gear and back up to my face, a smile spreading across his features. "Ah, a fellow early bird. Nice. Let's get you set up." He moves behind the reception desk as he waves me over.

As he starts processing my request, I take the opportunity to observe the gym more closely. The layout is efficient, with free weights on one side and various machines on the other. A group of people are engaged in what looks like a high-intensity interval training class in the far corner. Their focused expressions and the instructor's enthusiastic shouts add to the dynamic energy of the place.

Makai hands me a form and a pen. "Just fill this out, and you'll be good to go."

I take the form and start filling it out, keeping my responses as generic as possible. As I write, Makai leans casually against the counter, striking up a conversation.

"So, you must be new around here. I haven't seen you before."

I nod, not looking up from the form. "Just started renting the old Baker house. Figured I'd check out the local spots and start settling in."

He chuckles. "Well, you picked a good time. The weather's great, and there's always something happening around town."

I hand him the completed form and the cash amount listed as the fee for a week. He scans it quickly before nodding in approval.

"Looks good. Here's your pass." He hands me a card. "If you need any help with the equipment or have any questions, just let me know."

"Thanks, Makai," I say, tucking the pass into my pocket. "Is there usually someone here to help all day? I'll probably come back later after I explore some more."

Makai nods. "Yeah, there's always someone around. If I'm not here, one of the other trainers will be. We've got a pretty tight-knit team, and we're all happy to help out."

"Thanks, good to know. And you're open late, right? I thought I saw the lights on late last night," I ask, trying to sound casual. A strange look enters his eyes, and a chill slides up my spine.

"We generally close up around eleven at night. I was here late doing paperwork last night since I'm the owner. Here I thought you were a morning person, not a night owl." His grin is big as he teases me, but there is an edge to it now.

I force a laugh, trying to keep the conversation light. "I guess I'm a bit of both, depending on the day. Besides, it's always hard getting used to sleeping in a new place."

Makai nods, the strange look in his eyes fading as quickly as it had appeared. "Well, if you ever need a late-night workout, just let me know. I can make arrangements for you."

"Thanks, I'll keep that in mind," I say, heading towards the exit. "See you around, Makai."

"See you, Taylor," he calls after me, his voice carrying a lingering note of curiosity.

As I step out of the gym, I can't shake the feeling that Makai knows more than he's letting on. His reaction to my comment about the lights being on late was unsettling. Was he just caught off guard, or is there something more to it?

Either way, I think it is time to add more to my list on the owner of the gym.

Chapter 8
Hydessa

Instead of going straight back home, I decide to take some notes on my phone before heading to the tattoo parlor, Saints and Sinners Ink.

When I arrive, I realize it's dark inside, the doors closed. I guess it's a bit early for this sort of business to be open. Curiously, I look at the artwork in the window. The artist is talented. Intricate designs of dragons, flowers, and abstract patterns line the display, each piece showcasing a unique style and remarkable attention to detail.

As I move closer to the window to get a better look, I notice a small sign tucked in the corner. "Open at ten," it reads, accompanied by a rough sketch of a clock with the hands set to ten. I glance at the time on my phone to realize I still have another hour.

Turning away from the parlor, I decide to see if the art studio is open at this time instead. Heading across to the waterfront, I approach the front of the building where the gallery is. On this side there are a lot of pieces of art on display, various splashes of color across the canvases drawing the eye. Each piece is beautiful in its own unique way.

A bell jingles as I push through the glass door, the inside revealing glimpses of the beach and the painted surfboards through the back of the large open space.

"With you in a moment," a voice calls out from behind a wall that seems to separate the spaces.

Making my way in that direction, I pass the divider to see the space open out toward the crashing water. Big glass doors have been pushed to the side to allow an uninterrupted space between the beach and the shop.

To the side there are a lot of surfboards in the process of being painted, while several chairs and easels are set up facing toward the open back of the building.

A man is standing in the center of the space with his back to me. From the hints of the tattoo around his ripped tank, I believe it's the artist I saw painting the night before. He's spraying something on one of the canvases set up on an easel. The artwork in here is nothing like those in the gallery out front, making me assume he didn't create them all.

As he turns to set the bottle in his hand aside, he catches sight of me in the doorway and flashes a grin. A little stunned, I have to hide my reaction. There are highlights that shine through his black hair as he moves, almost like the pelt of a wolf. His smile reveals dimples in his cheeks that I'm sure capture the attention of a lot of women. He is handsome, and if he didn't keep a layer of stubble along his jaw he may have come across as a pretty boy.

But it's his eyes that have me startling, though I expect he gets that reaction all the time. One is brown, and the other is blue. I have heard of heterochromia, but I've never actually met someone with it before.

"Hi there," he greets, his voice warm and inviting with a slight English accent I didn't pick up on when he spoke earlier. "Welcome to my humble studio. I'm Chester. Are you interested in a tour or looking to buy some art?"

"Hi, I'm Taylor," I reply, stepping further into the studio. "I just moved to the island and wanted to check out the local spots. Your work is incredible." I gesture to the pieces around the room.

"Thank you, Taylor," Chester says, a confident look spreading across his face.

I nod towards the art he just finished spraying. "Are those ones done by someone else?"

Chester glances at the pieces and his lips lift to max capacity. "Should I take it that you aren't a fan of my latest work?"

My eyes widen as I realize I probably just not so subtly insulted him. "Oh, I didn't mean—"

He laughs and waves me off, picking up the piece to move it toward the other side of the room. "I'm joking. These aren't mine. I teach a class here in the evenings twice a week for the tourists."

I let out a relieved breath, smiling at his easy going demeanor. "That's great. I might need to come and try my hand at it too. Though, I'm not sure I'd be any good."

Chester chuckles, setting the canvas down and turning back to me. "It's all about having fun and expressing yourself. You'd be surprised at what you can do when you let go and just enjoy the process."

There is something about how he worded that, like he isn't talking completely about painting.

I don't know if it's his eyes that has me suddenly feeling uneasy, or the look in them. But as quickly as the feeling appears, it disappears again. Chester, like so many others on this island, seems to have layers beneath his friendly face. It's clear there's more to him than meets the eye.

"I might take you up on that," I reply with a smile, genuinely intrigued by the idea of trying my hand at painting. "Expressing myself sounds like just what I need right now."

Chester nods, his mismatched eyes twinkling with amusement. "Whenever you're ready, the studio is open. Feel free to drop by anytime."

"Thanks, I appreciate it," I say, glancing around at the artwork displayed throughout the studio. Each piece seems to tell a story, capturing moments and emotions in vivid detail.

He watches me closely, almost like he's assessing if my interest is real or not.

"Would you like to see some of my latest work?"

"I'd love to," I reply, genuinely curious.

Chester leads me over to a section of the studio where several finished canvases are displayed. Each piece is vibrant and full of life, with scenes of the beach, ocean waves, and local wildlife. The colors are striking, and the detail is impressive.

"You've got a real talent," I say, admiring a painting of a surfer catching a massive wave.

"Thanks," Chester replies, looking pleased. "I've been painting since I was a kid. The island's beauty is a constant source of inspiration."

I turn to face him, my curiosity piqued. "Do you ever stay open late? I thought I saw someone painting through an upstairs window pretty late last night."

Chester's smile falters for a moment, but he quickly recovers. "Yeah, sometimes I lose track of time when I'm in the zone. I do my best work at night when it's quiet and peaceful."

"That's understandable," I say, filing away the information. His momentary falter intrigues me further, and I decide to probe a bit deeper. "Is the piece you were working on last night here? I'd love to see something that I actually saw you in the process of painting."

He chuckles softly, but there's a hint of something guarded in his expression now. "No, that series is a lot different than these ones. Not exactly for the tourists' eyes."

We stand there looking at each other for a long moment before he speaks again, his grin more devilish now, the charm now feeling more calculated than genuine. "Maybe I might show you that series, eventually."

The bell above the door jingles again, announcing another visitor to the gallery. I turn to see an elderly couple entering, their voices filled with admiration as they discuss the paintings on display. Chester glances briefly at them, then back at me with a knowing look.

"Looks like I have more visitors," he says casually, gesturing towards the elderly couple before leaning closer and dropping his volume. "You should definitely come to one of the classes, for free, I'd love to see what you can do."

"Maybe, sounds like fun," I reply, trying to sound casual despite my swirling thoughts. "I might swing by again soon."

"Anytime," he replies with a smile that doesn't quite reach his eyes. "See you around, Taylor."

With that, I make my way towards the exit, casting one last glance over my shoulder at Chester as he engages the elderly couple in conversation. His charm seems effortless, yet beneath it lies an air of mystery that intrigues and unsettles me in equal measure.

As I step back out into the bright sunlight, I can't shake the feeling that I've only scratched the surface of what this island—and its inhabitants—have to offer.

Deciding to check the time, I find that it's almost ten o'clock, so I head towards the tattoo parlor again, hopeful that it's open now.

As I approach, I notice that the lights are on inside, and there is movement.

Pushing through the door, another little bell announces my presence.. I wonder to myself if all the small businesses here have the same quaint bell system for announcing customers. I guess it makes sense for places like this where the owner might be busy and not always stationed near the door.

Inside, the tattoo parlor is dimly lit with an array of flash designs covering the walls. The air is heavy with the scent of antiseptic and ink.

A gruff voice calls out, "Be with you in a sec."

I take a tentative step forward, glancing around at the various designs. Traditional anchors, skulls, and intricate Celtic knots vie for attention alongside more modern motifs of abstract art and Japanese-inspired designs. The contrast between the serene gallery and this edgier atmosphere strikes me. Both have beautiful art, but the difference in the tone is noticeable.

The space is small but open, with no walls separating the entryway from where the tattoo artist must work. It seems the tattoo chair is already set up, clean and waiting for the first customer of the day. What surprises me, however, is when I finally spot two men to the side of the room. One of them appears to be assembling new shelving while the other watches attentively. Both are heavily tattooed, but it's the one supervising the shelving who catches my attention.

As he turns towards me, I recognize him instantly from magazines and online articles. Tyson Santiago. He's a well known tattoo artist, and I knew he had left the city but I didn't know this is where he moved to. But he's not just famous for his tattoos, he is also the brother of Lucien, the lead singer of Saints in Hell. Seanna and I were fans of both the brothers. With us swapping jobs sometimes we steered clear of any permanent change in appearance though, plus we have different tastes in what we like so we would never be able to settle on a tattoo we both wanted.

Tyson is covered in tattoos from his neck down, and he wears a black shirt with the parlor's logo that seems to darken his brown hair further. I notice his blue eyes flare slightly as he taps the other guy on the shoulder to catch his attention. Without waiting for a response, Tyson steps toward me.

"Hey there," he greets, his voice deep and raspy. "Looking for some ink?"

I smile, trying to match his easy demeanor. I don't intend on getting any ink, but I would play along if it got me more information on the main residents of the island. "I was thinking about it, but probably not today. I'm curious to see what kind of designs you have. Do you have a portfolio I could flip through?"

Tyson nods, a smile of his own forming. "Got a bit of everything. I do custom work too, if that's your thing. Names Ty," he introduces himself, extending a hand.

"Taylor," I reply, shaking his hand. "Nice to meet you, Ty."

A huff comes from behind Tyson, and I glance towards the sound. The other man must have finished hanging the shelves. He, too, is covered in tattoos, but while Tyson is in his early thirties, this man looks to be around my age.

Glasses frame his clear, bright green eyes, and his messy brown hair gives him an almost windswept appearance. His stubble adds an edge to his otherwise unassuming demeanor as he shoves his hands into his pockets and avoids direct eye contact.

"Don't mind Telvin," Ty chuckles, glancing at the other man. "He just wants to go back and play with his wood."

Telvin shoots Ty a glare that quickly dissipates when he notices my gaze on him, then he ducks his head. "It's not what he's implying. I'm a furniture maker."

"Really?" I say, a little surprised by that information. "Do you have a store where I can see some of your work? I'm renting the old Baker house and it's partly furnished, but I may need to add my own charm at some point.,"

I don't realize I've taken a step closer until he takes a step back. Then I notice him tapping his fingers together nervously. He obviously doesn't do well with social situations, so I make a point of also taking a step back away from him.

"It's on the other side of the island. I don't really like the tourist crowds, it's nothing much," he mumbles, his voice barely above a whisper.

"He's being modest. Telvin does great work," Tyson interjects proudly. "He furnished most of this shop. When you need some more furniture, you should find him."

Telvin nods in acknowledgment, a small smile tugging at his lips. With a quiet murmur to Telvin, Ty directs me back towards the front of the parlor.

"Nice to meet you," I call over my shoulder to Telvin, who nods again before focusing back on what he was doing.

"Sorry, he's pretty shy. Now, let's talk about what you have in mind for a tattoo," Tyson says, guiding me towards a display of designs as we discuss possibilities.

Chapter 9

Hydessa

I left Saints and Sinners Tattoos with a smile and an appointment for the following week, that I knew I would have to cancel. As much as I was fan-girling on the inside, I needed to remember that just like all the others I have met, Ty is just another person of interest in my hunt for a murderer.

Since it's lunchtime, I decide to head to the café where I ate yesterday. The seafood salad was amazing, and I want to try something new today. Taking a seat at one of the empty tables under a pretty colorful umbrella, I look over the menu.

The chatter of other patrons and the occasional seagull's call create a soothing background noise. I listen in to the gossip, but it seems to all be the same as any other town. Mary something is seeing John and her dad is pissed. There's the occasional complaint about taxes being too high, and someone who knows how to fix the world if everyone would just listen to him.

It all feels so different than the city. There you have to fight to hear everyone. Instead of the calming sea, you are surrounded by car horns and police sirens. I can't remember the last time I ate outside without wanting to hunch my shoulders up to my ears just to make the noise stop.

The friendly waitress from yesterday notices me and makes her way over with a welcoming smile. "Back again, huh?" she says cheerfully. "Can't say I blame you. What can I get for you today?"

"Hi there, Lily" I greet her warmly. "I couldn't resist coming back. The seafood salad was fantastic after all, I can only imagine everything else will be too. What do you recommend today?"

She taps her chin thoughtfully. "If you're in the mood for something new, I'd suggest the grilled fish tacos. They're a hit with both locals and tourists and the fresh catch is some of the best."

"That sounds perfect," I reply, handing her the menu. "I'll have fish tacos and a lemonade, please."

"Coming right up." She swiftly jots down my order before heading back to the kitchen.

As I wait, I take the opportunity to people-watch and gather my thoughts from the conversations I had during the morning. Locals move with an easy familiarity, while tourists are more animated, their excitement evident as they take in their surroundings.

I pull out my phone and check my notes, going over the information I've gathered so far. Each victim had been a tourist, that detail had been easy to determine from the blog posts. That and the fact they all had limited resources.

Thinking back to the post from last night, I try to figure out if I can use it to help me narrow down the search a little. The writers always make it sound like the victims have been stabbed, and the fact that the one last night didn't struggle for long could be why there are no reports of her death.

I just can't seem to shake the feeling there is something I'm missing.

The waitress returns with my lemonade, placing it in front of me. "Your tacos will be out in a few minutes."

"Thanks, Lily," I say, taking a sip of the refreshing drink.

I'm still lost in thought when I notice a familiar face entering the café. The woman from the real estate office spots me and raises a hand in greeting before making her way over to my table.

"Hey, Taylor," she says, sliding into the chair across from me. "Mind if I join you?"

"Not at all," I reply. It takes a moment before her name comes to me. "How is your day today, Madeline?"

She waves her hand dismissively. "Oh please, call me Maddie. My day is going well. More importantly, how are you liking the island so far?"

I can't help but smile at her bubbly personality; it reminds me of Seanna. Who I make a note to call later today.

"It's nice here. The locals I have met have all been very friendly," I reply.

"Well, of course they are being super nice. At the moment, you're just one level up from a tourist. They will all just smile and wave at you until they can see if you stick around. Then the real fun begins."

I blink at her, but something tells me she is right. It's not going to be easy or quick to dig beneath the surface of this little town, but maybe the woman sitting in front of me might be able to help with that. Leaning back in my chair, I roll my eyes jokingly.

"Here I thought all small towns were a hive of gossip."

The grin on her face is huge as she leans forward almost conspiratorially. "Welllll, I could tell you a bit of gossip if you want. Best person for gossip around here, though, is Allegra. She hears it all."

I chuckle under my breath because Allegra kind of already told me as much. "I'll have to see if I can get some gossip with my coffee in the morning then."

Maddie grins. "You've met her already?" she asks.

At my nod, her lips lift even more. "That's great! Tell her I said hi when you see her."

She waves Lily over and orders a seafood salad for herself before leaning an elbow on the table. "Now tell me, who else have you met?"

With a laugh, I go through the list of people I've met so far. Maddie nods along but doesn't provide much more information until I mention Rye. Then she grimaces.

"Yeah, sorry about him. Unfortunately, he has a good reason to hate city girls. His ex-wife was one. Honestly, from what I know, the whole marriage was a shitty one, but then she ran away back to the city and divorced him within a month."

I wince, understanding helping me feel less personally attacked. Maddie suddenly motions with her head towards the café entrance. "What about the good doctor? Have you met him yet?"

Following her motion, I look over to see a man leaving the café entry, obviously having finished and on his way out. He doesn't look old enough to be a doctor, and I wonder if there should be some rule against doctors having perfectly tanned, tattooed skin because there is no way I could go to a man that pretty when I feel like shit.

His hair is dark blond, almost brown, and wavy, and like many others on the island, he wears it longer than usual. *Do they only have one barber here who can do only two kinds of cuts?*

But that's not what draws me in. It's his smile. It's big and charming when he stops by an older couple before exiting the door.

"No, I haven't," I reply, watching the interaction. I definitely need to create a profile for him, even if it is mainly to remember how pretty he is.

"That's Dr. Lachlan Hughes," Maddie says, leaning in a bit closer. "He's a general practitioner here. He's thirty and the youngest doctor we've had, and probably the most unconventional. But he's good at what he does."

"Unconventional?" I question, my mind slipping back to the way the stab wounds were described in the blogs.

"Yeah, he's practiced in a lot of different techniques and such." She waves her hand dismissively making me think she knows more than she is letting on, but I don't want to push my luck. Other than Allegra, she is one of the few who seems to speak openly to me and I can't afford to ruin that.

I watch as Dr. Hughes chats with the older couple, his demeanor warm and attentive. It's clear he's well-liked by the locals. But either way, something has me thinking I need to keep an eye on him.

"He seems nice," I say, turning back to Maddie.

"He is," she replies, her cheeks turning a light shade of pink. "And very dedicated. Moved here a few years ago and just fit right in."

"Let's hope you're saying the same about me in a few years," I say, trying to endear myself to her. Maybe if I'm seen to be fitting in well, then I will be able to dig deeper into the people.

She smiles and nods as our lunches are placed in front of us. Our conversation drifts to lighter topics as we eat our meal. Maddie's company is refreshing, and I appreciate her openness and friendliness. After a while, she checks her watch and stands up.

"I should get back to the office," she says. "But it was great getting to know you. We should do this again, okay?"

"Definitely. Thanks for the company, Maddie," I reply with a smile.

She heads in and pays for her lunch and I do the same, parting with her afterward with a wave. Deciding to head back to the house, I walk across to the beach, letting the sound of the waves and the salty breeze clear my head. The island has a charm that's hard to resist, but the underlying mystery still gnaws at me. I need to dig deeper.

The water brushing up against my toes makes me feel warm inside. It's calming to watch as families and couples enjoy their afternoon in the sun. The beach is a hive of activity, yet it feels peaceful. Nothing like the chaotic city I'm used to.

When I eventually arrive back at the house, I let myself in and make a beeline for the office. It may be strange to some, but my mother always seems to find peace while looking at her murder boards. Over time it has become the same to me.

It's almost like starting a five-thousand piece puzzle without knowing the image. The best place to start is to find all of the edge pieces. Once those are connected, more of the picture becomes clear. And it can't be perfect until the final piece is placed.

Sitting down at the desk, I open my notebook and start writing down all the interactions from the day and my thoughts. The border of my puzzle is starting to feel complete and this is how I plan to fill in the gaps.

I condense it all into a single list, tearing it out and sticking it prominently in the center of the wall.

Allegra - Bakery Owner

Daniel - Sheriff

Eli - Deputy

Rye - Construction

Jonah - Fisherman

Makai - Gym Owner

Chester - Artist

Ty - Tattooist

Jelvin - Furniture Maker

Lily - Waitress

Maddie - Real Estate Agent

Lachlan - Doctor

Satisfied with my work for the day, I step back and survey the wall, listening to the creaks and groans of the house as I try to make sense of it all. The women on the list don't strike me as the type to be killing tourists but I don't want to dismiss them entirely. After all, women can be the most deadly of us all when they want to be.

I flip through the profiles I've created, hoping that maybe the blogger will slip up and give me more information that can help narrow it down. The lack of a struggle could point to it being a woman. The victims could have felt safe until it was too late.

Or it could have been one of the charming men. They could take them out on dates, bring them to secluded areas under the guise of having sex or just being close and then, BAM.

At this point it could still be anyone and staring at this information is starting to cause a headache.

Instead of getting another cup of coffee, I decide to take out my phone and call Seanna. She answers immediately and I can hear her moving. I have a feeling she is finding a quiet spot to talk, so I wait until the sounds on the other end of the phone disappear.

"If I hide..." I whisper into the phone.

"Then I'll seek..." comes her reply. She sighs, her tone filled with concern. "You know I worry about you, especially with you on this mysterious island. How's the investigation going?"

I take a moment to gather my thoughts. "It's progressing, slowly. I've met some interesting people, but there are lots of pieces to this puzzle. There's something here, Seanna, something beneath the surface. I can feel it."

There's a pause on the other end of the line, and I can almost sense Seanna nodding in understanding. "Trust your instincts, Hydessa. You've always had a knack for finding the truth. You are so much smarter than me, believe in yourself. Have you even reached out to our parents or Uncle Max to help?"

"I don't want to involve them," I admit quietly, tapping my fingers against the table. "They're busy, and I want to do this on my own. I feel like I need to get to the bottom of this myself, to prove that I can handle it."

Seanna hums thoughtfully on the other end of the line, understanding my determination. "I get it," she finally says. "Just promise me you'll be careful, okay?"

"I will," I assure her, grateful for her concern. "And I promise to keep you updated."

"Good," Seanna replies warmly. "I'll be waiting for your updates. Now, back to the island life. You're surrounded by beaches and handsome men—please tell me you're having a little fun at least!"

I scoff softly, shaking my head even though she can't see me. "There are plenty of good-looking men here, but knowing my luck, I'd end up sleeping with the killer and he would stab me before I even climax."

Seanna bursts into laughter, her amusement contagious even through the phone. "Hey, you never know. You might have a knife kink and get off on being stabbed," she teases, her voice filled with mischief. "We both know our parents are deviant as fuck, maybe you inherited some of it."

Unable to hold back, I laugh along with her, the tension of the investigation momentarily forgotten. A faint memory niggles at the back of my mind but I dismiss it as I imagine Seanna's teasing grin. "You're terrible," I manage between laughs.

"I know, I know," she says, still chuckling. "But seriously, Hydessa, take a breather when you can. Don't let this mystery consume you completely. Enjoy the island while you're there."

"You're right," I agree, taking a deep breath. "I'll try to unwind a bit, too."

"Good. Now, go get some rest or do something fun. You've earned it," Seanna encourages.

"Thanks, love you Seanna," I say gratefully. "Talk soon."

"Love you, Hydessa," she says warmly before we hang up.

Reaching over to my tablet, I contemplate reaching out to Uncle Max to at least see if he can send me information on the names I have on my list. However, all thoughts of contacting him vanish when the screen turns on and there's a notification waiting for me.

My stomach drops—surely there can't be another murder so soon? Normally there is a few days, sometimes a week between each kill. If this timeline is accelerating, it could mean something far worse.

But as I read through the notification, I realize it's not another victim update. This blog post is different from the others entirely.

Come out, come out, wherever you are…

Are you looking for us? We are out in the open tonight, but you won't find us sitting up in that house. It's much too fun to run in the shadows.

Do you like playing games? How about hide and seek?

If you don't find us by midnight, then it's our turn. Let's count to twelve then, seems like a lucky number…

When it gets to twelve, you know what happens, right?

Tick, tock…

X X   X X

Chapter 10
Hydessa

I shouldn't be feeling excited that they are taunting me, but seeing that post has my heart racing in my chest. They are challenging me, and I have to admit to myself that I have never been called out like this.

They know where I am even now. Not only that, but it's almost like they can see me. They want to count to twelve after I just put a list of twelve names on the wall. They know more than I expected, and I have a feeling that the only way I am going to get answers is if I play their little game.

I look out the large window of the office, but all I can see is the trees of the forest. Are they out there right now watching me? I've had the feeling of being watched since I arrived, but apart from the moment in the forest yesterday, I simply put it down to being new in town.

A shiver runs down my spine as I sit back in the chair, trying to steady my breathing and think logically. Whoever this person is, they're trying to rattle me, to throw me off my game. But I can't let them. I have to stay focused.

Should I close the window to this room or keep it open so that I can use it to my advantage at some point? Did I miss cameras in here or are they climbing trees?

I glance at the clock on the wall. It's just past seven which means I have five hours until midnight. The blogger's taunt is clear—I need to find them, or they'll come find me. But where do I even start? I make a quick decision. If I'm going to find them, I need to be out there, observing. But I would still need to wear my mask and black clothes and do whatever it took to go unseen by others until the businesses all shut down for the day. Which means I still needed to wait another hour for true darkness to fall, not the navy sky that still shows the last of the setting sun.

Heading to my bedroom, I take a shower and dress in my black clothes, pulling on the mask and adding a concealed knife into a leg strap just in case. The bloggers were either just close enough to watch through my window, or they have a way of seeing inside which should be impossible. But I can't rule it out.

It makes me want to sweep the house again, but I don't have time right now.

I take a deep breath, trying to calm the adrenaline coursing through my veins. I need to be smart about this. Rushing in without a plan will only get me killed.

I go over each person on my list, trying to determine who might be the most likely suspects. The blogger revealed they are a team, so who would go together well?

Allegra, Daniel, Eli, Rye, Jonah, Makai, Chester, Ty, Telvin, Lily, Maddie... Each name conjures up different interactions and impressions. But nothing concrete. Nothing that screams "killer" or "stalker".

Some of the names don't have businesses along the main beachfront, and I suspect they are set up on the other side of the island. I would need to investigate that area, but with so many of the names concentrated along the beachfront, that direction feels like the better use of my time. Especially when the last victim was killed on the beach.

I pause for a moment with my hand on the door, a horrible thought crossing my mind.

I've never seen the bodies, there have been no legal reports. Could this all just be a game? Are these bloggers using made up stories to mess with my head?

My hand shakes as I take a seat by the door and try to get my thoughts in order.

No, Uncle Max said there was a case here, if only from how hard they try to conceal themselves. He said there was more to all of this.

These bloggers are in my head already, making me question myself. I hate it. I despise that they know so much about me and I know so little about them. It's clear they have been watching me, but for just how long?

The clock in the corner catches my eye, reminding me I have a mission. Find them before they find me.

Ready or not, here I come.

I slip out of the house, careful to lock the door behind me, and make my way through the quiet forest, sticking to the shadows. My heart pounds with every step, but I force myself to remain calm and focused.

My first stop is the bakery. As I approach, I see that the lights are still on inside. Slipping around the back, I find a vantage point where I can observe through the open back door without being seen.

Inside, I see Allegra cleaning up for the night. She looks up, as if sensing someone's presence, but quickly returns to her task. I stay hidden, but after a few minutes the bakery goes dark and Allegra locks up before getting in her car.

Feeling relieved but also frustrated, I move on to the next location: the police station.

This location is more challenging. The Sheriff and Deputy are still inside, going over paperwork and chatting, if how much their mouths are moving is any indication. I can't risk being seen, so I find a spot across the street more discreet than the previous night where I can watch from a safe distance.

As I observe, I see Sheriff Brooks come out for a cigarette like last night while Deputy Eli also leaves the station, talking on his phone. He looks around briefly before getting into his car and driving off. Nothing seems out of the ordinary here either, but the fact that the police are actively working this late is worth noting.

Would they really let me know if I found them? How would they know I did if I stay in the shadows? Taking a look around, my anxiety only grows. This is why I never like to seek. Hiding is easier, it's safer. This feels stupid as I wait out in the open for some strangers to confirm they are the ones watching me.

The restlessness under my skin pushes me forward toward the real estate and doctor's office. When they are closed with no lights on inside, my next stop is the café.

It's one of the last places open this late and the lights are still on. I approach cautiously, careful to keep myself hidden.

There are a few late-night patrons, and I can see Lily behind the counter chatting with a customer as she wipes down tables. She seems relaxed, no signs of tension or nerves. I scan the room for anything out of place, but everything appears normal.

Desperate to get answers, I watch for a few more minutes. It quickly becomes clear that I'm not going to glean any useful information from this spot. Frustration builds as I check my phone—9:30 PM. Time is slipping away, and I'm no closer to finding them.

I forgo being sneaky as I rush to the tattoo parlor. The lights are still on inside, making it easy to see everything even from a distance with its large windows. Tyson is still working on a client and I watch as he finishes up and tapes up the fresh tattoo before the client leaves.

When Ty starts cleaning up, I wait to see if anyone else shows up. But the place stays quiet, and eventually he turns off the main lights only to move over to a separate wooden artist desk toward the back that I can't get a clear view of.

I circle the building, crouching low when I get to the back and peek through a small window and see Tyson, focused intently on a sketch. He looks tired, unaware of his surroundings. If he were one of the bloggers, I'm sure he would have said something by now or given me a sign. If they are playing fair that is.

Who really plays fair anymore?

I watch for a while longer, but nothing unusual happens. Ty continues his work, and I decide to move on.

My next stop is the artist's studio right by the beach. It's almost 10:30 PM when I sit in the sand near some rocks.

Both floors of the studio are dark. I wait, hoping to catch a glimpse of anything suspicious. But the studio remains silent, and there's no sign of anyone coming or going.

It takes an immense amount of self control not to kick sand when I get to my feet and start the trek to the gym.

I'm slightly surprised when the bright lights of the gym spill onto the street as I approach, casting long shadows that I use to my advantage. Maika said he wasn't open late often, so I have to guess I've either won the game, or he has a client or two that asked to stay late like he offered for me.

I find a spot across the street to watch, giving me a clear view of the entrance. From my vantage point, I can see a few people still inside working out on the machines and lifting weights. I scan the room for any familiar faces or anyone acting out of the ordinary. Makai is at the front desk, doing paperwork from the looks of it. Everything seems normal.

I wait, watching as people finish their workouts and leave until the gym is empty. Makai finally locks up and gets in his car, leaving the building dark and silent. With nothing suspicious to note, I move along the beach. The moon casts a silver glow on the sand, and I see a few figures strolling along the shore.

Ducking behind some rocks, my adrenaline spikes. Is this them?

The beach is peaceful, the sound of the waves attempting to soothe my nerves. But as I watch the people walking by, I notice it is just an elderly couple enjoying a night time stroll

I want to scream while the time ticks down and I get no closer to finding these people. Are they watching me run around? Laughing while I go from place to place none the wiser to who they are?

Nothing seems out of the ordinary anywhere that I've observed tonight, but I can't shake the feeling that someone is watching.

Why would they taunt me to come out? What do they gain by drawing me out into the open? It's clear they know who I am and where I'm staying.

I can only think of a few reasons: they want to see how I react and observe my movements. The blogger's taunts aren't just idle threats—they're calculated moves designed to provoke and unsettle me. It's working, but I can't let it throw me off. I have to stay focused.

Am I missing something by concentrating so hard here on the beach and the businesses? Should I consider other locations or angles that I haven't explored yet? Am I even looking at the right people? Could there be suspects I haven't considered?

I doubt old lady Gladys is out killing tourists.

There's a nagging feeling that I might be tunnel-visioned on the locations and people I know, possibly missing crucial details or connections elsewhere on the island. The urgency of the blogger's challenge has narrowed my focus to those I've identified, but what if there's more to this puzzle that I haven't yet uncovered?

The blogger implied there is more than one of them, but I haven't really seen a lot of interaction between the names, with the exception of the Sheriff and Deputy, and also Ty and Telvin.

However, the impression Telvin gave me is that he is almost scared of his own shadow. Everyone else appears to lead completely separate lives. But I have only been on the island now for two days, that may not be enough time to actually grasp a good understanding of any connections. Just earlier today Maddie even spoke fondly of Allegra, could they be the bloggers and potentially murderers?

If this is a group effort, their cohesion could be masked by seemingly separate lives. Maybe they coordinate subtly, in ways I haven't observed. The challenge now isn't just identifying suspects but understanding their interplay, if any.

I check the time on my phone again—it's almost midnight and I feel like I've actually gone backward in my investigation. I have more doubts than answers now and nothing to show for my efforts. Their threat looms, but should I give it any credibility?

The phone in my hand buzzes with a message, my fingers moving to unlock it. When I open the message, my stomach drops to my feet and a cold sweat breaks out along my skin.

Tick, tock...

Chapter 11

Hydessa

I glance around, scanning the dimly lit street and the deserted beach. No movement, no hint of a lurking presence. It's as if the island has swallowed its inhabitants whole, leaving me alone in the stillness of the night.

With a sigh, I decide this is all a waste of time. In the end, they are going to come to me so the least I can do is be ready when they do. I need to find a way to create a more even playing field.

The risks of staying out in the open, exposed to an unknown adversary, outweigh the potential gains at this point. I'm not getting anywhere standing out here, let whoever it is taunting come for me directly.

Maybe I could get Uncle Max to trace the text message. No doubt they are using a burner phone though.

The clock on my phone reads five minutes to midnight. I've spent hours combing over the businesses and observing potential suspects, yet I'm no closer to unraveling the mystery. The island remains silent, almost conspiratorial in its tranquility, as if holding its breath.

As I turn into the forest, darkness presses down on me like a weight as I slowly start making my way back to the house. The chill of the night air seeps through my clothes, sending shivers down my spine despite the adrenaline still coursing through my veins.

The canopy above casts eerie shadows, and despite the mask concealing my face, I can feel the tension in every step. I listen for anything around me, but the silence is only broken by the rustling of leaves underfoot even as I tread carefully, and the sound of my own breathing within the mask.

I'm almost at the edge of the tree line, my house right in front of me, when a sudden flash of light to my right startles me. At first, it's a brief red glow in the distance, like a fleeting ember in the darkness. Just when I am about to assume someone is starting a bonfire, another pops up beside it, this one green.

They start to appear and disappear at random intervals, leaving me squinting into the semi-darkness watching as they move. The adrenaline that had just begun to settle spikes to an all time high, leaving my hands feeling jittery.

So much for trying to find an even playing field.

The rational part of my mind urges me to retreat and come up with a plan that makes me feel less like the prey. Yet, the investigator in me, fueled by a need for answers, compels me forward.

With each step, the shadows seem to grow thicker, the air heavier with an unspoken threat. Moments pass like an eternity as I move deeper into the woods, following the faint glimmers of light that appear and vanish like phantoms.

The lights disappear again, and although I push forward carefully, I have no idea if I'm still going in the right direction. Just as I begin to question my own sanity, the red light flares up again, this time closer, behind the silhouette of a large tree. My heart quickens, adrenaline coursing through my veins as I approach cautiously. The green light follows suit to the left, illuminating the darkness for a brief moment before fading into obscurity.

My eyes ache with the constant change from a glimpse of light then nothingness, making the darkness around feel even stronger each time they flicker.

I pause, my breath catching in my throat as a deep, echoing chuckle reverberates through the forest. It comes from my right, followed moments later by another echoing laugh from my left. My head whips around in both directions, but the darkness remains impenetrable, concealing whatever—or whoever—is out there.

Heart pounding, I fight the urge to run away. My body tenses, while silently cursing my own stupidity for putting myself in this situation..

Instead of creating neutral ground, I dove headfirst into enemy territory.

I inch closer, my nerves on edge while I try to get a tree behind me so that I feel like my back is guarded. But then I hear the chuckle again, closer this time. It's a taunting sound, low and mocking.

My eyes dart around, but I see nothing. A rustle in the underbrush to my left makes me freeze. The laughter comes once more, this time just annoying me. I feel like my heart is now lodged firmly in my throat, and when the red light appears again, it's a struggle not to scream.

"Looking for me?" A voice obscured by a modulator says as red illuminates the inches of space between me and a neon mask. It has X's for eyes and a stitched shut sinister mouth.

It's one of the creepiest things I've ever seen, and though I don't scream, I can't help the gasp that falls from my lips, making the person behind the mask tilt their head as they chuckle.

My hand twitches to reach for my knife, but they will see the move coming from a mile away. The person slowly steps back to lean against a tree as I begin to take a deep breath.

Swallowing past the lump in my throat I straighten my spine. I will not let him intimidate me, I am better than this, I have grown up surrounded by worse than this.

"Or is it me you're looking for?" Another echoing voice comes inches from my left, making me jump in surprise. I knew there was more than one of them, but I didn't realize they were this close.

I have to lock up my muscles to stop from showing them just how afraid I am. I may be a detective, and a damn good one at that, and I know how to use my fair share of weapons. But, there are two of them and one of me. They both easily tower over my small frame, like two devils looking down at a lost soul.

"I'm looking for a killer," I respond, my own modulated voice echoing through the trees.

The red-masked figure chuckles again, the sound low and sinister. "Well, you certainly found yourself two killers," he says, the neon X's in his mask flickering eerily.

My pulse quickens, but I force myself to stay calm. Panic won't help me now. "Why the games?" I ask, trying to keep my voice steady. "Why not just come for me directly?"

"Where's the fun in that?" the green-masked figure replies, taking a slow, deliberate step toward me. "We like to play with our prey."

"You've been very busy tonight," the red-masked figure continues. "Running around, looking for clues. It's almost... cute."

"Too bad you're not very good at it," the green-masked figure adds with another low chuckle.

Anger flares within me, momentarily overpowering my fear. "If you have something to say, why don't you come out and say it? Or are you too scared to face me without your masks?"

The red-masked figure's posture goes from relaxed and joking, to domineering and threatening in the blink of an eye. Pushing off the tree and taking a step forward, I get the feeling they don't appreciate not being in control.

"I think you're the one afraid to face the world without a mask."

Suddenly, fingers grip the mask covering on my face, turning me to look into the neon green smiling face that has my eyes wincing under the harshness of the light. I had let myself be distracted by the person in front of me and forgot the other one. I grab their wrist tightly to stop them from removing my mask, but they don't move to do more than just grip it.

It's a show of force, but they know as well as I do that once they remove my sense of security, I'll do everything within my power to remove theirs. We both freeze as we assess each other, time standing still for a brief moment.

I growl, my voice echoing through the modulator, "Let me go and stop playing games. I'm here to stop innocent lives from being taken. If I need to, I will kill you."

The green-masked figure laughs. "Bold words for someone who's clearly out of their depth. We like that," they say, leaning closer. The light of his mask is so bright it's almost blinding. "But are you willing to follow through?"

I tighten my grip on his wrist, my muscles coiled and ready to reach for my knife the moment I need to. "Try me. I will do what I need to to stop you killing innocent people."

The red-masked figure steps up close on my right. "Are we? No one we kill is innocent. But don't worry, we're not here to kill you. Not yet, anyway. We have plans, and you're a part of them."

"Plans?" I scoff, trying to keep the edge out of my voice. "What plans?"

The green-masked figure's grip loosens as they tilt their head. When I prove I'm not about to cower, they finally pull their hand away from my mask.

"You'll find out soon enough. Just keep playing the game, and all will be revealed."

I take a deep breath, trying to quell the rising anger and fear even as they seem to give me space. "What do you want from me?"

The red-masked figure steps closer, angling his body almost behind mine as they subtly cage me in.

Ah, so they weren't giving me space out of respect, it was so they could intimidate me further.

"Isn't it obvious? We want you," they say, their voice a low growl that sends a shiver down my spine.

I try to maintain my composure, my mind racing. These masked figures seem to have been watching me, studying me. But for what purpose? What could they possibly want with me? If they know who I am, wouldn't they want me far away from here if they are killing people?

The cold air surrounds my left hand as my glove is suddenly pulled off, leaving my hand exposed to the night air. Neon green light illuminates my fingers as the figure looks down at them.

I gasp behind my mask at the feeling of bare fingers sliding against my palm. Instinctively, I jerk my hand away. "I never gave you permission to touch me, asshole" I growl, pressing my hand firmly against my leg as if to wipe them off. But a strange memory tries to nag at me. I shake it away in favor of staying in the present because I have no idea who this is or what they want.

The green-masked figure just laughs in response, the sound echoing around us. "Oh, you cut me, darling girl. But we don't need permission. We own you and your darkness, even if you aren't ready to accept that."

My heart lurches at the use of the name. "Don't call me that. You don't even know who I am," I retort, my voice trembling with anger and fear.

The red-masked figure hums softly, the sound making me tense even more. "Oh, darling girl, we know more than you think."

The other steps forward. "Did you know a synonym for hide, is mask. Seems like fate that we discuss this while masked, given the meaning of your name." The green face tilts in front of me, as though assessing me, his fingers reaching out to touch my mask again.

I jerk my head back and slap the strong arm away even as nausea unsettles me. There is no way they know who I really am.

Maybe I can still fool them. Knowing my sister is back home and safe from this situation, I decide to pretend to be her to throw them off of my trail. After all, we learned to switch places even at young ages.

"Fine, you know I'm Seanna Darling. But that won't help you," I respond, but even I can hear the tremor in my voice.

Both masked figures shake their heads and the red-mask makes a tutting sound as if he were disappointed. "Nice try, but the two of you aren't as alike as you think you are. We can see the difference easily."

"For instance, Seanna has learned to embrace the darkness inside her, but you are still afraid of yours," the green-masked figure says.

My chest is heaving as I try to catch my breath while surrounded by them. "I'm not afraid of anything," I nearly yell in frustration.

Green-masks bare hand quickly wraps around my throat, his fingers pressing into my skin causing my pulse to speed up. "Funny, your heart rate says something different."

The red-masked figure steps more firmly up behind me, and I can feel the entire length of their body. When they speak, their voice is low and close to my ear. "Or maybe she's just turned on, brother."

My mind races as the situation escalates, trapped between these two masked figures who seem to know far too much about me. But they just gave me something. No, the body pressed against me gave me more. *They are both men. I am looking for two men. Two brothers.*

I was starting to come to the conclusion on my own based on their height and stature, but it's too dark to be sure.

The grip around my throat tightens as if they realize what they just did.

But that's when a terrifying realization comes to me. The feeling of being surrounded by them. The way their scents seem to tangle together while I inhale and the pressure of the warm hand on my neck is sending my mind into overdrive.

My thighs try to press together, craving something more. That's when it hits me. I'm fucking soaked.

I struggle against the hold, my hands gripping the masked figure's wrist, trying to pry his fingers away, but his grasp is unyielding.

"Let me go," I manage to gasp out, my voice strained and desperate. Panic threatens to overwhelm me as I realize just how much I like this feeling, but I force myself to focus on the fact that they are killers.

The green-masked figure chuckles darkly, his grip tightening ever so slightly to fully cut off my air supply. My ears ring as he whispers, his breath seeming to bypass the mask completely and drown me in the warmth.

"Oh, we're just getting started, darling." Shadows dance around my vision, and I can't tell if it's because of the glow of the masks or if I'm about to pass out.

He suddenly releases his grip on my throat, and I almost stumble from between them as I gasp for breath. I press my fingers to my neck, feeling the desperate need to remove my mask just to draw in a full breath, but I resist the urge.

They start circling me, their masks' lights flickering and weaving around me, disorienting me as they move.

I growl in frustration as I try to follow their movements. "Are you going to tell me your names at least?"

I may have walked into their little trap, but they have still helped me narrow down my list. Maybe I can get a little more from them so I don't feel like I failed quite as much tonight.

"Hmmm, yes, we do need to give you something to scream when you fuck yourself to our memory," the green-masked figure says, moving close to my back while I'm watching the red-masked figure. He inhales deep, as if he can somehow sense my arousal.

It makes me feel vulnerable and what surprises me even further is that it is yet another turn on. *What the fuck is wrong with me?*

"Should we tell you to call us something cute?" red mask taunts. "Batman and Robin? Thumper and Bumper? Bonnie and Clyde?"

The green-masked figure joins in, his laughter ringing out unsettlingly. "Ooooo you're Bonnie, I'm Clyde..."

The red-masked figure snorts dismissively. "We could go back to the classics with Romeo and Juliet?"

The green-masked figure laughs louder. "I'd rather she be the Juliet to my Romeo..."

That has me growling low in warning. I am no one's Juliet. I would never sacrifice myself for a man and I get the urge to claw their eyes out over the insinuation. People love to forget that the story isn't a romance, it's a tragedy.

"How about I just call you Tweedledee and Tweedledum?" I retort, trying to inject some defiance into my voice despite the fear simmering beneath the surface.

Abruptly, they stop moving, their masks' lights fading slightly. The red-masked figure steps forward, his demeanor suddenly serious like before, almost as if he has two personalities. "I know. You can call us Cain and Abel. After all, we are the sons of sin..." His words hang heavily in the air, and I narrow my eyes, trying to decipher their meaning.

"Didn't Cain kill Abel?" I ask in question, tilting my head.

"Oh, I did die," green mask says, "just not the way that the stories say... I died the day I met you."

Startled, I spin around to confront him, but he's gone. The red glow behind me winks out as I whirl back in that direction. I strain my eyes but suddenly see nothing except the impenetrable blackness of the forest.

There's no sign of either of them—they blended back into the shadows, leaving me standing alone in the eerie silence of the forest.

My hands shake as I begin the long walk home, but something tells me I won't be alone even in the dark.

Chapter 12
Abel

I have waited countless days for this moment, to be able to touch her again, to breathe her in. It won't be long now until she takes her rightful place between us. I know it's only a matter of time. We were always destined to be together, our souls bound by blood. I wasn't lying, I had died the moment I met her, because from that moment my soul belonged to her.

She became my obsession, the fire that consumed my thoughts and dreams. The anticipation of having her with us both now, of touching her, holding her together, it's damn near overwhelming.

Soon she won't be able to deny it, to deny us. After all, we are meant to be.

At first, my brother didn't understand. He thought she was a poison, something that infected my mind until the same fire that burned within me was kindled in him. He realized what I had known all along—that her darkness was a perfect match to our own. She is made for us, just as we are made for her. She will complete us in a way no one else ever could.

Even now it's as if my soul is on fire for her, calling for her heat to be between us again.

What Hydessa and I have isn't just an attraction or a fleeting desire. It's deeper, more profound—a connection forged by something ancient and powerful. Our souls are intertwined. She is our missing piece, the part of our existence that makes us whole.

The waiting has been excruciating, every passing day a reminder of the distance between us, but now the moment is almost within reach. Soon, she will understand. Our bond is inevitable, undeniable.

I can still feel her pulse under the pads of my fingers, smell the way she was turned on for the both of us as we caged her in. Most prey will fight when caught by a predator, but not her. Her grip was challenging as I felt her defiant eyes on me even through the mask.

She didn't want me to remove it and I was afraid that I would break her trust if I did. She may not be ready for the world to see who she truly is, but we are.

Until then, we will wait. The walls of that house won't stop me from watching her, from touching her. Soon Hydessa Darling will realize who she belongs to.

Bringing the glove I stole from her closer to my face, I inhale deeply, breathing in the scent that is uniquely Hydessa Darling.

Destiny cannot be denied. And no matter how good she is at sticking to the shadows, there is no hiding from fate.

Chapter 13
Hydessa

W ould it be childish to scream and stomp my foot? The thought crosses my mind, but I push it aside. I turn in circles, trying to determine which direction to go, but the oppressive darkness offers no answers. I thought I was headed the right way, only to realize I passed by the same fallen tree twice already.

Then, it hits me—my phone.

How did I allow the fear and adrenaline to cloud my mind so much that I hadn't even thought about it? It's moments like this when Seanna would shake her head at me, and I would deserve it too.

I pull it out, the screen lighting up the immediate area, and I quickly switch on the flashlight. The beam pierces the darkness, revealing the tall, looming trees surrounding me.

I try to backtrack my steps and look for the glove that was taken off when one of the assholes decided to touch me without permission. It's nowhere to be seen on the thick forest floor.

I let out a frustrated huff, my breath visible in the cool night air. Turning my attention to the trees, I try to determine the direction of the house.

Taking a deep breath to steady my racing thoughts, I try to move forward.. "Alright, Hydessa," I whisper to myself. "You've got this."

Using the flashlight, I carefully make my way through the forest, keeping an eye out for any signs of a path or familiar landmarks.

Every rustle of leaves and snap of twigs sets my nerves on edge, but I keep going, determined to find my way back.

After what feels like an eternity, I finally spot the edge of the trees and the back of my rental house. Relief floods through me and I quicken my pace, eager to leave the oppressive darkness behind. Ready to leave the memory of everything that just happened behind.

My hands shake as I unlock the door, constantly looking over my shoulder. They could have followed me and pushed their way into the house. They seemed to want so much more than what they got tonight.

But there is no sign of them as I rush inside, slamming the door at my back, taking a moment to catch my breath.

I pull the mask from my face, tossing it onto the dining table and pulling my hood off my head. I feel like I've been left with more questions than answers from that encounter

I make my way upstairs to the bedroom, shedding my clothes the moment I get there. Each piece of clothing feels like a weight lifted off my shoulders, a small relief from the tension gripping my body.

By the time I turn on the shower, I almost feel like a different person. The water runs hot quickly, so I step inside. The steaming water cascades over me, washing away the grime and stress of the night. I close my eyes, letting the warmth seep into my muscles, and for a moment, I allow myself to just breathe.

However, my moment of peace is assaulted by the memories of the night. The encounter with the masked figures replays in my mind, their cryptic words echoing around in my head as if they were trying to tell me even more.

What did they mean by knowing more than I think? Do I simply have to take their word for it that they don't kill innocent people? And what were their plans involving me?

I scrub my skin vigorously, as if trying to erase the touch of the green-masked figure's hand on my throat. Their words, "We want you," reverberate in my mind, sending shivers down my spine despite the heat of the water.

How is it possible to feel so completely owned by one simple action and a few simple words?

I finish my shower and wrap myself in a towel, before moving back into the bedroom. I sit on the edge of the bed with a sigh, not knowing where to go from here. It's already early hours of the morning and I should be getting some sleep.

Cain and Abel? I scoff to myself. I really think tweedledee and tweedledum fit them so much better.

The more I think about it all, the more I begin to realize how my body responded to them. Their echoing voices whispering in my mind. My hand reaches up to touch my throat, I can still almost feel where Abel's hand wrapped around it and squeezed.

A surprising shiver of arousal runs through me at the memory as my fingers dance around my neck. I never imagined something like that would be such a turn on. The way he had controlled me, the power in his grip... it was intoxicating. I find myself replaying the scene over and over, each time feeling a mix of fear and... maybe even desire.

I shake my head, trying to clear my thoughts. This is insane. I shouldn't be turned on by men who are clearly dangerous and unhinged. They are killers, they even freely admitted it tonight.

But then again, so am I... I just don't kill innocent people.

Standing, I try to force myself into action. Moving gets things accomplished, that's what I need to do now. I need to go to my office and make notes about everyone I saw tonight. Then I need to take specific notes of the masked mens stature.

I was close to them, too close. I wrapped my hand around Abel's bicep and felt the size, felt the muscles beneath his clothes. Not only that, but their height difference with me was clear. I know I can cross the women off the list for sure now, but are there any men I could cut too?

As I try to take note of it all, the sense of being surrounded by them makes me sit back on the bed. No matter how much I try to rationalize it, the feeling under my skin persists. The thrill of being caught in their game, the way they toyed with me. The dominance in their posture alone was intriguing, no matter how much I wanted to fight, my body seemed to want to obey them more. It all lingers in my mind, on my skin, making my pulse quicken.

I throw myself back onto the bed with a sigh, staring up at the ceiling. How can I be so aroused and yet so terrified at the same time? I let out a groan, covering my face with my hands. I need to get a grip, to focus on the real issues at hand. These men are dangerous, and I need to find a way to stop them, not sit here thinking about how addicting it could feel to be the center of their attention.

But as I lie there, I swear I can still feel Abel's hand and Cain at my back. Their strong arms surrounding me, but never actually hurting me.

They know who I really am, so why would they leave me alive? They know I am going to find them.

Is that the whole point?

My fingers trail down my body as I losen the towel, allowing one to dance over my hardened nipple. It's so sensitive that when I pinch it even lightly a moan escapes me.

I have never in my life been able to get aroused this quickly. I hate that they caused this, they awoke something in me I didn't want to acknowledge yet. I don't even know how I am supposed to deal with this feeling.

But then, I do.

I stand up and turn off all the lights, leaving the moonlight streaming in through the window, bright enough to cast shadows. The soft, silvery glow gives the room an ethereal feel as I walk back to the bed and drop the towel, letting it fall to the floor.

No one has to know what I do in the dark, and maybe that's the best part.

Crawling into the middle of the bed, I lay on my back and spread my legs.

This might be a mistake, I already know I have trouble bringing myself to climax and don't often get there with partners either. I can't help but try though. After all the running around town I just did, I think my body deserves this. Plus, it's not like trying would make things any worse.

My fingers touch my throat again, bringing Abel's possessive grip to my mind. The memory of Cain stepping up behind me follows closely as I let my fingers trail down my body. I squeeze my breasts, taking my nipples between my fingers, pain flashing through me as I pinch and twist them. Heat and desire flood me behind it.

I close my eyes, losing myself in the memory. Cain's voice, dark and commanding, whispering in my ear, "We want you."

Abel's presence, menacing and magnetic, making my heart race. My fingers move lower, tracing the curves of my body, wishing it was the echoes of their touch.

I let my mind drift, imagining their hands on me instead. How I want them to touch me together, one of them teasing my breasts while the other does the same to my aching clit.

As my fingers move lower, I bite my lip to stifle a moan. The memory of the brief glimpse at their dominance, their control, fuels my arousal. I circle my clit slowly, teasing myself, letting the pleasure build. My breathing becomes ragged, the heat pooling in my core growing more intense with each passing second.

But as much as I try, as close as I get, my climax remains just out of reach. After a few more minutes, I growl in frustration and sink back against the bed, hitting the mattress with the same fisted hand I was trying to use to get myself off.

I scrub my hands against my face with a sigh, catching the scent of myself on my fingers. A strange noise catches my attention and I drop my hands. The room is suddenly lit by neon from the TV on the wall facing the bed, where two neon masks fill the screen. My mouth drops open in shock before I scramble to find something to cover myself with.

"Stop," comes an echoing command, and my body freezes. The room has surround sound making the voice come from everywhere, wrapping around me like an invisible grip I am equally terrified of as I am turned on. My heart pounds in my chest, a mix of fear and an undeniable thrill coursing through me.

How did they hack into my TV? How long have they been watching me? How the fuck did I not find this camera?

"Hydessa." Something in the modulated voice tells me it's Cain, smooth and commanding as it fills the room. "We told you your time ran out. From that moment on, there is no hiding from us."

My breath catches in my throat. I feel exposed, vulnerable, and yet the same intoxicating fear and desire that haunted me earlier, grips me again.

"We told you we would come for you," Abel's modulated voice joins, darker, more menacing. "From that moment on, you belonged to *us*."

A shiver runs down my spine. I can almost feel his touch again, sending a jolt of arousal through me.

"Now, lay back," Cain's voice is softer now, almost coaxing. "Show us what belongs to us."

My eyes widen, a mix of fear and excitement flooding my senses. Shaking my head, I try to show them I won't do this. This is not me.

I shouldn't be listening to them, I should be fighting this even if there is something deep inside me that wants to obey them. My body feels frozen, caught between the desire to resist and the undeniable pull of their commands.

"Hydessa," Cain's voice continues. "We know you can hear us. There's no use fighting it now."

Abel's voice chimes in, low and chilling. "You belong to us. You felt it tonight, didn't you? The thrill of being ours."

Their words send another shiver down my spine. Despite my fear, a strange arousal pulses through me, mingling with the lingering frustration from not having an orgasm in months.

Is this what my body needs now? Crazy men who have threatened me and invaded my privacy but who command me to own my pleasure for them? Maybe I'm more fucked in the head than I realized.

"Lay back," Cain's voice is threatening now. "Show us."

The room feels surreal, bathed in the eerie glow of the neon masks flickering on the TV screen. Part of me wants to resist, to shut them out, but another part—buried deep within—craves their dominance, their control.

Slowly, almost against my will, I find myself sinking back onto the bed to obey. The moonlight and neon lights brighten up the room as I lie there, exposed and vulnerable. I hesitate for a moment, uncertainty clouding my mind, before slowly parting my legs.

The room feels charged with their presence, as their unseen eyes watch my every move. I close my eyes, giving in to the thrill of being seen like this, of being desired by these dangerous men. My fingers find their way lower, trailing down my body until they reach the soft warmth between my thighs.

"Spread yourself," Abel's voice cuts through the silence, gruff and unyielding. "Let us see everything."

My heart races, torn between the thrill of obedience and the terror of what I'm about to do. Slowly, I part my legs further, reaching down with my fingers to spread my pussy open.

"Good girl," Cain's voice whispers, smooth and approving. "That's it. Touch yourself for us. Show us how wet you are."

Goosebumps travel from my head to my toes over his praise. I get the feeling that not many people have been praised by this man, and I find myself wanting to earn more of it.

My fingers tremble slightly as I obey, sliding along my wet folds. I can almost feel their gaze on me like a physical touch. It's as if the room itself has become a stage for their desires, and I am now a willing participant in their twisted game.

A twisted game that might just bring me the thrill I have been craving for so long.

"More," Abel's voice commands, darker and more insistent. "Don't hold back. Give in to that darkness inside you."

His words send a thrill down my spine, igniting a primal need within me to please them. I slide my fingers lower, circling my entrance, teasing myself as Cain and Abel watch intently from wherever they are.

I tease myself, bringing my fingers back up to circle my clit slowly, the pleasure building with each stroke. The thought of them watching, of their dark desires mirroring my own, intensifies the sensations coursing through me.

"More," Abel growls, his deep voice making me yearn for his praise too. "Don't hold back. We want to see you come."

I arch my back, overwhelmed by the conflicting emotions—desire, fear, and the forbidden thrill of submission. Cain's voice echoes in my mind, urging me on, coaxing me towards the edge of pleasure. I moan softly, the sound echoing in the dimly lit room.

My fingers move faster now, seeking that elusive release. I'm so close, teetering on the brink as the intensity builds with each passing moment.

Suddenly, Cain's voice breaks through the haze of my arousal, low and commanding. "Did you like the pain earlier, Hydessa? When you pinched your nipple? Do it again."

I hesitate, my mind swirling with conflicting emotions, but the desire to obey them and finally get my orgasm outweighs my reservations. I reach up, fingers finding my nipple again, and I pinch and twist it roughly.

"Harder," Abel barks, his voice like a whip cracking through the air.

Without thinking, I obey, my fingers twist almost violently and my other hand jerks against my clit. It's an overwhelming feeling, the pain heightening the pleasure, driving me closer to that elusive climax. I moan louder, the sound reverberating in the room, my whole body now trembling.

"That's it, come for us, little shadow," Cain commands. "Let go."

With a desperate cry, the tension inside me snaps and I surrender to the pleasure they demand. My body shakes as waves of ecstasy wash over me, lost in the moment of release that Cain and Abel managed to pull from me.

As I lie there, breathless and sated, the room gradually returns to silence. The neon masks on the TV flicker and then disappear. Conflicting emotions swirl within me—shame, desire, and an unsettling craving for... more.

They could still very well be watching me. I make it my mission to find the damn camera tomorrow, but for now I will let them think they have won something. And to an extent, they have.

Cain and Abel have awakened something primal within me, a dark hunger that defies reason and logic. Despite the danger they represent, despite the rational part of me screaming to resist, another part—a deeper, buried part—already longs for them.

Chapter 14

Cain

I'm achingly hard and desperate to cum. Our darling girl is absolutely beautiful, the memory of her body completely spread out and flushed with pleasure has desire still pulsing through my veins.

It was perfect. *She was perfect.* And I don't think either of us will be able to hold out much longer.

My brother has already disappeared, her glove pressed close to his nose. No doubt going to fuck his own hand until we can fuck her pretty pussy ourselves. Him running off the second the call ends comes as no surprise; his impulsive nature often leads him to seek immediate gratification.

I should really be doing the same, but instead I continue to watch her as she gets beneath the covers and settles down to sleep. I know Abel will return to stare at her on the screen, driven by the same desire that consumes us both.

We have every little detail planned out, nothing will stand in our way from owning her. So far everything has gone like clockwork, but there is still so much more we have planned. She needs to accept the darkness inside of her, she needs to surrender to it before she can completely take her rightful place between us.

It is almost painful to watch as she holds herself back. We have witnessed her interact with the people here and she has a sixth sense for what lies just under the surface. It is clear why she has made such a great detective in the city.

But why is she still holding back here? She can feel it too, I know it. There is an extra energy to the island, warning everyone that comes that we are not what we seem. So why is she ignoring it? If Hydessa can't accept how dark and depraved she truly is, then she won't be able to accept that in us either.

Her taking our orders tonight was a good first step, but there is still a long way to go. We need to get her out of her head and smash whatever thoughts are in there that tell her to keep part of herself locked away.

As much as I hate being the voice of reason and control, that is my job in this dynamic. So I will keep watching, keep manipulating from the shadows.

Her orgasm has drained her of all remaining energy and I can hear her breathing level out. I adjust the camera to zoom in on her and those perfectly pouty lips I wish I could slip my cock between.

My finger hovers over the screen, tracing the contours of her face as if I could bridge the distance between us, as if I could feel the warmth of her skin through the cold glass.

We have been planning this for too long to jeopardize it now with impulsiveness. Even appearing to her tonight on the TV was perhaps too soon, but I could not have predicted how well she would surrender to us so quickly.

She must know that the facade she puts on for everyone else isn't real, that deep down her darkness is just as black as ours, that it wants to give in to ours. But it's not just about physical submission; it's about embracing her desires, her fears, and the complexities of her own psyche.

Only then can she truly belong with us.

I move to another screen, fingers dancing across the keyboard with practiced efficiency. The feed we recorded earlier flickers to life. I rewind the video, navigating through the footage until I find that pivotal moment—her surrender to the pleasure we orchestrated.

The screen illuminates with the scene of her abandon, her body arched in ecstasy, sounds of pleasure echoing through the room. Heat courses through me anew as I relive the intensity of that moment, feeling a shudder of anticipation ripple through my body.

I carefully select a section of the recording, capturing the essence of her surrender, the raw vulnerability that she unknowingly displayed. I prepare the clip and then my own personal message to go with it before I hit send.

Just because there is a plan, doesn't mean I can't give a gentle push.

***

Abel

M y knife scrapes over her body gently. It would be so easy to apply just that little bit of extra pressure but I don't, not yet. Her skin is so smooth, like silk. I could imagine it would be just as easy to cut through. She isn't pale like milk, more like tea or weak coffee, would she taste just as bitter or has she been sweetened by sugar. Would it wake her if I licked her?

The temptation is strong as I watch her breath in and out. But I won't. Not yet.

She's too beautiful to mark up with my knife, a vision that haunts my thoughts. She needs a more personal touch, I long to feel her skin beneath my bare fingers, leaving marks behind that are uniquely mine. Every curve, every line of her body calls to me. My life, my very existence, is tied to hers in ways she can't yet comprehend. The first time I saw her, I immediately noticed the pull we had to one another as if my shadows were screaming to press against hers and feel a familiar friend. She is a goddess to be worshiped, and I am her humble devotee, come to save her from herself in the black of night.

We will worship her.

I shouldn't be in this room with her, it's a risk and I know my brother will comment on my foolishness. But it's clear he's just as attached as I am. He understands even if he doesn't see her the same way I do. She isn't just a random soul, she is our everything.

Which is why I am here standing over her as she sleeps, drawn by that irresistible force. My fingers trace the outline of her face, memorizing every detail. She stirs slightly, and I freeze, holding my breath, my heart pounding in my chest. But she doesn't wake.

I can't wait for her to finally embrace her true self, the one that hides behind so many layers of what she perceives as normal, for us to dance together again in the shadows.

The thought of it sends a thrill through me. The anticipation is almost unbearable, but I know the wait will be worth it. For when she does accept her fate, we will be unstoppable, bound together for eternity.

As I stand there, mesmerized by her beauty and consumed by my thoughts, a faint smile twitches on her lips. Is it a dream, a fleeting moment of happiness, or is she somehow aware of my presence, even in her slumber? Does she know on some subconscious level that I'm here in her space with her?

The room feels charged with an unspoken tension, as if the very air around us holds its breath. I lean closer to her, breathing in the scent of cherries. It's been my favorite scent for a long time now.

The scent of her.

Chapter 15

Hydessa

I slept through my alarm. Either that or I never turned it on to begin with because the sun is flooding the room and the time on my phone reads after ten before I return to consciousness. There are also a couple of unread messages on there too.

Unlocking my phone, I narrow my eyes. There is a message from my parents waiting, but there is also one from the unknown number. Choosing to put off the one from the unknown number, I open the one from my parents first.

DAD

> Call us, you have your mother worried.

MOM

> Please… you keep forgetting the please… and when will you admit that it's you that worries too.

DAD

> *frowning emoji*

PAPA

> JFC *eye roll emoji* She is a very capable adult. She is fine, aren't you, munchkin?

PAPA

> Munchkin?

> *frowning emoji* Okay, I'm now team Dare... Call us, now.

Checking the time of the messages, I realize they were sent an hour ago. Huffing out a sigh, I know there is only one solution to their worries. Quickly getting out of bed, I use the bathroom to freshen up before throwing on leggings and a top and putting my hair up.

Picking my phone back up on my way to the office, I click on the video call icon as I mentally prepare myself to face my worried parents.

The video call connects, and within moments, the concerned faces of my parents appear on the screen. Their expressions soften with relief as soon as they see me.

"Hey there, munchkin," papa says, his voice filled with humor. "You finally decided to wake up, huh?"

My dad's eyes narrow slightly. "We've been trying to reach you for ages. Are you okay? Why didn't you answer earlier?"

I offer a sheepish smile, feeling a pang of guilt for causing them worry. "Sorry, I slept through my alarm. I'm okay, though, just a bit groggy."

Dad frowns, his eyes narrowing further as they assess me. It's almost like he can see something I can't. "How groggy, what does it feel like?"

I roll my eyes with a sigh, it's no secret that they had intentionally drugged mom at one point. "I was up until the early hours of the morning hunting, it's my own fault," I tell them reassuringly.

Dad shakes his head, though I can see the relief in his eyes. "Well, you're lucky you called us back. Your mom was about to fly over there on the next flight out."

Mom nods, her expression softening. "We just worry, honey. You know how it is. Especially with the vagueness surrounding your case, going undercover can take a toll on people."

"I know, Mom," I reply sincerely. "I appreciate you checking in, really."

Papa leans closer to the camera. "Is that a tan? In two days? Aren't you meant to be investigating, not sunbathing?" His laughter has me shaking my head with a smile.

"How is *your* investigation going?" I ask, hoping to divert the attention away from that topic.

Mom sighs and a look of frustration crosses her face. "It's going okay, I think we are closing in on our main suspect. How about you, are you getting closer?"

My pulse quickens as I remember the message waiting for me from the unknown number and everything that happened last night. "Yeah, definitely getting closer."

Mom's brow furrows slightly. "Are you sure you're feeling alright? You sound a bit off."

"Yeah, I'm fine, Mom," I reassure her. "Just a late start to the day, that's all. You know it always throws me off when I don't get in my early morning jog and cup of coffee."

I'm not sure they believe me, but Papa finally smiles brightly. "Alright, munchkin. Just remember to take care of yourself, alright? And keep us posted more often."

"I will," I promise, feeling a surge of affection for them. "Love you guys."

"We love you too," Mom replies softly.

We end our call and I sit back in the chair with a sigh, still staring at the phone.

Taking a deep breath, I click through to my messages again and pull up the one from an unknown number. I frown when I see it's a video, the initial preview shot is black so I don't even know what it is that I'm about to click on.

Bracing myself, I open it and press play, but there is no bracing myself for the loud audio. Whimpers, moans and cries echo around the office and I drop the phone onto the glass desk. I don't need to see it though, I already caught a glimpse before it slipped from my fingers. It's a crystal clear view of me spread out on the bed last night, bringing myself to climax.

When the voice starts talking over the video, I have to admit to myself it wasn't just my efforts that got me an orgasm, but those psychos behind the masks..

"Look at you, little shadow, look at how beautiful you are spread out, exactly like we wanted you. You're skin flushed and your pussy all wet for us. Look at what a *good girl* you were."

My whole body flushes again as the sounds continue to play on the phone, I slowly reach out and pick the screen back up and take in the scene. I can faintly hear their voices praising and encouraging me, but the voice talking over the video it's louder.

"Keep watching, little shadow, we are almost to the best part," his voice continues, and I know what part he is talking about as the sound of my moans grow. I see my fingers twist at my nipple and a cry escapes me.

"Right... there... mmmmmmm... perfection... I can't wait to hear the sounds you make while your pussy squeezes my cock."

As much as I want to slam the phone down and block the number, I equally can't stop watching in fascination. I have no control over how his words affect me, my body throbs without my permission as I watch myself panting on the screen.

How did I even end up in this situation? I should have stood up from that bed and demanded they show themselves, demanded answers, demanded they stop killing. I should have done anything except spread my legs like a good little frustrated whore.

"See you soon, little shadow," comes through just as it fades to black again.

Little shadow? He called me that last night too.

I'm very glad that I didn't open that message before I called my parents. Placing the phone back down on the desk with a heavy sigh, I now feel like I need another shower to cool my skin.

As I try to steady my breathing, I glance up at the wall with my investigation notes, hoping to distract myself from the video that is playing on repeat in my mind.

Frowning, I tilt my head as I look over my neatly positioned notes and printouts. Something seems off about them, yet nothing looks out of place. My skin prickles with the sensation of being watched, and I can't shake the feeling that I'm not alone.

They have a camera in my room, what if they have one here too?

I feel like I'm going to be sick, but I can't afford to lose my composure now. Yet, something doesn't feel right. Maybe it's paranoia, but some internal alarm is ringing. As a precaution, I snap pictures of the board with my phone. Next, I check the room and then the house for signs that anything is out of place, but everything appears undisturbed.

Then cursing myself for not even considering the possibility before now, I get the small scanner I have to check for bugs. It was given to me by Uncle Max, and he would be so disappointed in me for not using it when I arrived. I naively thought that a simple run through with my own eyes would do the trick.

The device is small, but still powerful enough to pick up most things. For the next hour I slowly make my way through each room, finding multiple devices, including one hidden near the television in my room as well as one in the office. I remove them all and store them in a small faraday box to block the signals.

It almost feels like a proverbial 'fuck you' to be able to do that. I have taken away their ability to watch me, but it still didn't help me solve this mystery.

How did they get them here in the first place? Were they here from the beginning or did they place them last night when I went out seeking them?

I huff as I once again look at the investigation wall and the list of names stuck to the center of it. The twelve names seem to taunt me, each one a potential lead to the identities of the killers. I could expand on the list, there are a lot of residents to look at, but these first twelve seem like a good place to start.

I'll work my way through them as quickly as I can before I add more to it, and if I need to stay longer then it's not exactly the worst place to be stuck. I just hope no one else is killed in the meantime. Given the frequency of the murders on the blog however, I need to make progress, and fast.

I'm about to reach for my tablet when my stomach makes a rumbling protest. Looking at the time, I realize that it's almost lunchtime and not only have I not had breakfast, I also haven't even had coffee.

No wonder I feel like I'm about to start dragging my feet. The sun is bright in the sky and I'm technically on holiday, so there's nothing to say I can't work from the beachfront. Grabbing my tablet along with my other necessities, I put on some shoes and make my way toward the sandy shores after locking the door to the house securely behind me.

There is almost always someone out and about in the sunshine who offers me a wave as I walk. I return their smiles and waves, trying to blend in, trying to appear just like any other local enjoying the beautiful weather.

As I walk, I ponder over the names, wondering if I can use the time during the day to find out more information on them without being too obvious. For me to look them up online I would need their last names, which would definitely fall into the obvious category. But perhaps there are ways to find them, like on social media platforms or simply looking at posts about the island and those who are tagged in images.

Even with it being lunchtime my feet still make their way to the bakery. I'm reminded of what Maddie said the day before, that the best person for any gossip or information on the island is Allegra.

Maybe if I eat there, I can wait out the lunchtime rush and find a moment to see if she might sit and talk to me. Maybe she could tell me all the information I want under the guise of gossip, even if she is one of the suspects on my list.

I know she wasn't one of the ones to wrap their hand around my throat, but she could be the perfect lead to me finding who was.

Chapter 16

Hydessa

The bakery is bustling with activity when I arrive, but Allegra still smiles happily when she sees me. The aroma of freshly baked bread and pastries fills the air, making my stomach rumble even more. I place an order for a coffee and a sandwich, and manage to find a small table near the window to settle in with my tablet to review my notes while I wait.

As the lunch rush gradually subsides, I notice Allegra moving more freely behind the counter, chatting with the remaining customers. When someone steps up next to my table, I look up to say something expecting it to be Allegra, but my words catch in my throat with my breath.

It's not Allegra at all—it's Ty. In his hands are a coffee and a brown paper bag.

"Hey Taylor," he says happily.

I smile. "Hi, I'm surprised you aren't midway through a tattoo right now."

He laughs, leaning his hip against my table. "I actually had a cancellation. I would have called you to see if you wanted the spot, but your number was mysteriously missing from the form."

I cringe, I had intentionally left my number off the form, hoping he wouldn't notice so quickly. "Oh really... I'm sorry, I must have overlooked it."

Ty raises an eyebrow, clearly not buying my excuse but deciding to let it slide. I'm sure tons of people get nervous about tattoos and leave out random bits of information like that here and there.

"No worries," he says, waving it off. He glances down at the tablet on the table in front of me. "Having troubles?" he asks, indicating the screen. For a moment, my heart speeds up, thinking that I've left something incriminating visible. But thankfully, it's just a search for computer companies on the island.

"Ummm, yeah, maybe," I say, trying to sound casual. "Do you know someone who might be able to help? The results on here aren't exactly promising." I avoid answering the question directly, hoping he might have some useful information.

Ty tilts his head, frowning. "I'm sorry, you're not going to have much luck here. Even I have to send my computer equipment to the mainland if I have an issue."

I nod, my disappointment clear but for different reasons than he thinks. I had hoped one of the masked men might have made a name for themselves by helping others with their tech problems because he is clearly good with computers, having been able to hide their identity from Uncle Max.

"That makes sense," I say, forcing a smile. "Thanks anyway."

"Sure thing," Ty says, taking a sip of his coffee. He glances back at the tablet. "You know, if there's anything else you need, feel free to ask."

I decide to fish for more information, following a hunch. "I will admit, I kind of fangirled a little when I met you. But I didn't realize you had another brother besides Lucien," I say slyly.

He laughs, shaking his head. "Who, Telvin? Nah, he's just a friend. It's a pretty small island in case you haven't noticed, and he is pretty much the only furniture maker here whose work gives me the look I want. I didn't know we looked related though."

His eyes twinkle as he grins, and I can't help but smile back, though my mind is already making a note of the new information. "That makes sense," I say.

Ty nods. "Well, got to get going, I should get set up for my next appointment. Enjoy your lunch, Taylor."

"Thanks, Ty. See you around."

As he leaves, Allegra comes over with a bright smile and a pot of coffee in her hand to top off my cup. "Looks like you already have a celebrity fan," she says with a laugh as she watches Ty walk away through the window.

I roll my eyes. "Then I have lots of fans because everyone seems to want to know all about me."

Waving her hand in the air she chuckles. "Oh hun, that's 'cause you're fresh meat."

Leaning back, I raise a brow and grin. "I feel like it's only fair that I know about all of them if they want to know all about me."

She takes the bait instantly, setting down the pot of coffee and glancing behind her. "Give me a second to grab a cup, and I'll tell you everything you want to know."

When she turns away, I have to restrain myself from patting myself on the back. This could be a goldmine of information. I take a sip of my coffee, trying to appear casual as I wait for Allegra to return.

The bakery's activity has slowed to only a couple of locals who just smile when she takes a seat at my table and pours herself a cup of coffee; this is obviously not out of the ordinary for Allegra during the slow times.

"Alright, where do you want to start?" she asks, leaning in con- spiratorially.

"Let's start with the basics." I shrug. "Tell me everything about everyone."

Allegra taps her finger on her chin, thinking for a moment. "Who have you met so far? We can start there."

"Well, yourself obviously," I say with a grin.

Allegra brushes me off with another wave of her hand. "Oh, I'm not important. But let's see... you've met the sheriff and his deputy, right? Both of them have been here their whole lives. Sheriff Brooks is a solid guy, very much by the book but fair. His deputy, Eli, is a bit younger and has a bit more fire in him. They're a good team, though."

I nod in acknowledgement, taking another sip of my coffee. "I've also met Rye, Jonah, Maddie, Telvin, Lily, Chester, Makai, and Ty as you just saw."

She leans back, thinking. "I heard you ran into Rye Anders, he's a character, for sure. He's a bit gruff, but he's got a heart of gold. He's also been here all his life and knows the island like the back of his hand. Maddie mentioned she told you about his wife. Maddie Graves, you know, she's a sweetheart, always looking out for everyone but loves good gossip just like I do. Same goes for Lily Holt, she works at the café and has a knack for making people feel welcome while also getting them to spill their secrets."

I can't help but laugh at her honesty. She really is an open book. I make a note to be careful around Lily if she is known for getting people to open up, I will have to stick to the story I created for myself like glue around her.

Allegra taps the edge of her cup with her nails thoughtfully. "Jonah Brine keeps to himself mostly, he's a bit of a loner. He's out on the water a lot of the time, but when he's in town, he's friendly enough. Chester Ryan is a bit of a free spirit and the resident heartbreaker.

He's sweet but can be unpredictable. Art types, you know? But his art is amazing."

She looks at me with a sly grin for a moment. "So has he talked you into his bed yet?"

I choke on my coffee "What?" I ask sputtering slightly.

She laughs loudly but doesn't move to help my lack of air. "Oh he must be on his best behavior, if you don't know what I mean, he is a charmer. There is always someone from his little art classes who will leave with a broken heart after being with him."

I huff but can't help smiling at her, he was a little flirty when I met him but not the charmer she seems to think he is. "I haven't taken one of his art classes, so I think I'm safe."

Allegra nods, smiling over the edge of her cup. "Then there's Telvin Quinn who is quiet but talented. He's got a small workshop on the other side of the island and makes the most beautiful furniture. He's not one for small talk and doesn't really like a lot of people, but if you get onto the short list of who he likes, he's a sweet friend."

I try to hold all of this information with my head, bringing up their image when she tells me about them and mentally making notes to add to their profiles.

"Makai Vinson runs the gym and is probably the most disciplined person you'll ever meet. Even though the gym is basically next door, you won't see him in here. He's ex-military and keeps everyone on their toes. He rides a Harley around here some weekends and has all of us ladies and even a few men flustered," she says, fanning her face with a hand while giggling.

I laugh along with her before moving the conversation along. "And Ty?" I ask, even though I already know a bit about him.

Allegra smiles. "Ty Santiago is a bit of a local celebrity, but he isn't a flirt or charmer like Chester. Everyone loves him, and his tattoo work is renowned even beyond the island. He's a good conversation-alist as you've probably noticed, and he's always in high demand."

I lean forward, curious. "Anyone else I should be aware of?"

Allegra taps her chin, thinking. "Well, there's also Dr. Lachlan Hughes. He's the island's only doctor and pretty much runs the clinic single-handedly. Then there's Gladys Bishop, she owns the grocery store. Took over when her husband passed away. She's been here forever and knows all the old stories."

"You do know everyone," I say, trying to absorb all the information. "So, have most of them been here their whole lives?"

Allegra frowns thoughtfully. "A few have. I've heard rumors that Jonah was born here but left for a number of years before coming back home, I don't remember him though. Chester, Telvin, Ty, and the good doctor all came at various times over the last tenish years, I believe."

I nod, intrigued. "Why do you think they decided to settle here?"

Allegra shrugs. "Different reasons for different people. Jonah never talks about why he left or why he came back, which is why it's only rumors you'll hear and I may be one to gossip but I do not spread lies."

I nod thoughtfully, appreciating her restraint and honesty. "Chester probably came for the inspiration—I'm not sure where he lived in England or what it was like there, but this island is beautiful and a bit wild, perfect for an artist. Telvin... well, he's got his reasons, I'm sure, but he's not one to share. Ty, though, he came here for a fresh start. He's got a past, like everyone, but he's made a good life for himself here."

"And the doctor?" I ask.

"Dr. Hughes is a bit of a mystery himself. He showed up one day, conveniently just before old Doc Mason died. He helped update the clinic and took charge of it, and that was that. He's dedicated, though. Takes care of everyone here like they're family. I even texted him in the middle of the night when I was having stomach pains and within minutes he was at my door, willing to do whatever it took for me to be able to sleep."

I take another sip of my coffee, mulling over all this new information. "It sounds like a lot of them have secrets."

Allegra nods, her eyes twinkling. "Doesn't everyone? That's just life on an island. We all know each other's business, but there are always a few secrets kept close to the chest. It keeps things *interesting.*"

I smile. "I guess I'll have to stick around to uncover some of those secrets," I say before tilting my head as I look at her. "And what about you? What's your story?"

She shakes her head as she stands, waving a finger at me jokingly. "Oh, I definitely have secrets too. Maybe one day I'll even tell you, if you stick around," she says with a wink.

With those parting words, she makes her way back behind the counter just as a new customer enters the bakery, leaving me to mull over all the new information she shared. The bakery's atmosphere shifts back into its usual rhythm with Allegra seamlessly slipping back into her role as the friendly and efficient baker and not the town gossip.

I take the time to add all the new notes onto my tablet, but Allegra's insights only helped add small tidbits to each of the suspects. It's evident that this island, with its close-knit community and picturesque charm, holds more than its fair share of mysteries. As I finish my sandwich and sip the last of my coffee, I decide that my next step should be to follow up on some of these leads.

Waving goodbye to Allegra, I gather my things and leave the bakery, intending to wander along the street in hopes of running into one of the suspects.

The warm afternoon sun greets me as I step outside, the fresh sea breeze carrying the scent of salt water while the scent of coffee follows behind me. The island's main street activity is starting to thin as it approaches the late afternoon and as I turn to make my way down the street, I'm stopped in my tracks by someone calling out my name.

Chapter 17

Hydessa

"Taylor!"

I turn around to see Makai approaching from the direction of his gym, a broad smile on his face. He's wearing workout clothes, his muscular frame accentuated by a fitted tank top.

"Hi, Makai!" I greet with a smile, noticing exactly what has Allegra swooning.

"I haven't seen you come into the gym yet," he says when he gets close enough.

"It's only been a day," I chuckle, feeling slightly guilty. "I know, I know, I've been meaning to. I've just been busy settling in and getting to know everyone."

Makai nods, his smile unwavering. "I get it. Moving to a new place can be overwhelming. But you should definitely come by. We've got some great classes, and it's a good way to meet people and stay in shape."

I think about it for a moment since I will probably be going for a run anyway, a class wouldn't hurt. "What classes do you have in the mornings?"

Makai's eyes light up with enthusiasm. "We have a yoga class and also a circuit training class in the mornings. Tomorrow happens to be a circuit day."

"Sounds interesting. What time is it at?" I ask.

"7:30 AM," he replies. "In the mornings, it's mostly locals because tourists don't exactly like getting out of bed that early to exercise while on vacation."

I nod, realizing he might be right and that it could be a good opportunity to gather more information about the locals. "I'll definitely try to make it in the morning."

"That's great! See you then, Taylor."

"See you, Makai," I reply, but he is already turning to jog back toward the gym.

Did he just come out here to get me to go to the gym soon? Was he watching and waiting for me to leave the bakery?

Shaking off the thought, I turn away from the gym and resume my walk down the street. The town is starting to feel more familiar as I stroll along, recognizing faces and exchanging friendly nods with locals going about their morning routines. It's becoming easier to distinguish between tourists and islanders—the relaxed pace and purposeful strides of the locals contrasting with the more leisurely and often bewildered wanderings of visitors armed with maps and cameras.

As I walk, I can't help but mull over Makai's friendly persistence. Was he genuinely eager for me to join his gym classes, or was there more to his encouragement? His timing, appearing just as I left the bakery, was almost too perfect. Like he had been watching me.

Lost in my thoughts I almost collide with someone standing squarely in my path. Startled, I jerk back a step, only to realize it's Rye. The slightly weathered lines of his face softened by a faint quirk of amusement.

"Sorry for startling you," he says, his voice carrying a touch of humor.

I blink at him, momentarily taken aback. "That's okay. I should have been paying more attention," I respond with a slight shrug.

His demeanor shifts slightly, the humor fading from his expression. "I was actually hoping I would run into you," he admits, his tone earnest now. "I wanted to apologize for what I said. I shouldn't assume things, and even if I had, I shouldn't have been so vocal about it."

I dip my head in acknowledgement, appreciating his candor. "It's fine. It's not like you know me," I offer softly.

He nods, a faint smile tugging at his lips again. "It feels like I know you though," he admits cryptically, then shrugs as if dismissing the thought. "You're the talk of the town. Everyone is saying something about you everywhere I go."

Internally, I cringe at the thought of being the center of attention, especially in such a small community where gossip can spread like wildfire. "Is that so?" I manage to say, trying to keep my tone neutral.

Rye nods, his expression thoughtful. His attention shifts to something across the street for a moment before he focuses on me again. "Anyway, maybe if you do stick around we could grab a coffee sometime," he says with a grin.

I huff a laugh at his dig about me staying before I shrug. "Maybe... who knows, I might run away to a different island instead," I joke and start to walk past him, but he just rolls his eyes good-naturedly and proceeds in the opposite direction to me.

As I continue down the street, I take a moment to find a spot on the bench where I can sit and observe, attempting to blend in while keeping an eye on those around me. Sheriff Brooks is once again outside the station, a cigarette in hand, his gaze sweeping over the tourists.

He seems vigilant, ever watchful for any signs of trouble. Across the street, Deputy Eli stands with his arms crossed sternly, addressing a pair of teenagers with a serious expression, likely reprimanding them for some misdeed.

My thoughts drift to the seemingly perfect façade of this town. It makes me wonder how much actually goes unnoticed here. With so many people coming and going, how many other transgressions slip under the radar? The bloggers brought attention to the tourist murders, but how many other crimes go unanswered?

I shift on the bench, my gaze drifting back to Sheriff Brooks, who is now flicking his cigarette to the ground and grinding it out with his boot. He smiles slightly as he watches a group of tourists pass by, their loud chatter piercing in volume. He seems to enjoy the happiness of the tourists, but I wonder if he could really enjoy so many people here.

Deputy Eli finishes his stern talk with the teenagers, who slink away with their heads down. He watches them go, it's clear that he takes his role seriously, but I wonder how effective they can be with the sheer volume of people coming and going.

As I continue to sit and observe, Eli starts wandering down the street, keeping an eye out and chatting with tourists. I'm surprised his surly demeanor doesn't make him less approachable, but I suspect the badge helps. It just makes me look at him a little more closely. I barely acknowledge when someone sits on the bench beside me, assuming it's just another tourist like the five others who have sat down and left before now.

"You're looking awful hard at my boy there," comes a gravelly voice. My head jerks around to see that it's the Sheriff who has taken a seat. His posture is relaxed, and the scent of cigarettes finally reaches me on the breeze.

I smile, masking my surprise. "Sheriff, nice to see you. I was just admiring how well he interacts with all the tourists. You seemed to be over there acting like a mildly grumpy old man wanting them to go away," I joke.

To my relief, he chuckles under his breath, a deep, genuine sound. "How old do you think I am then, lass?" he asks, his eyes twinkling with amusement.

Feeling emboldened by our easy banter, I grin. "Hmm, fifty-five? Sixty? I mean, it's an island. You could be a hundred but still looking young from the fountain of youth for all I know."

He bellows out a laugh, loud enough to draw attention from passersby. "I'm not even fifty yet. Still plenty of life left in me, Taylor," he responds with a wink, and I can't help the smile crossing my face. He is actually handsome for an older guy.

"Good to know, Sheriff," I reply, still smiling.

He leans back, his gaze following Eli as he continues his patrol. "Eli might be a lot sterner than me but it keeps the kids in line. Comes in handy with all the tourists we get."

"I can see that," I say, watching Eli approach a couple with a child throwing a tantrum. They immediately brighten up, grateful for his assistance. "So, Sheriff, with all these tourists coming and going, does it make your job harder? Do you see a lot of crime here?"

His expression turns thoughtful. "You'd be surprised. Mostly it's petty stuff—drunken brawls, theft, the usual tourist nonsense. But every now and then, something bigger happens. We do our best to keep things under control, but it's not always easy. Next week is usually our hardest week of the year."

I raise an eyebrow at him curiously. "Why next week?"

He clarifies, "Our annual carnival. It's not a huge thing but big enough to draw the crowds. They should be starting to set it up over the next day or two."

"Carnival, huh? I think I saw something about that," I muse, intrigued. "That must be a lot to handle."

The sheriff nods, a hint of a smile playing on his lips. "It's a good time, but yeah, it keeps us busy. Lots of extra folks around, more opportunities for things to go sideways."

I nod thoughtfully. "Sounds like you'll have your hands full."

He chuckles. "Wouldn't have it any other way. Keeps the job interesting."

We sit in silence for a moment, watching the ebb and flow of people on the street. The town's charm is undeniable, with its quaint shops and friendly atmosphere. Yet, beneath the surface, there's a complexity that piques my curiosity. As if there's an undercurrent running through the island that reminds me of the shadows inside myself.

"So, how are you finding our little island so far?" Sheriff Brooks asks, breaking the silence.

"It's growing on me," I admit. "It's different from what I'm used to, but in a good way."

"What are you used to?" he queries.

"City life." I respond simply.

He huffs a laugh. "Yeah, this is certainly not city life," he says. "If you need anything or have any questions, feel free to drop by the station."

"Thanks, Sheriff. I appreciate it."

He gives me a nod and a brief smile before standing up. "Take care, Taylor. See you around."

With a final wave, Sheriff Brooks heads back towards the station. I stay there people-watching for another hour, long after the deputy has also returned to the station.

I don't see any of the other people on my list except Lily, who waves at me between serving patrons at the café with a smile. Deciding to head back to the house to do some more social media stalking, I get up and start the trek.

As I walk, my attention is drawn to a bus pulled over ahead. As I approach, a girl stumbles out of it and into my path. She looks a few years younger than me, with stunning red hair —a mix of natural and dyed red that deepens the color — and a smattering of freckles across her nose.

"Oh my gosh, I'm so sorry," she says with a tired smile, quickly moving her backpack out of the way.

I chuckle softly. "That's totally fine. You look like you've had a long trip," I reply sympathetically.

"You could definitely say that. I'm Beth," she introduces herself with a friendly demeanor.

"Taylor," I respond, extending my hand, it doesn't hurt to be welcoming."Welcome to Amity Island"

"Thank you," Beth replies, glancing around as if taking in the surroundings for the first time. "Would you happen to know where the real estate office is?" she asks, adjusting her backpack.

"Absolutely, it's just over there," I point in the direction of Maddie's office, knowing it's not far.

Beth picks up her backpack again, a grin spreading across her face. "Thanks, Taylor. I'll hopefully see you around."

With a nod and a wave, I watch as Beth heads towards Maddie's office. Turning away, I resume my walk home, the familiar route now comforting after a day of observations and interactions. The sun is beginning to dip lower in the sky, casting a warm golden hue over the streets.

It is strange to realize just how much I am enjoying my time here even with the investigation aspect. I don't know at what point I started dreading the thought of leaving here, but I know I will need to at some point. Even with these murderers, I'm not sure this island is really the right place for someone like me.

Chapter 18

Hydessa

I'm contemplating calling Seanna as I walk back to the house. Typically we call each other every other day, but she is really good at helping me organize the information in my head.

My keys are in my hand when I notice a package sitting on my doorstep, beautifully gift-wrapped and about the size of a tissue box. A small card is tucked under the ribbon. I glance around but don't see anyone lingering nearby. Stepping closer, I tentatively pick up the box, narrowing my eyes at the blank card. I unlock the door and walk directly to the office, setting the small box down on the desk.

I pull the tiny card from beneath the ribbon. It's a simple gold color to match the ribbon. Turning it over, I see gold writing in an almost feminine script: "Welcome to the Island." Nothing else is written, and there are no distinguishing marks on the box. A gut feeling tells me to be wary, but I can't be sure if that's just my ingrained caution from childhood. Maybe it is a genuine gift from someone on the island like Maddie or Allegra.

Opening the box, I'm suddenly overwhelmed with the scent of cherries. My breath catches as I move the tissue paper aside to reveal cherry cookies. I faintly remember loving these as a child, but I haven't had them in forever. Setting the box aside on the desk, I stare at it for a few moments. It's probably a strange coincidence, but I decide not to trust them anyway.

With a sigh, I make my way to the kitchen. I have another long night ahead of me, so I prepare a pot of coffee and take a large cup back to the office, sipping it slowly before setting it on the desk.

I create additional notes to stick to the wall, reorganizing it so that I have one section for the victims with a separate section for the suspects on my list. It paints a picture that everyone thinks they know everyone, yet they all have secrets, and don't really know anything beyond the surface level.

With no details on the victims, I have no idea how they would even connect to any of the suspects. *How do they come into contact with the tourists? Why are those tourists in particular selected?*

I'm sure there are a lot of tourists that come to this island with no real prospects or home, but something tells me these tourists are specific. *And what was the trigger that started the killings? Was there a specific event that flipped a switch?*

I get myself another cup of coffee and when I return to the office, I glance at my phone on the desk as I lean back against it, my mind racing. Picking it up, I go to the message from the unknown number and taking a deep breath, I type out a response.

> Do you kill for a reason?

A moment later, my phone buzzes with a response.

UNKNOWN

> Hmmmm, I didn't realize we were playing twenty questions... careful, answers come at a price. Are you willing to pay it?

My heart pounds in my chest. This is not the kind of response I was hoping for but it's clear I'm talking to a psychopath so this is actually something I can work with. I take a deep breath, trying to steady my nerves. My fingers are trembling slightly as I type out another message.

> What sort of price?

UNKNOWN

> We will want something in exchange for each answer, it could be as simple as an answer from you... or it could be something bigger... you won't know until we ask for it or simply take it...

> ...

UNKNOWN

> How much are answers worth to you?

With how little I know in order to solve this mystery, I would be willing to pay a lot for some simple answers. But am I really about to play the equivalent of Russian roulette with some killers? There is a part of me, deep inside, that is buzzing with excitement. The part that reminds me that I've killed people too. My reasons were always justified of course, but it's still a part of me that feels more connected to murderers than the victims.

> Yes I'll pay the price.

UNKNOWN

> Let's test your willingness then shall we? You want to know if we kill for a reason? Yes we do, we always have a reason behind why we kill.

And this is the issue with playing this game with them, they can give me an answer without giving me any details to go with it if I don't ask the right question. And now simply because they responded to the question I owe them something.

The seconds drag as I wait for what will be my payment. I can feel my heart starting to beat faster in my chest. Finally, my phone buzzes again, and I quickly read the message.

UNKNOWN

> Your first payment is simple. Tell us something personal. Something no one else knows about you.

I take a deep breath, my mind racing through possible answers. I need to be careful with what I reveal. Giving away too much could be dangerous, but giving too little might not satisfy them. I decide on something that is personal, yet not too revealing.

> I sometimes wish I could be more like my sister.

I hit send and wait, my anxiety building with each passing second. The response comes quickly.

UNKNOWN

> Interesting. A small payment, but it will do for now. Keep asking, little shadow. Every question brings you closer to the truth, but also deeper into our game.

I need to be strategic here. I think carefully, trying to phrase the next question in a way that might yield more useful information.

> How do you choose your victims?

I hit send and take a large drink of my coffee, the warmth doing little to calm my nerves. My phone buzzes again, and I quickly read the reply.

UNKNOWN

> The people we kill are chosen carefully. They are not random. There is always a reason behind each of our kills and a lot of research goes into selecting them. But that's all you'll get for now.

Tell us about your biggest regret.

I swallow hard, feeling the weight of the question. My biggest regret is something I've never shared with anyone. It's deeply personal and painful. But I need to keep them talking, to get more information.

> Not admitting my feelings for someone before I lost him.

I hit send, feeling a pang of sadness wash over me. The response comes quickly.

UNKNOWN

> Regret is a powerful emotion. It shapes us in ways we often don't realize. You're doing well, little shadow.

So far, their answers are just vague enough to keep me guessing, yet they hint at a deeper, more intricate plan. I need to dig deeper.

> Was there a specific event that made you start killing people?

The response is almost immediate, as if they were expecting the question.

UNKNOWN

> There was a catalyst, yes. A significant event that set everything into motion. But what that event was... you'll need to earn that answer, little shadow.

> Why do you call me 'little shadow'?

> Wait, that wasn't one of my questions.

> Too late. We call you little shadow because you are living in the shadow of those around you. Your parents, your sister, both organizations you work for... We want you to see that. We want you to embrace that darkness you run away from and become its queen. Become our queen.

I'm speechless. Their words send a shiver down my spine. The thought of embracing darkness, of becoming the queen of it, is both terrifying and strangely alluring. But I can't let them manipulate me. I need to stay focused on uncovering the truth. If my darkness is so much like theirs as they claim, then I need to be doing everything I can to keep it at bay.

> What are you most afraid of?

My nerves suddenly make me jittery, my heart rate speeds up. I reach over and grab a cookie, shoving it into my mouth to calm my nerves. The flavor of the cherries bursts inside my mouth, and I moan at the taste. My heart rate calms a little as I wash the cookie down with some coffee before typing out my response, my fingers still trembling as I hit send.

> I'm afraid no one will love me for who I really am.

I'm still on edge and I reach for another cherry cookie, its sweetness offering a brief distraction from the intensity of the situation.

Picking up the coffee cup from the desk, I take another deep drink. Suddenly, a wave of dizziness washes over me. I blink rapidly, trying to clear my vision, but the room starts to blur. My heart races, not from anxiety but from something more insidious. I feel my limbs growing heavy, my head becoming foggy.

My phone buzzes, but I can barely focus on the screen. The words swim before my eyes as I struggle against whatever is in my system.

UNKNOWN

> You're doing so well, little shadow. But some-times, the darkness needs a little help.

Panic sets in as I realize what's happening. I stagger against the desk, but my legs are weak and unsteady. The room tilts and spins around me. I grasp at the edge of the desk for support, knocking over the coffee cup in the process.

Holy shit, they drugged me.

I need to call for help, but my phone slips from my grasp, clattering to the floor. With one last, desperate effort, I step toward the door, but my legs give out completely, and I collapse to the ground.

My mind races, trying to stay alert despite the overwhelming dizziness. Whatever they drugged me with hasn't rendered me completely unconscious, but I can't bring myself to move. It's like it wasn't a full dose, just enough to incapacitate me. My mind remains aware, trapped in a body that won't respond.

I see the moment they enter the room, their neon masks casting red and green glows as they walk straight toward me. My heart is hammering inside me as Cain kneels in front of me, his mask glowing a sinister red.

"The cookies," I manage to grind out, my voice barely a whisper.

Cain tilts his head, studying me for a moment. "It wasn't in the cookies," he says before reaching for me, picking me up like my weight means nothing and throwing me over his shoulder.

Chapter 19

Hydessa

H anging upside down makes the disorientation feel even worse. Whatever drug is in my system must have a very short shelf life because I can already feel the fuzziness beginning to fade away, my fingers tingling but still not cooperating with me.

How did they even get inside the house? I didn't hear anyone come inside, but I admit I was very distracted. Stupid me getting so engrossed in our texting conversation I didn't realize someone came in and poisoned my damn coffee.

Coffee is sacred and they ruined that.

I should have fucking savored those cookies more. Now I have to throw out everything in the house, because like hell am I trusting that it wasn't in the cookies.

My upper body sways with the movement of Cain's body as he walks up the stairs to the second floor. I already know where he's taking me; there's only one room I use up here, the bedroom.

With each step, I try to regain more control over my body, attempting to force my limbs to respond. Cain's grip on me is firm, his pace steady as if he has done this a hundred times before.

I can only faintly feel his muscular body under mine as he moves, like that numb feeling you get when your foot falls asleep. The eerie glow from his mask casts shadows on the dark walls upstairs, the sun having set as I worked, making the house feel more sinister, menacing even.

When we reach the bedroom, Cain gently sits me down on the bed. My head is still spinning, but I feel the dip of the bed behind me, the green glow of Abel's mask joining Cain's as he wraps his hands underneath my arms and drags me backward onto the bed. He takes a seat against my pillows, pulling me against him so that my back is pressed to his chest.

Cain moves around the side of the bed while Abel holds one of my arms out and Cain secures a cuff to it, pulling it tight against my skin, almost pinching.

Moving to the other side of the bed, they repeat the process with my other arm. By the time they are done, a lot of the feeling has started coming back and I'm able to jerk my arms and pull on the chains, but my strength is still weak and it just gets a low chuckle from both of them, the voice changer in their masks creating a sinister echo to the sound.

I can feel the leather cuff digging into my skin, the chains rattling softly with each movement. Abel's grip on me is firm but not painful, his body a solid, unyielding presence behind me.

He must have raised his mask because I can feel his breath against my neck, slow and measured, sniffing at my skin. It contrasts sharply with my own rapid, panicked breaths, but I can't move my head enough to see his face. Then I feel his tongue touch my neck, licking at me, tasting me.

The red of Cain's mask makes him look like the devil incarnate as he kneels on the end of the bed. He wraps his hands around my ankles, his grip firm while his gloved fingers press into the bare skin there as he spreads them apart. I'm surprised he hasn't bound them too, he leaves them free, but I can't get them to cooperate with me.

My breath hitches, a mix of fear and something else I don't want to acknowledge coursing through me. The sensation of being so completely at their mercy, so utterly controlled, stirs something deep inside me.

"Such a beautiful little shadow," Cain murmurs, his voice a dark caress. "You pretend to be so strong, but you crave this, don't you?"

I struggle against the chains and try to push against the strong body of Abel behind me, more out of instinct than any real desire to escape. The truth is, there is a part of me that is inexplicably drawn to this, to them.

They may be killers, but so am I. If they are going to enjoy the chase, I should be able to as well.

The loss of control—it's intoxicating in a way I hadn't expected. I can feel exactly how much Abel is enjoying my struggle, his hardening cock pressing against my back through our clothes.

Cain's touch is deliberate, his fingers trailing up my legs as he moves to kneel between them. "Feeling coming back now?" he asks with a tilt of his head. He reaches behind himself and when his hand reappears he has a knife held in it, making my heart race. "Because I want you to be able to feel this."

With a swift and deliberate motion, Cain slices through the fabric of my shirt and bra before he presses the edge of the blade against the sensitive skin of my breast. The sharp pain slices through the haze of fear, jolting me into a sharper awareness. I scream, a desperate sound mingling with the sound of rattling chains.

"That's it baby, scream for us," Abel's modulated voice whispers close to my ear with a groan. He must have pulled his mask back down when he was done sniffing me.

The knife traces a path, leaving a trail of blood in its wake. Each movement is deliberate, calculated to heighten my fear and discomfort. My body feels extra sensitive, still tingling and weak from whatever drug they had administered, but also like I'm now hyper focused on every touch against my skin.

He moves the blade across to my other breast, slapping the flat of it against my nipple and I whimper in response. Abel reaches around, his gloved hand sliding over the line of red blood starting to create a path over the curve of my breast. He smears it over my other nipple, spreading it like its paint as he circles a finger around the sensitive peak. He pinches the nipple between his fingers at the same moment Cain presses the blade into the skin at the side of my other breast.

I scream again, loud enough that I'm surprised that someone isn't beating down the door to the house. Abel's other hand moves to the new cut, spreading the blood over that breast too, and I jerk against the restraints when his fingers move over the fresh cut, probing for more.

"Why is no one coming to help me?" I grit out in frustration.

They both chuckle, the sound echoing around the room and making me shiver.

Abel brings one of his blood stained hands up to wrap around my throat, turning my face toward his, the neon green light shining brightly in my eyes. "You should be careful here, little shadow, the people in this town are just as twisted as we are," he whispers and my heart sinks at his words.

The blade suddenly digs into the skin of my upper arm, I try to jerk away but Abel holds me firm. I grit my teeth against the pain, but I refuse to scream now, I refuse to give them exactly what they want. And it won't make a difference anyway. Moments later he pulls the knife away again, trailing it gently down my body as I shake in agony and desire. It makes me want to lash out at him.

Cain's voice, distorted yet ominously smooth, fills the room. "Let's make this memorable, shall we?" With deliberate slowness, he traces the tip of the knife along the curve of my thigh through my leggings, leaving a cold, chilling sensation in its wake. He isn't applying enough pressure to cut the material of the leggings yet, it's just enough to tease, sending shivers through my body. Each touch feels calculated, purposeful, as if he's building and savoring the fear that pulses through me.

I swallow hard, my chest heaving with rapid breaths. The knife's tip moves to trace delicate patterns across the bare skin of my belly, leaving a trail of goosebumps in its wake. The sensation is both terrifying and strangely electrifying.

His other hand comes up to touch where his blade has already opened my skin. His fingertips move along each stinging cut, before spreading the blood. I hear the catch in his breath, the soft groan, almost like he is mesmerized by how it looks on my bare skin.

Abel's hand returns to my breast, twisting and pulling on my nipple as his other tightens around my throat. It's like his fingers have a direct line to my pussy, I can feel each pull and twist along the entire length of my body.

My body betrays me, responding to their touch despite my mind's protests. I can feel the heat pooling in my core, a flush spreading across my skin. My breaths come faster, more shallow, as the conflicting emotions war within me.

As the blade hovers dangerously close to my pussy, I struggle harder against the chains, my heart pounding in my ears. "Please," I manage to choke out, my voice trembling.

Cain's masked face tilts slightly, almost inquisitively, as if my plea intrigues him. "Please what, little shadow?" His voice is taunting, a dark amusement lacing his words. "Do you want me to stop? Or do you want more?"

My mind races with conflicting thoughts, fear battling against a disturbing curiosity that twists my insides. Every touch, every cut, seems to awaken a primal response within me, a response that both thrills and horrifies.

"Please," I manage again, my voice barely above a whisper, betraying my own conflicted desires. The chains rattle softly as I strain against them, my body taut with tension.

Cain's masked face looms over me, his eyes hidden behind the eerie glow of his mask. "You're trembling, little shadow," he observes with a hint of amusement in his voice. "And your body tells me exactly why that is."

Abel's grip flexes around my throat, his touch strangely possessive yet oddly comforting in its firmness. His other hand continues its torment, fingers twisting and pulling. It's as if he knows exactly how to play my body like an instrument, each touch resonating deep within.

The blade finally presses more firmly against me, tracing a slow, deliberate path along the sensitive skin of my inner thigh through the fabric of my leggings. The sting of the blade cutting my skin is sharp, making me hiss a breath because I didn't expect him to keep going. I arch against their hold, begging for more while straining to get away at the same time.

"Look at how she responds," Abel groans, his voice low and husky.

"She's perfect, brother," Cain says, his tone almost reverent, his eyes hidden behind the neon mask.

I am equal parts pissed off and turned on. My teeth clench and I wonder if I could throw them off. Could I hold my breath until I pass out? Could I pretend to pass out just to see what they do? Is there any way I can gain some kind of control here?

"I told you she would be," Abel responds.

I struggle to find words, my thoughts a chaotic whirlwind of fear and arousal. The pleasure that is swirling inside me with each touch is undeniable, a dark hunger awakening within me that I can't fully comprehend. They are right—I crave this twisted dance of pain and pleasure, even as it terrifies me to my core.

With a sudden movement, Cain slices through the rest of my leggings and underwear, the fabric parting under the blade's cold edge. The sensation of the last of my clothing being cut and pulled away adds to the feeling of surrender as he strips away my last shreds of control.

"Do you like this, little shadow?" Cain's voice echoes through the room, his words taunting me with the truth I've tried to bury. "Or do you wish you were somewhere else?"

I don't answer, torn between the shame of my arousal and the overwhelming need for more.

"Last night when you were spread open for us, were you imagining us buried inside you as you made yourself cum?" Abel whispers seductively in my ear.

The room seems to close in around us. In that moment, I realize I am truly at their mercy, bound not just by chains but by something deeper, something unsettling that stirs within me and talks to the darkness I have always kept at bay. The shadows strain toward them, trying to tear down the walls I built so long ago.

"Do you want more now, baby girl? Do you want our cocks?" Cain's question hangs in the air, a challenge and a promise wrapped in one.

I close my eyes, my breath hitching in anticipation. The answer comes unbidden, whispered from a place I don't fully understand. "Yes."

Chapter 20

Hydessa

M y heart races in my chest at my confession, I shouldn't be doing this, I shouldn't want this. But I do. I can feel Abel's mask against my neck, I can hear his breath hot and heavy inside it. His grip on my throat loosens just enough to allow me to breathe more freely, but he doesn't let go entirely.

Cain's fingers trail over my newly exposed skin, each touch sending a jolt of electricity through me. His gloved hand traces the curve of my thigh, his fingers toying with the fresh cut before moving closer to the heat pooling at my core. I am hyper-aware of every sensation, every brush of fabric against my skin, every shift of weight on the bed.

The anticipation is almost unbearable.

"You heard her, brother," Abel says, his voice dripping with dark satisfaction. "She wants more."

Cain's hand cups my pussy, the leather over his hand is cool against my heated flesh. He slides one finger between my folds, parting them slowly, deliberately, making me squirm against the restraints. I can't help the moan that escapes my lips, the sound betraying my need.

"She's so wet," Cain murmurs, his voice filled with dark amusement. "Such a good little slut, getting all worked up for us."

Abel's voice is low and husky near my ear. "Do you like being our slut, little shadow? Do you like being at our mercy?"

I bite my lip, trying to suppress another moan, but it's useless. The pleasure is building, an unstoppable tide that threatens to drown me. "Yes," I whisper, the word barely audible.

Cain's finger slips inside me, curling upwards to find that sweet spot that makes my entire body shudder. Abel's hand tightens around my throat again, his other pressing against one of the cuts on my breast before playing with my nipples again.

"Good girl," Cain says, adding another finger, stretching me. "Let's see how much you can take."

The rhythm of his fingers increases, each thrust sending waves of pleasure through me. Abel's hand moves from my breast to my sensitive clit, his fingers circling it with expert precision. My body arches against their touch, my breath coming in ragged gasps. The chains rattle with my movements, the sound mingling with the low, guttural groans from both men.

"Cum for us, little shadow," Abel whispers, his voice a dark command. "Show us how much your pussy is begging for our cocks."

The pleasure is overwhelming, a white-hot flame that consumes me from the inside out. My body shudders, every muscle tightening as I teeter on the edge. And then, with a cry, I shatter, the orgasm ripping through me with a force that leaves me breathless and trembling.

Cain's fingers continue to move inside me, drawing out every last wave until I'm spent, my body limp. Abel's hand slows its movements, his touch gentle now, almost soothing.

"There's a good girl," Abel murmurs, his mask brushing gently against my temple almost like a kiss. "You did so well."

Cain withdraws from me, his touch lingering on my thigh. "We're not done with you yet, little shadow." His voice promises more pleasure, and better yet, more pain.

I close my eyes, my breath coming in slow, ragged gasps. The fear is still there, a dark undercurrent that threads through my pleasure. But so is the arousal, the need for more. I am theirs, completely and undeniably, in this moment.

I feel Cain shifting away from me, leaving me with Abel at my back. Abel's gloved hands brush lightly up my arms before his fingers press against them, rubbing the tense muscles there. One then travels up further, opening my clenched hand and brushing against the skin of my palm. I must have cut myself with my nails without realizing. He then trails them back down to cup my breasts. It's like he can't stop touching me, like he wants to map every inch of my skin.

I hear the rustle of fabric as Cain undoes his pants, the sound sending another wave of anticipation through me. I can sense him watching me, his gaze burning with an intensity that makes my skin prickle.

"Open your eyes, little shadow," Cain commands softly.

I obey, my eyes fluttering open to see Cain's cock, hard and ready. He strokes it slowly, and the glint of neon reflected on metal has my breath catching. I've never been with anyone with a piercing before, let alone enough to look like the ornaments on a Christmas tree all lined up in a row.

"Do you want this?" he asks, his voice a seductive purr. "Do you want to feel me inside you?"

"Yes," I breathe, my eyes widening as I realize what I just said out loud. My body tenses up again as my nerves and anxiety start overwhelming me. Even without the piercings, his size would be a stretch.

I may go to the club and pretend to be my sister for a decent fuck here and there, but this is different. This isn't a fleeting fuck, these two man want to own me, and I just gave them the green light.

Cain leans forward, his gloved thumb brushing against my clit again in a soothing circle. "You're going to want to relax a bit, sweetheart, or this will hurt," he murmurs.

I try to focus on his touch, letting the pleasure distract me from the anxiety as he crawls between my legs. He positions himself at my entrance and then slowly, deliberately, begins to push inside me. The cold metal of the first piercing contrasts sharply with the heat of my body.

I clamp down on instinct, the feeling foreign and strange.

Abel's fingers pinch my nipple hard, sending a sharp jolt of pain that quickly morphs into pleasure and forces me to relax. The combination of sensations is overwhelming.

Cain pauses, giving me a moment to adjust. His thumb continues to circle my clit, coaxing my body to relax. The discomfort slowly fades, replaced by a growing need for more.

"Just a bit more," Cain whispers. "Get used to the feeling now, Hydessa, I won't always be this gentle with you."

He resumes his slow, deliberate push. I can feel my body stretching to accommodate him, each piercing creating a unique pressure that makes me gasp. Abel's fingers massage my full breasts before he squeezes, amplifying the sensations coursing through me.

My breath hitches as Cain finally fills me completely. His hands grip my hips, adjusting our positions, his fingers digging into my skin hard enough that I know I will have bruises in the morning.

"You're ours, Hydessa. Never forget that," Cain murmurs, starting a slow rhythm, each thrust measured and deliberate.

Abel lets go of me and slides out from under my body, kneeling beside me on the bed as his brother continues to thrust into me. With one hand he takes a handful of my hair, gripping it hard so he can turn my face to where he's using his other hand to pull his cock from the confines of his pants. He doesn't have all the piercings Cain has, but he still has one, right through the head currently glistening with precum.

Pain sparks along my scalp as the leather glove pulls on strands of my hair and I jerk against the chains, whimpering.

"Now, let's see how well you can please us both, little shadow," Abel murmurs, his voice low. "Don't bite or I'll choke you with more than just my cock."

When I don't open my mouth fast enough Abel pulls sharply on my hair again, making me gasp. He takes advantage of my open mouth to shove himself all the way into it, the metal of his piercing hitting the back of my throat. I gag around him and he groans, the sound echoing through the room.

Cain also groans, his hips jerking and slapping against mine. "Yes, that's it, she likes that," he growls, his rhythm getting harder, faster. The feel of the piercings moving inside me feels incredible, I've never felt anything like it before.

Abel's cock is thick and heavy against my tongue, the smoothness of his skin contrasting with the roughness of his glove as he grips my jaw with his other hand. He digs his fingers in until he has my jaw stretched wide for him. I taste the faint tang of salt and metal as I slide my tongue down his length, feeling him harden further in response.

I moan softly around him, the vibrations sending a visible shiver of pleasure through Abel's body. He tilts his head back slightly, his grip on my hair tightening even more.

"Suck it," he commands, his voice rough with desire. "Show us what a greedy little slut you are for our cocks." Forcing my head to stay in place, he thrusts deeper into my mouth.

The neon glow of both their masks dances over every surface of the room. For the first fleeting moment I wonder what the hell I'm doing, I've once again allowed myself to be pulled into this situation. These men are killers, the knife they used to slice my skin open earlier was probably the same one that took the lives of the tourists. I can feel the remnants of doubt flicker through my mind and I'm suddenly no longer in sync with their actions as my body begins to go numb.

Cain lets go of one of my hips, using that hand to slap my breast hard. "Stop thinking, little shadow," he commands.

His stinging slap reverberates through my body, snapping me out of my spiraling thoughts. My jaw flexes automatically and my teeth scrape against the tender flesh inside my mouth.

Abel gasps and he uses the tight grip he has on my hair to jerk my head back and off his cock. He brings a gloved hand to squeeze the head of himself to hold off his own climax, tilting his head at me. "Bad girl," he breathes huskily. "Are you trying to make me cum before I've felt you squeeze around me?"

His words send a shiver down my spine. I gasp as he tilts my head, forcing me to look down at what Cain is doing to me as he lifts at the back of my neck.

"You're enjoying this, aren't you? Being used by us." Abel murmurs.

I whimper in response, the sensations overwhelming as Cain's piercings move inside me, every thrust driving me closer to the edge. Abel's hand relaxes, rubbing soothing circles on the sides of my neck as he strokes my cheek almost tenderly.

"Our perfect little fuck toy, I knew you would be, you were made for us," he murmurs, his voice filled with dark satisfaction.

Cain's thrusts become even more demanding, making me gasp and moan with each stroke. His free hand moves until he is once again circling my clit with his thumb. I can't help the way they make me feel. It might be wrong, but maybe I'm just not right in the head. I want this and I want it with them, even if it's just for a little while.

The sensation Cain is building with his thumb pushes me closer to the edge. Abel's hand wraps around my throat again, applying enough pressure this time to make my head spin, my breath stuttering as I gasp.

The lack of air intensifies every sensation, my body reacting wildly to the deprivation. I can feel myself tightening around him. Cain's thrusts become more erratic, his thumb pressing down on my clit with a relentless pressure that has me wanting to cry with the need to come.

Abel's grip tightens, his fingers digging into my skin as he controls my breath, my pulse, my life, with such ease. It is intoxicating and yet, terrifying the amount of trust I am giving them. Somewhere in my mind something tells me that they may be killers, but they won't kill me.

"You're ours, every breath, every gasp, and every moan from now on belongs to us," Abel murmurs, his voice a dark, seductive whisper.

I can feel myself slipping, the edge of consciousness fraying as my body tenses in anticipation.

Just as I think I might pass out, Abel releases his grip slightly, allowing a gasp of air to fill my lungs. The rush of oxygen is like a jolt of electricity, sparking through me and sending me over the edge. My orgasm crashes over me in the same way I imagine lighting envelops a tree.

Cain's hips slam into mine one last time, his own release tearing through him as he groans my name. The heat of his cum fills me, the sensation prolonging my own orgasm. I'm still trembling when Cain withdraws from me, making me whimper.

Abel wastes no time, unclipping the restraint on my arm closest to him. He rolls my body over, and my mind, still hazy with pleasure and exhaustion, barely registers what he's doing until he has my ass raised in the air and me up on my knees.

His cock slams into my pussy with a brutal force, reigniting the pleasure that had momentarily faded. He sets an instantly punishing pace, tangling his hand in my hair to press my face against the bed, bending my back painfully.

I moan softly, the sound muffled by the sheets beneath me, he isn't as thick as Cain is, but he is bigger. He fills me completely, the piercing on the end of his cock sending sparks of both pleasure and intense pain through me with each thrust as it punishes my g-spot.

His grip on my hair tightens, jerking my body up with a force that leaves me gasping. He continues to thrust into me while arching my body back as far as he can. I try to gain purchase with my free hand. The arm still secured to a cuff stretches out, the chain rattling. My other arm reaches back, trying to find something to grab ahold of, what I don't expect to get my fingers on is the mask covering his face.

The neon green mask clatters to the ground but before I can do anything, Abel has his hand wrapped around my throat again, squeezing hard with a low growl.

The red glow of Cain's mask is bright as he comes to kneel in front of me. "Give us one more, little shadow," he demands, his hands reaching out to cup and squeeze my breasts, pulling on them as Abel continues to thrust into me.

I whimper, trying to shake my head but Abel's grip doesn't let me. "I can't..." I manage to rasp out.

My body is dancing along the edge, but I can't find a way to go over it no matter how much I want to. It's like when I'm alone with myself and I just want to give up because I'm not getting there.

Abel cuts off my air almost completely, his hold tilting my head up. He is relentless, to the point that I see stars dancing along my darkened ceiling. For a moment, I wonder if I was wrong. Would they really kill me now that they have had their fun?

Teeth sink into the soft flesh of my breast and bite down hard, making my release rush towards me like a freight train. I gasp loudly when Abel loosens his grip, crying out in desperation. I'm so close, I can feel it.

"Yes, you can," Cain growls, his fingers pinching hard at my nipples. The pain is sharp and intense, forcing the orgasm out of me as if he owned my pleasure.

Abel's pace stutters while his hand simply tightens around my throat once again. Darkness edges my vision and I struggle to draw breath. My whole body feels as though it is throbbing in time with the rapid beat of my heart and it doesn't take long for my vision to go completely black, my body and mind sliding peacefully into oblivion.

Chapter 21

Cain

I watch as her eyes flutter closed, her body trembling with the aftershocks of her release. The look of bliss on her face is enough to make me want another taste of her. Even though I just came, I can feel the desire building within me again. My brother's grip tightens momentarily before he begins to ease up.

"She's out," I say softly, noting the way her body goes limp. He slowly releases his grip on her throat, his fingers leaving marks that will no doubt linger for days. With a gentleness that belies the intensity of what just transpired, I put my hands under her arms and help lower her to the bed.

As I lay her down, I take a moment to admire her. The way she submitted to us, the way she surrendered so completely—it's perfect. I can see her starting to unfold like the most beautiful flower, our very own nightbloom. Her breathing is shallow but steady, her chest rising and falling in a rhythm that soothes something deep within me.

"I told you she was made for us," he murmurs, his voice filled with dark satisfaction. He traces a finger down her cheek, watching as her lips part slightly in her sleep.

I nod, my eyes roaming over her body, taking in every mark and bruise we've left. "She's perfect," I agree, my voice barely above a whisper. "But we need to tend to the cuts and bruises. We can't have her waking yet until we're finished and she's alone again."

He nods, his gaze sharpening on her. "I know," he says. "She's ours, and we'll make sure she knows it, even in her sleep."

Moving to the wall near the head of the bed, I press against two sections and hear the click as it opens the discrete panel hidden there. I pull out a breathing mask with some extended tubing and turn on the small tank, then I hold it over her face. Within moments, her breathing deepens, and her body relaxes further into the mattress.

Ensuring she remains unaware of our movements and actions is crucial, but she needs to wake up feeling both cared for and in control of her senses. The gas will help her rest while we take care of everything she needs, and it will help her body transition better to consciousness.

I pull the neon mask from my face, sighing as my brother fixes his clothes and retrieves his mask that she managed to pull free. I was thankful he was clear headed enough to restrict her movement or our plans would have been ruined.

"We'll start with the cuts," I say, moving to the side of the bed. Bending, I pick up the item I tossed there earlier and put it in my pocket. He retrieves a small first aid kit from the bedside table, its contents meticulously organized.

We work in silent harmony, cleaning each cut with antiseptic and carefully applying liquid bandages. On the deeper cut I apply a numbing cream to the area, it takes moments to do what I need to do, adding a small dissolvable stitch into her skin and sealing it. The bruises, though less urgent, are treated with a soothing salve to ease any discomfort she might feel upon waking.

As we tend to her, I can't help but feel a deepening connection to her. Each touch, each careful movement, solidifies my possessiveness of her. She's ours to protect, to care for, and to dominate.

Once we've finished, we move on to cleaning the rest of her body. Every inch of her skin is wiped down with a warm, damp cloth, removing any traces of sweat and blood.

Her breathing remains deep and even, the sedative ensuring she stays asleep through our care. I gently pull the bed sheets over her so she stays warm and comfortable.

I lean down, brushing a strand of hair from her face, my touch lingering for a moment. "Rest now, little shadow," I whisper. "We'll be watching you, always."

When I step back, I notice my brother doing something with her phone. Curious, I raise an eyebrow and ask quietly, "What are you doing?"

He glances up with a small smile playing on his lips, his fingers tapping away at her phone screen. "Setting her alarm for the morning," he replies casually.

I frown in confusion. "Alarm? Why?"

He looks at me knowingly and simply says, "Trust me."

His confident tone intrigues me, but I decide not to press further. Instead, I watch as he finishes and sets the phone back down beside her. The soft glow of the screen illuminates her serene face, casting a gentle light in the dimly lit room.

I know she doesn't understand everything yet. She only has a few pieces to the larger puzzle. But, she's ours now and has been for a long time, and we intend to ensure she understands that fully.

Chapter 22

Hydessa

I can hear the alarm going off from somewhere close by but I refuse to open my eyes. *Maybe if I don't open my eyes I don't have to face the reality that I did a very bad thing...*

Groaning, I roll over and bury my face into my pillow. Moving reminds me exactly what bad thing I did when I can feel all the little aches and pains that cover my body. The room falls silent as the alarm stops blaring and I sigh with relief. I don't even remember setting the alarm, or why I even would have set one.

I'm just starting to drift to sleep again when the alarm blares once more.

Annoyance flares within me as I grope blindly for my phone, almost knocking it off the nightstand before I finally manage to get ahold of it.

I pull the phone close to my face as I turn to squint at it against the bright light of the screen. 6:40 in the morning. Why would I set an alarm this early? It takes a moment before I remember the gym class at 7:30.

I don't even remember setting the alarm, and my body protests at the prospect of even going. But if I don't go, I will miss out on the opportunity to connect with Makai and anyone at the gym. As much as I want to skip the class and just sleep, I know I can't afford to.

With a deep sigh, I force myself to get up. The room is lit by the early morning light filtering through the curtains. I stretch my arms, feeling the tension in my muscles, and swing my legs over the side of the bed.

I take a moment to steady myself before standing up, my body protesting every movement. Slowly, I make my way to the bathroom, turning on the light and staring at my reflection in the mirror.

Instantly, I cringe, my hand going to my mouth in shock.

Surprisingly the cuts look like they've been cleaned, they even look like they have been sealed with surgical glue.

The cut on my arm aches the worst and I remember the knife digging in deeper there. I turn enough to look at it closer, my stomach dipping until I see the bump under my skin not far from it. I run a finger over it to assure myself that my birth control is still there before I look at the bruising.

There are finger marks in my hips, and my neck looks like I've been choked. Because I was.

Running my fingers gently across the marks littering my neck, I can't help but remember how they got there. The feeling of Abel's fingers wrapped around my throat, squeezing tight. How they possessed me and claimed me. How they *owned* me.

"Well, time to test the staying power of my makeup," I mutter to myself, trying to push the memories aside.

As I carefully apply foundation to cover the marks, I think about the day ahead in order to keep my mind out of the past. The gym class is just the beginning. I need to stay focused, gather information, and keep my guard up. I need to stop being distracted by masked men who fuck like demons from hell. *Maybe I need an exorcism.*

Once I've covered the worst of the bruises, I pull on my workout clothes. Taking one last look in the mirror, I nod to myself. I can do this. I have to do this.

Grabbing my phone and keys, I head out the door, locking it behind me. A sliver of annoyance creeps into my mind as I try to remember if I locked the door when I arrived back at the house yesterday, could I have unknowingly left it unlocked as an open invitation for my masked stalkers. The morning air is crisp and cool as I walk along the street toward the beach. My thoughts drift as I go, wondering what makes the killers tick, what motivates them to kill.

They said to me in our texts last night that they only kill for a reason, that they research and nothing is random, so why were those particular tourists killed? What connects them all, and what exactly did they do that made them targets?

As I make my way to the beach, I replay every interaction I had with Cain and Abel in my mind. Their words, their messages, their demeanor, the way they justified their actions—it all felt disturbingly logical in a twisted way. They seemed convinced that their actions were justified, that their victims deserved what happened to them. But why? What was the common thread that linked their victims together?

I pass by a few early risers, joggers and dog walkers, who nod and wave. I try to return their greetings with a smile, but my mind is elsewhere. My thoughts are churning, trying to connect the puzzle together but it's as if the pieces are upside down and no matter what I do I can't reveal the part of the picture I need to put them together on the other side.

When I reach the beach, the gym comes into view, and so does a large area at the end of the street where I can already see barriers erected and carnival rides starting to be set up. The sheriff did say that that would be happening, so it's probably a good thing I didn't make it to the beachfront last night.

Plus with the masked me distracted by me, they couldn't have been out killing anyone.

I push open the door to the gym and step inside, greeted by the sound of upbeat music and the sight of people either working out on equipment or warming up for the class. I recognize a few faces from around town, and I make my way to an empty spot near the back, hoping to blend in and observe.

Makai waves to me from where he is spotting someone on a weight bench. When that person sets the weight back in the cradle and sits up, I can see that it's Eli. I spot Maddie exiting the locker room and when she spots me, she comes over with a grin.

"Hey Taylor," she says, her voice as bright as her smile. I haven't had enough coffee to deal with that level of happiness this morning, as a matter of fact, I haven't had any coffee yet at all. She may be lucky I don't have any of my knives on me right then.

"Morning Maddie," I respond with a smile, mustering as much cheerfulness as I can. "Ready for a workout?"

She nods enthusiastically. "Absolutely! It's going to be a great class. Nathan, one of the trainers here that runs this class, always knows how to get us moving."

I force a chuckle, trying to match her energy. "Looking forward to it."

Feeling eyes on me, I look up and notice Rye sitting at one of the pieces of equipment not far from Eli and Makai. His eyes are on me as he takes a drink of water, offering me a small smile.

I momentarily wish that the dim lighting and neon colors during all the times I've been with Cain and Abel didn't make it so hard to pick up on more details of the men beneath the masks. I doubt the men around here would simply let me make them line up and drop their pants and let me look at their cocks. Though from some of the looks I get from them, maybe they would.

There are other locals there, shooting glaces in our direction, but none I can put a name to. I spot Telvin working out on the shoulder press in the corner, headphones in his ears as he manages to ignore everything and everyone around him. I wish I had that sort of focus.

A young guy suddenly approaches our group clapping his hands and smiling. He isn't as muscular as Makai and his brown hair is short. "Good morning, everyone! Ready for the circuit class?" His voice is upbeat, and he radiates energy. He must be Nathan, the trainer Maddie mentioned.

A chorus of affirmatives echoes around the room. I nod along, forcing myself to match the enthusiasm. Nathan's eyes scan the group, lingering on Maddie for a moment longer than anyone else. She returns his gaze with a smile that's just a touch more personal than casual.

Interesting. Maddie and Nathan have some sort of connection. Something to keep an eye on.

Nathan claps his hands again. "Alright, let's start with a warm-up! We'll do some light jogging in place, then move on to dynamic stretches."

As we begin the warm-up, I steal glances at Maddie and Nathan. They exchange more secretive looks, and Maddie seems especially animated whenever he's nearby. The circuit class begins in earnest, and I force myself to focus on the exercises.

My body protests, but I push through. Nathan's instructions are clear and precise, and he moves through the group, offering encouragement and correcting form. His interactions with Maddie are just a bit more familiar than with anyone else.

As I move from station to station, I try to listen to the conversations around me. People chat about the carnival, the latest gossip, and mundane life details. Nothing particularly useful, but I file it all away just in case.

During a break, I take a moment to breathe and grab some water. Looking around, I see that a few more people have come into the gym and started working out while I was focused on the circuit.

Makai is now chatting with Telvin as he works out on the leg press toward the back. Eli is on his own doing pull-ups, and Rye is making his way toward where I'm standing.

I take a long drink of water, trying to steady my thoughts. Rye approaches with a friendly smile. "Hey Taylor, how's it going?" he asks, wiping sweat from his brow.

"Hey Rye," I reply, returning his smile. "It's going well. This class is intense."

"Yeah, Nathan doesn't mess around," Rye says with a nervous chuckle. "It's a great way to start the day, though."

"Definitely," I agree, feeling the burn in my muscles.

Rye hesitates, as if he's about to say something more, but Nathan's voice cuts through the moment. "Alright, everyone! Time to get back to it. Let's keep that energy up!"

Rye glances back at Nathan with a scowl, then he is smiling again as he turns to me. "Umm, I'll see you around sometime, Taylor." He gives a quick nod and heads back toward the equipment.

As I watch Rye walk away, I notice him pass Makai, who nods at him before heading over toward Nathan. Makai murmurs something to Nathan, who nods in response before Makai moves on to help someone else. Nathan claps his hands together, calling everyone back into the circuit training one final time.

The rest of the class passes in a blur of movement and effort. By the time we're done, I'm drenched in sweat and my muscles are screaming. But I feel a small sense of accomplishment too. I managed to keep up and even learned a few more names and faces.

As I'm cooling down, stretching out my sore muscles, I see Makai approaching with a friendly smile. "Hey Taylor," he says, stopping in front of me. "How did you like your first class?"

"It was intense," I reply, chuckling despite the fatigue. "But in a good way. Nathan really knows how to push everyone."

Makai nods appreciatively. "Yeah, Nathan's great at what he does. It's good to see you pushing through. A lot of people don't come back after their first class."

"I can see why," I say with a laugh, stretching my sore muscles that aren't entirely from the workout. "I'll admit, I'm pretty stubborn. I'm determined to stick with it."

"That's the spirit," he says, his eyes studying me for a moment. "We have this class every week. We need more people with that kind of attitude around here."

I nod, genuinely appreciative of Makai's encouragement. "Thanks, Makai. It's good to know there's a regular routine I can stick to."

"Yeah, and if you're interested, we've got a few other classes that might interest you," Makai offers, his expression thoughtful. "Apart from this circuit and the yoga class I already mentioned, we also run Zumba, Pilates, and another high-intensity session. In the afternoons and evenings, there's also sometimes boxing and kickboxing, even mixed martial arts in the back room."

My ears perk up at that. "That sounds intriguing," I admit, "I do some kickboxing here and there."

Makai's eyebrows rise in mild surprise. "Oh, really? That's great to hear. You'll find a few enthusiasts here, especially in the evenings. It's a good way to blow off steam and stay sharp. Definitely a good workout."

I smile. "I might have to check that out sometime. Are you the one that does that training?"

Makai laughs and shakes his head. "Nah, I'm more into weights and strength training myself. It's actually Telvin who volunteers to handle the MMA and kickboxing sessions." He gestures subtly towards Telvin, who's now back to being deeply engrossed in his workout, oblivious to everyone else around him.

"Really?" I respond, glancing over at the man. He seemed so quiet and withdrawn when we met.

"Yeah," Makai chuckles again. "What's that saying? It's the quiet ones you have to watch out for? Apparently, it helps him focus or some shit."

I nod thoughtfully, considering this new piece of information. "Interesting. Do a lot of tourists attend those?"

He shrugs. "Some, but not many and it's not overcrowded during that time if that's what you're asking."

With a grin I stand up straight and shake my muscles out, then I start patting away any lingering sweat with the towel. Someone calls out to Makai and he glances over my shoulder for a moment, when his eyes return to me they flick down briefly.

He opens his mouth but before he can speak someone calls out his name again. He waves his hand in that direction but there's a momentary pause before he starts walking towards the person calling him, still glancing back at me.

"Maybe I'll see you here in the evening and you can really work up a sweat," he says with a grin. Then, not waiting for my response he heads off to attend to the gym's business.

Before I can react to Makai's parting comment, Maddie bounces up to me, full of energy. "Hey Taylor! Are you grabbing a coffee from the bakery before heading home too?"

I give an exaggerated groan, half-playful. "Yes, I need coffee. Just hook me up with an IV of it."

Maddie giggles, clearly amused by my dramatic response. "You might also need some more makeup," she points out, her tone teasing. "Your neck is a very pretty shade of bruised."

So much for the foundation's staying power.

Chapter 23

Hydessa

As we step out of the gym, I can see the carnival rides being set up more clearly now. A small thrill of excitement goes through me at the sight. The prospect of going to a carnival makes me giddy in the same way a child would feel. I never got to go to carnivals as a kid.

Maddie and I walk towards the bakery together, the morning seems to brighten with the promise of coffee and conversation. The small shop is already bustling with locals grabbing their morning treats and caffeine fix. Just as we're about to step inside, something catches my attention—a figure emerging from the waves at the beach, carrying a surfboard under their arm.

I can't see their details clearly from this distance, but their hair is slicked back and the wetsuit shows clearly defined muscles. It's still early, so seeing someone already out surfing indicates dedication.

Maddie pauses beside me and follows my gaze. When she sees who it is, she giggles softly. "Umm yeah, that's probably one board you don't want to ride," she remarks cryptically.

I turn to her, curiosity piqued. "What do you mean?" I ask, trying to decipher her meaning.

She grins mischievously. "Let's just say that board is well-ridden. Chester likes to keep it, um, available for rent at all times," she explains with a wink. "That saying 'Save a horse, ride a cowboy' does not translate to surfers and their boards... or at least not that one."

I can't stop the laughter from erupting from me. I haven't really had friends in a long time, not since I lost my best friend when I was younger. I could see Maddie, and perhaps even Allegra, being among those I would call friends now though.

"Got it," I reply, shaking my head slightly. "I'll keep that in mind. So Nathan doesn't ride a board?"

She exaggerates a look of shock, but the devious gleam in her eyes gives it away. "I have no idea what you mean," she says before looping her arm through mine. "But if I did, I'd defend that he spends more time on the mats than the waves."

She laughs at her own joke and the sound is loud and bubbly like her personality. There aren't too many people wandering along the beachfront area yet given the time, but it does catch the attention of the few that are. One of those is Chester himself who is still making his way toward his studio.

Looking away from him I see that our laughter has also caught the attention of Jonah, who is pushing a cart with tubs of what I am assuming is the catch of the day towards the cafe. He's paused to look back toward us for a moment but he doesn't linger, continuing on with his delivery after a short nod in my direction, his muscles flexing under his shirt.

There needs to be fewer hot men on this island. Maybe I should just kill a couple off to reduce the options.

Turning back to Maddie, she grins at me knowingly. "So, who else should I be staying away from then?" I ask with a laugh.

"Oh my god, dishing on the men in this town is my specialty. Let's grab caffeine first, though," she gushes as she pushes open the bakery door, leaving me no choice but to follow.

The scent of fresh coffee and baked goods is enticing but also reminds me that I need to go to the store for a fresh supply, as I can no longer trust what I have back at the house. Allegra grins and waves at the sight of us as we walk toward the counter.

"You two look like you could use a coffee, or a shower," she says in greeting and Maddie giggles. "And maybe a little less rough sex." She indicates to her neck while looking at mine and my fingers automatically reach up to touch the bruises there.

My heart speeds up at the memory of Abel's hand wrapped around it while they fucked me, but I push that aside quickly. "Both of you are just assuming it was a good time... what if it was some asshole getting violent?" I ask with a smile so they know I'm only joking.

Allegra moves to grab a pen and paper, writing something down quickly and holds it out to me. It's a phone number. "Then I would expect you to call me, so I can help you hide the body."

I take the note from Allegra, glancing at the phone number and giving her a playful smile. "And where would we hide the body?" I joke, but there's a hint of seriousness in my voice. "Do you have experience with covering up murder?"

Suddenly, there's something dark lurking behind her eyes. "You'd be surprised," she replies with a grin, her tone making me wonder how much of it is just a joke.

Maddie laughs loudly, drawing a few glances from nearby patrons, but she doesn't care. "Two large coffees, please," she says and Allegra moves to start preparing the order. "And throw in a couple of those chocolate croissants. We deserve a treat after that workout."

"So, Maddie, I heard there's going to be a dunk tank at the carnival. Any chance you'll be volunteering?" Allegra asks while she works.

Maddie grins and shakes her head. "No way. I've done it once, and that water is freezing. But I heard Sheriff Brooks might be in it, so that should be entertaining."

I chuckle at the mental image of the stern sheriff being dunked into icy water. "That sounds like fun. Maybe I'll have a go at it."

"You should," Allegra encourages. "It's all for a good cause. The money raised goes to local charities and community projects."

She finishes making our coffees and croissants, and we grab them with thanks. Maddie leads us to a cozy corner table by the window, where we can watch the town start to wake up.

"So, back to our conversation," Maddie says, tearing into her croissant. "Who else should you stay away from? Well, there's Chester, obviously. He's more trouble than he's worth. Then there's Bryce—he works at the bar and is a bit of a player. And maybe steer clear of Ryan, the lifeguard. He's nice, but he tends to get too attached too quickly."

I nod, mentally noting the names, two of them I haven't even met yet but will now be at the top of the suspect list, once I get through the first twelve at least. Well, nine if I crossed off the woman. "Got it. Anyone else?"

Maddie thinks for a moment. "I think that covers the main ones. Oh, and Ty," she says before leaning closer to me. "You know how his tattoo shop is close to the real estate office right? I was closing up late once and I saw him fucking one of his clients *on* the tattoo chair. I'd never wanted a tattoo so badly before that moment."

She sighs and her eyes flick down to my neck again for a moment before giggling again. "I mean, unless you already know what he's like, cause from what I saw, oh boy, it looked like he likes it rough too."

I take a drink of my coffee to avoid responding. It's not like I can even confirm or deny the comment considering I don't even know who was fucking me last night. I can feel heat rising to my cheeks at the thought, but thankfully Maddie moves the conversation along.

"So, besides avoiding the questionable men in town, what else do you like to do for fun?" Maddie asks, taking a sip of her coffee.

Killing people is not an appropriate response... hunting masked bloggers and being fucked senseless by them is not an appropriate response either...

I take a moment to steer myself away from those thoughts. "Well, besides exploring the island, I'm quite fond of photography," I reply with a shrug. It was always a hobby I enjoyed as a kid and teenager but rarely got time for. It helped me to see the beauty and light in the world while constantly being reminded of the darkness.

Maddie nods thoughtfully. "That's pretty cool! There are so many beautiful spots around here for photography. Have you been to the lighthouse yet? It's one of my favorite spots on the island."

"Not yet, but I've heard other people talk about it. I'll have to check it out," I say, genuinely interested. The idea of capturing the island's natural beauty through a lens did appeal to me, but my mind is too focused on the investigation to give it too much thought. Maybe once I unravel this mystery I can take a few days for myself. Before I have to leave.

I finish the last of the coffee and croissant as my mind drifts to the investigation that has me here. I feel torn, wanting to solve the mystery and stop tourists being killed, but so far I still don't have any solid evidence that it's actually happening. Not to mention that Cain and Abel told me that when they do kill, there are reasons for it. I know from experience working for my parents organization that some killings can be justified depending on the circumstances.

"So, what's it like working in real estate here?" I ask.

Maddie leans back in her chair, taking a thoughtful sip of her coffee before answering. "It's busy, especially with all the tourists coming in during the summer months. But I like it. You get to meet a lot of different people, hear their stories, help them find a place they can call home, even if it's just for a vacation."

"That sounds fulfilling," I comment, genuinely interested. "Meeting new people all the time must keep things interesting."

"Oh, definitely," Maddie agrees. "And you get to see how people connect with the island. Some fall in love with it instantly, while others take time to warm up to its charms."

"Have you ever had anyone just disappear without a trace, instead of checking out like they're supposed to?" I ask, thinking about the tourists that were killed and if Maddie may have noticed those victims disappear.

Maddie chuckles softly, shaking her head. "Nah, no one ever risks the fees we tack on if they don't bring back the keys," she explains, amusement coloring her voice. "But we do have an after-hours key drop that gets used pretty regularly. Sometimes people have early flights or catch late ferries, so they drop off the keys and head out without much fuss."

"That makes sense," I reply, mentally noting this detail with a touch of disappointment. But it could be a place to watch, see if anyone is regularly dropping off keys who is already a local.

"So, are you excited for the carnival?" I ask after a moment, trying to move my thoughts onto something happier.

She beams at the question. "Absolutely! It's one of the biggest events here, and everyone looks forward to it. There's so much to see and do—rides, games, food stalls. It's so much fun."

I smile, feeling a bit of the carnival spirit myself. "When does it start?"

"In three days," Maddie replies, practically bouncing in her seat. "There's a parade to kick things off, and then the carnival opens right after. It's going to be so much fun!"

I nod, already making mental notes to attend. "Sounds like a blast. I'll definitely be there." I frown for a moment, glancing at where the carnival is set up. "They are set up pretty early if it doesn't start for three days."

Maddie rolls her eyes playfully. "Yeah, they do some exclusive VIP things leading up to it. Trying to build up the hype, you know?"

I chuckle, wondering what sort of VIP events they hold and who the VIP's could be. "I guess so."

Maddie checks her watch suddenly and curses softly. "Speaking of getting ready, I have to run. I need a shower and then I have to open the office. Can't keep the tourists waiting."

I nod understandingly. "No problem. Thanks for the coffee and the company. We'll catch up later?"

"Definitely," Maddie replies with a bright smile, gathering her things. "I'll see you around, Taylor."

With a wave, Maddie heads off briskly. I get up and wave goodbye to Allegra on my way out of the bakery, heading toward the grocery store. I need a new supply of coffee, and maybe some cookies I can trust.

Chapter 24

Hydessa

G ladys greets me with a large smile and a wave when I walk into the grocery store. It feels good to be someone that people are happy to see, to be part of a community. After grabbing one of the baskets, I take my time to see what the store has to offer. Last time I was here I was so focused on getting just the basics that I didn't take time for anything else.

As I stroll, I find myself drawn to the section of homemade baked goods, hoping to find a pack of cherry cookies. However, my search turns up empty, which makes me ponder where the package from yesterday came from—did they buy them elsewhere, or did they actually bake them for me themselves?

Lost in thought, I begin filling my basket with various groceries, I'm lost in the array of coffee options when a voice behind me startles me. "You must really love coffee, didn't you get some only two days ago?" I turn to find Jonah standing there with a smile tugging at his lips.

I chuckle as I quickly think of an excuse for why I'm not drinking the supply I already bought. "Yes, I might have a slight coffee addiction," I admit sheepishly. "Can't start the day without it, preferably in large amounts."

Jonah nods knowingly. "I get it. Coffee is life. If you're into bold flavors, you should try this one," he says, reaching for a package himself. "It's one of my favorites. Helps me get out on the water before the sun's even up."

I glance at the green bag he's holding, noting the description. "Sounds perfect," I reply with a smile, adding it to my basket. "I could use a bit of extra motivation in the mornings."

Jonah chuckles. "Trust me, this stuff works wonders," he says before stepping back. "How are you settling in?"

"So far, so good," I reply with a genuine smile. "Everyone has been really friendly, and I'm starting to feel more at home. I'm also looking forward to the carnival. It seems like a big event here."

Jonah nods, his expression thoughtful. "The carnival's a blast. You'll definitely enjoy it."

"That's what I've heard," I agree, feeling a small thrill of anticipation for the festivities. My excitement must show because his lips twitch in amusement again.

Jonah leans casually against the aisle, his gaze thoughtful as he studies me for a moment. The soft light from the overhead bulbs highlights the laugh lines at the corners of his eyes. "Are you a cotton candy and games type of girl then?" he asks with a playful glint in his eyes.

I pause, considering his question. "I'm not sure," I admit honestly, a small smile tugging at my lips. "I've actually never been to a carnival before."

His eyebrows lift in surprise as he tilts his head. "Really? Never been to a carnival?" Jonah's tone is genuinely curious, as if trying to imagine what that must be like. "Did you live in a cult or something? Should I be concerned for the town?"

I can't stop the laughter from escaping and he half grins at me. If only he knew. "Not a cult, but maybe a bit sheltered."

Jonah raises an eyebrow, his curiosity piqued. "Sheltered, huh? That must have been interesting. Not often you meet someone who's never been to a carnival, even as an adult. So what is it that you said you do for work?"

My brain stutters for a moment, the gears almost grinding to a halt. That's the second time he has asked that, and as much as I do have a cover story, I can't help but feel a flash of stubborn defiance making me not want to give him an answer. With a smile, I decide to tease him instead.

"I'm not sure I want to answer that now that you seem so interested," I reply playfully.

Jonah laughs, his eyes twinkling with amusement. "Alright, I'll let you keep your secrets—for now." He gives me a playful wink before heading off to another aisle. I watch him go, feeling a mixture of relief and amusement.

When I reach the checkout counter, Gladys greets me with a warm smile. "Find everything you need, dear?"

"I was actually hoping to find some cherry cookies," I reply, placing my items on the counter.

Gladys frowns slightly, a look of genuine surprise on her face. "Cherry cookies? I'm sorry, but I've never stocked those here. I usually only carry the most common ones like chocolate chip, oatmeal raisin, and sometimes pineapple cookies during the summer. Did you try the bakery?"

Her answer has my thoughts swirling inside my mind, the only explanation could be they were made specifically for me.

Did Cain lie? Were the drugs in the cookies and not the coffee? I still can't trust either but it makes me wonder if they had gone to that extra effort of making them for me, and why those cookies specifically.

"I didn't see any when I was there this morning," I say, nodding when Gladys continues to look at me with a frown. "It must just be a city thing then."

"Could be," Gladys says, then she smiles as though a thought occurs to her. "But if you're looking for something specific, let me know. Maybe I can add it to our inventory."

"Thanks, I'll keep that in mind," I reply.

As she rings up my groceries, Gladys continues, "So, how are you finding our little community? Settling in well?"

"I am," I reply genuinely. "Everyone has been so welcoming, and it's nice to feel like part of a community."

"That's lovely to hear. I've always believed there's a place for everyone, even if it's not where you expect. We don't all find our place, but those that do know it right away. It's the same with people too."

Intrigued by her philosophical musings, I ask, "What do you mean by that?"

She pauses, her eyes thoughtful yet warm as she meets my gaze. "I believe that everyone has people out there that they are meant to connect with, whether as friends or partners in life. Sometimes, it's not where you expect to find them. Not everyone finds that connection, but when you do, you'll know it. Just like finding your place in a community."

Her words strike a chord within me, resonating with my own uncertainties. My mind becomes crowded with my own doubts and feelings, that I won't be able to find someone who will love me for all of me, darkness included.

Gladys places a gentle hand on mine to pass the grocery bags, startling me from my thoughts. "Fate is a funny thing," she continues softly. "You'll find those you need in your life when you least expect it, or perhaps they'll find you."

I nod slowly, gratefully. "That's a happy thought. Thank you, Gladys."

"You're welcome, dear." The way her eyes bring me comfort is almost like a parent looking out for their child. It's adorable and so sweet.

As I leave the store, Gladys' words linger in my mind. Her belief in fate and the idea that everyone has their place and a person meant for them is comforting, yet I can't shake my own doubts.

Deciding to take a walk along the beach on my way back home, I cross the road finding myself closer to the carnival. It's a hive of activity as workers finish setting things up, large signs across the main gates signaling that it's not yet open to the public. Turning away from the bustling scene, I head towards the soothing expanse of sand.

The salty tang of the ocean and the warmth of the sun are almost like heaven as I stroll along. Passing by the row of artfully painted surfboards, I notice Chester stepping out of his studio, adding another board to the rack. His hair falls casually to his shoulders, and the tattoo of a bird on his back ripples with his movements, looking almost like it's about to fly off his skin. His grin is infectious as he spots me.

"Hey Taylor, how are you?" he calls out warmly.

"Hey Chester," I reply, stepping closer to where he stands by the surfboards with my groceries in hand. "I'm good, thanks. How's your painting going?"

His grin widens as he turns fully to face me, his eyes dipping to my throat and flaring for a moment before he answers. "It's going great," he says enthusiastically. "I've had a lot of new inspiration lately. Been experimenting with some different techniques and themes."

"That sounds exciting," I comment, genuinely intrigued by his artistic passion. "I'd love to see some of your new work sometime."

Chester's eyes light up at my interest, and he leans casually against the surfboard rack, his gaze lingering on me thoughtfully. "I'd be thrilled to show you, love," he says, his voice carrying a hint of flirtation as his English accent thickens. "Maybe a private showing, when you're ready."

His use of the endearment catches me off guard, and my stomach dips. Chester's charm is undeniable, and his casual confidence adds an intriguing allure to his artistic persona.

"Private showing, huh?" I reply with a teasing smile, trying to match his playful tone. "That sounds like a special invitation. I might have to take you up on that."

Chester chuckles softly, his eyes turning intense. "I look forward to it," he replies smoothly, his voice dropping slightly. "Besides, I have a feeling you appreciate art in more ways than one, love."

If I hadn't already been warned about him by Allegra and Maddie, I may have fallen for his charm. It seems to come effortlessly to him as if his flirtatiousness were a part of him, like a second skin. But I keep my thoughts to myself in the hopes I can gain more insight into him.

"I... I guess we'll see," I finally manage to respond, hoisting my groceries on my hip.

Chester's gaze holds mine for a moment longer, his smile lingering as if he's savoring the exchange. "Indeed we will," he says, his tone a blend of amusement and intrigue. With a nod and a casual wave, he returns to his studio.

As I continue my walk along the beach, the rhythmic crash of waves helps steady my thoughts. This is my fourth day here and I still feel no closer to solving this mystery. Any one of the suspects could have interacted with the tourists at some point. I need more clues, more details to go on.

I stop by the cafe and grab a seafood salad to-go to eat back at the house. Lily gives me a large smile and an extra large serving despite my protests. She insists I need the extra portion and ushers me back out with a playful wink.

With salad and groceries in hand, I continue my walk home, enjoying the ocean breeze as my mind tries to make sense of my investigation. Nothing is adding up to me, and I can't connect the dots. The suspects, the clues—or lack thereof—everything seems to be at a standstill, leaving me frustrated.

The old man that lives down the road from the house waves to me on my way past and I smile and return the gesture. Arriving back home, I'm grateful to find nothing waiting on the doorstep today.

I head straight to the kitchen, placing the groceries on the counter. The sunlight filters through the window, casting a warm glow over everything. The now familiar noises of the old walls and floors are almost comforting.

With a sigh, I toss out the old coffee, replacing it with the new batch I picked up from the store. Despite Jonah's recommendation, I opt for a glass of water instead. Grabbing my seafood salad from Lily's cafe and the glass, I head to my office, eager to delve into the new information I've gathered today.

Placing the salad down on the desk, I turn as I take a sip of the water. The coolness of it soothes my parched throat.

As I turn towards the wall in my office, the glass slips from my fingers and my heart skips a beat as it shatters on the floor at my feet. There, among my meticulously arranged notes and printouts, are photographs. Photographs that were not there before. Each one is pinned next to different blog posts, each showing a different girl.

My hands tremble slightly as I edge closer, trying to make sense of this unsettling vision. The photos seem strategically placed, as if deliberately telling me a story. Each girl's face stares back at me, their images stark against the white paper printouts.

My breath catches in my throat as I move, my mind racing to comprehend what I'm seeing. I reach out to touch one of the photos, my fingers hovering over the image of a blonde girl smiling toward the camera. She looks carefree, unaware of being photographed. The realization hits me with a wave of unease—these are the dead tourists.

Up until now, I had hoped that the rumors of the dead tourists were just a cruel fabrication by the bloggers, a twisted lure to draw me—or any woman—into some bizarre game. But seeing these photos, the stark reality hits me like a punch to the gut. These are real people, real victims. My investigation just took a horrifying turn.

I force myself to take a deep breath, trying to steady my nerves. I know I need to clean up the spilled water and glass but instead I pull out my phone, intending to capture this new information first.

Instantly I notice there is a message waiting on my there; reading it has my heart racing in my chest.

UNKNOWN

> I wanted to scrub that makeup from your pretty throat when I saw it today. Keep trying to hide our marks and see what happens, little shadow.

Chapter 25

Hydessa

I struggle to control my breathing as I set the phone aside, turning away from the wall and placing my hands flat on the desk. My neck prickles, the feeling that I'm being watched washes over me and I suddenly wish I could hurt someone. I want to scream in frustration.

Turning back around, I stare at the photos as a cold reality begins to sink in. Each girl, captured in a moment of apparent happiness, now feels like a haunting echo of something far more sinister.

The chilling thought that these are the very tourists I've been trying to unravel the mystery of, makes my blood run cold. Their faces now have a grim presence in my space and I want to unleash my darkness on those responsible for extinguishing their light from the world.

Forcing myself to take another deep breath, I try to quell the fury boiling inside me, reminding myself that Cain and Abel told me they don't kill innocent people. I need to stay focused. My emotions are a weapon, but only if I wield them carefully. I grab my phone and after updating the contact for them, I start documenting the wall, capturing every new photo and which blog it's connected to. The methodical process helps calm my nerves slightly, giving me a sense of control in this chaotic situation.

I send the photographs to Uncle Max in a secure message, asking if he can find out any information from them. I can't bring myself to let him know how I came across the photos and I hope he doesn't ask. I trust Uncle Max, but the fewer people who know the details, the safer everyone will be.

As I wait for a response, I decide to double-check the house's security. I move through each room, ensuring windows and doors are locked. Not that it really makes any difference, they have proven at least twice now they can get past the locks. There is no denying that this time I did not simply leave the house open for them.

The unsettling feeling of being watched lingers, making every shadow seem more ominous. I return to my office, my mind still racing with thoughts of everything now pressing down on me.

I almost jump when a notification sounds on my tablet, it's a reply from Uncle Max. 'Received the photos. I'll see what I can dig up. Be safe.'

His brief message does little to soothe my nerves, but knowing he's on the case brings a small measure of comfort. I look back at the wall, the faces of the girls staring back at me. Each one represents a life cut short, a story that ended in tragedy. I can't let their deaths be in vain, I need to dig deeper and uncover the reasoning behind this, I need to find out why they killed these women. Is it possible that something more sinister lurks beneath these deaths.

Ignoring the message on my phone, I spend the next few hours combing through my notes and meticulously adding more information to the wall from the interactions I've had with the suspects. My lunch is forgotten as my mind buzzes with possibilities, but nothing concrete emerges. Frustration continues to gnaw at me, but I push through, determined to make sense of this puzzle.

The faces of the girls on the wall seem to watch me as I work, like that feeling now has a physical form. I start by listing the suspects again, re-examining each one's potential motive and opportunity.

The names and details intertwine with the blog posts, photos, and my notes. It's a tangled web, and I feel like I'm grasping at straws.

The clock ticks away, and the shadows in the room lengthen. The eerie stillness of the house presses in on me, interrupted every so often by the normal noises of an old house. My eyes strain to read the black and white printouts, and my back aches from hunching over the desk. But I can't stop. Not now. Not when I might be on the verge of a breakthrough.

Darkness falls, and I'm forced to turn on the light to continue working. Paper is scattered everywhere with my notes, and when my phone chimes with a notification, I have to dig under some of them to find it. Hoping it's a response from Uncle Max, my stomach turns when I see it's not.

PSYCHO MASKED STALKERS

> Care for a game of hide and seek, little shadow? I'll even give you a clue on where to find me.

A chill runs down my spine as I stare at the message. They're toying with me. Every instinct screams at me to stop, to pull back. But I can't. I won't. Any contact with them may lead to the answers I am looking for. With trembling fingers, I type a reply.

> I'll play.

Seconds feel like hours as I wait for a response.

PSYCHO MASKED STALKERS

> Good. Where laughter will soon echo and lights shine bright, now only shadows play in the dead of night. Come play with me at midnight, little shadow.

A riddle. I read it over and over, trying to piece together its meaning. The answer comes to me and my heart speeds up. *The carnival grounds.*

I glance at the time—midnight is only a few hours away. I mentally plan my next steps, ensuring I take my own knife with me. If this is my chance to put an end to this, even if it means putting an end to them, I have to be ready.

I take a moment to steady myself, then decide to have a quick shower. The photos on the wall distracted me from having one when I returned to the house, but the adrenaline coursing through my veins is making me jittery, and the shower might help clear my head.

I step under the stream of water, letting it wash away some of the fury raging inside me. The cool water soothes my heated skin. I allow a sense of calm to overtake me, a sense of control. I can do this, I can do what needs to be done.

As I start to put on clothes, I decide to go with the normal hunting outfit. They may already know who I am, but the black clothes and mask make me feel safe, like a shield I can hide behind.

With some time left before I need to leave, I pick up my phone again and call my sister. The phone rings twice before she picks up.

"If I hide..." I say softly into the phone. It's not lost on me that I'm about to go play the very game I'm talking about, and I'm playing the role I never wanted.

"Then I'll seek..." she responds with a sigh. There is something in her tone that makes me pause.

"Are you okay?" I ask gently, concern creeping into my voice.

"Yeah, just a lot going on. Don't worry about me," she says, trying to sound upbeat. "How's your investigation going?"

I don't want to burden her with the details of what's happening, so I keep it vague. "It's going well. I have a possible lead."

"That's great!" she replies, her voice brightening. "And have you taken the time to have some fun with a hot guy yet?"

I open my mouth to respond, hesitating for a moment. How could I tell her about the dark, twisted encounters with the masked men that I think murdered all of these girls. Or that they have now broken into my house not once but twice? Do I confess to her that being with them is the only time I have felt truly alive, that the war waged against my darkness seems to calm and I feel more like myself than I ever have?

Who am I kidding? I definitely can not disclose that I have two of the suspects stalking me and fucking me better than anyone has before. Yeah, she would send help immediately.

My hesitation must have been telling enough because before I can utter a word, she squeals excitedly.

"Oh my god, you have! Spill the details! Who is he? Is he cute? Tell me everything!"

My breath catches in my throat as I struggle to find the right words. How could I possibly explain the complexity of my situation without burdening her? I can't let her know the true extent of what's happening, not when I can already hear the stress in her voice.

I take a deep breath, torn between the desire to confide in my sister and shield her from what I'm dealing with. "It's... complicated," I finally manage, my voice wavering slightly. "I'm not sure it's about having fun. It's more... it's more like a dangerous game, and I'm not sure where it's going."

Her enthusiastic tone fades into concerned silence, and I can almost feel her worry through the phone. "Are you safe?" she asks softly, her voice now laced with a seriousness that matches my own.

"I'm doing everything I can to stay safe," I assure her, feeling a lump form in my throat. "But I need you to promise me something."

"What is it?" she responds immediately.

"I need you to be careful too," I say, my voice barely above a whisper. "Watch your back. Trust your instincts. Promise me, okay?"

There's a brief pause before she responds, her voice steady but something else lingers there too. "I promise," she says firmly. "And you promise me the same. Don't take unnecessary risks."

"I won't," I lie. I can't admit to her that I'm about to meet with the killers at midnight. "I'll be careful."

In that moment, I realize how much we're alike—needing each other like lifelines in the chaos and darkness, but hesitant to burden one another with our own stresses.

We exchange a few more words, trying to ease the tension that hangs between us. She manages to make me laugh with gossip from the organization, and for a moment, I can almost forget the weight of the situation I'm in.

After a while, we say our goodbyes. I hang up the phone, feeling a pang of guilt for not confiding in her, for not sharing the burden that threatens to overwhelm me. But for now, keeping her safe from this darkness feels like the only right choice.

I glance at the clock. Midnight approaches, and with it, the carnival grounds beckon ominously. I check my preparations—knife secure, mind focused, mask firmly in place. There's no turning back now.

Leaving my house through the back door, I lock up carefully, every creak and rustle of the forest making me hyper-aware. The moonlight filters through the thick canopy of the woods, casting eerie shadows as I make my way towards the beach. The path is familiar, yet tonight, it feels fraught with unseen dangers lurking in the darkness.

Moving along the darkened streets, I feel almost at home as I stick to the routes that are becoming familiar. The carnival grounds loom ahead, silent and foreboding. The signs warning people away are still in front of the gates and there is no movement beyond them.

Following the fence, I locate a side door with a note taped to it. My heart races as I read the message under the dim light of my phone flashlight.

If you hide, I will seek,
but be careful, little shadow,
the darkness holds secrets
deeper than your own...
and once you embrace it,
the light can't save you...

I hesitate for a moment, the message sinking in. The chilling words echo through my mind. But I steel myself, my resolve hardening as I prepare to confront whatever lies beyond that door.

With a steady hand, I reach out and remove the note, folding it carefully and tucking it into my pocket. Trying to control the shaking in my limbs, I push forward, my breath coming out in shallow bursts despite my efforts to remain calm.

The latch clicks softly as I push open the door, the hinges barely creaking, but feeling like a loud alarm in the silent space. I step through cautiously, the cool night air swirling around me, carrying with it the faint scent of ocean spray. The carnival grounds stretch out before me. The rides somehow looking sinister in the dead of night.

My footsteps are barely audible against the soft ground as I move deeper into the area. Navigating through the dark maze of tents and attractions, my senses are on high alert. Every rustle of leaves, every creak of metal, sets my heart pounding in my chest, my eyes straining as they dart everywhere.

As I move cautiously through the vacant carnival grounds, the soft strains of music suddenly catch my attention. Neon lights flicker to life in the distance, drawing me toward a carousel that stands still and empty under the night sky. I approach slowly, the music growing louder, beckoning me closer.

Just as I near the carousel, the music abruptly stops, and the lights dim until they fade into darkness once more. I pause, my heart racing, trying to make sense of the eerie sequence. Before I can gather my thoughts, another melody begins to play, this time from a different corner of the carnival.

I follow the new music, my footsteps light and deliberate as I navigate through the empty tents and rides. The lights guide me, promising answers just out of reach. But as I approach the source of the music, it too falls silent, leaving me standing in the quiet darkness once more.

After it happens a third time, a chilling realization dawns on me: I'm being manipulated, moved around the carnival like a pawn on a chess board. Each musical cue, each flicker of light, is designed to lure me exactly where they want.

I pause, my senses on high alert, scanning the shadows for any sign of movement. Another burst of music and lights draws me towards another corner of the grounds. This time, I ignore it, heading in a different direction instead. I want to see what they will do when I refuse to play the way they expect.

Creeping through the carnival rides, I'm moving around the center when the lights suddenly blare to life around me, momentarily blinding me after the intense focus on navigating the shadows. A chilling laugh pierces the air. I whirl around to see a figure perched on a table several yards away, his red neon mask making him look like the devil. His knife glints menacingly under the lights.

His deep modulated voice makes me suck in a sharp breath, taunting and menacing. "Little shadow, you aren't playing along like a good girl," Cain drawls, the words dripping with malice. My heart races, adrenaline pumping through my veins as I stand my ground, defiant.

"I'm not your good girl. I don't want to play this game," I retort, but even through the voice manipulator in my mask I can hear the strain. "Those girls deserve justice."

His laughter rings out again, a sound that seems to echo endlessly through the empty carnival grounds. "They will get justice, darling, but not tonight," he replies calmly, the edge of his knife tapping ominously against the table. "Tonight, we play."

I scan the surroundings cautiously, wondering where Abel is hiding, but Cain's next words answer me before I even ask. "It's just you and me tonight, darling girl."

"I'm not playing your games anymore," I declare firmly, my stubbornness flaring as I narrow my eyes at him.

"Is that so?" he taunts, and in an instant, darkness envelops us. The lights, including the eerie red glow of his mask, vanish. My breath catches in my throat as I strain to see through the impenetrable blackness.

Then, Cain's mask lights up again and before I can react, he lunges toward me with startling speed. Instinct takes over, and my body springs into action, fight or flight propelling me. He won't get to me easily this time.

Chapter 26

Hydessa

I run, sprinting away from him as adrenaline fuels my legs and I dash through the maze of attractions, heart pounding in my ears. The chilling laughter echoes behind me, urging me to push harder, faster.

The carnival begins to feel like a labyrinth closing in around me. I dart between games and booths, rides and creepy statues, the sound of my own ragged breaths mingling with the echoes of his laughter. It seems to come from all around me, almost as though it's being played on the speakers spread through the carnival. Each shadow seems to reach out, threatening to ensnare me as I navigate this random maze.

I dare not look back, fearing what I might trip over while Cain chases me through the darkness. Behind me, his taunting voice follows, a reminder that I'm now playing a game that only he knows the rules to. A game I told him I didn't want to play and ended up trapped in anyway.

"You can't hide forever, little shadow," he calls out.

A sudden burst of music and light from a nearby ride momentarily distracts me, but I force myself to ignore it, moving in the opposite direction. My feet stumble and I think I'm going to fall. My heart lurches as I spread my arms out for balance, gasping for breath. But

I recover and keep going, my pulse is racing as I take one corner after another.

Another ride erupts, this one even closer. I have to shield my eyes from how bright it is, and I growl under my breath as I veer sharply in the opposite direction.

When another ride lights up and I once again shift to go in the opposite direction, I curse my own stupidity. I'm being herded, just like the prey I am.

Spotting the darkened open door of a nearby attraction, I make a split-second decision and duck inside, moving swiftly through the entryway. The darkness envelops me like ink, swallowing me whole as I press deeper into its depths. There is no moonlight to rely on here, just my hand against the wall as I try to find a place to hide.

This is what I'm good at. Being out in the open is too vulnerable.

I strain my ears, listening for any sign of Cain's approach, but the silence is now absolute. Taking a moment to catch my breath, I lean against a cold wall, my chest heaving as I struggle to slow my racing heart. Sweat beads on my forehead, trickling down my temples as I try to calm the trembling in my limbs. Pulling the mask from my face, I shove it into my pocket.

As I stand there, the space around me gradually becomes clearer as soft lights begin to fill it. Startled, I glance around, but all I can see is my own reflection staring back at me—not just once, but multiple times.

Panic grips my chest as I realize I'm trapped in a hall of mirrors. Casting multiple reflections of myself in every direction. Each mirror reveals a slightly different angle, creating an unsettling illusion of infinite hallways stretching out before me.

My heart hammers against my chest as I reach back toward the door I came through, desperate to escape this maze of distorted reflections. I twist the handle, but it refuses to budge no matter how hard I push and pull. With a sinking feeling, I realize the door is locked.

He trapped me. How could he have even predicted that I would run in here?

Cautiously, I assess my surroundings, feeling a rising sense of dread. The mirrors taunt me with their endless reflections, each one a reminder of my vulnerability in this twisted maze.

I move cautiously forward, my footsteps echoing softly around the hollow room. The dim lights above cast an ominous glow, but the shadows seem to dance and flicker, distorting the reflections around me that warp in and out. I resist the urge to panic, knowing that clear thinking is my best chance of finding a way out.

As I move deeper, I run my hands along the glass on both sides, hoping to find a way out. Suddenly, my hand brushes against empty space.

Turning into the opening, I find myself in another hallway of mirrors, this one wider. I press forward, my senses on high alert, searching for any clue that might lead me out of this mirrored labyrinth.

As I walk, I notice subtle differences in the reflections—angles that shift imperceptibly, creating a maze of illusions that seem to stretch into infinity. Terror threatens to take hold, but I push it down, focusing on the task at hand: finding an exit.

I find another opening, moving into a space that seems to twist and turn with multiple wider openings. Frustration gnaws at me, not knowing which direction to choose.

Then, without warning, the dim lights sputter and die, plunging me into total darkness again. Panic fills me and I strain my eyes, but I can't see anything.

Just as fear threatens to overwhelm me, a faint crimson glow begins to suffuse the darkness. It flickers at first, then grows stronger, casting a red hue that distorts the mirrored walls. The room itself seems to come alive with the sinister light.

And there, in each mirror's reflection, is Cain.

He moves almost casually, his reflection rippling and moving around the room. Just when I think I know where he really is, the silhouette shifts out of the frame. "Had enough yet, little shadow?"

I don't know what's real and what's not. "I'll never let you win," I reply defiantly, my voice steadier than I expected.

Cain chuckles darkly, the sound bouncing off the mirrored walls, distorting and amplifying. "You've got spirit, I do love that," he muses, his red-masked reflection pacing in sync with his words. "But here's the thing, darling, you've already lost."

Reaching down, I pull the knife from the sheath strapped to my leg, letting the light of his mask catch on it as he tilts his head. "I don't think so."

He continues pacing as though undisturbed by my words. "A knife won't save you, Hydessa," he says and for a moment he pauses, looking less like a pacing lion and more like one ready to pounce. "This is a lesson for you, little shadow, there is no escaping us ever again. You're ours."

The lights go out again and before I can run, pain shoots through my wrist as something hits it and my only weapon slips from my grasp and clatters to the ground. The red light comes back on, almost blinding with how close it is in front of me.

My hand darts out, grabbing the bottom of his mask, but his fingers envelope mine, crushing them together until I whimper from the pain. He makes a tutting sound as he grabs the other hand I raise as well.

"Naughty girl, we may know who you are, but we'll keep our secrets a little longer. Don't make me bind those hands."

I struggle against Cain's grip, but my body is reacting to his, and I can already feel the ache in my core as he holds my hands captive. He twists my arms painfully behind me as he moves around my back, his movements swift and practiced.

I feel the cold bite of a belt tightening around my wrists. It cuts into my skin, restricting any hope of freeing myself. With each tug, my breath hitches, the pain radiating through my body.

The hood covering my head is ripped away, exposing my face to the light. His fingers snake around my ponytail, yanking it harshly until I'm forced into a painful arch, my back protesting the angle.

His masked face brushes against the side of mine as he leans over me from behind. His hard cock grinds into my ass as his other hand reaches around my body, lifting my hoodie and shirt to reveal my bra underneath and I whimper.

"I'm going to fuck you now, little shadow. I'm going to impale you on my cock and savor every delicious sound you make."

Jesus fucking christ, it would be helpful if my body didn't betray me, throbbing in time with each movement and word. I had wanted answers, I had been determined to get them this time.

But as I'm quickly learning, these men do what they want, when they want to. I'm not going to get answers tonight, and what he is going to give me is something I'm quickly starting to crave. His gloved fingers wrap around my bra at the thinnest part between my breasts, jerking on it until it snaps, exposing me to the mirrors and his masked gaze.

My hoodie and shirt drop again now that he isn't holding them up, covering me, but he just takes a hold of them and pulls them up and over my head, hooking them behind my neck. The material pulls tight as he releases my hair, pulling my arms and shoulders back even more. I groan as my muscles start aching quickly under the strain.

With my arms trapped, I offer no resistance when his hands move to my pants. Cain jerks them open and pushes them down my thighs with my underwear, sufficiently trapping my legs when they gather around my ankles. The length of my body is reflected over and over in the mirrors around us, the red light of his mask making the scene appear seductive as his gloved hands travel back up to my breasts.

My pulse races, my skin prickling with every brush of his gloves against my skin. "Please," I managed to whisper, my voice barely audible over the rush of blood in my ears.

"We spoke about this last night, little shadow, please what?" he growls. The fingers brush over the bite mark he left the previous night, trailing along the cuts as though enjoying the sight of them on my skin. When he finds my nipples, he rolls the already tender peaks. It's like he has a direct line to my pussy and I feel each twinge of pain deep inside my throbbing core.

The craving for him, for them, grows with each touch, each movement. I have gone out chasing release after release, searching for something I have rarely found. Even when I am able to find release with another man, it's fleeting. The feeling hardly lasts long enough for me to make it out of the club.

Not with these masked men. Maybe it's because I don't know who they are. Maybe I am just as twisted as them, maybe that's why my body becomes a willing participant in my own destruction, my own surrender is going to be my downfall.

I know this. I work hard and I have saved so many lives. I may not be full of light, I may fight hard against the darkness inside me, but in the end, I help people. So no matter how twisted this is, I am going to hold onto it until the last second because I deserve to feel good. I deserve to have something that thrills me like this, no matter how wrong it may seem.

I moan, words escaping me as I watch the erotic vision in the mirrors around us, the many reflections of his fingers exploring my body making it so much dirtier, so much more erotic. "Please, fuck me," I whisper finally.

One of Cain's hands travels up to wrap around my throat as the other moves down to cup my pussy, the fingers pressing firmly into my skin. I gasp, the ache inside me worsening with each caress.

"I told you last night, I won't always be gentle. This is one of those times that I'm going to hurt you, darling girl."

I open my mouth to respond but he proves his point by slapping my pussy. Hard. A cry escapes me as my legs almost buckle, my clit now pulsing with the beat of my racing heart. He shoves two of his gloved fingers inside of me, my own arousal making it easier for him as he grinds the palm of his hand against my clit. I whimper as my whole body trembles, pleasure swirling inside of me like a violent storm.

"And you're going to take everything I give you like my dirty little cock slut, aren't you?" he growls. My body burns for more. it wants his touch, those dirty low whispers, and his deliciously pierced cock.

I don't understand how my body can respond the way it is to a man I hardly know from Adam. Hell, I don't even know his real name. And yet, all I want to do at this moment is beg him harder to use me like he wants.

Never in my wildest dreams could I have imagined I would be watching myself get finger fucked by a masked killer, inside of a carnival maze of mirrors, and be wanting to beg for him to hurt me more. Because it feels good, the pain feels so damn good.

Quick fucks at the club were never like this. None of them ever trapped my throat or made me feel totally dominated. None of them took my control away and made the shadows within me submit to something greater. But Cain and Abel, they do.

"Answer me, little shadow." he snaps as he curls his fingers inside me and jerks up. I cry out as the move raises me to the tips of my toes. He grinds the heel of his palm harder into my clit and it's difficult to distinguish between the pleasure and pain it causes.

"Y-yes, p-please, I'll be your dirty little slut," I beg in a desperate whisper. I should be ashamed of myself for how needy I sound, how easily he's made me beg for him.

I gasp as Cain's grip tightens around my throat, cutting off my air supply for a moment before loosening just enough to let me breathe again. My head swims as the remnants of fear collide with the arousal inside me.

"That's right, little shadow," he purrs, his voice a dark promise. "Embrace that darkness inside you. You belong to me, Hydessa. You belong to me and my brother."

My heart pounds at the sound of my name on his lips, the way he says it, like I'm his obsession, like I'm his curse and salvation in one.

"Who do you belong to?" he demands, his voice vibrating through me.

"You," I breathe out, the word barely audible as it leaves my lips. "I belong to you."

Cain's grip tightens causing me to cry out.

"Louder," he commands, his voice dripping with authority. "Who do you belong to?"

"You," I repeat, louder this time, my voice trembling with a blend of fear and desire. "I belong to you."

His mask moves closer, a scent I swear I've smelled before surrounds me.

"And my brother?" he prompts, his voice softer, yet no less demanding.

"I belong to you both," I gasp as he starts pumping his fingers in and out of me. But the truth of those words settle over me as though the words themselves are embedded in my skin. "I belong to you both."

Cain's laugh is low and dark, filled with satisfaction. "Good girl," he murmurs. "That's exactly what I want to hear."

He releases my throat and pussy. My body slumps, my knees unsteady and almost giving out from the strain as his hands move on my body, leaving a path of tingling skin in its wake. He pushes on my back, bending me forward as the sound of his zipper echoes around us.

Cain positions himself behind me, his cock pressed against my entrance. "Beg for it," he demands.

"Please," I moan, my body aching with the need to feel him inside me. "Please, Cain. Fuck me."

I'm lucky that he has me so worked up already, because with a single, brutal thrust, he buries himself inside me, filling me completely. Each piercing along the underside of his cock catches at my opening as he pushes into me and the pain that radiates from where we are joined tells me just how much it's going to hurt the next day.

But right now, I couldn't care less. The sensation is overwhelming, a mix of pain and pleasure that leaves me gasping for breath. He doesn't give me a moment to adjust, his movements forceful and unrelenting as he takes me.

"Look at yourself," he growls, his modulated voice rough with lust. "Look at how beautifully you take my cock."

He wraps his hand in my hair again, yanking my head back and I force my eyes to focus on the reflections that surround us. I see from every angle as he fucks into me. My ass in the air, my back arched and my neck craning for him as his cock thrusts deep inside me. It's both shocking and arousing. His red mask glows ominously, the red stitching of the smile seems to grow even wider when he withdraws his cock and thrusts into me again.

I cry out, my pussy tightening around him. "That's it, keep watching," he groans, his other hand grips my hip, fingers pressing in to the point that I wince. "Take it all, just like the good little slut you are."

I can hardly process his command, my mind clouded with lust as each thrust drives me closer to the edge, my body responding eagerly to his every touch. The mirrors around us reflect every moment of my submission, the sight of Cain's masked face, and my own expression of ecstasy.

I'm so close to tumbling over the edge when he pulls out of me completely and the hand that was gripping my hip is suddenly between my legs. His fingers thrust inside me for a moment, then he pulls them back out of me. I whimper at the emptiness, my climax retreating like the tide.

When he lifts his hand toward his face, my stomach flips when I realize his intentions, his fingers disappearing behind the mask with a long low groan. Whatever he thinks of my taste seems to make him almost feral, his hand returns to my pussy, thrusting his fingers inside me again before he repositions himself and with a rough thrust, enters me once more with his pierced cock.

A cry tears from my throat, echoing in the confined space. He gives me no time to adjust again, his movements brutal and relentless, I can feel every inch of him moving inside me, his piercings rubbing against my sensitive walls. The pain is a sweet contrast to all of the other sensations, heightening until I can no longer tell where one ends and the other begins.

Cain reaches around and shoves the wet fingers of his glove into my open mouth. "Suck," he commands and my lips close around him, my body obeying instantly. I can taste myself there, and the groan he releases tells me I pleased him..

He pulls his fingers from my mouth and moves his hand down the front of my body until his fingers are pressed against my clit, rubbing in circles. I can feel the climax that had receded approaching again like a tsunami. The red light of his mask flares as if even it could grasp the intensity of this moment. My reflection blurs as tears fill my eyes, my emotions going haywire inside me.

"Come for me," he commands, his voice a harsh whisper in my ear. "Now."

The command sends me over the edge, my orgasm crashing through me with violent force. My body convulses as I scream for him. Cain follows moments later, his cum filling me as his pace stutters. All too soon the waves of pleasure subside, leaving me trembling, my muscles weak and my mind hazy.

Cain pulls out slowly, leaving me feeling empty and aching. For a moment, there's nothing but the sound of our heavy breathing filling the room. "Good fucking girl," he murmurs, leaning closer to me again. There's a sharp pain in my shoulder and the hazy feeling from moments before gets worse.

He catches me as my legs give out, his touch surprisingly gentle as he lowers me to the ground, the light of his mask dimming. "You're ours, Hydessa, remember that. You always have been and you always will be."

And then everything goes blank as I slip into unconsciousness.

Chapter 27

Cain

I walk into the room and find my brother already there, asleep on the bed set up to the side. On the monitors, our girl sleeps peacefully in her bed, exactly where I left her.

Anxiety races when I glance over to see my brother twitching in his sleep again, caught in another nightmare that I need to wake him from. I want to move to the chair to watch over our girl, but leaving him in that nightmare would end badly for us all. He's been doing so well, the nightmares staying at bay for so long, but I should have known they would come back this week.

I cross the room quietly, not wanting to startle him more than necessary. Kneeling beside the bed, I place a hand on his shoulder, shaking him gently. "Brother, wake up. It's just a dream."

He jerks awake, his eyes wide and disoriented for a moment before they focus on me. There's a flash of recognition, and he lets out a shaky breath, sitting up and running a hand through his hair. "Damn it," he mutters, the frustration clear in his voice.

"It's alright," I say, trying to keep my tone soothing. "It was just a nightmare. You're here and safe, and she's here now too."

He nods, though the tension in his body doesn't fully ease. "I thought I was past this," he says, his voice rough with exhaustion.

"Nightmares don't just disappear, especially not with what we've been through," I reply. "But we're managing. You're managing."

He sighs, his shoulders slumping as he leans back against the headboard. "Yeah, managing," he repeats, though he doesn't sound convinced. "I just... I can't shake the feeling that something's going to go wrong."

"That's the fear talking," I say, squeezing his shoulder. "We've planned for this. We've covered every angle. We're ready."

He takes a deep breath, nodding. "Some people are getting too close to her for my liking." His voice is tight with concern.

I nod, understanding his worry. "We knew they might," I reply. "The marks we left should deter most of them."

He frowns, and I can tell something is still nagging at him. "There's one that has been lurking a little too closely, I've seen him near her more than once," he says, and I already know who he is referring to. "You and I both know what he does to those he sets his sights on."

My jaw tightens at his words. "Then we take care of it," I say firmly. "And we use it to give her another clue."

Chapter 28

Hydessa

W aking slowly, I instantly wish I could go back to sleep to escape the pain. I groan as I roll over on the bed, every part of my body hurts. My phone chimes with a notification and for a moment I contemplate throwing it at a wall.

Is sex meant to make you feel so good but so bad at the same time? Is that what I've been doing wrong all these years?

Picking up my phone I click on the notification and almost sigh in relief when I see who it's from.

UNCLE MAX

> I looked into the images. I've sent you what I could find, which isn't much. Every single one of your suspected victims has what I would call a dubious background. Limited information, some bouncing between homes and streets, some other bad behaviors.

> I couldn't even find all of them, like some never existed. Something made them get on a bus to that island, and I can find the ticket purchase for a couple. There is then no record of them getting off the bus there and certainly no record of them on the island itself, no purchases, no accommodations.

Either they are paying it all in cash with a fake name or the records have been wiped clean and even I can't find a trace, so someone good with tech, or maybe a conspiracy. Could a group of people be in on it? Law, property rentals, etc? Let me know if you need anything else.

I sit up, ignoring the protest from my aching muscles, and read the message again, my mind racing. Uncle Max is the best when it comes to digging up dirt, and if he's still hitting walls, then something is off on a bigger level.

I quickly type back a response.

Thanks, Uncle Max. It's very strange. I'll need to keep digging on my end. Do you think there's a way to trace the cash payments? I've met the person who looks after rentals, she doesn't seem like the type to wipe records, it would have to be someone else or simply them hiding under fake names or something. But why?

Hitting send, I lean back against the headboard and close my eyes, thinking. But my phone buzzes again, and I see a quick reply.

UNCLE MAX

Like I said, kid, dubious and bad behavior. Something drew them to that island. As for the cash payments, it's unlikely we will find anything. People use cash for a reason. Stay safe.

I put my phone down and take a deep breath, trying to process everything. The pieces aren't fitting together, and the more I dig, the more questions I have.

I force myself to stand, ignoring the pain shooting through my body as I make my way toward the bathroom. *Piercings feel phenomenal in the moment... but the next day, not so much.*

Stepping into the shower I almost moan at the feeling of the water cascading over me, soothing my aching muscles. *Seriously, who needs the gym when you can simply have a masked man chase you through a carnival ground, then fuck you so good it hurts.*

Because I have to admit it to myself, the fucking is very good. I will be sad if this all leads to me having to take them out for killing innocent people. I will miss their cocks and the way they make me feel like they actually see me.

They talk about me accepting my darkness, but can I accept theirs if they do take innocent lives? The conflict within me churns as I struggle to reconcile the pleasure they give me with the darker realities of the investigation.

For a moment, I let myself relax under the spray, closing my eyes and just enjoying the sensation. I let my mind go blank with no regrets, no murderers, just nothingness as the steam builds in the room.

Reluctantly, when the water starts to grow cold, I step out and dry off, the steam filling the room as I wrap myself in a towel. Reality begins to set in again, and with it comes emotions I'm not ready to face.

Looking down at the cuts and marks on my body, my mind reflects on the message I received the day before. No covering the marks, huh? Surely that doesn't extend to clothing, I only brought a limited supply afterall, they can't really punish me for that right? Choosing a sleeveless turtleneck summer dress in a light blue, I am happy with how the look is casual but also beachy. It falls just below my thighs and the blue of it makes my eyes even brighter.

My stomach rumbles, reminding me it's been too long since I last ate. Deciding to head to the bakery, I make my way downstairs toward the office to get my tablet. The files Uncle Max sent should already be loaded.

Entering the room, I glance at the investigation wall covered with images of the victims, their faces staring back at me. What brought them to this island? What drew them into whatever dark web I seem to have been pulled into? The questions swirl in my mind like a storm threatening to break loose.

It's already late morning when I start making my way toward the beachfront, the sun is warm against my skin and the gentle breeze carries the scent of the sea. It warms something inside me, deeper than my skin and a smile spreads across my lips naturally.

I thankfully miss the morning rush at the bakery, and the comforting aroma of cinnamon rolls and freshly brewed coffee envelopes me, momentarily easing the weight of my thoughts when I push through the door.

Allegra greets me with a large smile. "Good morning, Taylor!"

"Morning, Allegra," I reply, feeling a twinge of guilt for not reciprocating her enthusiasm because my body hurts and I just need some coffee. She doesn't seem to mind as she takes my order for a large steaming latte and one of the cinnamon rolls. I choose a table by the window and she soon places my order down in front of me.

I'm grateful she seems to understand I'm not up for conversation today as she quickly retreats to the counter, giving me the space I need. I sip my coffee, savoring the rich flavor as I scroll through the files on my tablet. The faces of the victims continue to haunt me, their stories incomplete and shrouded in mystery.

Uncle Max's findings are frustratingly vague. There are too many gaps, too many unknowns. I flip through the images again, my mind racing with questions. *Who had the skill or ability to erase these people from existence?*

None of the locals I have interacted with seem to have the computer skills, even Ty said that there is no tech person on the island. But he could be saying that on purpose. Maddie has access to the rental records so could easily erase them, but I don't see her helping dispose of bodies, but then something about the way Allegra hinted at getting rid of a body made it actually seem possible. They aren't my masked stalkers, but could one of them be helping them.

The Sheriff and Eli could definitely make someone disappear, both physically and from police files, if I have learned anything from my parents it's how easily corruptible law enforcement can be.

I'm sure Jonah could dumb a body out to sea, but would a fisherman know how to make them disappear digitally? But then the lifeguard Maddie mentioned could also take the bodies into the water, I haven't even met him but already I want to add him to the list. Would either Telvin or Rye's businesses have access to a wood chipper to dispose of a body? And could they manipulate the records? Seems doubtful, but not to be dismissed.

Ty certainly knows how to keep a sterile working environment, he could certainly clean up after himself, and he was the one that told me there is no one good with tech on the island. Could that be a cover?

So many possibilities...

Finishing the roll and coffee I make my way to the beach. The sun warms my skin and the salty breeze tangles my hair. The rhythmic sound of the waves crashing against the shore is soothing, offering a brief respite from the turmoil in my mind. The sand is soft beneath my feet and even though my thighs ache,, I let my thoughts wander as I walk along the water's edge.

Up ahead, I spot someone coming out of the waves. As I get closer, I recognize the striking red hair—it's Beth from the bus stop. She's just emerging from the surf, droplets of water glistening on her skin as she pushes her hair back and spots me.

"Hey, Beth!" I call out, waving as I approach.

She smiles warmly and waves back. "Hey, Taylor! Enjoying your morning?"

"Yeah," I reply politely, matching her smile. "How about you? How are you settling in? Enjoying the island?"

Beth wrings out her hair and nods. "It's been great so far. The island is beautiful, and the people are super friendly. It's a nice change of pace from the city."

"Yeah, I completely agree," I say, surprising myself with the enthusiasm in my voice. "The island has such a different vibe. It's like stepping into another world."

Beth raises an eyebrow and looks at me curiously. "You sound like a city girl," she remarks, a hint of amusement in her tone.

I laugh softly, nodding. "Guilty as charged. I grew up in the city and have been living there most of my life. The hustle and bustle, the noise, the constant activity—it's what I'm used to. But I have to admit, the island's charm is really growing on me."

"Really?" Beth says, genuinely intrigued. "I would have thought the city life would be hard to leave behind."

I think about it honestly for a moment, not having really stopped to assess my feelings properly until now. "It was, at first," I admit. "But there's something about this place. The slower pace, the sense of community, the natural beauty... it's refreshing. And I think I needed a change."

Beth's eyes reflect a shared understanding. "I get that. Sometimes a change of scenery is exactly what we need to gain a new perspective on things."

"Exactly," I agree. "And honestly, the people here have been so welcoming. It's made it easier."

"Yeah, I've noticed that too." She wrings out the last of the water from her hair. "Everyone seems genuinely friendly and interested in getting to know each other. It's a nice change from the anonymity of the city."

"Are you planning to stay here long term, or is this just a vacation for you?" I ask, curious about her plans.

Beth hesitates for a moment, a shadow crossing her face before she quickly masks it with a smile. "Just here for a few days, actually. I needed to escape some stuff," she says, her voice trailing off as a haunted look fills her eyes. It vanishes as quickly as it appeared.

I nod, understanding more than she realizes. "What are you doing for dinner tonight? We could eat together if you want to talk about it," I suggest, hoping to offer her some company. Besides, it will be nice to have some conversation where I'm not digging for information.

She lights up with excitement for a moment before she slumps in disappointment. "Oh, I signed up for one of the painting classes tonight. They provide finger food, so I'm kind of tied up."

"How about coffee tomorrow morning then?" I suggest, as I don't want to stress her further with making her choose. "Meet me at the bakery at 9:30? That way it's not too early."

Beth's smile returns, genuine and grateful. "That sounds perfect. I'd love that. See you then, Taylor."

"See you, Beth," I reply, waving as she heads off towards the water again.

I spend a few more hours walking along the beach and then people-watching while eating a late lunch at the cafe. I take my time walking back to the house before making myself a coffee with one of the new bags, and then heading to the office to go over all the notes again and add missing details to the wall. Still, nothing is standing out.

Realizing that the cookies distracted my social media stalking the other day, I sit down at the desk with my laptop. Bringing up the popular platforms, I get to work. Now that I have last names I start by searching for each of their profiles.

As suspected I don't find all of them. The ones I do find are filled with posts about their businesses, presenting a professional front for anyone who might look. Even old lady Gladys has a profile to promote her little grocery store. There are only small and infrequent posts across most of them that are personal. The woman posted the occasional selfie at the beach, while the men posted selfies at Makai's gym.

It's late afternoon when my phone chimes with a message, interrupting my thoughts. Glancing at the screen, I see it's from an unknown sender, sendings a chill down my spine.

PSYCHO MASKED STALKERS

> I told you not to cover our marks, little shadow.
> Did you really think a dress was a better idea?

I stare at the message, my heart pounding in my chest. My fingers hover over the screen before I finally respond.

> You do not control me or what I wear.

PSYCHO MASKED STALKERS

> Is that right?

> YES

PSYCHO MASKED STALKERS

> We don't want to control you, little shadow.

That doesn't mean we can't do something about the other men who see what's ours and think they have a chance of taking it from us.

My jaw tightens, irritation and apprehension mixing in equal measure.

> You're being ridiculous.

PSYCHO MASKED STALKERS

> Try us. We will always be watching.

Anger and defiance surge within me as I read their last message. I refuse to be intimidated. My fingers fly over the keyboard.

> Fine, you want to watch me? Then watch this.

I hit send, a sense of rebellious determination coursing through me. I won't let them dictate my actions or my choices. They can watch all they want, but they won't control me.

Storming toward the bedroom, I strip out of the dress and my underwear, digging through my clothes for something that would make a statement. My fingers brush over the smooth fabric of my bikini, pulling it out of my bag, and then I find it—the sheer overdress with delicate embroidered flowers. It's completely see-through, every cut and mark on my skin will be visible, but at that moment I don't care.

They want their marks on display, then they will be on display.

Chapter 29

Hydessa

I probably shouldn't have let my temper get the better of me. I have worked so hard to never give into impulsiveness. I have a feeling if I did, then that part of me I keep locked deep inside would seek justice in the most brutal ways.

I couldn't help it though. These men keep getting to me, pushing me. I think it's time I pushed back a little more.

After checking the time, I decided to take some advice from Maddie and take a walk to the lighthouse to take some photographs at sunset. The fact that I would have to stroll through the entire beachfront area to get there was just a bonus.

Those psycho masked men can kiss my almost completely bare ass. Oh but wait, that would require them to remove their masks, which the assholes won't do.

Since I don't have my professional camera with me, I decide I'll improvise using my phone camera instead. Making my way to the beach and then toward the tall impressive building on the distant bluff, the fading sunlight casts a mesmerizing array of colors across the sky, painting it with hues of pink, orange, and purple. Despite my earlier frustrations, a sense of satisfaction washes over me as I weave through the bustling crowd of tourists and locals.

The idea of Cain and Abel watching me among the crowd in my minimal attire brings a defiant smirk to my face. Several heads turn in my direction, their gazes lingering as I smile politely.

Reaching the end of the beach, I turn towards the path leading to the lighthouse. The air is filled with the salty tang of the sea, making me lick my lips for a taste of it. The sound of waves crashing becomes a soothing backdrop to my thoughts.

The silhouette of the tall red striped building grows more distinct against the colorful sky. I pause for a moment to admire the view, the vibrant hues of the sunset painting the scene in a surreal beauty. Pulling out my phone, I switch to the camera mode and begin capturing the scene before me.

Each click of the shutter captures a different aspect of the lighthouse and its surroundings: the stark contrast between the darkening sky and the illuminated structure, the play of light and shadow on the rugged terrain, and the distant horizon where the sun dips below the edge of the world.

As the sun sinks lower, casting a final blaze of color across the sky, I capture one last photograph. Satisfied with my efforts, I take a moment to simply absorb the beauty of the moment before turning to head back.

Deciding to walk back on the beach I take the path down the side of the cliff the lighthouse sits on. The walk back feels different now, my thoughts quieter. *Maybe I needed that moment after all.*

This area is quiet and nearly empty, too far away from the main street for tourists to bother with. There are a few jagged outcrops of rocks and hills, and the whole area is beautiful.

I can see rocks sticking up from the sea close to the cliff. I pause for a moment, taking a seat on the sand to watch the first stars come out. The sky turns from a deep blue to dark navy before all color disappears.

I lean back on my elbows, gazing up at the night sky. It's a perfect moment to reflect on everything that has happened, and I find myself feeling more grounded and centered.

Feeling as though the moment will help me tackle the investigation with a clear mind, I get back up to my feet and start to make my way back, intending to return to the house. Not far ahead, I can vaguely see that the cliff edge gets close to the water again, but the prospect of wading through the water doesn't bother me.

When I get closer, I notice lights moving close to the cliff. They're not completely distinct, but the red and green colors make me frown. The lights disappear again, but after days of being taunted by Cain and Abel's neon masks, I can't simply dismiss what I saw. My pulse quickens as I keep moving closer to the rock face.

I may be going crazy, it's highly probable, but then the possibility that Cain and Abel might be nearby propels me forward. As I approach the cliff face, I move cautiously, trying to stay out of sight. My skin prickles with the feeling of being watched again, but there is no chance of seeing anyone in this darkness.

Creeping slowly, my back against the cold rocks, I try to remain as silent as possible. The crunch of sand beneath my feet seems deafening in the quiet night. My heart pounds, every beat echoing in my ears. Suddenly, the rocks are no longer at my back. Before I can react, a hand wraps around my mouth and jerks me backward.

My instincts kick in, and I struggle against the grip, but it's firm and annoyingly familiar. The red and green glow I know all too well flares to life again as Cain continues to move me backward into what I can now tell is a cave.

The panic that was there only a moment before fades quickly. Cain stops moving me and says, "Do I need to bind your hands, or will you behave like a good girl?"

I don't respond, and he takes my silence as acceptance. The moment he releases me, I turn and shove him in the chest with a frustrated growl. It moves him only a step, and they both laugh.

"Ooo, someone's feeling feisty today, brother," Abel says, causing me to turn my anger on him. I move to shove him in the chest too, but he simply captures my hands in one of his and holds them to his chest. The neon green of his mask is bright in my eyes, and not for the first time, I wish it was a face I was looking at and not a mask.

Cain moves closer, his gloved hand trailing down the sheer over-dress I'm wearing. "I do love the gift wrapping," he says before he swats my ass. The thin material makes the pain sharper.

My yelp echoes in the cave, blending with the sound of waves crashing against the rocks outside. Anger pulses through me, but I reign in the impulse to lash out again. Instead, I narrow my eyes at them, seething silently.

"You don't get to tell me what I can or can't wear. I will wear whatever the hell I want, in front of whoever the hell I want to," I snarl, and they only chuckle in response. *How do these men make me feel so good, but also so downright furious at the same time?*

Abel's other hand comes up to wrap around my throat, a feeling I am becoming quickly accustomed to. "As we said, we won't control you, you are free to do whatever you want. But make no mistake, you are ours, and we won't hesitate to kill anyone who thinks they can touch what's *ours*."

I've come to the conclusion they are insane, but fuck if his words don't make me swoon a little.

"How did you even know I would be down here?" I ask stubbornly.

Cain brushes a finger across my cheek, his touch surprisingly gentle yet sending shivers down my spine. "Because we know you, darling girl," he murmurs, his voice low and intimate. "Maybe even better than you know yourself."

Abel leans in, the side of his mask brushing against my other cheek as he speaks. "We love your spirit, little shadow," he adds with a hint of amusement. "We knew that by telling you not to do something, you would make a point of doing the exact opposite where everyone could see you."

I huff in annoyance at their high handedness. Mostly because I just proved them right.

"Don't be upset with us," Cain says and his voice is almost soothing, yet laced with an undeniable edge. "We did bring you in here for a couple of reasons."

Abel releases me as I turn to face Cain, my jaw clenched in defiance, though a flicker of curiosity burns beneath my anger. "And what would they be?" I challenge, folding my arms across my chest, unwilling to show any vulnerability.

Abel steps closer, his masked face unreadable yet somehow comforting in its familiarity. "Firstly, we needed to clarify something for you," he begins, his voice steady.

Cain tilts his head, his expression unreadable behind the mask. "We aren't your enemy, Hydessa," he adds, his tone softening slightly. "And we also aren't who you are looking for."

I frown, perplexed by their cryptic statements. "I don't understand," I admit, pressing my fingers against my temples as if to massage away the confusion.

"Don't get us wrong," Cain continues, his voice taking on a serious edge. "We are killers. We have no issues taking a life when it's the right thing to do."

I look at them with pinched brows, some of the puzzle starting to come together but definitely not all of it. It's like the pieces that were upside down are finally right side up, but I still have to put it all together. "I still don't understand."

"We aren't the ones killing the tourists," Abel states simply, his tone leaving no room for doubt.

I blink, momentarily taken aback by the unexpected revelation. I try to reconcile their words with everything I have seen and felt since arriving on Amity Island.

"But why should I believe you?" I finally manage to say, my voice laced with skepticism.

"We have our own code," Cain responds, his voice low and deliberate. "We don't take innocent lives."

A part of me is relieved it's not them killing innocent people but yet another is frustrated. "Do you know who it is?" I asked.

"Yes," Abel says. "But you need to solve this case for yourself."

"Why not just tell me?" I demanded, my tone sharper than intended.

Cain's gloved hand rests lightly on my shoulder. "Because understanding this case requires more than just knowing the identity of the killer," he explains. "It requires understanding their motives, their methods. To truly grasp their darkness, you must be willing to confront your own."

"Embrace the darkness inside you, Hydessa," Abel says, his voice calm yet insistent. "It's not a weakness; it's a strength."

I bristled at his words, the notion of embracing my darkness conflicting with everything I have struggled to be. "I've fought against that part of me for as long as I can remember," I reply, my voice tight with emotion. "I've done everything I can to keep it locked away."

Cain hums quietly. "We know," he says quietly. "But sometimes, embracing it is the only way to truly understand the mind of a killer."

Abel claps his gloved hands together, startling me. "Which brings us to the other reason we brought you here, or at least to this cave."

"We have a present for you, little shadow," Cain says, and I frown. I'm not sure I trust any of their presents after the cherry cookies and coffee incident.

Abel turns away, moving toward one of the walls of red and yellow rock near us. Pushing a button, lights suddenly flare inside the cave, almost blinding me. When the spots clear from my eyes, I realize we aren't alone. Toward the back, bound by chains to the wall and gagged, is a man. It takes a moment for what I'm seeing to register.

"Rye?" I gasp, my voice barely above a whisper.

Chapter 30

Hydessa

Looking at the man bound to the wall, my brain is struggling to understand what is happening. Rye's eyes widen with recognition as he struggles against the chains binding him. I take a step toward him, but Cain's hand on my shoulder stops me.

"Why?" I ask, my voice filled with confusion. "Why is he here?"

Abel turns back to face me, the neon green of his mask glowing ominously. "Rye has been a very bad boy," he says simply, his tone almost casual.

"We thought this could be a lesson for you, darling girl, but also, think of this as an offering," Cain says.

"An offering?" I echo, still struggling to comprehend their twisted logic. "I'm not some sort of goddess."

"No, but you are our queen," Abel says with a dark chuckle. "And we will worship you as such."

Cain's grip on my shoulder tightens slightly. "Yes, an offering," he says, his voice calm and controlled. "But first, if you could ask one question of the killers you investigate, what would it be?"

I blink, thrown off by the sudden shift in conversation. My mind races, trying to think of the most crucial question amidst the chaos. "Why do they do it?" I finally ask. "What drives them to kill?"

Cain tilts his head in acknowledgement as he considers my question. "Good question," he says, his voice thoughtful. "It's a common debate, right? Nature versus nurture? Everyone wants to understand what makes a killer do what they do. Are they born with that killer instinct or was there something that made them do it, that made them snap."

He pauses, looking over at Rye. "Take Rye here. He is an example of nurture, and I'll explain that in a moment. But the three of us, what we do, who we are, that's definitely nature at work. We're born this way, it's in our DNA."

Abel laughs, a short, bitter sound that echoes off the cave walls. "We won the genetic fucking lottery," he says, his tone dripping with sarcasm.

Cain hums in agreement before continuing. "But with our current serial killer, the one killing the tourists, because they are by definition a serial killer now, their reasons could be either or both. They certainly have something evil in their genetic makeup, but there was also an event that influenced them and went a long way to explaining why they killed those tourists."

I stare at Cain, trying to grasp the full weight of his words. "And what event would that be?" I ask, my curiosity getting the better of me.

"The ultimate event," Abel interjects a little too cheerfully. "Death."

I can almost hear Cain gritting his teeth from here. "Yes, death," Cain continues, his tone more measured. "Our killer had a brush with death, a near-fatal experience. It brought them face-to-face with their own mortality, and from that moment, they became obsessed with it. They want to know what others see, what they experience in that final moment."

I feel a chill run down my spine. "So, they kill to understand death," I say, more to myself than to anyone else.

"Precisely," Cain says. "Their own experience wasn't enough. They need to see it reflected in the eyes of others, to understand the fear, the realization, the acceptance."

"But how do you know all this?" I ask, still trying to piece together the enormity of the situation.

Abel steps closer, gently tucking a strand of hair behind my ear. "Even the streets on this island have ears and eyes," he explains.

I frown as I realize the implications. There must be cameras in the beachfront area, watching everything and everyone. I sigh, giving them both a resigned look. "I don't suppose you might be willing to give me that footage?"

"Nope," Abel says, laughing.

Frustration wells up inside me, but I know that arguing with them won't get me anywhere. I rub my temples, already feeling a headache coming on. "Well then, if you aren't going to simply tell me who the killer is, can we get back to the man hanging from the wall of this cave?" I motion toward where Rye is still staring at us wide-eyed.

"That's right," Cain says, returning to the earlier topic. "As I was saying, Rye is an example of nurture. He also had an event that would be considered a trigger."

"Okay, I'll bite. What was his trigger?" I ask.

"Abandonment," Abel says, his tone subtly changing, almost as if he has personal experience on the subject.

I look at him curiously, noting the shift in his demeanor. "His dad died when he was younger," Cain continues, "but then his mother left the island to move south not long after he had become an adult and established his business, so he couldn't move. Which I'm sure would have been fine, until his wife left him too. That was the trigger."

I frown at Cain's words. "But there haven't been any other murders here. I checked as part of my investigation."

Abel scoffs, and Cain looks at him briefly before turning his attention back to me. "You're forgetting Rye has a particular hatred for city girls. Remember the cases you investigated that went cold, the random club overdoses?"

I had spent months investigating a string of dead women, the captain had pulled me from the case when I became too emotionally invested in trying to bring them justice. It was hard to look at the photos of women who had been raped and then injected with enough drugs to kill them without feeling a burning need to kill the person responsible.

The new lead investigator on the case had pronounced it cold when the killer stopped, but I felt that he hadn't, he just got better at covering his tracks.

My eyes nearly bug out of my head as I realize what he means. Rage fills me, almost blinding me. Without thinking, I take a few steps toward where Rye is until both Cain and Abel grab onto my arms.

"Careful," Abel says, pointing to the ground where there are valleys and wells in the sand and rocks forming pools of water. "I like you wet, but let's save that for later, okay?"

"We normally don't kill in our own backyard, but then Rye decided to turn his attention to the wrong city girl," Cain says, his tone darkening.

Abel leans closer to my ear, his voice dropping to a whisper. "You," he says, before turning and walking closer to Rye. I notice this time that his steps miss the wells of water with practiced ease.

"Do you use this cave often?" I ask, wondering how many times they have killed here.

"You'd be surprised at how many hidden spots there are on this island. But this one is even more special," Cain says.

"Why?" I ask curiously.

Abel, now standing near another wall, responds without turning around. "Because the tide will come soon and wash all the evidence away."

I shouldn't ask, I already know what he is about to say, but I need him to say it. Deep down, I want him to say it. "What evidence?" I finally question, my voice barely above a whisper.

"The blood, the footprints, the DNA, everything," Cain says, almost casually. "The tide rises, and with it, all traces of our activities vanish. It's nature's perfect cleanup crew."

Abel turns to face me, and the item in his hands makes my heart race, but not out of fear. "Do you believe us yet, Hydessa? We will kill anyone who thinks they can touch you. And to us, knives are for the bedroom. When getting rid of people like Rye here, we prefer to make a statement," he says as he twirls the barbed wire wrapped bat in his hands.

My lips part on a breath. *Why is that the hottest, most possessive thing I've ever heard? And why is it such a fucking turn on?*

Cain lets go of my arm, making his own way over to where Abel is holding a second bat also wrapped in barbed wire out to him. Taking it from his brother, he moves to where Rye is chained. He pauses for a moment, tilting his head as though he's savoring the fear radiating from him.

"I'd remove the gag, except we wouldn't want any tourist coming to find out what all the screaming is about," he says.

Abel chuckles, the sound slightly disturbed. "Damn shame."

Cain raises the weapon, adjusting his grip and preparing to swing it at Rye.

"Wait." The word escapes me before I consciously think about it. I almost take a wrong step more than once on my way across to where they are standing. When I'm close enough, Abel makes a show of kneeling before me and raising the bat to me as though presenting a sword.

"My queen," he says and I have to swallow my laughter.

I take the bat and twirl it in my hand, feeling the weight of it. Cain steps aside and suddenly I'm standing in front of Rye, wondering what I'm doing. But deep down I know, the darkness inside me knows what to do, what I want to do.

For the first time in my life, I slowly loosen the tight reigns I have on it inside my mind. I can almost feel the moment everything shifts. The lines between right and wrong are blurred, and a sense of injustice takes over. I let it flood my veins as I inhale.

Abel steps up behind me, his mask brushing against the side of my face as he whispers in my ear, his voice dropping to a seductive whisper. "You know you want to, little shadow. Just imagine how good it will feel, getting justice for all those women finally. Have you ever used that pretty knife of yours to cut someone open?"

My breath catches and my heart races in my chest. There is a memory that is just out of reach, but it disappears again as Abel runs a hand down the arm holding the bat. He adjusts my grip until I am ready to swing, turning my body until I'm positioned exactly how he wants me.

"It's a beautiful and deadly weapon, like the woman who wields it. I love watching how easily it slices through the layers of flesh, how quickly the blood spills from the wound." A soft caress on my cheek has me closing my eyes for a brief moment, wondering if I can actually do this.

"It's different with you though, my darling girl. I could spend hours watching how the crimson beads on your pale skin. I would happily trace the path of a single blood drop with my tongue," he continues, his voice a dark promise that has me panting in response to the imagery he's painting in my mind. I can almost imagine his tongue on me. I would gladly spill a million drops of blood if he traced every single one.

With that realization, any doubts of if I could do this or not disappears.

His hands continue to brush against me as he makes tiny adjustments to the way I'm standing, each movement has my body responding, growing hot and needy. I'm practically panting for him and I can feel how much he needs me too.

"The bat isn't as sophisticated as a knife, it's not made for pleasure. It's built for pain, for tearing flesh from the bone. There is nothing elegant about the damage you can inflict upon someone with a weapon like this. But that darkness inside you, it needs violence, it feeds on it, it needs to hurt those who hurt others. Embrace that part of yourself, Hydessa, become our dark queen."

Looking Rye in the eyes, I see the terror. But what has me tightening my grip is that I can see without a doubt he did exactly what Cain and Abel accused him of.

Without hesitancy, I swing the bat. There's no turning back now.

Chapter 31

Hydessa

E ven with the gag, Rye still manages to let out a high-pitched squeal as the bat makes contact with the side of his body. My rage takes over as I remember each and every one of the women I now know he killed. The part of me that I tried to bury deep inside, the darkness that I fought so hard to suppress, it's no longer something I can ignore. I can feel it taking control, pushing me to exact vengeance for all the pain and suffering he's caused.

The barbed wire wrapped around the bat catches on his shirt, and the skin beneath it, but the momentum of my swing tears it free, leaving deep, jagged gashes. Rye's muffled cries grow louder, the sound almost inhuman, as I prepare for another strike. Each scream only fuels the fire inside me.

I think of Hannah, and how he tore her clothes so violently. Then, Rachel; her body was so bruised it was like he used her as a punching bag before he overdosed her. Cindy's lips were twisted in pain, even in death. And lastly, Olivia. The one that made me lose my mind on the case. I had never seen a woman so violated, as if pure hate itself came out of another being just to assault her.

I lost sleep and even had to see the department psychologist to work past her death, especially after the case was deemed cold. I would dream at night of finding a way to bring them justice and now I finally can. They had given that to me.

I swing again, and again, each hit more brutal than the last. The room fills with the sickening sounds of the bat meeting flesh, of Rye's muffled screams, and the raw power of my anger unleashed.

Blood now sprays with each impact, splattering across my face and clothes. I feel the warmth of it, the sticky wetness, and it only drives me further into my frenzy. My vision blurs with tears of rage, but I don't stop. I can't stop. Not until he feels a fraction of the pain he's inflicted. Not until the darkness within me has been satisfied. It's almost as if it whispers to me in my head.

Finally.

The bat catches his ribs this time, and I hear the unmistakable crack of bone. Rye's body convulses, his eyes wide and terrified. And I wonder if he enjoyed the terror in his victims' gaze. I wonder if he ever stopped to think about them and how he robbed others of their futures. I think of their families, forever broken by his cruelty.

Rye's struggles weaken, his cries becoming more pitiful, but I don't relent. Not yet. The darkness inside me demands more, cries out for blood and retribution. Eventually, when my arms can no longer hold the weapon up, I take a step back, panting, the bat slipping from my grasp and clattering to the floor. Rye hangs from the chains, crumpled, a broken, bloody mess, barely recognizable. His eyes are glazed over, empty. Just like all his victims.

The room is eerily silent now, the only sound is my ragged breathing. Blood drips from the body, forming a dark pool on the floor. I can feel it on my skin, the metallic smell filling my senses. The adrenaline is still pumping through me, my heart racing in my chest.

I reach up with bloodstained hands to wipe at my face, but I'm startled when someone steps up behind me, his hands stopping mine.

"Don't, you look so fucking beautiful," Abel says, his hands running down the side of my dress, dragging it up my body until he can touch my skin unhindered. "Did that turn you on, little shadow? Are you wet with more than just that blood?" His fingers make their way beneath my bikini. I can't help but moan when they slide through my wet folds.

Abel thrusts two fingers inside of me, his other hand coming up to wrap around my throat and hold me in place just as he always does. It should be strange that it's now feeling like a comfort to be collared by him.

I watch as Cain moves toward the body, checking for a pulse before resting the bat in his hand against the cave wall. He turns back to watch as Abel continues to thrust his fingers into my pussy, the red neon of his mask not as bright in the light but still sinister. Abel presses and swirls his thumb against my clit, making me whimper. In the silence of the cave, you can hear how wet I am, how turned on the scene here made me.

Cain takes a step toward me and away from the body, his head tilting as he watches us. "Is my good little slut needy for my cock?" he asks.

Abel's fingers move faster, pushing me to the edge. His grip on my throat tightens just enough to send a thrill through me, intensifying every sensation. I can barely think, my mind consumed by the mix of lust and the adrenaline still coursing through my veins from the violent act I just committed. My body trembles, caught between the primal need for release and the raw power of my anger.

"Yes," I gasp, my voice barely more than a whisper. "Please, Cain."

Abel chuckles, a dark, pleased sound as he continues his relentless assault on my body. "Hear that, brother? Our little shadow is begging for you."

Cain closes the distance between us, his movements almost predatory. He brushes a hand along my cheek, his touch surprisingly gentle compared to the brutality we just unleashed.

"Good girl," he murmurs, his fingers trailing down to join Abel's, teasing the sensitive skin of my inner thigh. "So needy for us."

I gasp, arching into their touch, my body craving more. Cain's fingers slide through my slick folds, joining Abel's in a maddening rhythm that has me on the verge of breaking. The intensity is overwhelming, every nerve ending alight with sensation.

"Tell me," Cain demands, his voice a rough whisper. "Who do you belong to, Hydessa?"

"You," I breathe, my voice betraying just how strong my need for them is. "Both of you."

Abel growls in approval, his fingers thrusting deeper, matching the pace set by Cain. "That's right, little shadow. You're ours."

I'm so close to the edge already, only they seem to be able to provide me with this pleasure so quickly and so completely. But then they both pull away, making me whimper again.

Cain opens his pants, pulling his already hard cock out and stroking it, I can see the red smeared on his thick length from where his glove touched the lifeless body. His other hand comes back up to my face, a finger pressing past my lips. "You're going to let me use this mouth with my cock, aren't you, darling girl?"

Abel presses down on my shoulders and I drop to my knees. Water flicks up, and I realize that it's slowly rising, spreading along the cave floor as the tide starts to come in. Cain presses the head of his cock against my lips. "Let me fuck that pretty throat," he demands.

I open and he presses forward, groaning as my lips wrap around him. The piercings along the underside of his length are cold compared to the warmth of my mouth, and I flick my tongue against them, wondering if they are sensitive. I hear the catch in his breath as his cock twitches inside my mouth, so I do it again.

My eyes flick up to look at Cain's mask, his head is tilted down and I know he's watching me as I take him deeper. The coppery tang of blood mingles with the taste of his skin, a reminder of what happened, of the body not far from us.

Cain's gloved fingers thread through my hair, guiding my movements as I work my mouth along his length. Each thrust is met with a low groan, his fingers tightening as he starts to take control. I hollow my cheeks, sucking harder, my tongue moving along his piercings, and he rewards me with another sharp intake of breath.

"Fuck, you're perfect," he mutters, his voice rough with pleasure. "Our perfect little slut."

Abel's fingers slide around the sides of my waist, pulling the lower part of my body up until I'm on my hands and knees. He pushes the dress up to my waist, pulling my bikini bottoms to the side and running a finger through my wetness. "You're doing so good, little shadow," Abel purrs. "Taking him so well. But I think it's time for you to take me too."

The water is rising steadily now, lapping at my knees as Abel moves behind me. I feel the cold tip of his pierced cock pressing against my entrance, and I brace myself, knowing this will be rough especially with how sore I already am. Abel doesn't disappoint, thrusting into me with a force that has me crying out, my body arching as I struggle to adjust.

The mix of pain and pleasure sends shockwaves through my body, my cries muffled around Cain's cock. Each thrust from Abel forces me forward, taking Cain deeper, filling my senses with the overwhelming intensity of being used by them both. The rising tide adds a chilling contrast to the heat coursing through my veins, heightening every sensation.

Cain's grip forces me to take him all the way past where I thought was possible, his thrusts becoming more erratic as he loses control. "Relax your throat, show me again what a good little fucking cock slut you are," he commands, his voice a strained growl.

I try to obey, forcing myself to relax despite the overwhelming sensations. My throat opens for him, taking him deeper, and the groan that escapes him is almost feral.

Abel's rhythm is relentless, his hands gripping my hips tightly as he pounds into me from behind. The cave echoes with the sounds we are making and the distant waves.

Cain's movements become more urgent, his breaths coming in ragged gasps. My throat protests the abuse, making me gag, but he is unrelenting. "That's it, gag on it," he groans, his pace quickening.

I can feel his cock swelling in my mouth, making me gag even more, but I don't pull away. Abel's pace slows and if I could have growled in frustration I would have. With me kneeling, the water is now up to my thighs, the chill a stark contrast to the heat between my legs.

Cain pulls my head back, forcing me to release his cock with a wet pop, his length glistening with my saliva. My lips are swollen, my throat raw from the rough treatment. He strokes himself furiously, the sight and sound of me gagging on his cock must have been too much for him to handle.

"Fuck, your mouth is perfect, little shadow," he growls, his hand tightening in my hair. "Open wide."

I obey, opening my mouth as wide as I can, my tongue out to catch every drop. Cain groans loudly, his hips jerking as he cums, coating my tongue and lips. My eyes stare into the neon red of his mask, wanting to please him.

"Good girl," he pants, stroking my cheek with surprising tenderness. "Swallow every drop."

I do as he commands, the taste of him sliding down my throat, my tongue darting out to chase the taste of him. I don't have time to recover before Abel pulls out of me, turning me toward him. He lifts me and wraps my legs around his waist, impaling me on his cock again with one thrust.

"Fuck, she feels so good," he growls, his voice rough with lust as my hands try to grasp onto his shoulders. He shifts slightly, rolling his hips in a way that makes me moan, the piercing in the head of his cock dragging against my sensitive walls. One of his hands moves to take a handful of my ass, while the other wraps around the front of my throat. "Take a deep breath, little shadow."

My mind is a whirlwind of confusion and sensation, but I obey, taking a deep breath as instructed. Seconds later, Abel uses the grip he has on my throat to shove me backward. My back hits the water, which is now significantly deeper, plunging my head under the surface while keeping where we are joined just above the water.

My head is completely submerged, the water distorting my vision and muffling every sound. The only thing clear is the renewed rhythm of Abel's cock plunging into me. His grip on my throat is firm, holding me in place as he takes what he wants. The force of his movements sends waves rippling around us.

His thrusts are savage, the intensity of it becoming overwhelming as the glow of their masks dances above the water. My hands grip at his wrist as I become lightheaded, my need to breathe clashing with the pleasure I feel. But even as I struggle, the intensity of the pleasure coursing through me only increases.

I can feel myself tightening around him as the pressure builds inside me, the need for release becoming unbearable. Abel's thrusts grow more erratic as darkness fills the edges of my vision, my chest tightening from the lack of air.

My lips part on a soundless scream as my orgasm crashes over me, more violent than the sea that now surrounds us. Water rushes into my mouth and I start to choke on it. Abel's hips slam into mine and I feel his cock pulse inside me as he comes. Just as my consciousness starts to slip away, he jerks me back up and out of the water.

I gasp as the cold air fills my lungs, coughing as I cling to him. My body shudders and clenches around his cock again, aftershocks making us both moan. But I'm weak, my body feeling incredibly heavy, sleep and exhaustion pressing against me. I fight against the pull of it as Abel gets to his feet and Cain lifts me out of his arms.

They murmur to each other, but I can't grasp onto what they are saying, my body and mind already surrendering to the pull of unconsciousness.

Chapter 32

Abel

"Take her home the long way, not via the beachfront. No one but us gets to see her like this," my brother says, passing Hydessa back to me after I straighten my clothes, and I couldn't agree more. "I'll take care of the body."

I don't need to ask what he's going to do, we have done this enough now that there is a system. We hadn't lied to her, we are killers; we just hunt a particular brand of sick souls. Ones who prey on the weak and the innocent.

I know Hydessa's family hunts the same brand of criminal as we do.

Turning, I make my way slowly toward a section of the rock face that twists out of view, treading as carefully as I can through the water that's now up to my knees. Once past the slight turn, it opens up further before the tunnel starts to slope upward. I have to duck my head at some points, but after a while it levels out again. When the tunnel finally opens up, I continue out and into the forest.

I veer left, taking the long way around the back of the beachfront area and continuing through the trees toward the rental house. As I walk, I can't help but replay the events of the night in my mind.

I've never seen anything as stunningly beautiful as Hydessa exacting justice on Rye. Watching her swing that bat, the blood spraying through the air. It was like watching a masterpiece in motion.

The raw, unfiltered rage in her eyes, the way she channeled it into each brutal swing, it was mesmerizing. She was powerful, primal, and utterly breathtaking.

As I navigate the forest, careful not to stumble over roots or rocks, I keep glancing at Hydessa. Her wet hair clings to her face, but even in this disheveled state, she looks ethereal, like a warrior goddess after battle. I feel a surge of protectiveness, a fierce desire to keep her safe.

Finally, the house comes into view, its familiar shape a welcome sight. I approach the door, shifting Hydessa's weight to get the keys. The lock clicks open, and I push inside with my shoulder, stepping into the quiet, dimly lit interior.

Carefully, I make my way up the stairs, my steps light to avoid waking her. The bedroom door creaks slightly as I open it, the room beyond bathed in soft moonlight filtering through the curtains. I lay her gently on the bed, her body sinking into the plush mattress. She barely stirs, a small sigh escaping her lips.

Using the gas hidden in its secret compartment, I make sure she slides deeper into sleep, it will keep her under long enough to do what I need to do..

I kneel beside the bed and begin the delicate task of removing her dress and bikini, my movements slow and careful. Discarding the wet clothes toward the bedroom door, I make a mental note to wash them for her.

Rising, I head to the bathroom, filling a bowl with warm steamy water and soap, then grab a clean washcloth and towel. I return to the bedroom, setting everything on the nightstand.

I sit on the edge of the bed, gently lifting one of her arms and dipping the washcloth into the soapy water. I start to clean her, the cloth gliding over her skin, washing away the events of the night.

Her breathing remains steady, and I take my time, wanting to ensure every inch of her is cared for.

When I'm finished, I dry her off with the towel, doing my best to dry her hair without disturbing her yet. I brush a few strands from her face, my fingers lingering. I have never known anyone as beautiful as her, not just her looks, but her personality. That beauty is a beacon to the dark and depraved people in the world and unfortunately something will need to be done to warn others away.

I draw the sheet over her body, standing and picking up the water bowl, towel, and clothes on my way out of the bedroom. Silently, I move through the house with practiced ease, and before long, I have the clothes and towel washing and the bowl rinsed.

Next, I move to a hidden panel underneath the stairs, opening it and retrieving the items there. Closing the panel again, I make my way back up the stairs and into the bedroom. I lay the items out on the bedside table, picking up two of them. I switch one of them on and press the button down at the top.

I did love that outfit on her earlier, and I did say I would never control what she wears or doesn't wear. But everyone would soon know, she belongs to us.

Chapter 33

Hydessa

I wake screaming, torn from my sleep as it feels like fire rips through me. The heat searing and the smell of burnt flesh has me choking, but it's nothing compared to the pain. It overwhelms my senses so quickly that the darkness of unconsciousness saves me from it within moments, the pain too much for my body to cope with. But with it comes a memory I tried to forget...

***

17 Years Ago

My dad is cooking when someone comes to the house. It's late, the sun has already set. Seanna is staying with a friend; she has always been the popular one. She tries to take me along with her, but tonight, I just wanted to stay home.

The adults are talking in the living room and I know not to interrupt. Walking quietly into the kitchen I can see something cooking on the stove, I know it's been forgotten about because the water is overflowing a little, the sound of it sizzling as it drips is soft enough that they won't hear it from where they are.

Dragging a chair over I hop up onto it, reaching over to turn it off like dad showed me, but it's still dripping and making that sizzling sound. Reaching out to move it away from that spot, my fingertips brush against the metal and I gasp as pain flashes through me from where I touched the pot. Tears fill my eyes, but I don't want to get in trouble so I swallow the cry that instantly builds in my throat. A whimper still escapes as I look down at where two of my fingertips are now pink and stinging sharply.

"If you suck on them it will help." A voice comes from behind me and I gasp, turning too fast and almost toppling from the chair. Hands steady me, but they aren't adult hands, they are the hands of a child.

"I'm sorry, I didn't mean to scare you," he says and I find myself looking down into big green eyes. His dark hair has been cut so close to his head there is barely any of it, making his eyes stand out.

I quickly get down from the chair and move away. "Who are you?" I ask, sticking my burning fingers inside my mouth.

His lips twist to the side, as though he is chewing on the inside of his cheek. "No one," he says after a moment. He looks really sad.

I tilt my head, confused, letting my hands drop to my sides again. "Your name is 'no one'?" I ask with a giggle, and he smiles, even though the sad look doesn't leave completely.

"No, it's Lincoln," he says, shaking his head. Can't say I blame him for wanting to be called something else.

I try to stop laughing but I can't. "That sounds like an old man's name," I point out and he rolls his eyes at me. "I understand why you would want to be called 'no one' instead."

That look completely returns to his face and it makes me confused so I stop laughing. I didn't mean to upset him.

"I don't want to be called 'no one'. It's just what my parents would say to me all the time. That I'm nothing and no one," he explains, making me instantly want to cry.

He pulls out one of the chairs at the table and sits down, so I hop down and drag the chair back over next to him to sit as well. Folding his arms onto the flat surface, he lets his head fall against them and for a moment I think he might be crying. I've never seen a boy cry before.

"They're wrong," I say, laying a hand on his shoulder like papa does to me when I cry. "And those names don't suit you at all anyway." I can see him peeking at me out of the corner of his eye. The voices in the living room get louder for a moment but then go back to being quiet again while I think of a better name for him. "I think Link would suit you better."

I can see a small smile come back to him as he thinks about it, nodding a little as he lifts his head again. "What's your name?" he asks softly and I giggle again. I'm so used to everyone already knowing my name, it seems silly that he doesn't.

"Hydessa," I respond and his face twists a little into a frown.

"I don't think that name suits you either," he says, making me frown too.

"It's the only name I have. Well really it's Hydessa Darling, " I explain. I've never known any other name.

He laughs finally and I pout. I don't understand why he's laughing at my name, but then again, I did laugh at his name too.

"Maybe you should get called 'little darling'," he says between giggles and I cringe, my face twisting in disgust.

"Ewww, no, that's what my dads call my mom," I tell him, there is no way I'm allowing anyone to call me that.

His laughter dies down and he takes a moment to think about it. "Okay then, I'll just call you Dessa," he finally says with a smile.

"I like that name," I say, smiling back at him. "But only you can call me that."

*Link nods, a hint of pride in his eyes. "Then only you can call me Link,"
he says. He leans in closer, his voice dropping to a whisper. "Did you say
'dads'? Are both of those men your dads?"*

I giggle and nod. "Yes, silly. Well, I call one Dad and the other Papa."

He frowns, trying to make sense of it. "How do you have two dads?"

*"Well, they both love my mommy, and they are brothers, so they
decided to love her together," I explain.*

*Link's frown deepens, as though he's trying to wrap his head around
the concept. Then, his expression turns sad. "I wish I had a brother. I don't
have any family."*

*This time, it's my turn to frown. "I thought you said it's your parents
who call you those mean names."*

*He huffs and I'm not sure if he is cranky or upset at the reminder
now. "They aren't my real parents. They made that clear too. I don't have
anyone."*

*I reach out and take his hand in mine, giving him a smile. "You have
me now."*

***

With a pained groan, consciousness starts to slowly return. The
burning sensation has dulled down, but fingers are moving over the
skin of my arm. As my eyes part, I see the neon glow of Abel's mask,
but his attention is on my arm as he wraps something around it. I
whimper and he glances at me, reaching a hand out to brush hair
away from my face.

"What were you dreaming about?" he asks, his voice low and
almost soothing despite the situation and the modulator.

I groan, shifting slightly. "That's none of your business."

As I finally look at what he is doing, I notice he's wrapping my arm in something clear, like the kind of wrapping used for a fresh tattoo. But it's certainly not a tattoo under the covering.

"You fucking branded me?" I snap, the realization hitting me like a cold shock as I stare at the two red and raw mask shapes burnt into my skin.

Abel doesn't respond, simply finishes wrapping it before standing and moving to lean against the wall, his attention never leaving me. I wish I could see his expression, but even then I doubt I would see regret.

"Why?" I demand, my voice filled with anger and confusion. "Why did you do this?"

He doesn't flinch, his mask glowing softly in the dim light of the room. He watches me with a calm demeanor, seemingly unaffected by my anger.

"You're ours, and now everyone else will know it too," he finally responds.

I growl, frustrated as I let my head fall back. But that means I can't see him, and I obviously can't trust what he will do if left unattended, which makes me wonder where Cain is. I push through the pain and sit up, breathing out a sigh when I lean back against my headboard.

"Seeing our mark on your skin just makes me want to fuck you again," Abel says suddenly, his voice low.

I give him a droll look, my patience wearing thin. "My pussy can't take much more of your obsession with it."

He tilts his head slightly, as if considering how to respond. "Your pussy isn't the part of you that I'm obsessed with," he says finally, his tone serious.

I roll my eyes, frustrated. "Would you have done this to any woman who came to investigate these murders?"

"No," he answers without hesitation. "But no one else was going to come looking."

"Anyone could have seen that blog and looked into it," I argue.

"Could they?" Abel counters cryptically, a subtle change in his tone catching my attention.

"You're speaking in riddles," I snap, annoyance sharpening my tone.

"The person who needed to see the blog saw it first," he says with a shrug, looking away for a moment.

"Why me?" I press, frustration building. His gaze returns to me, his head tilting again.

"You'll know why soon enough."

My frustration finally snaps. "If you knew who was murdering tourists, why haven't you taken them out?" I demand, my voice tinged with anger. "People have died since you started trying to get my attention."

Abel remains silent for a moment, his mask betraying nothing. When he finally speaks, his voice is measured and deliberate. "It's not that simple," he begins. "What's that saying? The reason you fall for the villain over the hero of a story is because the hero will choose the world over their lover but the villain will burn it down for insulting his queen... We aren't good men, don't mistake us for good men. We would burn it all down for you."

I feel like my heart stops beating in my chest, but he doesn't even give me a chance to respond before he quietly walks out of the room, leaving me to my own thoughts and a restless night ahead.

Chapter 34

Hydessa

A bel had been considerate enough to leave painkillers on the bedside table, but sleep was still limited. I honestly hoped it was them drugging me just to escape from my thoughts. But no, the one time I actually want that they seem to disappear.

I find I'm having to drag myself from the bed the next morning when it gets closer to when I said I would meet Beth for coffee. The brand is still red and raw, my arm aching as I try my best to shower and wash my hair while not getting it wet. It doesn't help that I swung a bat for the first time in my life probably a hundred times.

Why can't these assholes consider these things when they decide to RANDOMLY FUCKING BRAND ME??

My frustration is simmering as I choose an outfit that will cover the mark on my arm. I silently wonder if this is an extreme way of simply getting me to not wear next to nothing in public again. Even if they did say they won't control what I wear.

I end up choosing a pair of leggings and a light shirt that is strategically cut across the shoulders with sleeves to my elbows, but covers my upper arms where I need it.

Locking up the house I start to make my way toward the beach-front. I walk down the now familiar path, waving to the elderly man outside his house like I always do, and appreciating the fresh sea air and warm sunlight.

I try not to think about the crime scene I left behind last night, about how the water has washed it all away. My thighs brush together as I move and I refuse to let my thoughts focus on why they are so sore. I push it all away in favor of having coffee with someone and trying to forget for just a little while.

Hey, at least I can take a name off my list.

Before long, I'm pushing through the doorway to the bakery. Allegra smiles happily at me as I walk up to the counter.

"Morning, Taylor," she says cheerfully.

"Morning, Allegra," I respond with a smile. "I'll just grab a coffee for now. Someone is meeting me here shortly."

She raises an eyebrow and gives me a sly grin. I roll my eyes. "Not like that," I say, flicking a hand at her. "It's a tourist I met the other day. She's super nice and a city girl like me, so I figured I'd be friendly."

Her laugh is light and carefree. "Don't get attached to the tourists; they disappear before you even know it."

My heart thuds in my chest at the thought of that being exactly why I'm here. But she wouldn't know anything about that, would she? She hadn't given me any impression she was involved and now that I know the masked men aren't the murderers, it could be anyone again. Well, anyone except Rye.

I force a smile and nod, hoping she doesn't notice the sudden tension in my eyes.

I settle at a table close to the window with my coffee, watching the town waking up, tourists starting to venture out for breakfast and taking to the beach. I can see that the carnival has new additions, like a large Ferris wheel, and there are workers already in there stocking up the sideshow prizes and food supplies. Excitement fills me briefly as I think about it opening tomorrow and what there is to look forward to.

And then I flush as I'm filled with heat at the thought of what I have already done there.

Taking a sip of my coffee I finally allow my mind to reflect on everything I learned last night about the killer, and about myself. I momentarily wonder what happened to Rye's body, did they let it float out to sea with the tide? I doubt it. They have to know that without anything to weigh it down, it would just make its way back to the beach and cause more issues than I'm sure Cain and Abel want.

What near death experience did the murderer I'm chasing experience to turn him into a killer?

The thought plays on my mind, gnawing at my curiosity. It must have been something traumatic, something that twisted his mind so profoundly that he felt compelled to inflict pain and suffering on others.

I'm lost in thought about the suspects and investigation when the door to the bakery opens again. I glance up eagerly, expecting to see Beth. But it's Makai.

I glance at Allegra to see her just as surprised as me. She had been the one to tell me we would never see Makai in the bakery given his dedication to fitness. His smile is big enough to show his teeth as he makes his way over to me.

"Good morning, Taylor. Sorry, I saw you through the window," he says by way of greeting.

I return his smile. "Morning, Makai. That's okay, I'm meeting someone for coffee," I respond, and something enters his eyes that I can't identify before disappearing again.

"I won't keep you then. I just knew you were interested in the kickboxing nights, and we have one this evening. I wanted to make sure you didn't miss it," he says.

I nod appreciatively. "Thank you. I'll definitely try to make it."

"Great, hope to see you there." He gives me another warm smile before turning to leave.

After he disappears out the door again, Allegra hurries over to me carrying the coffee pot, making a show of refilling my cup.

"What the hell was that?" she whispers, and I stare at her wide-eyed.

"I have no idea. I thought you said he would never come in here?" I whisper back.

She laughs. "Ummm, you will notice he didn't get anything from me. He just wanted to speak to you. Looks like you have yet another fan," she says with a wide grin.

I roll my eyes. "Don't be silly, there is absolutely nothing special about me at all," I say, trying to resist the urge to fold my arms across my chest. I'm probably too old to pout, and the brand on my arm would hurt like a bitch if I did.

She scoffs at me. "Excuse me, are you one of those girls who can't see how fucking stunning you are?"

I gape at her, but she ignores my astounded look and says, "When you get tired of all the boys chasing after you, maybe come over to the dark side... we have cookies," she says with a wink, turning to walk back to the counter as Jonah comes in.

My heart races slightly at her offhand comment, but I quickly dismiss it, shaking my head. As much as I appreciate the distraction, my mind drifts back to the investigation. Each encounter, every piece of information, feels like a small step closer to understanding the truth behind this mystery that I still don't have a clear picture of.

Jonah gives me a nod as he heads back out of the bakery with his coffee, but doesn't stop to talk. Obviously conscious of Allegra's interruption the last time he tried.

Beth still hasn't shown up, and a pang of worry starts to set in. I glance at my phone, checking the time with a frown. It's already 9:45am, past the time we agreed to meet. She didn't seem the type to simply not show up.

I decide to wait a little longer in case she is just running late. I continue to watch the people outside through the window of the bakery, sipping my coffee. Twenty minutes later, Allegra comes back over to my table, offering another top-up, but I decline with a frown.

She shrugs when she notices my look. "As I said, don't get attached. They always disappear."

My frown deepens as I decide to take the opening she gave me. "Do they?" I ask.

She glances back at me as she gets back to work. "'Do they what?" she asks.

"Disappear? Are there a lot of tourists that simply go missing? Is that a thing here?" I ask.

She laughs, but there is a tension in her tone that wasn't there before. "I mean they decide to leave early or forget they have to check out before they commit. It's why you can only trust the locals," she responds.

Her words are turning over in my mind when a notification comes through on my phone. For a moment, I think that maybe it's Beth, before I remember she doesn't have my number.

PSYCHO MASKED STALKERS

> Do we need to write you a blog post, little shadow? Do we need to tell you how her blood was as red as her hair?

My breath catches and emotions I didn't expect well up inside me as I read the message for a second time. It's one thing knowing that it's happening with vague details, it's another having met a victim before they die. There is no escaping what they meant, but a part of me is glad that they spared me the details this time.

Beth is dead.

Taking a deep breath I type out a message and hit send.

> How? Why? She wasn't homeless. She was a city girl like me. Was it Rye before we stopped him?

PSYCHO MASKED STALKERS

You know it wasn't. Think about it, darling girl, what would cause the change?

I think about it for a moment, running the theories through my mind.

> He's accelerating. Losing control of his urges. His ideal target wasn't available and he needed to satisfy a need.

PSYCHO MASKED STALKERS

It's a good theory.

Really? That's all they are going to give me? I can't even curse out one of them specifically, because they are both as frustratingly vague as each other.

I sigh deeply, feeling the weight of exhaustion settling in as I close my eyes. After a moment I open them again and pull up a contact on my phone and hit dial. After a couple of rings, the call is answered.

"Hey munchkin, everything okay?" The familiar voice of Papa on the other end soothes me momentarily.

"Yeah," I reply, my voice soft with emotion. "Just..." I pause, not sure what to say while I'm sitting in the bakery and not at the house. But I needed to hear the sound of home suddenly.

"Just what, honey? Are you okay?" my mom's voice comes over the line.

I sigh, just hearing her voice has warmth spreading through me. "Hey mom, I'm okay. I just met a tourist the other day here and now she's gone." I know that they will understand what I mean with the way I said it.

"Oh, honey," my mom says softly. "I'm so sorry. It's always hard to lose someone while on a case."

"Are you safe?" Dad's voice cuts in, concern evident.

My mind momentarily flashes to the several times I have absolutely not been safe. "Yeah, I'm safe," I reassure him, lowering my voice and trying to keep it steady.

I can hear one of them hum on the other end of the line which I know means they either don't believe me or they are thinking about something. *Which, let's face it, they shouldn't believe me, I almost let another killer drown me last night. But the sex was too fucking good.*

"Go to the local police there," Dad finally says, shocking me from my one way thought train to depravity.

Frowning, I look at the screen of my phone, yep it is my parents I'm talking to. "I'm sorry, have you been taken over by pod people?" I jokingly ask and their laughter has a smile spreading across my face.

"Think about it, if you go to the local police about someone you have physically met there and know wouldn't have just disappeared they will need to look into it. If they don't, then you will know they are involved," Dad explains, his reasoning does make sense. Especially because the sheriff and deputy are on my list of suspects. It's the first time I've had the opportunity to press for action without it being obvious I'm here investigating.

I hear Papa chuckle as though he's thinking about something specific. "And if they *are* involved and you ask them to look into it, they might mess up by trying to get rid of her. You have your knife, right munchkin?"

"Yes," I respond, rolling my eyes. "Okay, I'll do what you suggested and see what happens."

"Make sure you stay safe, no unnecessary risks," Dad commands and I choose to ignore the last part.

"Hey honey, have you spoken to Seanna recently?" Mom asks and I frown, they never ask that, she speaks to them as regularly as I do.

"Yeah, about two days ago like normal. Is something wrong?" My heart thuds in my chest at the thought.

Mom quickly reassures me, "No, well, not as far as we know. She just seemed a bit stressed or off when we spoke to her last. Maybe give her a call today?"

"Okay, I will," I promise, the concern for my sister now mingling with everything else I'm dealing with.

After promising again to be safe and telling them I love them, we say goodbye and end the call. I take a deep breath, trying to focus on my next steps. I need to get to the bottom of this, and quickly.

Chapter 35

Hydessa

Waving goodbye to Allegra, I start walking towards the police station, determined to follow Dad's advice. If there's any chance that the Sheriff or Deputy are involved or complicit, I need to know, and this is the best way to find out.

The beachfront is now buzzing with activity, tourists are everywhere as I make my way through them toward my destination. It doesn't take long until I'm pushing open the front door to the station. It's a small building, just big enough for the two of them. They don't even seem to have anyone looking after the front desk.

I'm surprised when I see the Sheriff inside a glass walled meeting room having what looks like a tense conversation with Chester. While the Sheriff looks calm and composed, Chester appears frustrated and uses his hands in an exaggerated way to convey whatever he's trying to say. Whatever it is, the glass walls are keeping their conversation private and I have to assume there is some sort of soundproofing in that room for interview purposes.

Eli looks up, scowling from his desk close by. Perhaps he is expecting trouble this morning, but the snarl vanishes from his face when he sees that it's me standing at the counter.

Without hesitation, he gets up and starts moving toward me. "Hey, Taylor," he greets, but his steps are interrupted when Chester starts storming out of the station with angry steps and his face twisted in rage. But just like Eli, the look disappears when he sees me standing there. I smile in greeting at all of them.

"I'd say good morning, but it's almost lunch already," Chester says. "And I didn't see you at the bakery earlier, sooo... have a late night?"

I laugh. The police station is not going to be where I admit that, yes, I had a late night killing a man who preyed on innocent women. "Something like that," I say in response.

"Then maybe I should take you to lunch," he suggests.

"Uh, I actually came to talk to the Sheriff," I say, glancing over at Sheriff Brooks, who is now observing us.

"Well, don't let me keep you," Chester says with a wink, but there's a seriousness behind his eyes. "Maybe later?"

"Maybe," I reply noncommittally, my attention shifting to the man I need to see.

He gives Chester a narrow-eyed look. "Chester, didn't you need to go sort those permits? Wasn't that what you were just complaining about?" he says pointedly, making Chester grind his teeth in frustration..

Chester sighs, clearly annoyed. "Yeah, yeah, I'm going," he mutters, giving me a quick nod before heading out of the station.

Eli watches Chester leave, then turns back to me. "What brings you in today, Taylor?"

"I need to report a missing person," I say, my tone serious.

Sheriff Brooks gestures for me to follow him to his office. "Let's talk in here," he says.

Once we're inside, he leaves the door open behind us, and I know Eli is listening in as he returns to his desk. "Who's missing?" he asks, getting straight to the point.

"A tourist I met a couple of days ago. Her name is Beth," I explain. "We were supposed to meet this morning, but she never showed up, and I haven't heard from her since."

The Sheriff listens attentively, jotting down notes. "When was the last time you saw her?"

"Yesterday, when we made plans to meet for coffee," I reply. "She seemed fine, excited even."

He nods. "Did she mention any plans? Anyone she was going to meet?"

"No, she didn't," I say, shaking my head. "She was taking one of the art classes but nothing else. She said she's met a lot of people since arriving here and she did hint at some issues back in the city she was trying to escape from. She was renting a place through Maddie."

Sheriff Brooks leans back in his chair, contemplating. "We'll look into it. But you know, sometimes tourists get caught up in the excitement and lose track of time. She might just show up later."

I appreciate his attempt to reassure me, but I already know differently. "I hope you're right."

"We will need to wait another day but I'll have Eli put out an alert as soon as he can and keep an eye out for her," he says, standing up. "In the meantime, if you hear anything, let us know."

"Of course," I say, getting up to leave. "Thank you, Sheriff."

At least I will be able to have Uncle Max see if they do create the missing person report. If they do, then it will eliminate them from my suspects at least, and it will have more people looking into it.

Sheriff Brooks walks me out of the station, his expression softening slightly as he tries to reassure me. "I'm sure she's just fine," he says. "Tourists here can be unpredictable. We'll find her."

"Thanks, Sheriff," I reply, trying to sound hopeful.

As we reach the front of the station, Eli calls out a goodbye from his desk. "Take care, Taylor."

"You too, Eli," I respond, waving back at him.

Sheriff Brooks gives me a final nod at the door. "If you need anything else, don't hesitate to come by."

"Will do," I say before stepping out into the bright midday sun. The bustle of the beachfront and the throngs of tourists suddenly feel overwhelming. The noise and activity are too much today.

Deciding to head back to the house, I make my way through the crowded street, my mind racing. When I finally reach the house, I let out a sigh of relief as I step inside. I feel so frustrated with everything today, my mind and body on edge.

I head to the kitchen, brewing myself a strong cup of coffee. As I sip it, I think about my next steps as I head toward the office. I decide to give Seanna a call, maybe hearing her voice will help and then I can be assured that at least she is okay.

I plop down in my chair, the warmth of the coffee soothing my frayed nerves. I dial Seanna's number and wait for her to pick up, tapping my fingers on the desk in a rhythmic pattern. The phone rings a few times before I hear the click on the line.

"If I hide..." I whisper into the phone.

"Then I'll seek..." comes her instant reply.

Her sigh down the line is an echo to mine, maybe we both needed to hear from each other today.

"You okay?" I ask, concerned.

"I was about to ask you the same thing," she responds, giving what can only be a self deprecating laugh. But she doesn't answer the question, and neither do I. We really are a matching pair after all.

We sit in silence for a moment, the weight of our mutual concern hanging in the air. Finally, Seanna speaks.

"Please make sure you're being careful, look after yourself first. What you're doing there comes second remember."

Her words have my concern rising. She has always been the one to throw herself headlong into an investigation. She isn't one to tell me to be careful, she's the one who tells me to seek adventure. Just as I go to press, try to make her tell me what is going on, she clears her throat.

"I'm sorry, I have to go, I love you," she says softly. We say a brief goodbye before the line goes dead.

I take a deep breath, trying to shake off the unease. Seanna is as capable as I am, and we have our own code words if we need to raise an alarm. She didn't say any of them. Maybe she's just as stressed with her investigation as I am with mine.

Pushing the thoughts away since it's not something I can solve right away, I place my phone on the desk and look over at the wall filled with my notes and the photographs of the victims. The list at the center catches my attention, twelve names, though I know I can cross at least one off the list now.

Now that I know that Cain and Abel aren't the ones killing the tourists, I wonder if the questions I asked them previously related to them, or the case I'm investigating. Picking up the phone I bring the messages up again. One of them stands out in particular, so I type a new message and press send.

> You said there was a catalyst in our messages, were you talking about you two, or the serial killer?

As usual, I only have to wait a moment before a response comes through.

PSYCHO MASKED STALKERS

> Both would be accurate. But unlike the others, ours didn't specifically cause us to kill. There were events that set this in motion, but it's our DNA that predetermined the darkness inside us.

> Are we playing twenty questions again, little shadow? You know a question comes with a price.

I huff at the reminder, I should have known I wouldn't get the information for free. But at this point, maybe any price they offer will be worth it for answers.

> I'll pay it.

PSYCHO MASKED STALKERS

> Are you sure, darling girl? Remember, it won't always be as simple as a question.

I hesitate for a moment, my heart speeding up. I would bet by the wording that it's Cain on the other end of the phone. Is Abel there too? Could they potentially ask for something I wasn't able to give? Was I agreeing to something I potentially wouldn't agree to normally?

I guess that's their whole point. They want me to embrace a part of myself that until now I locked away inside.

They already claim that I'm theirs, I even have what I can only assume is their brand burned into my arm. How much fucking deeper could I possible get into their twisted web? Would they even let me return home once I have this solved? Do I want them to?

> I'm sure.

PSYCHO MASKED STALKERS

> Good girl. That mark on your arm needs caring for. Clean it and leave it uncovered. There are supplies in the bathroom.

I huff in annoyance. That isn't what I thought they would respond with and it means taking the time to do what they requested, instead of being able to ask more questions. But I know if I don't, they won't keep playing either. It's a test again, to see if I will pay the price as asked.

> Yes, sir.

PSYCHO MASKED STALKERS

> Don't play that game, Hydessa. Or that brand on your arm will be the least of your issues.

I shake my head, frustrated by Cain's cryptic warnings and commands. Cleaning and tending to the branded mark on my arm becomes my immediate task, though my mind churns with questions and uncertainties.

As I follow Cain's instructions begrudgingly, the feeling of being watched prickles at my skin again. I've combed this place for cameras a hundred times by now, how can they see me? It's like I can feel them watching at all times. Waiting.

Once the brand is cleaned I return to the office, leaving my shirt off so that the wound is left uncovered. I glance at my phone, wanting desperately to ask more details about the men beneath the masks. But as much as I want to know more about them, I need to find the serial killer first.

> Why is the killer targeting tourists?

PSYCHO MASKED STALKERS

> The tourist part isn't as important as the homeless part, or more specifically having no one who will care that they disappear. No one to walk into the police station and lodge missing persons reports…

My heart races at their reference to me doing exactly that this morning.

> You know why I did it though, right?

PSYCHO MASKED STALKERS

> We know.

> Why were you so resistant to embracing a part of who you are?

Sadness threatens to overwhelm me as I think about the answer to their question. I had hoped for simple questions, simple tasks, but I should have heeded their warning. Nothing about the answer they are asking for is simple. But perhaps I can make my answer simple.

> Embracing it doesn't always end well. Not everyone is able to handle the darkness inside me, they haven't in the past. Why risk it when I know how it will inevitably end?

PSYCHO MASKED STALKERS

> Why not risk it for the chance of happiness? For the chance of the love you're afraid you will never find?

Because I've seen what embracing it does. It's not about risking happiness; it's about avoiding the pain it causes.

PSYCHO MASKED STALKERS

But what if that pain is just the start of something beautiful? A love greater than you've ever known, a connection deeper than any other?

That kind of love is a fairytale. My parents were lucky to have found it. But owning and embracing my darkness just led to pain.

PSYCHO MASKED STALKERS

Then you've seen only part of the story. Darkness can lead to light, pain can lead to healing. It's all about balance, little shadow.

I don't know if I believe in that balance anymore. It feels like darkness just consumes everything.

PSYCHO MASKED STALKERS

Then maybe it's time to change your perspective. Look beyond what you've seen and imagine what could be.

I huff out a breath. When did this turn into a debate about my life?

Easier said than done.

PSYCHO MASKED STALKERS

True, but sometimes the hardest paths lead to the greatest rewards. You've already embarked on a journey; why stop now?

I sigh heavily. They already asked this but in a different way, avoiding it this time isn't an option.

> Because I'm afraid of where it might lead.

PSYCHO MASKED STALKERS

> Fear is natural. It keeps us safe, but it also holds us back. Only you can decide if the risk is worth the reward.

> I wish it were that simple.

PSYCHO MASKED STALKERS

> Life is rarely simple, Hydessa. But the choices we make define who we are. Embrace your darkness or fight against it—it's your choice, but it won't simply disappear. And you know which side of that choice we will be on.

> Did I not make that choice with what happened last night?

PSYCHO MASKED STALKERS

> Think of it like a fork in the road. You want to think that you can turn back and take the other road. That not all choices are permanent unless you let it be.

Frustration fills me momentarily, my fingers clenching around the phone until I'm surprised the screen doesn't crack. Some choices are definitely permanent. Death is absolutely permanent. Losing my best friend as a child, also permanent.

Taking deep breaths, I try not to let that frustration out as I type my response.

> Really? Because this brand on my arm feels aw-fully fucking permanent.

Oops.

PSYCHO MASKED STALKERS

> Maybe you should have asked if that step would have been taken if you hadn't taken the one in the cave. If you hadn't taken many of the steps you have taken since stepping foot on this island. Each step you took was a choice, including coming here.

> I've gotten the impression that even if I had chosen not to come here, you would have come after me.

PSYCHO MASKED STALKERS

> And now you're learning, little shadow. Everyone gets to make their own choices in life, and you can't control them all. You chose to stop this serial killer, you chose to kill in that cave, you chose to start this game with us.

> And we chose to never let you go.

Chapter 36

Hydessa

I set the phone aside after their last message, the questions turned into a rabbit hole that I wasn't sure I was prepared for the reality of. Frustration and annoyance is like a thunderstorm inside me. It builds and builds until reaching a point that I can't concentrate on the investigation at all.

I need to vent, I need to find an outlet that isn't being fucked by masked strangers. I need to hit something.

Glancing out the window I can see that the sun is starting to set, the sky turning shades of orange and pink in the distance. I'm not sure what time Makai said the kickboxing was on at the gym, but even if it's over I should still be able to use the equipment to expel some of this anxious energy.

Quickly changing into my gym clothes, I glance at the brand on my arm. My tank leaves my arm bare, and I can't wrap it again or it will put me at risk for infection when I sweat while I'm working out. I pull out the anti-bacterial cream that was left in the bathroom cabinet for me, applying it to the little mask outlines marked into my skin.

Grabbing my jacket, I head out of the house, the door slamming behind me. I walk quickly down the street toward the beachfront, watching the sun creep toward the horizon as I make my way toward the gym.

The beat of the music and the smell of sweat hits me as I push through the door. I can already see Makai toward the back, talking with Telvin. I make my way toward them, and Makai spots me as I approach, giving me a wide grin.

Telvin turns in my direction to see what has caught his attention. He gives me a small, tentative smile, dipping his head before he turns away and proceeds through an archway, his fingers tapping together nervously.

Makai, on the other hand, approaches me with practiced ease. "You made it," he says. "I was worried you weren't coming. We're about to start."

I laugh in response. "Well, you didn't actually tell me what time to be here," I say. He pauses, frowning as he looks me over.

"Didn't I? Sorry, I must have been distracted," he confesses before his face clears and he motions toward the archway Telvin just disappeared through. Following after him, I'm surprised to see that on the other side of the archway there is a whole boxing and martial arts training center.

The sight of the space immediately lifts my spirits. The sound of gloves hitting bags, the smell of equipment and sweat—it all feels invigorating. I spot Telvin on the far side, already wrapping his hands. There must be some rule against face shots, because his glasses are still on. He looks up briefly and gives me another small smile before returning to his task.

"This place is incredible," I say to Makai, genuinely impressed.

"Yeah, it's a bit of a hidden gem," he replies with a grin before he turns and calls out, "Anyone taking part in kickboxing, prepare and head to the mats!"

He faces me, and gestures to the mats. "Have you done much kickboxing before? Do you know how it all works?"

"Yeah, I have," I reply confidently.

"Great," he says, handing me some tape. "Wrap your hands and let's get going."

Once I've got the tape just how I like it, we make our way toward where Telvin and several other men are waiting. Telvin narrows his eyes, tilting his head as I approach.

"We have no woman here for you to spar with," Telvin says when we stop near him.

I frown, glancing around and seeing that he's right. There are several men I don't know, along with Eli, and surprisingly, Ty is also there.

"I'll spar with her," Makai says with a smile.

Ty laughs. "The poor girl wouldn't survive your muscles. I'll do it."

Telvin shakes his head with a sigh. "I'm the closest to her build, and besides, it would be irresponsible of me as the trainer to risk her getting hurt by any of you," he says softly, but his voice still holds enough weight that it has the others shrugging and starting to pair off instead of arguing. He looks at me. "We will do some pad work so I can see where your strengths are then go from there."

I nod, feeling a mixture of relief and excitement. Telvin hands me a pair of lightweight gloves while he grabs some focus mitts, and we move to an empty spot on the mats. He demonstrates a series of combinations, and I follow his lead, focusing on the rhythm and precision of each strike.

"Good, keep your guard up," Telvin instructs. "And remember to breathe."

I nod, adjusting my stance and throwing a few more punches. The repetition is soothing, and I find myself slipping into a comfortable rhythm. Telvin occasionally stops to correct my form or give me pointers, but overall, he seems pleased with my performance.

"Not bad, not bad at all," he says with a slight smile. "But let's see how you handle some real pressure."

Telvin starts to call out more complex combinations, pushing me to move faster, hit harder. He starts striking my arms and legs lightly with the mitts at random times between strikes when I miss.

"Is that all you've got?" he taunts quietly as I miss another strike. "I thought you said you've done this before."

I grit my teeth, trying to channel my frustration into my punches, but his words start to get under my skin. He knows exactly what he's doing, and it's working.

"Come on, you can do better than that," Telvin challenges. "Maybe you should stick to something less intense, like *yoga*."

I can feel myself growing hot, the need to prove myself pushing me harder. I throw a punch with more force than I have skill to back up and my form slips.. Telvin catches the mistake immediately, tapping my arm harder in response. It just happens to be the same arm as the brand and it does nothing but remind me of the reason I came out here in the first place.

"Not bad, but you hit like a tourist," Telvin says, his lips curling into the hint of a smirk.

I narrow my eyes but keep my focus. "I'm just warming up," I retort.

"Maybe, but if you keep hesitating like that, you'll never land a hit in a real fight," he shrugs, not taking me seriously.

Anger bubbles up inside me like boiling water, but I channel it into my punches. "I'm not hesitating," I snap back, aiming a particularly hard punch at the mitt.

"Sure, sure," he says, sidestepping. "I've seen more aggressive sparring from beach bums."

I aim a kick at him, but he grabs my leg and sweeps the other from under me in a swift move I didn't see coming. I land heavily on the mat, my breath escaping me in a rush. Before I can move, he's kneeling beside me, a focus mitt held under my chin.

"Lesson for the day," Telvin says gently, looking down at me. "Control your emotions. Anger makes you sloppy."

I lay there for a moment, trying to catch my breath. The mat is cool against my back, a stark contrast to the heat burning through my chest. He's right, of course. I let him get to me, and I paid for it.

I'm letting everything get to me lately. It's causing my mind to be too distracted and making it impossible to look at the investigation objectively.

"Got it," I finally manage, pushing myself up.

Telvin offers me a hand, and I take it, pulling myself to my feet. "Good," he says. "Now, let's try that again, and this time, keep your cool."

I nod, determined to prove myself not just to him, but to me too. We go through the motions again, and this time, I focus on staying calm and controlled. I match my breaths with my punches, settling into a practiced rhythm. Telvin pushes me hard, but I don't let his comments get to me again.

After a particularly grueling round, he steps back and nods. "Better. Much better."

"Thanks," I say, wiping sweat from my brow. I feel proud of the way I was able to recover and the turmoil in my mind has actually seemed to calm a bit.

"Remember," Telvin says, "it's not just about strength or speed. It's about control. You could potentially win a fight with the strongest man, if you keep your cool and your control in the heat of a fight.

You've got the basics down. Now, work on keeping your head in the game."

"I will," I promise, feeling a renewed sense of determination.

Makai walks over, grinning. "How'd it go?"

"Pretty good," I say, feeling exhausted but satisfied. "Thanks for the push, both of you."

"Anytime," Makai replies. "You did great."

Telvin nods in agreement, stepping further away now that the training is over. "Keep coming to the sessions. You've got potential," he says before turning to walk away.

As I gather my keys and phone, Eli walks over, giving me an approving nod. "Nice work out there," he says. "You've got a good punch."

"Thanks," I reply, still catching my breath.

Eli looks around the gym, then back at me. "It's late. Want me to walk you home?"

I appreciate the offer, but I shake my head. "Thanks, Eli, but I'll be fine. I could use the walk to clear my head."

He nods, though I can see a hint of concern in his eyes. "Alright, but be careful."

I wave goodbye to Eli and the others as I walk out. The cool night air is a refreshing change from the heat of the gym, and I take a deep breath, savoring the freshness. The sky is dark, with only a few stars visible, and the street is quiet, adding a sense of calm to the night.

Starting the walk back to the house, my mind can't help but replay the training session, feeling good about all of my work. Telvin's words about control echo in my head.

I'm almost back to the house when something catches my attention.

Frowning, I look toward the house I'm passing. The blinds are open slightly, just enough to see inside. My heart skips a beat as I notice what looks like someone tied to a table, blood running in rivulets down pale skin. A knife is held above the bare chest, glinting in the dim light.

Adrenaline shoots through me, my heart racing inside my chest.

Sneaking quickly toward the window, I try to get a better look at what's going on inside, but the angle is wrong, and I can't see much more detail. I start creeping further around the house, trying to find a better vantage point. Just as I'm passing a door, a piercing scream shatters the silence. I decide not to wait for more detail and throw the door open, rushing forward.

I'm going to catch the killer red handed this time.

But the next sound has me stumbling over my own feet as the scene in front of me unfolds. It's not the killer in action at all, unless you consider what the man is doing to that woman's pussy murder as she screams in ecstasy. A deep moan echoes around me and my mouth drops open.

Lily, the woman who serves me seafood lunches and ice cold lemonade, is strapped to a St Andrews cross, legs spread, and shallow cuts adorn her chest. Kneeling between said legs is the perfect face of the chef at the cafe where she works. I see the moment his tongue sticks out, pushing into her and her body arches in ecstasy.

I'm so caught up with what I'm witnessing that I don't even realize there are more people in the room.

Another sound comes from behind me, drawing my attention in that direction. I regret it immediately, my hands coming up to cover my eyes when they connect with a sweet old man who is watching Lily and her chef as he pounds into none other than the woman I buy my groceries from.

Oh my god, I'm never going to be able to look at old lady Gladys the same. And like fuck am I waving at that old man ever again.

Something touches my arm and I startle almost violently, my hand striking out on instinct. The person side steps me, holding his hands up in a placating gesture. His muscular and tattooed bare chest is on display and his jeans are partially open, giving a clear view of the trail of hair leading down into them.

His light brown hair is disheveled and falling slightly into his green eyes. The smile he flashes is nothing but white teeth and charm. "How about we step out and give them some privacy?" he suggests, motioning toward the door I just barged through.

I turn in a daze and walk straight back out of the house as he follows, closing the door behind him. I take a moment, trying to process what I just witnessed. The scene was startling and entirely unexpected to say the least. It seems that Cain and Abel aren't the only ones with knife and blood kinks in this town.

As I turn, frowning, I meet his emerald green gaze again.

"I guess I should formally introduce myself. I'm Lachlan Hughes. Nice to finally meet you, Taylor," he says, his voice carrying a hint of amusement. "Didn't expect you to barge in like that. I take it you weren't expecting the scene you walked in on?"

I finally find my voice, still reeling from what I saw. "No, I... I definitely wasn't." My words come out in a rush, my cheeks burning with embarrassment. "I thought... I thought I was interrupting something much worse."

Lachlan chuckles softly, his green eyes studying me. "Well, I suppose that depends on your perspective. I can see why you might have thought something bad was happening, but I can assure you everything in there is consensual."

I shake my head, trying to clear the image from my mind. There is no doubt in my mind that they were all consenting adults. "I should have just kept walking. I... I didn't mean to intrude like that."

He shrugs casually. "Don't worry about it. These things happen. I have an open door policy if you ever get curious." There's a casualness to his demeanor that contrasts sharply with my own embarrassment.

I glance at him, noticing the tattoos on his arms and the easy confidence in his stance. "You seem... unfazed by all this," I manage to say. "H-how often exactly do 'these things happen'?"

Lachlan laughs as he meets my gaze with a wry smile. "Pretty often. I've seen my fair share of surprises living here. Nothing much fazes me anymore."

"Right," I respond, drawing the word out, before shaking my head and turning to leave.

As I'm walking away, Lachlan calls out, his voice trailing after me, "I'd ask you to join us, since I have no partner tonight, but... you know..."

I stop abruptly and turn sharply to look back at him, but Lachlan has already retreated inside, closing the door behind him. This has got to be some sort of alternate reality.

Chapter 37

Hydessa

I shouldn't be surprised that after the memory that came to me the previous night, my dreams are now filled with more memories of that time.

***

17 years ago

Each night I hear Link whimper from his nightmares where he is sleeping in the guest room. And each night I sneak in there to hold him to help him sleep like my parents do for me. He may think he deosn't have anyone, but I meant it when I said I will be there for him.

"Shh, it's okay, Link," I say quietly, my voice barely above a whisper. I settle beside him, the mattress barely moving or making a sound under my small weight. He stirs, as though sensing me there, and I reach out to gently stroke his hair, mirroring what my mom does for me.

The moonlight is shining into the room, casting shadows across Link's face. He relaxes under my touch, his breathing slows as the last of his nightmares fade away. I don't want to leave and have his nightmares return like a monster under the bed, so I stay there, watching over him while he sleeps, trying to protect him from something I can't see. My hand finds his in the dark and he clutches at it like a lifeline.

The nights are hard for him, but we always find something to keep us busy during the day. When I'm lucky I can make him smile, and he knows just how to make me giggle.

It's been two weeks since he came to stay with us and while I always loved having my twin, I find a different kind of comfort with Link. We are behind the house, playing close to the forest. But we can still hear the sound of my parents' music in the distance. We aren't allowed to go into the forest, so we play as close as we can. Seanna is at a friend's house again. She doesn't like Link, so I wasn't upset when she left me behind.

"Your parents like strange songs," he says.

I giggle as I slowly spin around to one of the songs. "Yeah, they do. Some are good, some are weird."

Speeding up, I keep spinning until I'm dizzy and fall down into the grass. He laughs at me, that rare smile making my heart feel like it's full of butterflies. Walking over he looks down at me and then lays down at my side. We stay there in silence for a while, listening to the music, giggling over the music and funny words.

"This one is not a normal song," he says with a laugh as a familiar tune comes on again. They seem to be playing a list on repeat. "What is it even about?"

Listening to it I try to figure out what the lyrics mean. "I think maybe the singer met someone that hurt her?" I suggest with a shrug.

He hums and when I look toward him I can see that the thought has upset him. I'm not stupid, even being little I know that someone hurt him. I can tell he's scared of something when he goes to sleep. The fear in his eyes when he wakes from a nightmare only confirms it.

"I don't like that someone hurt her," he whispers. I know he means himself.

I sit up and look down at him in the grass. "Me either. Maybe we should pretend it's about something different," I suggest and offer him a smile.

He sits up, his lips twitching as though he likes that idea, but then a frown creases his face, his eyes squinting as he thinks about it. "I'm not sure you can change it to something nice with the words she keeps singing."

I tilt my head, listening again. It's a catchy tune but it is sad. "Maybe we can pretend that we are burying treasure. When she says about digging a heart's grave it's like burying all the secrets and everything that makes our hearts happy and sad like it's treasure."

His face lights up then, happy again. I stand, excited as the idea builds inside my mind. He props himself up on his elbows and watches me with a smirk as I do a spin to the song.

"My mom says that we all have shadows and darkness inside us. She says my dad's are her partners in shadows and darkness. One day I hope I'll find the same, someone who will look after my heart's grave. The treasure of everything I love and the things that make me sad too."

His face is serious again when he stands up. "I could be your partner," he says simply. I giggle but he reaches out and grabs my hand. "I mean it, Dessa."

I shake my head. "We aren't old enough, silly. Mom says we won't know who our partner is until we're old."

He shakes his own head in response. "But I already know."

And so do I, but my mom is right, we aren't supposed to know yet.

He huffs, his frown deepening. "I'll prove it. All those stories in movies say we should have a bond. I watched one where they said a blood bond is the strongest of them all."

I screw my face up. "We aren't vampires."

Giggling he shakes his head. "We don't drink it. I think they called it an oath. It's like a promise."

Understanding what he means I bounce on my feet. "Yes! That's exactly what we can do. I even have my pocket knife."

Reaching down, I pull it from my shoe. It's little but it has a knife in it.

"Why do you have that with you?" he asks with a laugh.

"My dad always tells me to be prepared," I smile in response as I flick the knife out. Then I pull a face at the thought of it cutting me. "Ummmm, I think you need to cut me, I can't cut myself."

Link rolls his eyes, taking the pocket knife from me. I hold out my hand, feeling a mix of excitement and trepidation. "Should it be a heart? Like the song?" I ask. He nods quickly, and when he starts to press the knife to my skin, I whimper and look away.

It hurts a little, but I concentrate on the feeling of Link holding my hand. Before I realize it, he says he's done. I blow out a breath and look down at the mark. It's not a huge heart and it's mostly shallow, but blood stains the outside.

"Your turn," I say as I take the knife back. "Which hand?"

He shakes his head and pulls on the neck of his shirt. "It's meant to be a heart, right? Then put it over my heart."

I stare at him wide-eyed, but he isn't changing his mind. I'm glad his shirt is black and my mom won't see the blood. Leaning closer, I use the point of the knife to cut the shape of a heart into his skin. He makes a noise a few times, but he doesn't cry either. When I'm done, there's blood trailing down his skin. I'm strangely proud of the heart I made.

He grabs my hand where he cut it and puts it against his.

"You dug my heart's grave," he said, eyes wide and solemn, locked on mine as if sharing a profound secret. "And now you're the keeper of its secrets, my partner in shadows and darkness."

"Forever," I whisper, and he nods, a small smile tugging at the corner of his lips that feels like a promise too.

Chapter 38

Hydessa

Today is the day.

The day the carnival opens and all of the rides, lights, foods, and games will be on display. Since the moment I saw the flyer in the bakery the day I arrived, I've felt an undercurrent of energy every time it's mentioned.

It has absolutely nothing to do with Cain fucking me in the house of mirrors.

But first, I needed to spend the day working on the investigation. I feel like I'm getting somewhere now.

When I finally dragged myself from the bed, I decided that I was going to go back to basics. I will clear everything from the drawing board and start with a clean slate. There are no masked stalkers, no twin with her own issues, no weird kinky sex clubs in random houses down the street.

I shudder at the memory. *Honestly, this island should really come with a warning label.*

All of the cuts and bruises on my body are healing nicely. Even the brand has started to heal as well, though I know it's a lot more permanent than the other marks. I trace the edges of it lightly with my fingertips, feeling the raised skin. It reminds me that I need to call and cancel the tattoo appointment with Ty, though somehow I doubt that Seanna and I will be able to still get away with changing places now that I've been marked like this.

Dressing in casual leggings and a loose shirt, I make myself a strong coffee, grab some of the cherry cookies I never ended up throwing out and proceed to the office. Putting my treats on the desk I turn to look at the investigation wall. It's a mess of notes, photographs and printouts.

Taking a deep breath, I proceed to take everything down.

The empty wall feels both daunting and liberating. I sit down with my coffee, taking a long sip as I let the caffeine fuel my resolve. I pull out my notebook and start from scratch, jotting down everything I know, everything I've learned, and the questions that still linger.

I need to focus on the facts, to strip away the distractions and the noise. I start with the basics: the victims, the locations, the timelines. Slowly, methodically, I begin to piece together a clearer picture, looking for connections I might have missed before.

Hours pass and before I know it, the sun starts to set. My third coffee is long gone, and the rest of the cookies have been reduced to crumbs. Remnants of a sandwich sit on a plate on the desk, but I've made progress. The wall is starting to take shape again, this time more organized, more coherent.

The puzzle is being filled in, and there's just a few more pieces to go before the picture is clear in front of me.

As I step back to review my work, a sense of accomplishment washes over me. I'm far from done, but I feel like I'm on the right track. And for the first time in days, I feel a glimmer of hope that I might actually crack this case.

Checking the time, I realize the carnival is already well underway and I missed the grand opening. I think after working all day I deserve a night out to just enjoy myself.

I quickly clean up, changing into a flowy black skirt and a bright blue sleeveless top. After locking the house, I walk down the darkened street toward the beachfront.

As I approach the carnival, the atmosphere envelops me. The air is filled with the smell of popcorn and cotton candy, the sounds of laughter, and the distant roar of rides. The bright lights reflect off the ocean, creating a magical scene.

Wandering through the array of people and flurry of excitement, I take in the night and all it has to offer. Children run past me squealing in excitement and I find myself smiling, the stress of the investigation momentarily forgotten.

As I walk, I notice familiar faces in the crowd. Near the house of mirrors, I pause, feeling a rush of memories from my encounter with Cain. Shaking my head, I push the thoughts aside and move on. This is a night for fun, for escaping the heaviness of my current reality.

I see Maddie and Allegra walking toward me, both of them grinning and waving enthusiastically.

"Hey, you made it!" Maddie calls out as they reach me.

"Of course," I reply, smiling. "Wouldn't miss it for the world."

We spend the next hour wandering the carnival together, laughing and enjoying the various attractions. And it's the first time in years, besides the moments with Cain and Abel, that I have felt truly alive in my own skin. I have my own friends and I'm actually enjoying my life.

At one point, I see Dr Lachlan Hughes in the distance and he grins and waves at me. My face flames at the memory of what I saw the previous night so I turn away from him quickly. When I do, I'm met with the curious faces of Allegra and Maddie.

"Ummm, I may have stumbled across a secret kink party last night," I confess to them.

They both laugh so hard that tears start streaming down their faces and my cheeks are on fire.

"Oh, babe, that is not secret at all. Lachlan has been the host since he arrived on the island, we're a bunch of kinky fuckers here," Maddie says between giggles.

"I believe we did try to tell you, this island is fucking twisted. Well, the locals are anyway. Now I'm sad I missed it last night, I could have given you a show," Allegra points out with a smile.

I stare at them both wide eyed. *Jesus fucking Christ, is everyone here as dark and twisted as I am on the inside?*

"Are you about to tell me you kill people in your spare time?" I jokingly say, and then almost stumble with the look they give each other. "Are you fucking kidding me?"

"Ummm, we kinda thought that was why you moved here to be honest. I mean you and your family aren't exactly unknown in certain circles of our community. But when you introduced yourself as Taylor, we figured you just wanted to hide for a bit, no pun intended," Maddie says with a grimace as we edge away from the crowds and toward a quieter area of the carnival.

My heart is officially racing in my chest. *They have known who I am since the start?* "Does everyone know?" I ask in astonishment.

They glance at each other again and I'm already dreading the answer. "Well, no, only some of us. And also just to clarify, Maddie hasn't killed anyone at all, her hands are totally clean, well murder clean anyway," Allegra responds quickly.

I slump against a wall at the edge of the carnival. Does this mean my investigation is tainted? Does the serial killer already know who I am? No, I think Cain and Abel would have told me if my cover was completely blown, right?

"But you have?" I ask Allegra, and a look crosses her face. I see it instantly, the darkness lurking beneath the face of the pretty baker.

"Let's call it self defense," she says with a shrug. "My ex-boyfriend chose the wrong woman to try to rape. The fact that I found out I wasn't the first one may have also had something to do with it too."

The revelation hits me like a freight train. Allegra's admission is both shocking and oddly comforting. In a twisted way, knowing that the people I've come to trust and care about have their own dark pasts makes me feel less alone in mine.

"Right, self-defense," I repeat, more to myself than to her. "Tha t's... understandable. Even encouraged in those circumstances."

Allegra nods, her eyes softening as she looks at me. "We all have our skeletons. The island just seems to attract people with... complicated histories."

Maddie steps closer, her usual light-hearted demeanor replaced with a rare seriousness. "We may have our secrets, but we're here for you. Whatever you need, we've got your back."

I feel a warmth spreading through me, despite the chill in the evening air. This island, with all its quirks and secrets, is starting to feel like a place where I can belong and be accepted for who I really am. Hydessa, and not the mask of Taylor that I hide behind.

"Thanks," I say, my voice a little shaky. "I appreciate that. More than you know."

We stand there for a moment, a silent understanding passing between us. The noise and lights of the carnival fade into the background as I process everything.

After a few minutes, Maddie breaks the silence with a grin. "Come on, let's go find something fun to do. Enough heavy stuff for one night."

"Umm, I think I'm going to go for a walk. I have a lot to think about," I say, the weight of my reality pressing down on me. I need to know how many people know who I am, and then I might need to start over on the whole investigation. Maybe Sheriff Brooks will team up with me and we can figure it out together?

They both smile in understanding and give me hugs before returning to the main part of the carnival. As they leave, I take my time to wander alone. It feels like a curtain has parted, and now I'm looking at everyone in a different light. I knew Rye killed innocent people for his own pleasure, but the way the girls talked, the others had reasons or did things that were justified. They know who my family is, and our whole mission is to protect and save innocent lives.

Lost in my thoughts, I wander into a quiet room. It's empty in this part of the carnival, and the dim lighting gives it an almost eerie feel. I stand in the center of the room, trying to clear all the doubt and uncertainty from my mind. I sigh heavily, unsure of where to go with my investigation from here.

Glancing up, I notice a series of frames around the room. The dim light is due to the walls being painted black to match the content of the frames. Each piece is done in blacks, reds, and golds, and they look breathtaking. I'm surprised no one else is in here looking at them, but I suppose the main attractions at carnivals are rides and sideshows.

The frame directly in front of me is of a heart, so I move toward it. There are cracks throughout the piece, tiny lines that at first almost look like veins until I get closer. There's a little sign beneath it, and I glance at what it says: "Bethany's Beating Heart."

I frown, wondering how long the piece has been around if it's cracking like this. I reach out, touching one of the cracks and a tiny part of the picture comes away with my finger. I try to look at it closer but the lights are dim making it hard. Rubbing my fingers together, it feels like the paint has become powdery so I bring it to my nose. The scent of copper assaults my senses.

I hear someone enter the hallway behind me. 'Can I ask who did this art piece?' I ask, assuming it's the attendant for the attraction, but only silence answers me.

Turning to look behind me, I'm surprised by the neon green mask. *Abel, why are you here, now?*

I smile as he moves toward me silently, and I'm half anticipating his touch already. The flash of his knife catches my attention and I step back, my back pressing to the art piece. Abel has never played with me using a knife, it's always been Cain's thing. But there is no mistaking the sharp edge of the blade when he holds it under my jaw.

My heart rate picks up as the cool metal presses against my skin, my lips part on a silent gasp. He still hasn't said anything, and now something feels off. He tilts his head as he presses the sharp edge harder until I feel the sting of it, a whimper escaping me. I feel the warm trickle of blood, running down my throat and into the valley between my breasts.

Something still doesn't feel right though.

When he pulls the knife away, holding the blade up to the limited light of the room, I see crimson droplets drip from it. His posture almost looks like he's entranced as he stares at it. My stomach drops, and I shove hard against his chest, but he's immovable.

When I try again, he brings the knife back down sharply. Pain explodes at the side of my head and the last thing I see before everything goes black is the neon green of his mask.

Chapter 39

Hydessa

17 Years Ago

Link doesn't know when his birthday is, so I told him we are baking a cake today and from now on, today would be his birthday. It makes me sad that he's never had a cake before, let alone a party. We have one every year, and the thing I like about it the most is the cake.

But instead of letting me make it for him, he said he would help. So now we are in the kitchen and there is flour all over our faces. I giggle as I throw some more in his direction. Mom won't be happy, but seeing Link's smile is worth it.

"Gotcha!" Link shouts, throwing a handful of flour back at me. We both burst into laughter, the kitchen quickly becoming a battleground.

"Okay, okay, truce!" I say, holding up my hands. "Let's make a cake."

Link grins and nods, his face and hair dusted with flour. We start measuring ingredients and mixing them together. The kitchen is a mess.

Suddenly, Link stops and his face goes pale. He falls to the ground, and I can feel my heart beating faster the longer he stays there.

"Link? Link, stop playing," I say, my voice trembling.

He starts shaking, and I drop the mixing bowl and kneel beside him. "Mom! Mom!" I scream.

She rushes into the kitchen, her eyes wide with alarm. She sees Link on the floor and she quickly kneels beside him, her hands moving over his face.

"Dare, call 911!" she shouts.

My Dad rushes into the room, holding a phone to his ear. My Papa comes in too but he comes toward me, wrapping his arms around me and picking me up. He carries me out of the kitchen.

I don't want to leave Link. I want to be with him, but Papa isn't listening to me. No matter how hard I try to push away from him, no matter how hard I scream or yell, he won't let me go.

Minutes later, though it feels like forever, the paramedics arrive. My mom and dad leave with them when they take Link away, they wont let me go too.

"Papa, please let me go with him. I need to be with Link," I beg, tears streaming down my face.

Papa holds me tighter, his own face etched with worry. "Hydessa, they need to take care of him. We need to stay here. We'll go to the hospital soon."

I cry and plead, but Papa doesn't change his mind. Eventually, I feel so tired, and he carries me to my room where I cry myself to sleep.

In the middle of the night, I wake up to my mom lying beside me. She's holding me, gently stroking my hair. Her eyes are sad, but she tries to smile for me.

"Mom, can we go see Link?" I ask, my voice small.

Her face falls, and she looks so sad. "I'm so sorry, honey. He's gone now."

I feel like the world is falling down around me, and for a moment, I can't breathe. I clutch my mom tighter, sobbing into her chest as her words keep repeating inside my head. Link is gone.

Days pass like this, and I don't want to see anyone but Link. I know I can't though, and it makes the tears start all over again. Everything hurts and I don't understand it. It's like I can feel the darkness and shadows inside me screaming for us to be reunited, but he's no longer here.

I had two whole months with him. Waking up every day to see his face, and making it my mission to get him to smile. He was doing better, the darkness in his eyes didn't seem to linger as much and he didn't wake with nightmares as often.

So why did the world take him away from me? I was doing the right thing. I finally felt free to be me with someone.

My parents keep trying to talk to me, but I don't want to listen. Nothing is the same anymore. He was my partner, and now I don't have my partner anymore. Every time they try to comfort me, it just feels like another reminder that he's gone.

After a week of them hovering, I finally get tired of my parents trying to tell me everything is fine and I run away.

I sprint into the forest to hide before they can catch me. I don't want to speak to anyone. I don't want to go back to the life I had before Link arrived anymore.

Once I've gone too far for me to hear them, I find a spot under a large tree and curl up, trying to make myself as small as possible. The forest is quiet, and it feels like the only place where I can be alone with my sadness.

How can I tell them that nothing feels right anymore? How do I explain that Link saw a deeper part of me than they ever have? How do I tell them that having him by my side was helping me embrace the darkness inside? That I'll never be able to embrace it without him next to me.

I can hear them calling my name from my hiding spot, but I don't want to move. I just want to hide and be sad, even if I've run out of tears.

It feels like hours pass before I hear a noise near me. I don't bother looking, I don't need to look to know it's Seanna. She crawls into my hiding spot with me and wraps her arms around my body silently, letting me continue to cry.

"I just want to hide," I whisper finally.

"And you know that if you're ever hiding, then it's my job to seek," she says softly.

"What if I don't want to be found?" I reply, struggling not to sob.

"Then, I'll sit here with you in the dark," she responds with a shrug.

She keeps holding me while I shake with silent sobs, and everything continues to hurt. I can feel the darkness inside me calling out for him, crying for him like I am.

"It hurts without him," I whisper to her when I feel like no more tears will fall. "He said he would be my partner in shadows. Just like mom told us our dads are to her. Who will help me control my darkness now that he's gone?"

She takes a minute to think. I've never talked about this part of me with anyone but Link until now, and she must sense it's a big deal. "Then hide the memory of him in your heart with your darkness. Keep it safe there. No one has to know what you keep locked away."

It takes a long time for the words to make sense to me, but finally I let her pull me from my hiding spot.

There are moments in life that leave a lasting impression. Moments that shape who you are as a person moving forward. Mine was when I lost my best friend and partner.

Chapter 40

Hydessa

My head is hurting so much that I can't stop the whimper that escapes me, even before I manage to force my eyes open. My hope that I was having a nightmare is quickly dashed when I see the figure standing in front of me, his green neon mask making my heart pound.

I can immediately see we're no longer at the carnival. Trees surround us, the canopy blocking out the moonlight. It's not hard to see he brought me to the forest, but I can't figure out why. I try to move, but I can feel something binding my hands together behind my back where I'm propped against one of the trees.

I'm not sure what he has planned, but I get this feeling that something has changed. Abel always stands tall when he's near me, but this masked man is slouched over. Abel always controls me with my neck, his hand around my throat like a collar while unable to put space between us. This man tied me to a tree and is keeping his distance.

"Why are you doing this?" I finally growl. The mask on his face tilts to the side, assessing me. Using my bound hands against the tree behind me, I manage to get to my feet. I will not cower on the ground for anyone.

"You have been asking too many questions. Annoying little questions that draw too much attention," he says. But even with the voice disguiser, I can tell something is off. How does someone change so quickly? Even the shadow of his build looks different.

"And you think killing me won't raise bigger questions?" I ask, scowling at him.

He steps closer, his gloved fingers brushing down my arm over the brand there. "Oh, that will be easy. You decided that the island wasn't for you after all. Your stuff will be gone, and it will be like you just went home to the city. Besides, maybe you ran away from the island because you feared for your life. Enough people know what this brand means to assume you got scared off."

His gloved hand reaches for me, but I turn my face away from it with a growl, not wanting him to touch me. The mask is shining so brightly it's distracting, but I try to focus elsewhere, staring into the trees surrounding us. He hums as he starts to trail his finger against my skin.

"It will be a shame to kill something so beautiful," he whispers, and I narrow my eyes.

"You seem to have forgotten an important detail," I respond, and he tilts his head, waiting for me to continue. But I don't need to.

"Us," comes a voice from behind him before a fist hits the imposter on the side of the head, sending him sprawling to the forest floor.

Two more masks flare to life on the figures now standing between me and the one on the ground. The red and green neon is so very similar to the one that had just been in front of me, but now I see the slight differences, and only these ones make my heart race.

"They do say imitation is the highest form of flattery, right?" one of the figures says. The way he speaks, I instantly know it's Cain. He turns to look at Abel. "Do you feel flattered? I certainly feel fucking flattered right now."

Abel growls, "Nah, I just feel fucking twitchy. You know, the kinda twitchy I get when someone else touches what's ours!" He kicks out at the figure on the ground, and the impact has a loud crack echoing around us as I hear the person groan.

"I didn't know," the masked figure wheezes.

Cain gives a derisive laugh. "You just said you saw the brand! You knew exactly who you were messing with."

Abel crouches down, getting closer. "You think because you've killed all those tourists you're untouchable now?" He reaches out and takes hold of the mask on the imposter, pulling it off his face and throwing it toward the trees. "The only reason we let it go on this long was because we needed to draw her to the island, otherwise we would have killed you ourselves."

My stomach does a flip as I see the face of the serial killer, and suddenly every little piece fits together in my mind. I shudder at the thought that I ever looked at him with anything but disgust. His mismatched eyes widen in fear as Cain also crouches down closer to him.

"We thought that with her arriving and starting to ask questions you would lie low, but you couldn't help yourself, could you, Chester," he says. "You had to take the one opportunity you had to kill again. You somehow knew exactly when we were taking out the other trash polluting our island."

"But you didn't realize you were killing a tourist that our girl had made friends with," Abel says, standing and moving closer. When he reaches me, his fingers deftly work to untie the bindings on my wrists. "Are you okay?"

I nod, though my body is trembling from the adrenaline. But with it, comes a realization. "Yeah," I manage to say, before looking at the man on the ground.

My mother is one of the best profilers in the world, and growing up surrounded by her work has taught me a few things. I walk over to Chester, all of the pieces finally fitting into place. "That was her blood wasn't it? On the painting at the carnival? This was about more than just your need to understand death."

Chester looks up at me, and for the first time, I see the darkness lurking there, but there is a selfish kind of evil swirling in his gaze. "They were my greatest masterpieces," he finally whispers.

A chill runs down my spine at his words, the sheer depravity of his confession almost too much to bear. Cain leans forward, grabbing Chester by the collar and pulling him to his feet.

"You won't have the chance to create any more," Cain says, his voice cold and unyielding.

Chester looks at each of us before he turns his gaze back to Cain. "You know you won't get away with killing me." There is a hint of a challenge in his voice. I frown, but Cain simply scoffs in response, shoving Chester away and moving toward where the gleam of the blade can be seen on the ground.

"Oh, I think we will," Cain says, picking up the knife. "You're not the only one who can make a body disappear, remember?"

"Was it even worth it? Did you get what you were searching for?" I ask him, taking a step toward where he's standing.

He shrugs, a twisted smile on his face. "Not sure. How about you let me know," he says, and before anyone can react, he charges toward me. The impact of his body is like a freight train, sending us both back to the ground, but this time he's on top of me, his hands wrapped around my neck.

"If they are going to kill me, I will at least take the woman they love with me," he growls, his hands squeezing so hard I can't breathe. My pulse pounds inside my head, and I scratch at any part of him I can reach, but his grip is unrelenting.

Just as my vision starts to blur, I see a flash of green and I watch in slow motion as Abel's hand takes a hold of Chester's head and gives a sharp twist.

Then there is silence. I can't hear anything past the sound of my own heartbeat pounding in my ears. The world seems to dim for a moment, and then Chester's grip loosens, his body going limp and collapsing onto me. Abel instantly pulls him off and tosses him aside.

Abel pulls me up and into his arms, his hands running over me as though making sure I'm alright.

"I'm okay," I manage to say, my voice hoarse. Everything feels dull, as if my body is moving but I can't feel it.

Cain steps forward, looking down at Chester's lifeless body. "He's done. It's over," he says, more to himself than anyone else. He then looks at both of us. "Take her back to the house, make sure she's okay, I'll deal with him."

My legs feel like jelly, but the adrenaline is keeping me upright.

Abel instantly grips my hand and starts to move through the forest with me. I stumble twice before I pull him to a stop in frustration. The light of the moon is now shining brightly through a gap in the trees, making his mask dimmer. It's as though the darkness has moved away from us now that Chester is dead. I stand for a moment, catching my breath and trying to steady my legs as my mind races with everything that happened today.

"What did he mean about us not getting away with killing him?" I ask finally. Abel looks back in the direction we came from, as though he can still see the body we left behind.

"Don't worry about that just yet," he says, moving to take my hand again. But I growl and hold mine up, making him stop.

"Then tell me how you found us so quickly. We are in the middle of a forest, there aren't any cameras here," I nearly shout, but my voice is strained and my neck sore. But when he glances back where we came from again, I realize I will get no answers without Cain present.

"Let's get you back to the house," he says after a moment.

"No! I'm tired of the lies and half-truths and manipulations. I want answers!" I shove my hands at his chest. Anger, hurt, frustration, and relief all try to course through me at once, but I don't know what to focus on so I just keep pushing.

"Hydessa," he sighs, but I've had enough. I shove at him again, then again, and the next time I just yell.

"I want the truth!" I demand, trying to shove him back once more, but he gently grabs my hands.

"Little shadow, stop," he says more firmly, planting his feet in the ground and becoming immovable.

"NO! I'm done. I can't do this anymore. I can't let both of you keep doing this to me!" I yell. Tears fill my eyes as my words tumble from my mouth loud enough that I'm sure the whole island can hear me at this point.

"Dessa!" Abel yells, causing my blood to turn to ice. I freeze, barely able to breathe.

"Don't call me that. *Never* call me that." I'm no longer shouting, but my breaths are heaving as I try to find a sense of control. "Only one person was ever allowed to call me that," I whisper. Abel brings my hands to his chest, and this time I don't push.

"I know," he says softly in response. I can barely comprehend what's happening as he unzips his hoodie, revealing a heavily tattooed chest. He moves my hand, and I try to pull it away, but he holds firm, placing it against his skin. I feel it instantly—a raised scar in the jagged shape of a heart.

"You dug my heart's grave," he whispers. Tears trail down my cheeks as I look up into the neon green face of his mask and I realize who's behind it.

"Link?"

Chapter 41

Link

17 Years Ago

I can hear a faint beeping sound, like an alarm but softer. I struggle to wake up, but everything feels so heavy, my whole body feels like it's weighed down with sand. There's something taped to my hand, but I can't force my eyes open to look at it.

What happened to my cake? I was looking forward to my first birthday cake. Dessa convinced me that I needed to celebrate a 'birthday' each year. Weren't we making a cake?

I can hear whispered voices close by, and it takes a moment to recognize Dessa's mom and dad.

"I'm worried, Dare," I hear her mom say.

"I thought we agreed not to hold the sins of his father against him?" comes a quiet male response. I don't understand what they are talking about.

"That's not what I'm talking about, I know he isn't his dad, he is a sweet boy and I know he won't make the same choices," she responds, but her voice is getting softer. Maybe they are leaving, or I'm falling asleep again. I do feel very tired.

"Then what is it?" comes a faint question, but I don't hear the answer, sleep is already dragging me down into darkness.

I'm not sure how long I sleep for, but when I slowly hear the beeping sound again, it's louder. My body doesn't feel as heavy this time and I'm able to force my eyes open, blinking at the harsh lights above me.

"Hey Lincoln," comes a man's voice at the side of my bed. When I turn my face toward it, I see Dessa's dad.

His kind eyes soften with relief as he notices I'm awake. "You gave us quite a scare, buddy," he says, his voice gentle but filled with concern.

I try to speak, but my throat feels dry and scratchy. He quickly grabs a cup of water with a straw and holds it to my lips. I take a small sip, feeling the cool liquid soothe my throat.

"What happened?" I manage to croak out, my voice barely above a whisper.

He sets the cup down and sits back in his chair, his expression serious. "The doctors said you had a little seizure, they aren't sure what caused it, they said it could be anything. But you're going to be just fine."

My mind struggles to process his words. Seizure? I don't understand, but the worry in his eyes makes me feel scared. I try to remember what happened, but everything is a blur. My thoughts drift to Dessa, and fear grips me.

"Where's Dessa?" I ask, my voice quivering with anxiety.

He sighs deeply, his expression softening further. "Can we talk for a moment, buddy? Man to man?"

I nod slowly, my heart pounding in my chest. He leans forward.

"We found a family who would love a little boy like you. They're a good family, and they will care for you like their own. You won't want for anything ever again," he says, his eyes searching mine.

I frown, confusion and fear swirling inside me. "Do you not want me anymore? What about Dessa? I thought we were partners?" My voice is soft, and I hate that I can feel tears in my eyes. I'm meant to be a big boy; I shouldn't be crying.

"Of course we do, Lincoln. Dessa is so worried and upset that this has happened," he says, sighing again. He leans closer, his eyes filled with sadness and understanding. "We know you want to be her partner, buddy, but Hydessa isn't ready for your darkness yet, okay? Maybe someday, but not yet."

I swallow hard, blinking fast to try to see past the tears, but I can't make them go away. Why won't they go away? "Will you be a big boy for her? Just give her some time to grow up, you too. Then maybe you guys will find each other again."

I nod, even though I don't really understand. The tears keep coming, and I feel so lost and alone. "I'll try," I whisper, my voice breaking.

He reaches out and squeezes my hand. "That's all we ask, Lincoln. You're a brave boy, and we're so proud of you."

I want to ask him to tell her I love her, but I can't bring myself to voice it. I know it's silly and that I'm young, but I feel it deep inside me. I simply nod again, trying to be brave, trying to be the big boy they want me to be. But inside, all I feel is a deep, aching sadness.

I don't want to leave Dessa. I don't want to be with another family. But I don't say any of that either. I just lie there, holding onto Dessa's dad's hand while hoping that somehow, someday, everything will be okay.

I'm so scared and worried. My whole body feels jittery, like there's too much energy trapped inside me, fighting to get out. I want to hit something, to scream at how unfair everything is, to cry and curse my life, but I don't. Instead, I force myself to retreat into that safe part in my heart, the part that belongs to her, my tears slowly drying up as I wait for my new family to come for me.

At one point, Dessa's dad takes both of my hands in his to stop my fingers from tapping nervously. All I can do then is stare blankly at the wall. The beeping of the machines, the sterile smell of the hospital room, *it all fades into the background as I try to hold onto the part of me that feels connected to Dessa. My shadow in the dark.*

It's all I have left now, that darkness inside me that calls out to her. I won't ever let that go. Nothing else matters but keeping that connection alive. I will do that for her, until she's ready.

Chapter 42

Hydessa

Pulling my hand free, I reach up and push the mask off his face, the hood going with it. I'm not surprised when his hair falls forward, almost hiding the green eyes that I don't know how I didn't recognize.

A sob escapes me as I finally see the boy I knew in the man in front of me. "I thought you were dead," I whisper, my voice trembling.

His eyes, those same familiar emerald green eyes, look back at me, filled with pain and regret. "It needed to be that way, Dessa," he replies softly, his voice carrying the weight of years lost and memories buried.

My fingers touch his face, needing to confirm that he's real, that this isn't some cruel dream. The moment they brush against his skin, warm and solid, and another sob breaks free from my chest. He catches my hand in his, holding it tightly, as if afraid I might disappear if he lets go.

"Why did you leave me?" I ask, my voice breaking.

He looks away briefly as though trying to reign in his own emotions before he looks back into my eyes. "For the longest time, I didn't understand why I had to. But you weren't ready back then for my darkness, little shadow. There was so much I didn't know about myself back then. If I had found out while we were together, it could have destroyed us."

He reaches out and wraps his hand around the front of my throat as he leans close to my face. "*I* would have destroyed you, my darkness wouldn't have cared what we were to each other. It was the hardest decision of my life back then, but in the end, even without knowing, I did it to protect you."

Tears stream down my face as his words sink in. "I didn't need you to protect me, I needed you with me," I whisper as I imagine him all alone again.

He tucks me against his chest, strong arms wrapping around me tightly. "I know, Dessa, and I'm sorry. I wish I could make you see that it was the right thing for us. I never stopped thinking about you, not for one moment."

I frown, frustration taking place in the front of my mind. I shove him backward again and this time he does move. "Really? Then why the fucking games, why the masks, why not tell me exactly who you were from the start, *Telvin?*"

He grimaces, at least having the sense to look apologetic as he shoves his hands into his pockets and he looks upward at the canopy above us.

"You don't even act the same," I whisper, my heart aching a little less as I look at him alive and safe in front of me.

He chuckles as he seems to take me in. I'm so focused on how nice it is to see his eyes that I don't even realize when his hand snaps out. He grabs a fist full of my hair, dragging me against the front of him again. "You know I hated my name. And would you have suspected sweet, quiet Telvin of fucking that pretty pussy raw?" he asks, his voice going husky.

Well fuck, now that's a reminder of the change between boy and man if I've ever seen one.

He starts to walk me backward, his body completely controlling mine until my back is pressed against a tree and it turns my insides to liquid. "We had our reasons for doing what we did, the way we did it, we won't apologize. There are still things at play here that you don't know about."

"Link, you can't just come back into my life and expect me to accept everything without question. I need to understand. I'm not that child anymore either. I changed too," I breathe out.

His lips twitch and there is definitely nothing boy-like in the look he gives me, his grip remains unyielding, tugging harder on my hair. "No, you're not. We'll tell you everything, Dessa. But first, you have to trust us. Trust me."

I open my mouth to ask, but he must see the question on my face before I voice it. "Don't ask me who he is," he says, his voice low. "He has his own story to tell."

I huff, frustrated by his evasiveness. He grins at me, the mischievous glint in his eyes unmistakable. "Come on, little shadow," he says, his tone teasing. "Let me walk you home like a gentleman."

I laugh, giving him a disbelieving look. "You are *not* a gentleman."

His eyes grow hooded, like a predator looking at his next meal. "So nice of you to notice," he murmurs, and then his lips are on mine, stealing my breath. He continues to speak between each brush of his lips, his words igniting a fire inside me. "I've spent 17 years... obsessed with everything about you... every part of you... your body and mind... I want to devour you... possess you... I'll never be a gentleman... I'm the needy orphan who begs for more..."

His words send shivers down my spine, and I cling to him as he deepens the kiss, his tongue dancing with mine as my fingers grip his hair. The intensity of my need for him is overwhelming. I feel myself melting against him, so ready and willing to surrender to the passion that simmers between us.

But then he abruptly steps back and away, leaving me weak in the knees, trying to hold myself up as I catch my breath. *Maybe I underestimated the whole mask thing. I should be glad he hasn't kissed me before, his mouth is just as dangerous as his cock.*

Tangling our fingers together, he starts leading me through the forest toward the house. His grip is firm, reassuring, and I find myself squeezing his hand in response. Despite everything, a part of me wants to trust him, to believe that there's a reason behind all the secrecy.

When we finally reach the back of the house, he barely stops, somehow producing a key and unlocking the door.

"You have a key to my house?" I ask incredulously, and he shushes me. I almost stumble as he continues to pull me along behind him, my mind struggling to focus on anything but the fact that he has a goddamn key. I knew they were able to get in easily, but I didn't realize they didn't have to work for it.

"Don't you dare shush me right now," I snap, but he simply turns back towards me, his shoulder digging into my stomach as he throws me over it and continues through the house. He carries me up the stairs, and when I start protesting, one of his hands lands heavily on my ass making me yelp.

Link kicks open my bedroom door and throws me onto my bed, my body bouncing slightly. My skirt rides up my legs, revealing more skin and the knife that's strapped to my thigh. Both of them have a seriously annoying habit of manhandling me, but at least Cain placed me down gently last time.

I open my mouth to protest again, but he starts talking at the same moment he begins pulling off his gloves, followed by his jacket.

It's far easier to see all of his tattooed and tanned skin now that we're out of the forest. The heart that was etched into his skin is now framed by one of ink. If he had been shirtless at kickboxing I would have seen it instantly.

"You want to know the only difference between now and when I had that mask on and you didn't know who I was?" Before I can answer, he wraps his hands around the back of my knees and jerks me toward the edge of the bed. "This," he says, ripping my underwear from my body with one swift motion.

And then he kneels, his head presses forward while holding my eye contact, and then his mouth is on me. *Oh holy mother of God... His tongue needs to be considered a lethal weapon.*

I moan, my breath stuttering as his tongue moves and flicks over my clit before sliding down to my entrance. I can barely breathe, the sensation of his hot mouth on me making my entire body tremble. He is relentless, teasing and exploring, driving me to the edge of sanity before pulling back and teasing again. I grip the sheets, my knuckles turning white as I try to ground myself, but it's impossible. My body is reacting to him in ways I never imagined.

The knife in its sheath inches from his head doesn't even concern him, he simply digs his fingers into the skin of my thigh next to it, holding me open for the war he's waging on my pussy.

"Link," I gasp, trying to form coherent words. "Stop... I need... we need to talk."

He doesn't stop, though. Instead, he glances up at me, his green eyes dark with desire. "Talking can wait, Dessa, I've waited far too long to taste you," he murmurs against my skin, the vibration of his voice sending another wave of pleasure through me.

My protests die in my throat as he continues his assault, his hands gripping my thighs firmly, holding me in place. Every touch, every lick, every bite is pushing me closer to the edge, and I know I won't last much longer. The heat building inside me is too intense, too overwhelming.

"Please," I whimper, not even sure what I'm begging for anymore. Release, maybe. Or perhaps for him to stop before I completely lose myself.

But he knows exactly what I need, and he's determined to give it to me. His pace quickens, his tongue working me with a precision that leaves me breathless. He thrusts two fingers inside me, curling them in just the right way to have me moaning like a porn star. My vision blurs as the pleasure builds, until finally, it crashes over me like a tidal wave.

I cry out, my back arching off the bed as the orgasm rips through me. My body trembles uncontrollably, every nerve ending on fire. He doesn't bring me down gently, he just continues until I'm gasping as another smaller orgasm rolls over me. I start to wonder if gentleness is even possible for this man outside of the mask he portrays to the town.

He finally stands, releasing his hold on me as he opens his pants and shoves them down his legs, revealing his already hard cock. I'm trying to catch my breath as I watch his finely toned muscles bunch and shift with each movement of his body. *All of him is a lethal weapon.*

I don't know what comes over me, but I don't resist at all as he strips the clothes from my body, leaving only the knife on my thigh. His bare hands are warm but hard as he moves me exactly how he wants, the feeling of his calloused fingers make me weak in a way no one else has before. Until them.

He has the length of his body pressed against my back as I kneel on the bed before him, and his hand wraps around my throat, his lips brushing against my ear. "You were always destined for us, Dessa. Do you understand that now? You were always meant to be the partner to *our* darkness, just like we are the partners to yours. No one was ever going to satisfy you like us."

I whimper as his fingers flex, digging in and making me arch back against him. His other hand trails down the side of my body, leaving a path of goosebumps in its wake before he grips my hip.

"Do you feel it, Dessa? Do you feel how perfectly we fit together?" he whispers, his voice a blend of lust and something deeper, something possessive. And hearing his voice, his real voice, does something within me.

I nod, unable to form words as I feel the heat of him pressing against me. My breath hitches, and I feel my body responding, a fresh wave of arousal washing over me.

He releases my hip, his hand sliding between us, his thumb parting my ass cheeks and pressing firmly against my entrance. I buck against him, but I can't stop the moan from escaping me. "Now, your going to be a good fucking girl, and let me fuck you here while my brother fucks that needy pussy," he murmurs, his voice a dark caress.

I hadn't even realized that Cain had entered the room. But the thought of them both inside me at the same time has my nipples hardening and my mind desperate to feel them both.

I'm going to die... Here lies the corpse of Hydessa Darling... killed by cock.

Chapter 43

Hydessa

Link doesn't give me any time to protest, no time to even think as he pushes me forward until I'm on my hands and knees. He spreads my legs apart and I hear the cap of a bottle before cold liquid drips down and onto my overheated skin and between my ass cheeks. My breath catches as his fingers move against me, rubbing in slow circles before pressing harder against my back entrance.

I whimper as one pushes into me, gently moving in and out, spreading the lube. It's intense, but I'm already relaxed because of the double orgasm his mouth just blew my mind with.

I sigh when he adds another, my heart racing at the sensation of his fingers moving and stretching me open while my mind is caught up in the pleasure he brings. No man has ever touched me here, and yet with him it feels natural.

All too soon he guides his cock to my tight hole, the metal piercing cold and hard as he grips my waist and pushes in slowly. The sensation of being filled by him, the way he stretches me, it's overwhelming. Like I'm lost in a haze of pleasure and need, and all I can do is cling to sheets beneath my hands and give into every sensation he offers.

His movements are slow and deliberate at first, each thrust measured and controlled, but I can feel the tension in his body, the way he's holding back. The initial pain of the stretch gives way to pleasure and I press back against him, urging him to go harder, faster.

Link growls low in his throat, the sound sending shivers down my spine. His body blankets my back as he rolls his hips a little harder and faster.

I moan, one hand reaching back to ask him for more, but I don't know what more he could give me. "You want it rough, little shadow?" he whispers against my ear, his voice a dark promise.

I nod, unable to speak, my body trembling with need. He doesn't need any more encouragement. He reaches around and grips my throat tightly as he starts to move faster, his thrusts hard and deep, driving me to the edge with each powerful stroke. The intensity of it, the raw, primal need, is unlike anything I've ever felt.

And then he stops.

I whimper when he releases my sore neck and moves us both while he stays buried inside me. He wraps his arms around me, lifting and rolling us over until I'm looking up into the bright neon red of Cain's mask.

My heart slams against my ribcage, racing as the sinister color shines down on my body from where he is standing at the end of the bed. His gloved hand is wrapped around his hard cock as he spreads lube along the pierced length.

Link doesn't move as Cain reaches out and runs his fingers through my wet pussy. He crawls onto the bed and presses his cock against my entrance, teasing me with just the tip. The anticipation is maddening, and I want to pull him forward, needing him inside me. He chuckles softly as I shift my hips, my thighs spreading wider and causing Link to go deeper.

"So eager," Cain murmurs.

"She needs you too brother," Link says. "You should feel how hard she's clamping down on my cock right now."

He rolls his hips under me, causing me to let out a gasp and a whine. I need them both. Now.

Instead of pushing forward, Cain pulls the knife from where it's strapped to my thigh. My breath stutters as I reach out to stop whatever he intends, but Link grabs both of my arms, pulling them up until my back arches and I'm whimpering at the pain.

Cain chuckles, his echoing voice low and dark as he taps the flat of the blade against the flesh of my breast, returning my focus to him. I shiver as the cold metal touches my skin, a sharp contrast to the heat radiating from my body.

"Such a needy little cock slut," Cain murmurs. He presses the tip of the knife just hard enough to leave a mark but not break the skin, tracing a slow, deliberate path across my ribs. My pulse races as he continues down my stomach, the flat edge leaving a line of goosebumps in its wake. Link's grip on my wrists is firm, holding me in place as Cain toys with me.

When the blade pauses just above my pussy, he begins pressing lightly against my skin, not hard enough to cut, but enough to remind me of the danger of its presence. My breath catches in my throat, every nerve in my body on high alert.

"Do you trust us?" he asks, his distorted voice feeling so different to Links. .

I nod, swallowing hard. "Yes," I whisper, trembling with anticipation.

With one swift motion, he flips the knife, the handle now pressing against my clit. The unexpected pressure makes me gasp, my hips jerking involuntarily. Cain chuckles, clearly pleased with my reaction.

"Good girl," he says, sliding the handle along my folds, sending shivers through me. His other hand grasps my thigh, holding me open.

Link's grip on my arms tightens, his body a solid weight behind me, his cock still buried deep inside.

Finally, Cain pushes the handle of the knife inside me, the hard unyielding metal sending an electric shock of sensation through my body. I cry out from the sensation especially when he tilts it just right that it presses into my g-spot.

"Yes," I nearly scream. "Right there."

Link rewards me with a kiss to my cheek as he whispers, "Don't you worry, Dessa. We are going to give you everything."

Cain's movements are deliberate and controlled as he thrusts the handle in and out. My body quivers with every motion. He doesn't let up even when waves of pleasure cause my moans to grow louder as the intensity builds.

Just when I'm on the edge, he pulls the handle out of me. Leaning forward he holds it up to my mouth and my eyes widen.

"Open," he commands, making my heart skip a beat. I comply immediately and he shoves the handle into my mouth. "Bite down, little shadow. And be careful, you wouldn't want it to fall and stab anything vital." I shudder at the taste of myself as my teeth bite into the handle of the knife before he lets it go.

He repositions himself at my entrance and pushes forward slowly, each of his piercings catching as he fills me inch by inch. The sensation of both of them inside me is overwhelming, the stretch and fullness almost too much to bear. I whimper loudly and my teeth clench as my eyes roll to the back of my head. My body trembles as they both start to move in sync, their thrusts deep and hard.

Link's grip on my arms adjusts as he pulls me back against his chest, his movements perfectly synchronized with Cain's relentless thrusts. The sensation of both of them inside me is a heady mix of pleasure and pain, the lust in the air building with each powerful stroke. My body trembles uncontrollably, caught between them.

Cain's dark laughter fills the room as I beg for more. "You like this, don't you? You like being our dirty little slut," he taunts, his voice a dark, seductive purr even when it's distorted. "Being used by both of us."

I can only whimper in response, the pleasure too intense to form coherent words. My hips move of their own accord, pressing back against Link and thrusting forward to meet Cain, desperate for more.

Cain increases the pace, his movements becoming more forceful. They both push deeper, the cold metal of their piercings scraping against my sensitive walls with each thrust. My body arches, every nerve on fire as I teeter on the edge of release.

Cain's hand reaches up and twists one of my nipples, sending a jolt of pleasure directly to my clit. The sensation is like a live wire coursing through my body, and I cry out around the knife handle, my back arching even more.

His nails dig into the skin of my thigh as he pounds into me. The whole bed is shaking with their movements and I wouldn't be surprised if it broke. *Wouldn't be surprised if they broke me too.*

Link's mouth finds my ear, his teeth scrape over it before doing the same to my neck. "Do you like the way my brother fucks you? Do you like being full with both of us?"

"More," I beg, needing them to give me what I want, what I crave just as much as I know they do. Every thrust from them is perfectly synchronized, filling me completely, the sensation a delicious torment that makes it almost impossible to breathe.

Cain's grip on my nipple tightens, then he draws circles around the stiff peak before flicking it. I can actually feel myself clamping around them when the pain registers.. "You're such a good little whore, taking us so well."

Link's hand moves from my wrists to my throat, his grip possessive and unyielding. "Do you feel that, Dessa? How every part of you belongs to us? You're ours," he growls, his breath hot against my ear. "And now, you're going to come for us."

I think they thought I would go after the knife in my mouth first. But I could always handle a knife. My hand snaps out and rips the mask away from Cain's face.

I'm sure he could have stopped me if he really wanted to, but he doesn't. And if anything, the intensity of his thrusts become more brutal, more primal. He pulls the knife from my mouth, the blade making contact with my breast more solidly this time. Pain flashes through my body like lightning as Link's hands tighten around my throat, cutting off my air.

My eyes widen for a brief moment before they roll back as pleasure overwhelms my senses. The intensity of their combined movements, the way they claim me so completely, is too much. I shatter around them, my orgasm ripping through me with a force that leaves me breathless and boneless.

His voice cuts through the haze of pleasure, low and commanding. "Look at me, little shadow," he growls. My eyes, heavy-lidded and unfocused, manage to lock onto his. "You're ours," he continues, each word punctuated by a deep thrust. "Every. Single. Inch."

I try to cry out, his name on my lips, but Link releases my throat the same moment he buries his teeth into my neck. Air rushing in as my body spasms, another orgasm ripping through me. But then my cries are being swallowed by a mouth pressed to mine. My body clenches around them and I feel the moment they both cum, their deep groans echoing around the room and making my whole body throb in time with my beating pulse until I'm a quivering, broken mess between them.

I feel like I'm floating as they both gently withdraw from my body. Then I'm being lifted into solid muscular arms. I shiver when I feel the cold marble under my ass and finally manage to focus again. My breath hitches but he simply slides his hand along my jaw, gripping it before brushing his lips against mine again.

His lips are warm, and for a moment, the world outside fades away. When the kiss deepens I moan, he tastes like everything I have come to love about this island.

Chapter 44

Hydessa

The taste of saltwater lingers on my lips as he pulls back, his forehead resting against mine.

"I should have punished you for doing that, I should have edged you until you begged me to stop," he whispers, his tone teasing but his green eyes intense. They are different than Links. His eyes are like a turquoise sea, drawing me into their depths.

"I think you've murdered my pussy enough for one night, don't you? If you did anything else you would have had another body to dispose of, and that wouldn't have been as easy," I counter with a tired grin.

He huffs a chuckle under his breath. "You'd be surprised, the ocean takes two just as easily as one."

I arch a brow as I lean back with a sigh. "I guess having a boat does have its advantages."

He gives a full throaty laugh at that, the sound filling the small space. The moment I saw his face above me, the last of the puzzle seemed to slip into place.

I watch as he steps back, stripping out of his clothes quickly before starting the shower. He checks the temperature before returning to scoop me up and carry me under the warm water as the steam starts to build around us.

Taking a seat on the bench inside the shower, he continues holding me, letting the warm water soothe my tense muscles. "Jonah," I sigh softly, and his hand threads through my hair, gently pulling my head back so he can look into my eyes again.

"Say it again, little shadow," he murmurs, his voice low and intimate, "let me hear my real name on your pretty lips."

A smile spreads across my face, but I remain silent as his eyes narrow on mine. His hands clench in my hair, fisting and pulling at the strands hard enough to have a breathy moan escaping me. "Jonah," I breathe out and his eyes flare with heat and satisfaction. But then quickly turn serious.

"For the longest time I wanted to kill you, little shadow," he says and I frown. I try to shift back but he doesn't let me go. "I wanted to slaughter you, the same way your parents slaughtered our dad."

My stomach drops at his words. *What the ever loving fuck is he talking about?*

When I try to get up again, he simply tightens his hold on me and growls. I whimper and not the good kind, my frown deepening as confusion and a thread of fear washes over me. "Link never said–"

"He never knew," he interrupts the tension in his voice unmistakable. "I was eight years old when our mother packed me and my newborn brother up and headed to the city to visit our dad. Imagine our surprise when we got there to find out he was dead. Our mother decided then and there that she wouldn't be able to raise me and a newborn baby alone, so she left him at a fire station on our way home."

My breath catches in my throat as I process his words, the revelation hitting me like a punch to the gut. I feel cold, despite the heat of the shower around us. "I had no idea... I didn't know any of this."

The emotions in his eyes make my heart ache. "She hired some-one to find out what happened, and she told me who was responsi-ble. For the longest time I hated your family. If they hadn't killed my father, my mother wouldn't have given up my brother and I hated you all for that too. But fate has a funny way of working out," he says, his voice raw with emotion.

He closes his eyes, a look of anguish crossing his face. "I stewed in my hatred, darling girl. It became a black hole inside me," he admits quietly. "I spent a long time learning how to hack into all corners of the internet to try to find my brother. When I couldn't learn any more, I left for the city to learn to hack all corners of the dark web too. But when I finally found my brother all he could remember was the family who saved him from an abusive foster home, and the raven haired girl who owned his heart."

When he opens his eyes again I can see the pain in them, the years of anger and sorrow that have shaped him into the man holding me now. "It wasn't easy to dig deeper and find that family, but what were the odds that it was the same family that put him there to begin with. He also told me about the little things he heard while he was there. That our dad was evil, that he hurt and used women. I did my research then and found out he also led a whole world of corruption and drugs." Jonah's grip on my hair loosens, and he pulls me closer, his forehead resting against mine once more. "And that he killed both of your grandmothers."

I reach up, cupping his face with trembling hands. "Jonah, I—" I start, but he shakes his head, silencing me.

"All that time, I thought I knew what I wanted. Revenge, justice, call it what you will. But finding him, learning the truth about every-thing... learning about you... it changed it all," he continues, his voice breaking slightly.

I swallow hard, my heart pounding in my chest.

"From that moment on, learning everything about *you* was all that mattered. My brother's obsession became mine too, to the point where we both needed you in our lives but we weren't entirely sure how to do that."

I shake my head, my voice barely above a whisper. "But, I'm nothing special. Both of you could have anyone you want."

His eyes flash with intensity, and he grips my face gently but firmly. "Don't you ever say that," he growls, his voice filled with emotion. "You're everything, little shadow. You are the missing piece of our dark souls."

Tears prick at the corners of my eyes, but I blink them back.

Jonah's expression softens, and he leans in, his lips brushing against mine in a tender kiss. "You don't simply settle for someone that you may see yourself with in twenty years. You find that someone you simply can't live without because the thought of not being with them in sixty years is still not enough. And when you find that someone, you never let them go."

I melt into him and he holds me close, the water continuing to rain down around us. Eventually he starts to help me get cleaned up, gently washing my body before doing my hair. Once he turns off the shower he tends to my cuts before carrying me back to the now empty bed. I frown as he covers me in the sheet and I look around, wondering where Link is.

"We'll be back, we have a few things to take care of, little shadow. Get some sleep," Jonah whispers softly, his kiss on my cheek leaving a lingering warmth as he quietly slips out of the room, closing the door behind him.

Alone in the quiet aftermath of Jonah's departure, I succumb to exhaustion. My eyelids grow heavy as sleep envelops me, pulling me into its depths despite the questions that linger in the recesses of my mind.

As darkness claims me, I find solace in the knowledge that despite the uncertainties ahead, I'm not alone anymore. Jonah and Link have chosen me, flaws, darkness and all, to be a part of their lives—a realization that brings a sense of belonging that I had only ever hoped to find. Link. My Link. I can hardly believe it.

The doorbell of the house startles me awake the next morning. Blinking sleep from my eyes, I manage to quickly throw on a pair of leggings and a shirt as I make my way downstairs.

To my shock, standing on the doorstep when I open the door is Sheriff Brooks and Deputy Eli.

"Good morning, Taylor," Sheriff Brooks greets me, his tone measured. "We were hoping to chat with you about the report you filed the other day?"

My heart skips a beat as it takes a moment to remember about the report I filed for Beth. I nod, inviting them inside. "Would you like some coffee? I'm just about to put a pot on, I only just woke up."

Sheriff Brooks and Deputy Eli exchange a glance before Sheriff Brooks nods. "Coffee sounds good, thank you, Taylor."

I lead them into the kitchen, starting the brew before turning back to face them. "Please, have a seat," I say, gesturing to the table. As they settle in, I retrieve mugs from the cupboard before pouring them each a cup.

Once we're all situated, Sheriff Brooks clears his throat. "We wanted to follow up on the report you filed regarding Beth."

"Of course," I reply, my mind still groggy from just waking up. "I haven't heard anything further since filing it. Is there any update?"

Sheriff Brooks leans forward, his expression serious. "Actually, Taylor, it's been brought to our attention that a local has gone missing this morning. Did you happen to hear or see anything unusual overnight?"

My heart is suddenly racing in my chest. "No, I'm sorry. I didn't hear anything out of the ordinary last night," I respond, my whole body filling with unease. "Who is it that's missing?"

Deputy Eli hesitates for a moment, as if considering how much information to disclose. "It's Chester," he finally reveals, his voice low. "According to what we know he was supposed to meet with some friends early this morning, but he never showed up."

I freeze, the name ringing in my ears. *Oh yeah, him. Last time I saw him was when he was trying to kill me and one of the men I love was snapping his neck.* My breath hitches and my heart skips a beat, but it has nothing to do with Chester, and everything to do with me realizing I'm in love with my men. And they are my men.

"Do you have any leads?" I manage to ask, trying to focus despite the whirlwind of emotions.

Sheriff Brooks' gaze remains steady, his expression unreadable. "We're gathering information and interviewing witnesses," he replies cautiously. "Any details you can provide, no matter how small, could be crucial."

I nod, my thoughts racing. "He mentioned something about an art project he was excited about," I offer, trying to think quickly. "Let me see if I made note of it on my phone. He did tell me about a few different art shows in the city if that helps."

I stand, making my way from the room as Deputy Eli scribbles down notes. I'm not sure where I left my phone but I'm making my way toward the office, turning the corner in the hallway when I hear the Sheriff and Deputy behind me starting to have a heated discussion. I can't make out what they're saying, so I pause, turning back toward the corner in an attempt to listen in.

Suddenly, I hear a shout and the sound of smashing glass from the kitchen. When a loud noise echoes through the house, I peek around the corner to see a body laying in the open doorway to the kitchen, heavy footsteps starting to move toward the hallway. I have to suppress my gasp as I jerk back away from the corner, my heart racing. I can't tell from this distance if he's dead, but it didn't look good.

I keep my back to the wall and start sliding quickly and quietly along it toward the office. My knife is upstairs but my gun is hidden in the desk. The footsteps are getting closer when the wall vanishes from behind me, and before I can react, a strong hand clamps over my mouth and jerks me backwards.

Chapter 45

Hydessa

P anic rises within me as I struggle against the grip, until a familiar scent in the air washes over me. I relax back against his hold as the opening in the wall he just pulled me through silently seals shut.

Slowly releasing the hold he has on my mouth, he captures my hand and starts pulling me along the narrow hall we are in. My mouth drops open as I try to understand what I'm seeing. When the hall opens up into another room, my eyes widen and I stumble to a stop, forcing Link to stop with me.

"What the fuck is this? Where are we?" I demand in a low hiss, still trying to process what I'm seeing. But I don't know why I bother, he just grins at me, letting go of my hand and turning toward Jonah.

They have a secret fucking room in the house I'm renting?!

I'm both speechless and furious all at once. There are an array of screens showing different areas of the house, while another smaller screen shows a GPS map with a little red dot on it over this address. It's a stalkers paradise.

Maybe it wasn't love after all, maybe it was indigestion. I'm sure there's medication for that shit right?

I'm just about to give them both a piece of my mind when a voice starts talking, and it's not any of us in the room.

"Do you think I don't know you're connected to his disappearance, you show up and days later he's gone? I'm not that stupid sweetheart."

Jonah gives a low chuckle, glancing in my direction before pressing a button on the keyboard in front of him. "You mean, the same way we aren't stupid and how we know you were helping him."

I finally see the man on one of the screens, looking around as though he can identify exactly where the voice is coming from. "Jonah? Is that you? Now why are you involving yourself in this?"

"Oh I don't know, Sheriff, why are you looking for our woman in her house with your gun drawn?" Jonah retorts. I watch the way the Sheriff frowns, his eyes narrowing as he keeps looking around.

He doesn't answer, and he doesn't put his gun away either. "Come on now, son, I've known you your whole life, are you really going to choose a fucking meddling tourist over me?"

Jonah exchanges a glance with Link before leaning forward to speak again. "She isn't some random tourist, but either way why would I ever choose you? It really shouldn't have surprised me that dear old dad put one of his own men in charge of the island where his mistress lived. You knew mom and I came home without the baby after dad was murdered. And I know you went and made sure my brother ended up in that foster home. The one that almost killed him."

The Sheriff apparently has no regrets about what he did, his own chuckle echoing slightly through the room we are in as he keeps moving through the house trying to find me. "Oh? He's alive then? Good for him."

Link narrows his eyes at the screen and I can't help but reach out and lace my fingers through his. He offers me a sad smile, but it just makes me want to wrap my arms around him even more. The same feeling I had when we were children.

But those feelings don't quell the rage building to boiling point. How dare that man put Link in harm's way. Even if him doing that was the only reason he came into my life, that darkness inside me calls out for vengeance, it wants to hurt the sheriff for ever hurting my men. And I'm no longer keeping it buried now, the cage is gone.

"There's that heartlessness that my dad loved so much," Jonah responds, his tone carefully even. "You have that down to a fine art, pity you weren't quite so detached from your own son."

A lamp is tossed across the room, the crashing sound echoing on the walls around us. I can see the anger on the sheriff's face as he keeps moving carefully, room by room. "What did you do to him?"

Jonah tilts his head and it reminds me of the way he would look at me when he had the mask on. "You almost had everyone fooled. If we weren't already watching you because of your connection to dad, we may not have even known. I mean, who could have possibly suspected that Chester was your son. But you couldn't resist helping him."

The sheriff finally makes it to the office and I see the look of shock on his face as he takes in the investigation wall set up there. A storm of anger feels like it's twisting and swirling under my skin, anger that the sheriff was involved in killing and disposing of all those victims.

"Oh, did you not realize that just because you burned the bodies for him it didn't get rid of the video evidence?" Jonah continues, his voice filled with a dangerous calm.

The sheriff's face contorts with rage. "You think you're so smart, don't you, Jonah? What did you hope to achieve with this?"

Jonah looks at me before answering. "I didn't do that, Sheriff, our girl did."

I've had enough of listening at this point, my darkness is at the surface and now that I've decided to embrace it, I'm ready to play. I know they say don't take a knife to a gunfight, but seeing the knife on the desk Jonah is at, I know it's my only option.

Letting go of Link's hand, I pick up the knife and turn around quickly. Link and Jonah both try to protest as I turn and walk back to the wall I was pulled through. But when I give them a look, they begrudgingly open it again and follow me out.

"What's she going to do, she's nothing, a nobody," I hear the sheriff say as I close in on the office. He exits the room at the same time, but his attention is still on the investigation wall, allowing me to get the upper hand.

"Actually, I'm a Darling," I snarl as I strike out with the blade in my hand.

It doesn't hit anything vital though, he moves his arm to block me, but I don't think he realized there was a knife in my hand. The blade cuts into the flesh of his arm and when he jerks it away automatically, it sends his gun sprawling onto the ground.

He lunges toward me instead of the gun, but he's intercepted by Link.

The two of them grapple fiercely, and for a moment, all I can see is a blur of limbs and raw fury. Jonah moves quickly, scooping up the gun and training it on the sheriff.

"Enough!" Jonah commands, his voice ringing with authority.

The sheriff freezes, glaring at Jonah with a mixture of hatred and disbelief. "You're really going to shoot me, son?"

Jonah's hand is steady, his gaze unwavering. "If it means protecting her and making sure you can't hurt anyone else, then yes."

The sheriff's eyes flicker with something dark, and in a desperate move, he lunges at Jonah. The shot Jonah fires goes wide, and the two men crash to the ground, grappling fiercely. I try to find a good angle from the narrow hallway, my heart pounding in my ears, but I can't get close enough to strike again.

Suddenly, they roll, and the sheriff rears up, having gained control of the gun once more. Panic surges through me, and I rush forward, but before I can get close enough, a gunshot rings out, the sound echoing through the hallway.

I cry out, almost stumbling, but Link grabs me and wraps his arms around my waist, holding me steady. Seconds feel like eternity before I see the blood spreading across the sheriff's shirt, a look of shock and pain etched across his face. He falls backward to the floor with a heavy thud.

A grunt behind us draws our attention, and that's when I see Deputy Eli leaning against the doorway to the kitchen, his gun held loosely by his side. His face is pale, there is blood dripping down the side of it and he looks like he's barely holding himself together, but his eyes are sharp and focused.

"Can't say I understand all of what I heard just now, but I heard enough to know I needed to do that. I hope you do have evidence or my ass is going to be on the line," Eli grits out.

I glance at Jonah and Link before looking back to Eli. "Yeah we do, but you shouldn't stress too much, I know some people who can help take care of it."

He scowls suddenly as he looks at me. "Please don't tell me your FBI or CIA or some shit?"

I can't help but laugh, not that he isn't close considering who my mother is. Shaking my head I move a little closer, holding my hand out to him. "I'm Detective Hydessa Darling," I respond and for once I'm proud to tell him exactly who I am because I think I've just figured it out myself

He grunts again as he reaches out and weekly shakes my hand, his body sliding a little more down the door frame. My eyes widen and I turn back toward Jonah and Link. "Umm, you may want to get Lachlan here to help him."

Jonah nods, walking back into the hidden hallway. I follow, leaving Link to stay with Eli. Jonah is already on the phone to Lachlan when I get to the room with the cameras, shaking my head at the whole setup. Have they really been watching me all the time since I arrived here?

My eyes catch on the GPS screen again as Jonah hangs up on the call and I frown, looking at him as the gears turn in my mind. "How exactly did you know where to find me last night?" I ask and my stomach drops when his eyes flick to my arm.

No the fuck they didn't.

My fingers graze the place where there is a healing scar left from days before, nothing felt out of place when I first checked.

Like last time there is only one thing that I can feel under the skin of my arm. But if the item under my skin is actually a GPS, then it means it replaced what was originally there.

Jesus fucking christ, I'm going to kill them. Since when did obsession mean cutting out my FUCKING BIRTH CONTROL to replace with a TRACKER?! Is Eli here because he may need to arrest me for murder.

I glare at the man in front of me, and I hope he realizes that if looks could kill he would be ash and dust about now.

He simply grins and gives a shrug of his shoulders. "Not sorry," he says before his hand snaps out and drags me against him, his mouth landing on mine with a need that melts my insides.

After a moment I shove him backward, turning and walking back down the hallway toward the main part of the house. "You both owe me a lifetime of fucking orgasms for this shit," I mutter over my shoulder, trying to hide the smirk tugging at my lips. Jonah's laughter follows me, echoing down the narrow hallway.

Link looks at me with a grin as I walk straight into his open arms.

I guess I did ask for the same sort of obsessive love my parents have. Who needs flowers and chocolate when you can have hearts carved into flesh and stalker tendencies.

Epilogue
WARNING!

I know you like me, you made it this far without throwing your book/kindle at the wall. I really want you to keep liking me so I feel it is only right to give you a teeny tiny warning at this point of the story.

We all love happy endings, I do too... and technically this is Hydessa's happy ending right here...

HOWEVER...

Past this point right here there is what you call a cliffhanger...

It's not about our girl, but it will have you potentially screaming at me for the next book... which won't be out until (hopefully early) 2025.

SO...

Turn back... turn back before it's too late...

No?

Still reading?

You only have yourself to blame now...

Hydessa

S itting down at my desk, I look at the investigation wall. A sense of satisfaction fills me that all those women got the justice they deserved, that their stories weren't simply forgotten because they had no one who cared about them.

I cared. My men, they cared.

Link and Jonah had gone with Eli to fill in all the missing details on what the Sheriff and Chester had been doing. Which now also meant that there would be a job opening in the Amity Island police station that the guys had made it clear they wanted me to fill.

This island, this community, it feels like home. Strangely enough it had felt like home the moment I got here. Until now I hadn't believed in fate or destiny, but now everything feels like it was meant to be.

I would miss living with my family. But I did love this house, their house as it turned out.

I just hope Seanna can understand why I'm staying here.

Picking up my phone I pull up her number and hit the call button. The phone rings a few times before it's answered, I've just opened my mouth to speak first when she interrupts me. "Hey, sis."

My heart stops. My breath catches in my lungs and the blood in my veins turns to ice.

"Hey, sis," I respond to her softly.

I close my eyes, taking a deep breath. I can't hear anything except her voice.

"How's the investigation going?" she asks cheerfully, but I can hear the tension beneath her tone.

"We got the bad guys, we always get them, remember," I say softly and she hums. I hear her shift slightly and there's a catch in her breath.

"I'm glad. I have to go, sis," she says. I can hear the sadness creeping into her voice and it takes everything inside me not to cry.

"I love you, Seanna," I say quickly, my voice filled with emotion. I need her to know that.

"Love you too," she responds softly before the call disconnects.

I feel the tears on my cheeks as I quickly pull up the next contact in my phone, my fingers trembling.

"Hey munchkin, we were just–" Papa's voice comes on the phone.

"Seanna's been taken," I interrupt, closing my eyes to try to stop the world from spinning.

***

UNKNOWN

She hands me back the phone, smiling that fake smile she has perfected so well.

I can see past it though, she can't hide from me.

Humming I shove the phone into the pocket of my utility pants. She growls at me when I grab her free arm, securing it once more to the chain attached to the bed. She tries a well placed swipe with her claws at the mask on my face, but I'm out of reach before it lands.

"I'm not stupid," I say simply, my voice distorted by my mask. "Don't worry, S, you'll be punished for that."

She screams in frustration as I turn and walk out of the room, closing the door and bolting it behind me.

Her screams echo through the dimly lit hallway as I walk away, each note filled with a mixture of rage and desperation. I ignore them, knowing she'll soon tire herself out. My mind races, but my steps are steady as I make my way through the old house.

Once I'm in the main room and a good distance from her, I pull the mask from my face. Getting my phone out, I bring up the contact I need. It's pretty much the only one that gets called from this burner phone. He answers almost immediately, making a humming sound instead of saying anything and I know to keep my voice low, that there is someone near him that shouldn't overhear what we talk about.

"We have to move again," I whisper into the phone, my voice barely above a breath. "Her sister knows. This location is now compromised."

"Make it happen."

seek me darling

Coming Soon

Author's Note

I hope that you enjoyed hide me darling!

Please don't gather your pitchforks and flaming torches after that cliffhanger if you read it... I did warn you.

First off, thank you to my husband for always supporting me and putting up with my random obsessive personality that gets me totally lost in my writing etc. and also helping to answer all the questions that would land me on a federal watch list... If I'm already on it though, hey there, how you doing?

I want to thank my amazing team which has grown so much over the last year and a bit of publishing. All of you in my dream team, you are amazing and thank you so much.

Special thanks to my PA Nikki, Sarah and Taylor for all your help from start to pure panic mode...

And lastly thank you to you, my readers, for picking up this book and taking a chance it, and me, I completely appreciate it and you.

xx

Maree Rose

About the Author

Maree is an indie author who, although she has been writing most of her life, never thought she would ever get something published, which is now why she published this herself. She has always been an avid reader since a young age after roaming through book exchanges with her mum when she was just starting to read serious big girl books.

Maree lives on the East Coast of Australia with her wonderful husband, her son, and her two gorgeous squishy british bulldogs.

When she is not writing, she is working in a financial career (for something completely different to the creative side) or she is working on her photography (which is just as hot as her books).

Stalk Me

Please feel free to stalk me.
Like metaphorically, not literally of course!

Also By

SHATTERED WORLD

Shattered Safety Duet:
Untouchable & Unbreakable
Shattered Memories Duet:
Unforgettable & Unstoppable

DARLING WORLD

hunt me darling
hide me darling
seek me darling (COMING SOON)

DEAD DEVIL'S WORLD

Dead Devil's Night
Dead Devil's Playground (COMING SOON)

SIERRA VALLEY

Home Sweet Home

BLACKSTONE SECURITIES

All We Want